I0822770

PRAISE FOR GLOSSER BROS. HOLIDAY TALES

"Nostalgia takes center stage in this collection of tales, as Jeschonek immortalizes beloved members of the Johnstown community throughout the seasons and the decades. Hope, love, and the power of the people are what truly make this book shine."

– Malena Colon, Reviewer, Bloomfield, NJ

"*Glosser Bros. Holiday Tales* feels familiar the instant it begins. The characters are warm, lovable people who will remind you of loved ones in real life, and the numerous acts of kindness that take place will restore your faith in the power of community."

– Abby Morgan, Reviewer, Pittsburgh, PA

"Jeschonek binds GLOSSER BROS. HOLIDAY TALES with place—specifically, Johnstown, PA department store Glosser Bros., home to magic and memories. Though the store isn't the main character, its atmosphere—warm, welcoming, and, as with all department stores, a tad chaotic—suffuses each story in this collection."

— Sonia Beltz, Reviewer, Dayton, OH

"Readers will be immersed in nostalgia for Glosser Bros. and won't forget the magic in each of these holiday stories."

– Kendra McConnell, Reviewer, Minneapolis, MN

GLOSSER BROS. HOLIDAY TALES

ROBERT JESCHONEK

GLOSSER BROS. HOLIDAY TALES

Published by Pie Press
411 Chancellor Street
Johnstown, Pennsylvania 15904

ALSO BY ROBERT JESCHONEK

A Glosser's Christmas Love Story

Christmas at Glosser's

Death by Polka

Easter at Glosser's

Fear of Rain

Fourth of July at Glosser's

Halloween at Glosser's

Long Live Glosser's

Old-Fashioned Bargain Days at Glosser's

Penn Traffic Forever

Richland Mall Rules

Thanksgiving at Glosser's

The Glory of Gable's

The Masked Family

Valentine's Day at Glosser's

To the men and women of Glosser Bros., who brought such passion to everything they did, especially during the holidays.

INTRODUCTION

BY ROBERT JESCHONEK

Let's face it: Some days, we could all use some roasted nuts from Glosser's.

If you ever visited the Glosser Bros. Department Store in Johnstown, Pennsylvania, you know what I'm talking about. As soon as you walked into the place, the incredible smell of roasting nuts enfolded you, making your mouth water and your stomach growl. It taunted you as you shopped, distracting you until you finally went to the candy and nut counter and bought a bag for yourself…at which point, as you devoured them, every taste bud in your mouth groaned with pure bliss at the warm, sweet, salty goodness.

Mmmmmmm.

Even if you were never there, I think you get the idea. The Glosser Bros. Department Store had its own special comfort food, its own special brown-and-white striped bags (and matching delivery trucks), its own special wooden escalator and basement supermarket (at least until the 1977 flood) and its own special salespeople dedicated to treating customers like family and showering them with personal attention. Glosser's had its own special way of making you feel at home...and it stayed with you. It inspired memories so vivid, it isn't hard to imagine yourself within its walls even though it's been closed since 1989. It just makes you want to go back there again and again, reliving the experiences that created such an unforgettable impression.

Is it any wonder I've written so many books about the place?

I started with the fantasy tale *Christmas at Glosser's,* then followed that with *Long Live Glosser's,* a definitive history of the store and its founding family. In writing those books, I truly felt as if I'd gone back in time, returning to the store I'd loved so much for so long...and best of all, I'd taken along readers who shared my affection for Glosser's and what it represented to us all. To the members of Glosser Nation, it was just as memorable and addictive as those legendary roasted nuts.

If you know the story of Pandora's Box, you can already guess what happened next. With the doors of Glosser's reopened for those two books, I couldn't resist keeping them open for more. It was just too much *fun,* slipping back into that classic store as if no time had passed, enjoying the familiar sights, sounds, and smells that I recalled so well. Whether writing about the bargain basement, the ground floor, the cafeteria, or any other corner of Glosser's, I felt as if I'd resurrected the place and was taking a tour in defiance of the laws of time and space.

In the process, I got to relive the celebration of different holidays at Glosser's—Christmas, Valentine's Day, Easter, Independence Day, Halloween, Thanksgiving...even Old-Fashioned Bargain Days. It made the books all the more special, since Glosser Bros. was such an important part of so many holidays for me and my family. It was where we went to buy food for holiday get-togethers...decorations to make our home festive...cards and presents to exchange in the spirit of giving...and outfits to wear at seasonal celebrations.

As important as the time and setting was to these books, the characters were always the heart of them... including a few who'd stepped right out of real life onto the page. Through the magic of storytelling, I was able to revisit and honor some of the incredible people associated with the store, like Hunt Room Mary Schuster, queen of the Hunt Room Restaurant; Bill, Fred, and Izzy Glosser, all key sources in making *Long Live Glosser's* a reality; and the beloved Ruby Shaffer, who worked at Glosser's soda fountain with her twin sister, Ruth, for 38 years.

Looking back on these books, I'm hard-pressed to think of a writing project I've enjoyed more, for deeply personal reasons. Bringing the store back to life—if only in the pages of a work of fiction—and bringing along so many readers who share my love for it, has been extraordinarily rewarding. How could I resist going back to the well just one more time?

The answer is, I couldn't resist. The result is in your

hands or on your screen or playing on your sound system —a compilation of the full *Glosser Bros. Holidays* series... and more. To make this book extra-special, I've added in two brand-new novelettes, unavailable anywhere else in any form: "Saint Patrick's Day at Glosser's" and "New Year's Eve at Glosser's." I wrote them just for this book, after thinking about them for ages.

"Saint Patrick's Day at Glosser's" is a historical tale centered on Glosser Bros., grounded in the reality of very specific, factual events. "New Year's Eve at Glosser's" also explores historic happenings—including the very early days of the store—but the action is driven by elements of fantasy. In the tradition of Charles Dickens' *A Christmas Carol,* "New Year's" brings the past to life in magical ways that open up astounding possibilities. Come along for the ride, and you will *love* the payoff that awaits you.

I've added a few more surprises, as well, including a chapter from *Long Live Glosser's.* "The Last Day of the Glosser Bros. Store" recaptures exactly what its title promises...the events of May 26, 1989, the very last day the store was open to the public. Appropriately enough, it goes in a poetic, haunting direction, and I think it makes the perfect ending to this book.

Might it be the end of the series as well? If so, it's a fitting one. You'll see.

But it's not necessarily *that* final. After all, I still have ideas for stories set at Glosser's...maybe even novels. I even have a finished cover for one of them.

If the muse strikes, and you, the readers, support this book, it's safe to say I might spin some more stories in this direction. Frankly, it's hard to imagine not revisiting Glosser Bros. Department Store and Gee Bee again...celebrating special occasions with a shopping spree and lunch in the cafeteria...meeting up with old friends like Ruby and Fred one more time.

Meanwhile, you have this big new book with brand-new novelettes to enjoy...and, hopefully, share with others. I still believe we'd do well to learn from Glosser Bros. and what made it so special; spreading the word to those who never experienced Glosser's themselves can only help expand its positive influence in our wayward world.

As you and I know, Glosser's was more than a department store. It was a gathering place, a cultural center, and a monument to the American experience. It was a symbol of unity, shared values, and shared history, a place where customers, management, and staff were all treated as friends and family. It was a source of magic in the modern world—the magic of business, the magic of community, the magic of tradition. It was a place that, if you were lucky enough to go there, you would never forget.

That's why I wrote these stories, and that's why I've invited you to have another taste of the lovely lost world in which they are set.

Help yourself. The roasted nuts are as delicious as ever.

Johnstown, Pennsylvania, July 4, 2022

GLOSSE

A GLOSSER'S CHRISTMAS LOVE STORY

JOHNSTOWN, 2016

Even before Jason kissed her, Emma thought it was a perfect moment.

Snowflakes fluttered down around them, drifting lazily out of the night sky. The cold air was barely moving, only lightly stirring her long black hair. Strings of white lights clung to the spindly tree branches around them, giving off a magical glow.

Best of all, the giant Christmas tree in the middle of Johnstown's Central Park danced with colorful patterns of light, flashing and changing in time to the holiday music playing from nearby speakers.

Jason's face had been bathed in the blinking light from that tree when he pulled her close. "I'm so happy when I'm with you." His cheeks had flashed red and green when he'd said those words. "I mean, *every* time I'm with you."

Emma's heart had been pounding. She could have

sworn it had been beating in time with the song that was playing—"Let it Snow."

"I feel the same way," she'd said. "It's like we were made for each other."

Smiling warmly, he'd reached out and traced the line of her jaw with the tip of his finger. "You're the greatest Christmas gift I've ever gotten in my entire life." Breath misting in the cold December air, he'd leaned closer. "I love you, Emma."

That was when their lips had met, after he'd said those words for the first time.

For that one perfect moment, Emma felt transported. The wintertime city of Johnstown, Pennsylvania melted away around her, leaving her suspended in another realm of perfect warmth and happiness. All she could feel were Jason's lips pressed against hers...Jason's arms wrapped around her body...Jason's heartbeat through the coats they wore.

There were people around them (the tree drew big crowds for the holiday season) but Emma was blissfully unaware of any of them. Only the man who was kissing her seemed to be real. Only Jason Halloran seemed to matter.

It was like something out of a dream...

Only when the song changed to "White Christmas" did they break the kiss. Even then, they stayed close, with foreheads touching.

"I love you, too," she told him softly.

He kissed her again, longer this time. People around them were singing along with the music, which somehow made the second kiss more romantic than the first.

Emma knew she would never forget this night. It was the first time the two of them had said those words, announcing they loved each other. And it was the first time they'd been together during the holiday season. After all, they'd only met three weeks ago.

And in just a few days, they would spend their very first Christmas together. She could hardly wait.

But she also wanted to savor every magical moment, to enjoy it for all it was worth.

The music changed again, to "Rockin' Around the Christmas Tree." Jason broke the kiss...but again, did not pull away. "Want to get some hot chocolate or cider?"

Emma nodded. "Okay." Something hot to drink sounded like a good idea on a cold night.

The truth was, anything seemed like a great idea as long as he was with her. She had a good feeling about him, a *great* feeling, unlike any other boyfriend she'd ever known in the 27 years of her life so far.

It was a feeling that stayed with her as they left the big, flashing tree and headed for the lights of the busy Press Bistro up ahead, across the street on the corner of Locust and Franklin.

THE PLACE WAS PACKED when they walked in, full of people in a festive mood. Ever since the tree had gone up, the

Press had become one of the hottest places in town, especially on Saturday nights like this one.

At first, Emma thought they might not find a table...but an elderly couple sitting by one of the windows waved them over from across the crowded room.

"The table is all yours." The man, who might have been in his seventies or eighties, pushed himself to his feet. "We were just leaving."

"That's very kind of you." Emma smiled. "We were just enjoying the tree."

"We know." The woman, who looked about the same age, grinned and nodded. "We saw you two canoodling out there."

Emma blushed. Jason laughed and kissed the top of her head.

"Young love at Christmas time." The old woman sighed as the man helped her up by the elbow. "It's good to see."

"Brings back memories," said the man. "Walking through the park in the old days, then looking at the holiday decorations in the windows—right here." He gestured at the window by the table. "Back when this was Glosser Bros. Department Store."

"It was a magical place during the holidays." The old woman nodded as the man helped her on with her heavy brown coat. "So many lovely decorations in the windows and all through the store. People coming and going, buying presents. Christmas music playing, everyone feeling good."

"That's why we still love coming here so much," said

the man. "Glosser's store is gone, but this restaurant brings back some of the same good spirits."

"My grandmother used to work here," said Emma. "At Glosser's."

The woman blinked from behind her thick glasses as she buttoned her coat. "What department, dear?"

"The grocery store and a few others," said Emma. "She always says how much she loved it here."

"Then you and your beau have certainly come to the perfect place tonight." The old woman smiled and patted Emma's arm. "The perfect place to get to know each other better."

With that, she and the old man said goodbye and worked their way through the crowd to the door. Emma and Jason sat down beside each other, holding hands.

"What a cute couple!" said Emma.

"Want to hear something crazy?" Jason squeezed her hand. "*My* grandfather used to work at Glosser's, too."

"For real?" Emma felt a thrill of excitement ripple through her.

"I know, right?" Jason smiled and shook his head. "What a coincidence."

"I wonder if they were here at the same time!"

"I wonder if they knew each other."

"I wonder." Emma loved the thought of another connection between them, another link that seemed to confirm how meant-to-be they were. It was like the dream-come-true just kept getting better.

"We need to find out," said Jason.

"I'll have to talk to Gram," said Emma. "Ask her what she remembers. What's your grandfather's name?"

"Frank," said Jason. "Frank Halloran. What's your grandmother's name?"

"Sarah Jensen," said Emma. "She's my mom's mom."

"Cool. So I'll call my grandpa in Michigan and see what he says about Glosser's," said Jason. "And Sarah."

"I'll see her tomorrow," said Emma. "So I'll talk to her then."

"Awesome." Jason drew her hand up and kissed it. "Wouldn't it be cool if they knew each other back in the day?"

IT WAS SNOWING hard the next afternoon when Emma pulled up to the apartment building in Richland Township, the suburb of Johnstown where Sarah lived. At least the parking lot was mostly clear; someone had plowed it so the usual crowd of Sunday visitors would have plenty of open spaces to occupy.

Parking her ten-year-old blue Honda Civic at the edge of the lot, Emma walked around front and entered the vestibule. When she hit the button for Sarah's apartment, the inner door buzzed open, and she stepped through.

The big front lobby was overflowing with holiday decorations. There were fully decked trees in each of the four corners, each with a different color scheme and theme. Evergreen boughs entwined with red ribbons and colored lights ran along the chair rail on the wall and wrapped around the pillars in the corners. The big mahogany table in the middle of the room was covered with festively wrapped packages trimmed with gold and silver bows. Somewhere nearby—in the dining room, maybe—Christmas music played softly.

Emma winced at the sight and sound of it all. She could only imagine how much her grandma hated it.

As far back as she could remember, for reasons she never knew, her grandmother had always hated Christmas.

Passing through the lobby, Emma swung right and headed down the hallway, which was also strung with boughs, ribbons, and colored lights. Every door was decorated, too—covered in wrapping paper, ribbons, and bows like gift-wrapped presents.

As Emma walked, she smelled something baking, though she couldn't quite figure out where it was happening. She got her answer when she followed the bend to the one door that wasn't gift-wrapped—number 116, her grandma's place. The baking smell was coming from there, no question.

When Sarah opened the door—before Emma could knock, as always—the smell rushed out and engulfed her. There was nothing like it in the world, nothing better (except, perhaps, the smell of Jason's cheek). It instantly made her think of childhood and Sunday dinners at Gram and Grandpap's big old house on Highland Avenue in Moxham.

Sarah ambushed her with a hug the second her toe

crossed the threshold into the apartment. "Emmy Lou!" She always called Emma that, though her middle name wasn't Lou. "Get your coat off and come help me with these cookies!"

"Only if I can have one first!" Emma's eyes widened when she saw the racks of cooling chocolate chip cookies in the little kitchen behind the door. Was there anything more delicious than warm cookies straight off the rack?

Warm cookies baked by *Gram? So what* if they were distinctly un-Christmaslike, in keeping with Gram's rejection of anything associated with the holiday.

"Coat first, hon." Sarah, 86 years old and barely five feet tall, was still a bossy, brassy individual. "And wash those hands! Twenty seconds and plenty of soap!"

"Yes, ma'am." As Emma stripped off her black-trimmed bright red coat, she looked around the little apartment. As with every Christmas season, there wasn't a holiday decoration anywhere to be seen—no tree, no boughs, no ornaments, not even a card set up on a table. It was like Christmas wasn't even happening, as far as Gram and her apartment were concerned.

In years past, at least, Grandpap Mike had put up a few decorations in keeping with tradition. But things weren't the same with him gone, and the old house sold, and twelve years passed since things had stopped being the way they used to be. There was no one else who could convince Sarah to put up a sprig of holly or a Christmas stocking.

After washing her hands in the bathroom, Emma returned to the kitchen and snagged a cookie. "Mmmm." It was every bit as melty and delicious as she'd expected. "Thank you, Gram, thank you."

"Mm-hm." Sarah straightened her apron—which was more like a sleeveless housecoat, white with red plaid hip pockets and a blue back—and handed over a spatula. "Now less eating, more working, sweetheart. We've got another batch coming out of the oven in..." She glanced at the old egg timer on the counter. "...one minute."

Emma automatically started stacking the cookies on a plate on the counter. "Say, Gram. Back when you worked at Glosser's, did you know a guy named Frank Halloran?"

"A guy named what?" Sarah was a little hard of hearing sometimes.

Emma spoke up. "Frank Halloran. Jason's grandfather. He moved to Michigan ages ago, but he lived in town and worked at Glosser's. Did you know him?"

Suddenly, Sarah froze. She just stood there and stared into space.

"Gram?" Frowning, Emma stopped plating cookies and took a step toward her. "Gram, are you all right?"

"I haven't heard that name in ages." Sarah's voice was hushed. Her fingers clutched the silver locket that she always wore around her neck. "Frank Halloran."

Just then, the timer dinged. The cookies in the oven were done.

"Who is he, Gram?" asked Emma.

Sarah's eyes glittered when she met Emma's gaze. "The love of my life," she said. "And we met at *Glosser's*."

Johnstown, 1953

"You dropped something." The young man with the bright green eyes and red hair held up a 20-lb. frozen turkey and grinned. "Here you go."

Sarah Jensen stopped in the frozen food aisle of the Glosser Bros. grocery store and shook her head. "Not *my* turkey, thanks."

"But it is!" The guy pushed the frozen turkey toward her. "I clearly saw it fall out of the pocket of your sweater."

Sarah shrugged and sighed. She wasn't in the mood to goof around that morning, not after the letter she'd gotten before coming to work. "You must be confusing me with someone else."

"Not a chance." The guy's smile turned charming. "There's *no way* I could ever confuse you with anyone else."

The smile made Sarah hesitate. She was 23 years old, after all, and he was...he was...

Not completely unattractive. His eyes were bright as emeralds, his hair red as firelight. He was six feet tall, with a slim, athletic build and muscular shoulders. And he was about her age or a little younger, perhaps a little older.

But no. She had her reasons for not socializing these days. And besides... "I need to get back to my register," she told him. "My lunch break is over."

"So?" He lowered the turkey, revealing the Glosser

Bros. nametag pinned to the chest of his white button-down shirt. "I'm not even *on* break."

The tag, stamped with the name "Frank," caught Sarah off guard. She hadn't known he was a fellow employee. She'd never even seen him before he shoved the turkey in her face.

Not that it made any difference. "Look, I really have to get back to my register," she said.

"Then what am I supposed to do with *this*?" He turned the turkey over in his hands, looking forlorn.

It was then she was seized by the inexplicable impulse to throw him a bone. "Put it in the oven for six and a half hours at 325°," she said. "Either that, or roll it down the aisle and use it to bowl for customers."

"Brilliant!" Frank perked up. "You're a genius..." He peered at the nametag pinned to Sarah's gray sweater. "...you *Sarah,* you."

"That's what they tell me." Sarah smirked. "I'm a genius, all right."

As she started to walk away, Frank stepped in front of her. "See you around?" He smiled expectantly.

"I guess so." Reaching up, she pushed a lock of her chestnut brown hair behind her right ear. "Though I've never seen you around before today."

"That's because this is my first day on the job." He winked. "But you'll be seeing me a lot more from now on."

"Is that so?" Sarah looked toward the checkouts in the front of the store. If she didn't get back to her post soon, someone would come looking for her.

"Absolutely." Frank nodded enthusiastically. "I'm like a bad penny. I keep turning up."

Sarah shrugged and headed for the checkouts. Frank backed away and disappeared in the frozen food department.

Up front, she returned to her register, apologizing for being late to the girl who'd been covering for her. The girl, a chatty redhead, didn't seem to care as she stepped away from the checkout and Sarah replaced her.

As the next customer put her items on the counter, Sarah punched their prices into the register. She slid cans of corn and green beans into the bagging area at the end of the counter, and someone caught them.

At first, Sarah didn't look to see who was doing the bagging. But as she finished ringing everything up, she turned...and there he was.

Frank Halloran himself grinned back at her as he loaded the items into big brown paper bags.

Sarah just stared. She hadn't expected to see him there.

"Ma'am?" Frank was talking to the customer. "Shall I carry these upstairs for you?" Offering to haul purchases was expected, since the grocery store was located in the basement of Glosser's department store. It was a long walk up and out to the parking lot or on-street parking, especially with a heavy load of groceries.

"Yes, please." The customer, a heavyset middle-aged woman in a pale green coat and squat cream hat, nodded. "My car is out back in the lot." With that, she paid Sarah, got her receipt, and briskly started toward the nearby flight of stairs to the first floor.

Frank followed with a bag in each arm. He winked at Sarah as he followed the customer, mouthing four words that made her smile in spite of herself.

Penny for your thoughts?

FRANK WASN'T KIDDING about the bad penny stuff. He worked as a bagger at her checkout every day. When she went on break, he showed up beside her at the lunch counter in Glosser's cafeteria. When she left at the end of the day, he walked out with her.

And soon enough, he started hinting around about going out with her. She brushed it off, pretending she didn't hear him...but she knew she couldn't keep playing dumb forever. Sooner or later, she had to tell him the truth.

She had to tell him exactly why there could never be anything between them.

Though the truth was, she didn't really mind the attention. It was nice for a change, even though he was a little too persistent. It had been too long since anyone but Mike had acted that way with her, and Mike...

Mike wasn't around. He'd been overseas for two years.

But Sarah knew she had to put her cards on the table at some point. If only Frank wasn't *there* so much, and wasn't so *nice*...maybe it would be easier. If only he didn't make her *laugh* so much. If only...

Then, one morning, she got her wish. Billy Cruikshank, not Frank, stepped up to bag groceries at her checkout stand.

"Where's Frank?" she asked.

Billy shrugged. "Dunno." As usual, he had a blank look on his face. A tubby, swarthy guy in his thirties with a crewcut, he had a reputation for not being "all there" since returning from fighting in Korea.

Talking to him made Sarah's heart sink, and she quickly turned away. Now that Frank wasn't there, she instantly missed him.

And hated herself for feeling that way.

LATER, Sarah sat down at her usual spot at the lunch counter in Glosser's cafeteria and pulled out a pack of Lucky Strike cigarettes. She was just about to light one when the place erupted into chaos.

"Ho ho ho!" A man dressed as Santa Claus burst into the room, shouting to the high heavens. "Who's been *naughty*, and who's been *nice*?"

"Nice!" hollered the Shaffer twins, Ruth and Ruby, from behind the counter.

"Naughty!" shouted sassy Mary Schuster from the adjacent Hunt Room restaurant.

Howling with laughter, Santa grabbed a gift-wrapped present out of his sack. Bells on his sleeve jingled as he waved it overhead. "Today, *everyone* gets a present, naughty *or* nice!"

"Got any hooch in there, Santa?" asked Mary—known as Hunt Room Mary to her customers and colleagues.

"Open your present and see!" Santa tossed the wrapped gift her way, and she caught it. "Better hope it's not a lump of coal!"

"I'll kick your fat behind if it is!" said Mary.

"Ho ho ho!" Santa handed gifts to Ruth and Ruby, then made his way around the counter to Sarah. "And what about you, young lady? Naughty or nice?"

Before Sarah could answer, he pulled a small box wrapped in silver paper out of his sack. "Wait! I already know!" He bowed at the waist as he handed the gift to Sarah with a flick of his wrist, sleeve bells jingling. "You're *always* on the nice list, aren't you?"

Smiling, Sarah took the package and undid the red ribbon crossed around it. With one fingernail, she broke the single piece of adhesive tape sealing the paper. Then, she slowly unwound the silver paper from the box.

Frowning, she studied the cubical Glosser Bros. box underneath. It sat in the palm of her hand, big enough for some kind of jewelry...or whatever little surprise Santa might have in store for her.

"Go ahead and open it, Sarah." Santa pointed a red-gloved finger at the box and winked. "Don't you want to see what Santa brought you?"

It was the wink that gave him away. Finally, Sarah saw through his disguise and realized who was under the beard and costume.

And she froze. She couldn't bring herself to open the box.

"C'mon, honey!" shouted Hunt Room Mary. "Show us what Santa brought you!" She pulled a green and red plaid sweater out of her gift box and shook it with glee. "Just look what *I* got!"

"Yeah, Sarah!" said Ruby. "Let's see it!"

"Let's see it!" said Ruth.

Still, Sarah hesitated. Since that was Frank in that Santa Claus costume, she could only imagine the gift he might have brought her.

She had a pretty good idea how he felt about her, after all. And the box in her hand was the exact size commonly used for gifts of jewelry.

And jewelry was something she could *not* accept from *him*.

"I can't." She tried to give the box back to Frank. "I really can't."

He wouldn't take it. "I insist. You've been very nice lately, and you deserve this gift."

Sarah shook her head. "No, really." She put the box down on the counter. "I have to get back to work."

"You've really lost it, haven't you, sweetie?" said Hunt Room Mary.

"Santa Claus always knows best!" Frank grabbed the box, tipped the lid open, and held it out for Sarah to look inside. "See what I mean?"

She did...and how.

Her eyes flew wide open, and a huge smile flashed onto her face. She let out a little yelp of delight and quickly flung her hands over her mouth as if to keep any more yelps from escaping.

"What?" Ruth and Ruby said it simultaneously as they crowded in from behind the counter.

"What the heck is it?" snapped Hunt Room Mary.

Sarah giggled and reached into the box. "It's the best gift ever!" She pulled out the object resting on the cotton padding inside and held it up to watch it glint in the bright cafeteria light.

"Huh?" said Ruth and Ruby.

Hunt Room Mary hustled over and squinted at what Sarah was holding. "Well that is one cheap gift, if you ask me. Santa Claus can be a real *skinflint.*"

"But it's not just *any* penny," said Sarah.

"It's a *bad* one," said Frank. "The kind that keeps turning up! Ho ho ho!"

It was then, in that moment, that Sarah had the urge to hug him. Because the truth was, she had been so very lonely for such a long time...and she cared for him, and she liked the way he treated her.

And the way he made her laugh.

So she did it. She went ahead and hugged him.

And she made a decision. She wasn't going to talk about Mike, not with Frank. At least for a little while.

AFTER HER SHIFT THAT AFTERNOON, Sarah spent some time shopping in the store upstairs, searching for gifts. She did all her shopping at Glosser Bros., since she got to use her employee discount to save money on purchases.

She'd had her eye on a thing or two for Mom, and she knew it was time to buy. With just a few days until Christmas, the place would be completely picked over soon.

As it was, Glosser's was packed with shoppers, grabbing items off tables and racks. Twice, Sarah got elbowed by women in the accessories department...but she didn't mind. Holiday music was playing, and decorations hung everywhere. The smell of fresh chocolates and roasting chestnuts filled the air.

Even with all the heartache in her life, Christmas at Glosser's was her favorite time of year.

"Your mother is going to *love* these." Margie the sales clerk draped the pretty white kid gloves in a gift box on the counter. "And that beautiful *hat* you picked out...! Such lovely gifts, Sarah!"

"Thank you." Sarah smiled. "I can't wait to see her open them."

Margie, a pretty brunette just a little older than Sarah, put the lid on the box of gloves. "There's a nightgown upstairs that I've had *my* eye on for a while." Smoothly, she pulled a piece of gift wrap out from under the counter and folded it around the box.

"Sounds perfect for your mother," said Sarah.

"Who said anything about *her*?" Margie cocked her head, looking dead serious...then laughed. "So how much more shopping do you have to do?"

"This is it." Sarah had already bought her dad a new lunch bucket and overalls. An only child, she didn't have any brothers, sisters, nieces, or nephews to buy for. "All done."

Margie stuck a bow on the box and handed it over. "So you've already bought something for your fiancé then?"

"Oh yes." Sarah had bought and shipped the gift over a month ago. It took a while to get to Korea, after all.

And it took even longer to get back, sometimes. That was what she'd read in the depressing letter the other day —that Mike, her fiancé, who'd already been gone two years, wasn't coming home for at least another six months.

The damn Korean War didn't seem to care what she felt. Though the truth was, these days, she wasn't so sure what she felt anyway. She didn't even wear her engagement ring to work anymore, though she said it was because it got in the way when she handled groceries and ran the cash register.

"Good for you." Margie punched buttons on the cash register, ringing up the sale. "Won't that be something when he finally comes home?"

"The best gift ever." The words came easy, but they felt hollow. Had Mike been gone too long? Had they lost whatever was special between them?

Or was it something else?

Just then, Sarah heard jingling bells from across the store. Instinctively, she looked in that direction, expecting to see Frank in his Santa Claus costume.

But this time, it was just a sales girl shaking jingle bells for a laugh. Sarah slumped.

"Why so disappointed?" Margie followed her gaze. "Did you think it was Santa?"

"No, no," lied Sarah.

"He *is* a handsome boy under that beard, isn't he?" Margie smiled, then dropped her voice to a whisper. "Do you think I should go sit on his knee and tell him what I want for Christmas?"

Sarah shrugged and pulled the change purse out of her pocketbook. "That's how it works, isn't it?"

"I suppose." Again, Margie spoke in a whisper. "I wonder if he'd bring a present down *my* chimney?" She giggled.

Sarah smiled as she paid for her purchases...but wasn't amused. For the first time, in fact, she felt something new toward Frank, something she hadn't expected.

She felt *jealous*.

SARAH WAS WORKING at her checkout the next day, ringing up a customer, when a conical deep green cap was suddenly thrust in front of her face.

"Quick! Put this on!"

Startled, Sarah quickly looked to see who was pushing the cap at her, even as her housewife customer's two small children called out his name.

"*Santa*!"

"That's right, kiddies!" Naturally, it was Frank in costume again. He spent all his working hours dressed as Santa Claus these days. "And this fine lady is my very special *helper* today!"

"I am?" said Sarah. "Says who?"

"Says Rudolph!" Frank winked at the kids—a little boy around 6 or 7 and a girl around 4 or 5—and they cheered again. "He said you're the best elf in all of Glosser's!"

Sarah didn't love the idea of dressing up like an elf. "Tell Rudolph I'm very busy here at my register today."

"Lucky you, Elf Sarah! Mr. Glosser himself gave you special permission to work with Santa for the day!" Again, Frank shoved the green cap in her direction.

"Which Mr. Glosser?" asked Sarah.

"*All* of them!" With that, Frank reached up and lightly placed the cap on her head. "You can come upstairs to the North Pole as soon as you finish ringing up this customer."

"Yes, please." The housewife customer sounded annoyed. "Finish ringing me up, please."

"Sorry, ma'am." Flustered, Sarah returned her full attention to the groceries and cash register. She punched in the prices of the few remaining items, announced the total cost, and got the correct amount of cash from the customer. No change necessary.

Meanwhile, Santa Frank took care of bagging the groceries, since Billy the bagger was away at the moment. The kids loved it and watched his every movement.

"Are you gonna carry our stuff up to our car?" the little girl asked excitedly.

"Ho ho ho! Of course I am!" said Frank. "As for *you...*" He grinned at Sarah as he scooped up the two bags of groceries. "I'll meet you at the North Pole when I get back."

Sarah was stuck and she knew it. If Mr. Glosser—*any* Mr. Glosser—had given the go-ahead, she had to play ball.

Taking off the elf cap, she turned it over in her hands, thinking how ridiculous it would make her look...and then she smiled. Frank was certainly full of surprises. And she had to admit, once again, that she was flattered by the attention. It was nice, even if it could never go anywhere. It was nice to make believe for a while, after being so lonely for so long.

Laughing to herself, she put the cap back on her head and switched off the light above her register, closing the checkout. She would give the elf business a try.

There were worse ways to spend an afternoon.

"YOU WANT A *WHAT*?" Santa Frank sounded stunned by what the little boy on his knee had said. "A *real* rocket ship?"

The kid, who couldn't have been older than six or seven, nodded so decisively, the red-and-black hunting cap with the giant brim and ear flaps flopped forward over his eyes.

Grinning, Sarah stepped up and raised the cap so it sat back on his head. She had to admit, she was having fun playing elf for the day.

"Can we even *do* that, Elf Sarah?" Frank asked her.

"Hmm." She pretended to think hard about it. "Rocket

ships take a long time to build. What about a really neat *toy* rocket ship until we get the *real* one ready to go?"

"Ho ho ho!" Frank gave the kid a shake. "What do you say to that, sonny?"

The little boy thought it over, then nodded. "It's a deal!" The hat flopped down again, and he pushed it back himself this time.

"Good for you! Now watch the birdie!" Frank pointed at the camera mounted on a tripod ten feet away, manned by an overweight middle-aged photographer in over-stretched green tights and a cap like Sarah's. "Smile for Harry the Photo Elf."

"Dat's me." Harry, who usually manned the loading dock, peeked around the camera, looking like he'd rather be somewhere far away. "Say cheese, kid."

The kid said it, the camera flashed, and Frank helped him down off his knee. Sarah held out the basket of candy canes for him to take one...but the kid took three and ran off to rejoin his mother.

Before the next kid in the very long line could move in, Sarah stepped in front of Frank. "Do you want to take a break?"

"No, ma'am." Frank shook his head. "Keep 'em coming."

"But you haven't taken a break since we started," said Sarah.

"Maybe in a few minutes." Frank leaned forward and winked. "I love this, you know."

There was a twinkle in his eye when he said it. He really did make a great Santa Claus, Sarah realized.

It made her like him all the more.

"Well, you just let me know if you need anything," she said.

"As a matter of fact, I *do* have a question," said Frank. "What do *you* want for Christmas, Elf Sarah?"

She shook her head. For the longest time, she'd wanted one thing, but now she couldn't have it. If Mike wasn't coming home for Christmas, she couldn't think of anything else she really wanted.

Or maybe she *could*.

"What about you?" She turned the question around on Frank. "What do *you* want for Christmas, Santa Claus?"

"I already have it." His eyes locked with hers, and he smiled warmly behind his bushy white beard. "You don't even have to ask."

Sarah's heart raced. His gaze, his voice, his words—the message was unmistakable. The feelings were there in him...but did she *share* them?

And what could she do if she did? She was *engaged* to another *man*.

Suddenly agitated, Sarah cleared her throat and spun to face the crowd waiting in line. "Who's next?"

"I am! I am!" shouted a sweet little girl with curly blonde hair and a black fur-trimmed coat.

"Santa will see you now." Sarah waved the girl forward.

"My name is Grace!" said the girl as she hopped up on Frank's knee. "I want a dolly and a milkshake!"

"What flavor?" asked Frank.

"Chocolate!" said Grace. "For the milkshake!"

Frank chuckled. "Have you been good this past year?"

"No." Grace shook her head. "The op'site."

"Well, at least you're honest." Frank patted her on the head and grinned at Sarah. "Santa likes honesty."

Sarah felt uncomfortable and looked away.

"Time for your picture, Grace." Frank pointed at the camera. "Smile nice for Harry the Photo Elf."

"Dat's me." Harry lit a cigarette off a match and peeked around the camera, looking bored.

"What about the *other* elf?" Grace pointed at Sarah. "Could she get in the picture, too?"

Frank laughed. "I don't see why not. Come on over here, Elf Sarah."

Sarah hesitated but wanted to make little Grace happy. She stepped behind the ornate throne on which Frank sat and leaned down to smile over his left shoulder.

"Say cheese," said Harry, puffing smoke from his cigarette.

It was then, with a bright flare of the camera's flash bulb, that he snapped the shot.

WORKING as an elf could be exhausting. That was why, as Sarah trudged outside after her shift, she only wanted to go home.

Standing on the corner of Franklin and Locust streets, she pulled a cigarette out of her coat pocket and lit it. The tip glowed red as she drew the warm smoke into her lungs, relishing the taste of it.

Just then, as she prepared to head for the bus stop, she

heard the door crash open behind her and a familiar voice call her name.

"Elf Sarah!" It was Frank. "Need a lift?"

"No thanks." Sarah was still a little stung by his earlier comment about honesty. Did he know about Mike? Had someone told him? "See you tomorrow, though."

Frank—in a navy blue pea coat and watch cap instead of the Santa suit—looked crestfallen. But then he quickly shook it off and smiled. "May I walk you to the bus stop, at least?"

Sarah puffed on the cigarette and blew out some smoke. "Okay, sure." Maybe he'd clue her in about the honesty comment along the way.

They started down the walk along the Locust Street side of the Glosser Building, lit by the glowing display windows. Those windows were the showpieces of Glosser's, especially at Christmas time. People came from all over to see the elaborate holiday displays even if they didn't plan to actually shop at Glosser's.

"So that was a fun day today, wasn't it?" Frank walked between Sarah and the street, hands folded behind his back.

"It was." Sarah smiled as she remembered the parade of children who'd come to see Santa.

"I love making kids happy, don't you?" said Frank. "And Christmas is my favorite time of the year."

"Mine, too," said Sarah.

Frank drew a deep breath, then let it out. "It makes *me* feel like a kid again." With that, he darted around behind her to look into the nearest display window. "I remember it like it was yesterday."

Sarah paused for a look, too. Inside the window, the figures of three happy children were posed around a grinning snowman wearing a top hat and corn cob pipe—Frosty himself, in the middle of a one-window winter wonderland.

"Now *that* is Christmas to me." Frank pressed his hands against the glass. "I used to stand here for ages and look in at those wonderful visions and *dream*."

"I've always loved these windows, too," said Sarah. "I look forward to them every year."

"People always make such a big deal about Penn Traffic's windows. Not me." Frank tapped his finger on the glass. "I was *always* a Glosser's fan."

Continuing on, he stopped at the next window and smiled. Sarah thought he looked handsome in the reddish glow from inside.

"Working here was a fantasy of mine when I was a kid," said Frank. "But getting to play *Santa Claus* is something I never imagined! It's the best ever!"

Stepping over beside him, Sarah gazed into the window. This time, the scene was right out of a typical living room on Christmas morning. There was a fully-decorated Christmas tree off to one side, and two little boys unwrapping gifts. Mother and father mannequins watched over them in bathrobes and slippers, holding presents of their own.

"I think I've finally found my calling." Frank reached under his pea coat and pulled out his red Santa hat with the white fur trim. "Forget the steel mill. I wanna be Santa Claus." Grinning, he pulled on the hat and posed for her with arms folded over his chest.

Sarah chuckled. Mike had never been this funny or surprising. In her time with him, she'd forgotten how much she missed it.

"So you never answered my question, Elf Sarah," said Frank. "What *do* you want for Christmas?"

"I really don't know." Sarah took one last puff on the cigarette, then dropped it to the sidewalk and crushed it out with the toe of her shoe. "Maybe I'm too old for that sort of thing."

"Never!" Frank jabbed an index finger overhead. "You are *never* too old for Christmas!"

Sarah shrugged. She didn't think he understood, and she didn't want to try to explain. "It's for children, anyway."

"There *has* to be something you'd like." Frank marched to the next window and stopped. "Maybe a little more window shopping will help?"

Sarah checked her watch. It was almost time to catch the bus.

"Sometimes you don't know what you want until you see it." Frank hiked his thumb at the window. "Sometimes it's right in front of your face."

Curious, Sarah walked over to stand beside him. Frowning, she peered into the window...and froze.

On the other side of the glass, a mechanical Santa Claus sat on a red wooden rocking chair. As three pointy-eared elves looked on expectantly, Santa read an enormous paper scroll that could only be his nice/naughty list. But the part of the scroll he'd finished, the part that flopped over his red-mittened hand and was readable to Sarah, wasn't what she would have expected. Another scroll of paper had been laid over the list, inscribed with a message in big black letters—and affixed with the photo of Sarah, Frank, and little Grace that Harry had snapped earlier.

"ELF SARAH," read the message. "YOU ARE INVITED TO ATTEND GLOSSER'S CHRISTMAS EVE PARTY WITH SANTA CLAUS!"

Sarah stared for a long moment, stunned. Frank had caught her off-guard.

"Like it?" Frank rapped on the glass, and the faces of two male employees popped out from behind the green background curtains. Sarah recognized them but didn't know them by name. "The guys in the display department set it up for me." The guys behind the curtain waved, then popped back out of view. "I owe them big time, but it was worth it."

Sarah's head was spinning. She had hoped to keep pretending a while longer, but she was going to have to tell him. She was going to have to own up about Mike.

"Well?" Frank was grinning, oblivious. "What do you say?" He shook his Santa cap, swinging the white puff on the tip back and forth. "Will you go to Glosser's Christmas Eve party with Santa?"

Sarah's eyes were burning. Why couldn't he have left well enough alone?

"We'll have fun, I promise." Frank crossed his heart. "The most fun ever."

"I can't." Sarah backed away from the window. "I just *can't.*"

"Because you're engaged?"

Sarah's heart felt like it stopped. "You *knew?*"

Frank shrugged. "People talk, Sarah."

"You *knew,* and you kept...you did this *anyway?*" She flung up a hand at the window with the invitation inside.

"I *like* you. So sue me."

"But I'm *engaged.* I have a *fiancé.*"

"Who isn't here," said Frank. "Does he still make you happy, Sarah?"

"That doesn't have anything to do with this!"

Frank pressed his hands to his chest. "*I* make you happy, don't I?"

Sarah didn't answer.

"It's true and you know it," said Frank. "Just like I know that *you* make *me* happy."

"I can't do this." Sarah took another step away from him.

"You don't have to do anything," said Frank. "It's *your* life, isn't it?"

"No, no." Sarah turned away. She was going to miss her bus. "I made a promise to him."

"Then why don't you wear your engagement ring?" asked Frank. "People talk about that, too, you know."

"Leave me alone!" With that, she hurried off across the snowy street, heading for the bus stop with tears streaming down her cheeks. "And find yourself another elf while you're at it!"

Frank didn't follow but called out after her. "The invitation stands! The party's tomorrow night!"

Sarah didn't answer him. She just kept running toward Main Street, waving frantically as the bus pulled up to the stop.

THAT NIGHT, Sarah lay in bed and read the latest letter from Mike, the one about him not returning for at least six months. She read it again and again, crying harder each time.

"Honey?" Her mother knocked on the door of her bedroom. "Are you all right?"

"I'm fine," said Sarah.

She could hear Mom's hand on the doorknob. "You don't *sound* fine."

Sarah took a deep breath to steady her voice. "I am, thanks."

Mom hesitated. "Do you want to talk?"

Sarah was sure she already knew everything Mom would say. "No, thanks. Goodnight."

Again, Mom hesitated. Then, the doorknob turned, and the tall, slender woman leaned into the room, her dark brown eyes full of concern. "Oh, honey. Is it Mike?"

Sarah wiped tears from her face. "I said I'm fine."

Mom walked all the way in and closed the door behind

her. She was still wearing her housedress and Christmas apron after cleaning up the dinner dishes. "It's that letter he sent, isn't it?"

Sarah tossed the wrinkled and tear-stained letter on the bedside table. "Why can't things be simpler?" she said.

Mom sat on the foot of the bed. "What things?"

Sarah sighed and rubbed her eyes. "If Mike was here—if my *fiancé* was here—I'd know just what to do."

Mom tipped her head to one side. "There's someone else, isn't there?"

Sarah's instinct was to deny it, but she nodded.

"I see." Mom crossed one leg over the other and tapped her bottom lip with a fingertip. "And you have feelings for him?"

Sarah felt the tears welling up, and a sob escaped her.

Mom nodded. Reaching up to pat her short brown hair, she stared at Sarah for a long moment. She looked like she was thinking something over, trying to decide whether or not to say it.

Then she said it. "I had a similar situation myself once, you know."

Suddenly, she had Sarah's undivided attention. It wasn't at all what Sarah had expected to hear.

"That's right." Mom lowered her voice. "When your father was in Europe during the War, before we were married, there was...someone else."

"What?" Sarah sat up straight. *"Really?"*

"Shhh." Mom raised an index finger to her lips. "I don't want your father to know."

"Dad doesn't *know?*"

Mom's eyes widened. Emphatically, she struck the finger against her lips.

Chastened, Sarah lowered her voice. "Who was it?"

Mom shook her head. "What matters is, it was a similar situation. Your father and I got engaged in '43, and then he was gone for almost three years. And I...met someone."

"You mean...did you...?"

Mom slashed a hand through the air. "I wasn't that kind of girl. It was all very innocent." She shrugged. "If you don't count kissing."

Sarah leaned forward, seeing her mom with new eyes. "I just can't believe this. You never mentioned it before."

"It wasn't important to anyone else," said Mom. "But I'm not ashamed. Loneliness is a terrible thing, honey. And love..." She gave Sarah's ankle a squeeze. "Love is *rare* in this world."

Sarah sat back and looked over at the letter on the bedside table. "So you loved him?"

In reply, Mom gave her ankle another squeeze.

"But you married Dad anyway. You waited for him."

Mom nodded. "He's a good man. I did what I did."

"What about the other person?"

"Sometimes I wonder what happened to him." Mom sounded wistful. "But I don't suppose I'll ever know."

Sarah thought for a while, then flung her head back and blew out her breath. "I still don't know what to do."

"Whatever makes you happy," said Mom. "You're a 23-year-old woman, and your life is your own."

Again, Sarah was surprised by what Mom told her.

She'd always thought of Mom as a straight-laced goody-two-shoes type...and now this. "Do you ever regret what you did or didn't do?"

Mom gave her ankle one more squeeze and got up from the bed. "Sometimes, yes. I wonder what life would be like if I'd chosen differently." Crossing the room, she reached for the doorknob. "But whatever you decide to do, remember that things have a way of working out." She opened the door and glanced back over her shoulder before leaving. "Especially at Christmastime."

THE NEXT MORNING, Sarah was back to ringing up groceries. It was Christmas Eve day, and Glosser's grocery store was mobbed with folks stocking up for Christmas dinner—so the store manager had put a stop to Sarah's North Pole duty. He needed all hands on deck at the checkouts.

Which was probably just as well, after what had happened with Frank the day before. The display window he'd altered was back to normal...but Sarah was still sorting out her feelings. It might have been uncomfortable for her to go back to playing the role of Elf Sarah with Santa Frank for an entire shift.

So she really didn't mind being back at her checkout with Billy Cruikshank the bagger. It was actually a relief, a chance to forget about her problems and just throw herself into her work.

At least until a familiar hand shoved a familiar green cap in her face again.

"Put this on," said Frank. "And hurry."

For an instant, Sarah was furious. She spun, ready to give him a piece of her mind for interrupting her shift...and then quickly lost her rage.

She could tell from the look on his face that he wasn't goofing around, though he was wearing his Santa getup. Something was terribly wrong, and Frank was deeply upset.

"What's going on?" asked Sarah.

"We need to leave right now." Frank gave her the hat, then handed her the rest of her folded-up elf outfit. "It's important."

"But what—?"

Frank whipped around to jab a finger at Billy. "Get another cashier to cover for her. If anyone asks why, say it's an emergency."

Sarah was worried and confused at the same time. "What kind of emergency would I need an elf suit for?"

Billy scowled. "You don't give the orders around here, Frank Halloran."

"No, but David Glosser does, and he's the one telling you to get someone to cover for her!" Frank turned to Sarah and bobbed his head hard to one side, indicating that she should follow him. "Now let's go! We need to get to Lee Hospital right away!"

"Frank, wait!" Sarah ran after Frank as he charged toward the stairs. She was starting to panic a little. "Please tell me what's going on!"

Frank bounded up the stairs in a most un-Santa-like way, nearly bowling over shoppers on their way up or down. "It's Grace! The little girl from the photo! She's been in a car crash, and she's asking for us!"

AFTER CHANGING into her elf costume in a ladies' restroom at the hospital, Sarah followed Frank to Grace's room. Over his shoulder, Frank lugged a full Santa sack, which a Glosser's co-worker had loaded and handed off on his way out of the store.

The good news, according to the duty nurse on the ward, was that the little girl's injuries weren't life-threatening or permanently debilitating. The bad news was, her Christmas had taken a turn for the worse.

"Ready?" Frank asked in a hushed voice in the hall outside Grace's door.

Sarah straightened her green felt cap. "That poor child." Her heart was racing. "Two broken legs and a broken arm..." She shook her head.

"And *we* are going to cheer her up." Frank shifted the sack on his shoulder and gave her a wink. "Are you okay with that? After last night?"

Sarah looked away, then returned her gaze to his face. Her mother's words came back to her. *Your life is your own.* "Yes." She nodded. "I'm okay."

Frank's bright green eyes held her, glittering. Slowly, a

smile emerged beneath his bushy white beard. "Good. That's good."

He took a deep breath, then turned and marched through the doorway. "Ho ho ho! Merry Christmas Eve!"

As Sarah followed him in, she saw little Grace on the bed. Both legs and her right arm were bound in white plaster casts and suspended by traction apparatus mounted in the ceiling. Gauze was wrapped around her head and left eye, too, and there were bruises on her face and bare right arm. She looked like she ought to be utterly miserable—yet she still lit up at the sight of her visitors.

"Santa!" Grace's voice was weak and shaky, but her excitement still shone through. "And Elf Sarah! You came!"

"Of course we did!" Frank swung his sack onto a nearby chair. "A little bird told us we should stop by on the way to the North Pole!" He nodded at the girl's gray-haired grandmother, who sat in a chair beside the bed. Grandma nodded back.

"How are you feeling, Grace?" Sarah stepped up beside the bed and smiled down at the child.

"Worried about my mommy." Grace frowned. "But Grammy says she's okay."

"She got banged-up, too, but no broken bones," said Grammy. "Poor Grace got the worst of it, I'm afraid."

"Well, you're a brave and very talented little girl," said Frank. "Fixing those legs and that arm of yours like that."

"The *doctors* fixed those." Grace giggled.

"But I'll bet you helped them, didn't you?" Frank folded his arms over his chest and frowned. "Or were you *bad* again?"

Grace thought for a moment. "I cried. Does that count?"

"Of course not, honey." Sarah grinned and shook her head. "Especially after what you've been through."

"I *want* to cry now," said Grace. "'Cause Christmas is *ruined*."

"Put those teardrops right back in your tummy!" said Frank. "Christmas is *never* ruined."

"But *look* at me! Doctor says I can't go home for Christmas! I won't be there when you bring my presents!"

"Oh, wait, that's right." Frank scowled as if deep in thought. "If only we had some way to get you those presents that didn't require you to be home."

When he flashed a wink at Sarah, she immediately caught on. "Santa?"

"Hmm." Frank folded his hands behind his back and paced across the room. "If only we could somehow bring them here to you."

Sarah cleared her throat. "I said, Santa!"

"But that's impossible, isn't it?" Frank paced to the doorway and leaned against the jamb, wagging his head. "It could never, ever *work*, could it?"

Eyes wide with feigned frustration, Sarah looked at Grace. "Doesn't he *remember*?" she said in a loud whisper.

Grace looked at the sack of gifts on the chair across the room and giggled.

"Oh, woe is me." Frank paced over to stand by the window, gazing out at the falling snow. "If only there was some way I could perform my Christmas duties for this sweet, sweet child!" He glanced over his shoulder at her and winced. "I mean, this *bad* child, but at least she's *honest* about it."

"Oh, San-ta!" Sarah tiptoed over to the chair with the sack of gifts and slid it toward it him. "I *have* something for you!"

"What shall I do?" Frank plunged his face into his red-mittened hands and pretended to weep. "How can I live this down?" Suddenly, he whirled and flung his arms out wide. "I'm not fit to be Santa Claus any..."

Just then, Sarah bumped the chair full of gifts into his legs. Again, she cleared her throat, louder than before.

"Oh, my." Frank pretended to notice the sack of gifts for the first time. "Look at that, won't you? What do you think is in that bag of mine, Grace?"

"*Presents*!" Grace laughed.

"I get so forgetful when I haven't had my milk and cookies!" Frank shook his head. "Thank you, dear Elf Sarah!"

"You're welcome, Santa." Sarah curtsied.

"A good elf is hard to find," said Frank. "I don't know what I'd do without her."

"You should give her a hug!" said Grace. "Elf Sarah needs a hug!"

Frank shrugged. "Well, she knows how much I appreciate her."

"Hug her, please?" said Grace. "For me?"

"Don't you want your presents first?" asked Frank.

"Hug her, Santa!"

Sarah looked at him, thought about it...then walked toward him with a kind of "let's humor the kid and get it over with" attitude.

This time, it was Frank's turn to clear his throat. "All right, then." He reached out and wrapped his arms around Sarah, as she did the same to him.

"And a kiss!" said Grace. "A hug *and* a kiss!"

Still in Frank's arms, Sarah leaned back and met his gaze. Smiling, she considered the promise in his eyes and what it might mean to her future.

If the future even mattered anymore. Maybe the only thing that did matter was this moment in time, and this person who made her feel happy and less alone. Who accepted her and wanted her in his life as much as...

As much as she accepted and wanted him. And this kiss.

She closed her eyes and leaned toward him, and he did the same.

Their lips met, softly, through Santa's beard...and the feeling was electric in spite of the abundant whiskers. Her whole body tingled, and everything but him melted away around her.

It was the first time she'd kissed anyone since Mike had left for Korea, and it was magical. It was perfect.

Then, Grace cheered, and the moment was broken. Frank pulled away from her, smiling. She knew she was blushing as she smiled back at him.

"Oh no!" said Grace. "You forgot the mistle-toad!"

"No, he's right here." Frank tugged his Santa hat up and down and made *ribbit* noises. Grace giggled louder than ever. "Now how 'bout if we open those *presents,* huh?"

"Already got my present." Grace smiled contentedly.

"Tough beans." Frank slid the chair up beside the bed and opened the sack of gifts. "You got more where *that* came from, kid. Now repeat after me: Ho ho ho!"

"Ho ho ho!" said Grace.

Frank winked at Sarah, and she joined in, too. "Ho ho ho!"

"God bless us, every one!" said Frank as he pulled the first gift out of the sack.

SARAH AND FRANK stayed with Grace for hours, reading her stories and playing games and just talking. They stayed until she fell asleep, just as visiting hours were ending, and then they each kissed her forehead and left.

It was snowing hard when they stepped outside, big white flakes slashing down in the golden glow of the streetlights. All around, it was deeply quiet, amazingly peaceful for downtown Johnstown on a Thursday night, when the stores were usually open late and the streets full of people and cars.

As the two of them walked up Main Street, it seemed like they were the only people in the world. It felt to Sarah like a perfect moment, so magical that she couldn't resist when he reached to take her hand.

"Thank you," said Frank. "Thank you for coming along tonight."

"I wouldn't have missed it." Sarah walked close to him, enjoying the way his arm brushed against hers. "It was so wonderful, giving that poor girl a nice Christmas Eve."

"We did, didn't we?" Frank's smile was plain to see now that he'd taken off his Santa beard and stuffed it in his pocket. "We make a great team."

A car drifted past, laying tracks in the freshly fallen snow. For a second, Sarah thought about letting go of Frank's hand—but then she caught herself and kept her hand right where it was.

"Can you think of a better way to spend Christmas Eve?" asked Frank. "Helping a little girl in the hospital?"

"I can't." Looking over at his smiling face, she had a rush of feeling for him—admiration and affection all at once. She was so proud of him for doing what he'd done and taking such obvious joy in it. He was a good person at heart...a good man.

"So much for the Christmas Eve party," said Frank. "But I don't mind, do you?"

Sarah shook her head. "This was more fun."

When they got to Central Park, they followed the snow-covered walk to the Christmas tree, its multi-colored lights glowing through the falling flakes. They stood there a while, side by side, gazing at the lights.

Then, he turned to her, his face blushing with reddish glow. "This is all I want for Christmas," he said softly. "All I could *ever* want."

When he leaned to kiss her, she didn't pull away.

THE NEXT MORNING, Sarah woke up bright and early and sailed across her bedroom, getting ready for Christmas Day. Frank had driven her home in his Chevy the night before, leaving her with one more kiss at the front door...and sweet dreams the whole night through.

As the sun streamed through her window that morning, Sarah realized she was happier than she'd been in a long time. The past two Christmases had been punishing, full of sadness because her fiancé was in Korea—but this one was full of hope. There was someone else who cared about her now, someone she cared about in return...and she was going to see him soon.

The night before, Frank had asked if he could come by around noon on Christmas Day, and she'd said yes. She hadn't told her parents yet, but she had a feeling it would work out fine. Dad might not be thrilled, but she knew Mom was on her side. Hopefully, Frank could even eat Christmas dinner with them.

The thought of it made her heart pound. She felt like she was finally moving forward after being frozen in place for so long.

The morning hours fell away like snowflakes as Frank's visit drew closer. After the family exchanged gifts around the tree, Sarah helped Mom with preparations for Christmas dinner. It was then she asked Mom if it was okay for Frank to join them...and Mom said yes.

Sarah was more worried about asking Dad, though, and put it off. She wasn't sure he'd appreciate the situation, as he'd once been in Mike's shoes himself, overseas with a fiancée at home during World War II.

Around noon, the doorbell rang, and Sarah knew it was too late. She would just have to wing it and hope for the best, hope her father would come to like Frank as much as she did.

"I'll get it!" She stopped peeling potatoes in the kitchen and dashed to the front door. One thing she didn't want was for Dad to get there first.

As the doorbell rang again, she straightened her hair, smoothed out her top, and took a deep breath. Smiling, she reached for the knob...so happy to be about to open the door and see *him* there. To know her Christmas was going to be *special* again.

She swung the door open, beaming expectantly. Her muscles tensed as she thought about holding him, kissing him...

And then, the world suddenly stopped turning.

Sarah's eyes locked on the face on the other side of the door, and she gasped. It wasn't Frank. It was the last person in the world she'd expected to see that day.

It was *Mike.*

"Merry Christmas, beautiful!" he said. "Miss me?"

SARAH WAS in a state of shock. She just stood there in the doorway, gaping, speechless.

"Great surprise, huh?" Mike laughed amid the flurries glittering around him. He looked different from the last time she'd seen him, different even from the photos he'd sent from time to time—leaner, bonier, tougher. His dark eyes and big nose stood out more sharply from his knobby brows and sunken cheeks.

To Sarah, he was almost a stranger. "But your letter..."

Mike laughed again. "It was a setup! I've been discharged!"

"You mean...you're home?"

"Well, obviously! So is this the biggest surprise ever, or what?"

Sarah felt light-headed. She still couldn't believe this was happening. She still couldn't believe, after *everything,* that she'd opened the door to see *him* instead of...

Just then, a familiar blue Chevy pulled up at the curb. And Sarah's heart didn't just sink...it *nosedived.*

"So come on." Mike pointed at the sprig of mistletoe pinned to his olive drab cap. "Aren't you gonna give your fiancé a kiss?"

He spread his arms and grinned. Over his shoulder, Sarah saw Frank get out of the Chevy and walk toward them.

"Mike!" At that moment, Dad popped up behind her in the doorway. "You're back!" He was so excited, he pushed past Sarah to hug Mike himself.

Frank slowed down as he got closer, taking in the scene. Looking at Mike in his olive drab army fatigues and combat boots. Doing the math.

His eyes met Sarah's, and a world of understanding passed between them. She saw a flash of pain and disappointment, and she wanted to run to him. She wanted to comfort him, to take him in her arms as she'd intended and *care* for him. *Choose* him.

But she just stood there, frozen on the outside as she was tearing herself apart on the inside. She just *stood there*...thinking she needed more time, she needed to figure this out, she needed to do what was *right* for her.

It was one of those moments, she realized years later, that change a life forever.

As she watched, Frank gathered himself up and walked the rest of the way up the sidewalk. "Merry Christmas," he said brightly.

Everyone turned to look. "Who's this?" asked Dad.

Sarah cleared her throat. "This is Frank Halloran." She felt like she was speaking in a dream. "He works at Glosser's."

"As Santa Claus." Frank's smile was wide. Probably only Sarah could see how forced it was.

"Can we help you with something?" asked Dad.

Before Sarah could say a word, Frank answered. "I just stopped to give Sarah something." He dug in the pocket of his pea coat, came out with a closed fist. "Here you go." Leaning past Mike, he dropped the contents of his fist into Sarah's hand. "A little Christmas present for a co-worker."

He smiled then, only for her. For an instant, it was like before between them.

And then he whirled and hurried back to his car.

"What is it?" asked Mike.

Sarah opened her hand. A shiny penny rested head-up on her palm.

"A little money I owed you!" Frank said over his shoulder. "I always pay my debts, especially on Christmas!"

Sarah's eyes burned. Mike reached for the penny, and she snapped her hand closed around it.

"Merry Christmas!" shouted Frank. "God bless us every one!"

Sarah wanted to run after him. Almost did, for an instant...but then she didn't. She stayed instead.

As Frank drove off through the snow, the rest of his life somewhere in the distance.

JOHNSTOWN, 2016

Sarah almost didn't get out of the car.

"Come on, Gram." Emma stood on the street with the car door open and reached in to help. "Jason and his grandfather are waiting."

Sarah frowned and shook her head. It had been 63 years since she'd last seen Frank Halloran, since he'd driven away from her house on Christmas Day. He'd moved away shortly thereafter and had never come back or reached out to her. The thought of seeing him again filled her with curiosity...but mostly panic.

"I shouldn't have let you talk me into this." She studiously kept her eyes from drifting toward the big Christmas tree in Central Park, just fifty feet away, which was where Frank was supposed to meet her. "I've changed my mind."

"Too late for that." Emma was determined to get her grandmother out of the car. She had high hopes that meeting Frank after so many years might restore Sarah's love of Christmas. Losing him, after all, was what had ruined the holiday for her in the first place.

"No." Clutching the silver locket at her throat, Sarah watched the reflected light from the tree flash and flicker on the windows of the car. "Not after the way things ended."

"He wants to see you, Gram." Emma smiled encouragingly. "He's okay with it. Otherwise, he wouldn't be here tonight."

"*He's* okay with it..." Sarah's voice trailed off. In 63 years, she had never forgiven herself for letting him go. She had never let herself celebrate Christmas.

Emma hunkered down and put a hand on her arm. "You have regrets, I get that. But you'll regret *this*, too, if you don't go to him now."

Sarah let out a long, shaky breath. She wished she could snap back to her usual sassy self with her take-no-crap attitude...but that part of her was switched off now. On the verge of reuniting with her long-lost love, all she felt was fear.

"Come on, Gram," said Emma. "He's a widower now. It's time for a second chance."

"What if you're wrong?" said Sarah. "What if it all goes south?"

Emma gave Sarah's arm a tug. She wanted this reunion for Sarah so much, wanted to bring some joy back into her life. "If things go south, I'll run you outta there like a bear out of a bee swarm."

Sarah stayed put another moment...then let Emma pull her out of the car. "The *second* they go south?"

"The *second*," said Emma, though she prayed she wouldn't have to keep her word.

"You better." Sarah snapped her fingers. "Or I will disinherit you like *that.*"

Emma laughed. "Now *there's* my Gram."

"Not for long if you don't get me outta there *pronto*." Sarah glared as she pushed past her granddaughter and headed into the park.

THE CROWD around the tree in Central Park was huge that night. After all, it was Christmas Eve.

Sarah moved slowly among the people, mindful of the coating of snow on the sidewalks. The big tree, like a beacon, guided her onward, its multicolored lights blinking and dancing amid the swirling flurries in the air.

Emma walked by her side, keeping one arm around her shoulders and holding on lightly to her elbow. She was a good girl, that Emma—even if she *was* pushing Sarah to do something she didn't want to do.

Just then, a little boy charged past, almost knocking Sarah over. Another child followed, with a young mother bringing up the rear. "So sorry." She smiled apologetically on her way past.

It was amazing, what a difference that tree had made

in such a short time. Funded by donations, spearheaded by a partnership of business people and volunteers, it had given new life to downtown Johnstown during the holidays. Practically deserted at night for many years, Central Park now reminded Sarah of the old days, when Glosser Bros. had still been packing them in.

It was appropriate, then, that as she approached the big tree, she suddenly saw Frank Halloran smiling back at her.

Even if his grandson, Jason, had not been standing nearby, Sarah would have recognized him instantly. Frank's hair was white instead of red, but his face was the same as ever. His body was as lean and athletic as before.

And somehow, as his green eyes met hers, the sparks were there between them again.

Sarah caught her breath. Her heart leaped in her chest like a bird taking flight.

Emma was saying something, but Sarah didn't hear a word of it. No one else mattered at that moment but him.

He called to her across the crowd, over the music from the flashing, blinking tree. "Elf Sarah!"

Tears ran freely from her eyes as she shuffled toward him. *To think,* she thought, *I almost didn't come here tonight.*

Frank didn't wait for her. Grinning, he rushed across the snowy walk and threw his arms around her, holding her tight against him.

WHEN EMMA SAW Sarah and Frank embrace, she flung up her hands in their wooly white gloves and clamped them over her mouth. She couldn't help herself from crying tears of pure joy to match those running down her grandmother's cheeks.

After all the wonderful things Sarah had done for her through the years, Emma was thrilled to give her this gift from the heart. She'd wanted to give her grandma back her love of Christmas, so she could enjoy it as much as Emma did...and now she had done just that. And more.

For there was *another* gift coming, a surprise.

"This is so great!" said Jason as he rushed over and threw an arm around her. "I think this is the happiest I've ever seen him!"

Sarah wiped tears from her face and nodded. "We did it! Oh my God, we did it!"

"Not like it took much work, though." Jason chuckled. "As soon as I mentioned her name, he was online checking plane fares! I think he was packing while we were still on the phone!"

"She was scared," said Emma. "But now look at them."

"And she doesn't know?" asked Jason. "About the surprise?"

Emma shook her head. "Why spoil it?" She grinned and turned to kiss him. "She should hear it straight from the horse's mouth."

SARAH SHUT her eyes and savored every moment. How many times had she dreamed of this very thing happening over the past 63 years? How many times had she wished for this man to return to her?

Now there they were, a widow and a widower, basking in the light and magic of that special tree, across the street from the Glosser Bros. building where they'd first met in 1953.

"I told you I was a bad penny," he whispered in her ear. "Always turning up."

Sarah smiled with pure, boundless joy in his arms. She couldn't believe she'd been afraid.

"I'm so sorry," she said.

Leaning back, he shook his head. "Not me." Reaching out, he stroked the side of her face with his warm, rough hand. "Just *imagine* how good this *kiss* is going to be after all that time!"

As he leaned toward her, she saw Emma and Jason kissing out of the corner of her eye. She felt so overcome with emotion, she thought her heart might burst.

"By the way," said Frank. "I have a request."

"What's that?" asked Sarah, gazing lovingly into his bright green eyes.

"Do you know anyone who could help me get settled?"

"Settled?"

"I'm moving back to town," said Frank. "Effective immediately. I'm sending for my things."

Sarah couldn't believe what she was hearing. "Really?" Her heart, which had already taken flight, was soaring into the loftiest heights now. "Immediately?"

Frank shrugged. "I've been considering it for a while, with my son and grandkids here. *Now* just seems...like the right time."

Sarah's smile widened. Her tears of joy quickened.

"So what do you say?" asked Frank. "Know anyone who could help..."

Sarah didn't let him finish his sentence.

As the tree played "I'll Be Home for Christmas," she lunged forward, pressing her lips against Frank's...and it was every bit as glorious as she'd imagined. She stopped thinking about fear and regret and second chances, stopped thinking about anywhere but *there,* anyone but *him,* and anything but that *kiss.*

And the penny he'd given her on that last day long ago, which she'd worn in a silver locket around her neck every day since, seemed to warm and glow like an ember between them, breathed back to life by the heat of their beating hearts.

LOVE, MISS GEE BEE

VALENTINE'S DAY AT GLOSSER'S

THE CONTENTS of the mail sack poured onto a round table in the break room of the Gee Bee Department Store—hundreds of postcards and letters addressed to a woman who didn't exist.

Though the woman sitting at the table was known to answer to her name.

"Just look at all those cards and letters," said Gary the mailroom guy. "Every one of them made out to you, Miss Gee Bee."

"What can I say? My fans adore me." The smiling woman at the table was young and pretty, with deep green eyes and shoulder-length black hair. "I guess 1973 is the year I hit it big." Though she wasn't really named "Miss Gee Bee," she played that character in ads for the Gee Bee discount department stores, offshoots of the legendary Glosser Bros. store in Johnstown, Pennsylvania.

Her *real* name was Emily Bradley.

"Well, enjoy the adoration." Gary shook out a few last cards and slung the empty bag over his shoulder. "Looks like you've got a couple *hours'* worth to keep you busy, Miss Gee Bee."

"Feel free to jump in and give me a hand." Emily scooped up a stack of cards and letters and shook them emphatically. "Come on, Gary! Don't tell me you don't love romantic *poetry.*"

"Okay, I won't tell you." Gary chuckled as he headed for the door. "But I *might* have been known to *write* some from time to time."

"Oh my God! You mean..." She scooped up some mail and gazed at it wonderingly. "One of *these* could be *your entry* for the big *contest?*"

"You never know, Miss Gee Bee." Gary grinned and spoke along the back of his hand as if telling her a secret. "P.S., I *might* have signed it with a *pen name.*"

"Then how will I know it's yours?" asked Emily.

"You'll know when it makes you swoon," said Gary.

"*Throw up* is more like it," said Emily's friend and co-worker, Tina Fontana, as she strolled past Gary into the room. "Save it for the girls at the warehouse, Gare."

"I've got a poem for you, too, Tina," said Gary. "It starts with 'There once was a girl from Nantucket.'"

"Always so charming, Gare." Tina rolled her eyes and gave her long blonde hair a toss.

"Then why did you go out with me that time?"

"Beats the heck outta me." Tina spun to smile at Emily as Gary slunk out of the room, mumbling. "So check *you* out, honey. You're really raking in the *valentines.*"

"Don't be jealous," said Emily. "They're for Miss Gee Bee."

"You must feel so *special.*" Tina picked up a postcard, read the message on the back, and fanned herself with it. "All these romantic *poems.*"

"Which aren't even all from *guys.*"

"They aren't?"

"I can tell." Emily nodded emphatically. "The really *good* ones are from *women.*"

"I'll bet they said that to Bill Shakespeare."

"Shakespeare didn't write love poems to win a 10% Sweetheart Shopping Spree at Gee Bee Department Store." Emily picked up a handful of mail and let it dribble down onto the pile. "Trust me, there's no Shakespeare in *this* mess."

"Whose idea *was* this contest anyway?" Tina scowled as she read another card, then threw it right in a nearby trash can. "Jack Shepherd?" She was talking about the manager of the store.

"Straight from the top, I heard." Emily rolled her eyes. "Mr. Black himself."

Tina chuckled. "You really *are* on the radar, girl! Better mind your P's and Q's."

Just then, Gary leaned in the doorway and whistled. When Emily and Tina looked, he threw a paper airplane, which floated in their direction...and suddenly crashed.

"Geez," said Tina. "You can't even make a *paper plane* right."

"Just what we needed, Gary." Emily didn't bother picking up the plane. "More *poetry.*"

"Not poetry." Gary smirked. "A message from the *boss*."

"But Mr. Shepherd could've just walked back here and told her himself," said Tina. "Why the paperwork?"

"I'm talking about the *big* boss." Gary nodded as he backed out the door. "The boss in downtown *Johnstown*."

Tina bugged her eyes wide. "Speak of the devil!"

Emily jumped up and grabbed the plane from the floor. Before she unfolded it and read the note inside, she already knew who'd written it. She knew exactly whom Gary was talking about.

Gee Bee was a suburban store in Richland Township. The mother store, Glosser Bros., was located a few miles away in downtown Johnstown. That was where the biggest bigwigs could be found, including the company president.

Getting called to see him, Emily knew, could be a big deal—for better or worse.

"Have fun, Miss Gee Bee!" said Gary as he slipped back out of the break room.

"Go Gee Bee yourself, Gare!" Tina told him.

Emily folded the note and stuck it in the pocket of her black slacks. "I guess I'd better get going. The note says I need to see the president right away."

"About what?" asked Tina.

"It doesn't say." A feeling of dread crept over Emily. She couldn't think of anything she might have done wrong—but she still worried about the summons. Her profile had been raised three months ago, when the bosses had chosen her as the real-life version of company mascot Miss Gee Bee; ever since, as a company representative, she'd had to stay on her best behavior and had been more worried about getting in trouble.

It wasn't easy being Miss Gee Bee.

"Maybe he just wants to give you a love poem, too," said Tina.

"Good." Emily straightened her floral print button-down blouse, checked her hair in the mirror, and grabbed her purse from the back of the chair where she'd been sitting. "It has to be better than anything *Gary* comes up with."

WHEN EMILY WALKED in the front door of the Glosser Bros. Department Store in downtown Johnstown, the first thing that struck her, as always, was the wonderful smell of roasting peanuts and cashews. It was a smell that always made her feel at home, a smell that had been part of her life for as long as she remembered. It made her feel welcome, whether she entered as an employee or shopper.

And it drew her onward, through the first floor of the store, which was busy even then, at lunchtime on a Wednesday in early February. The source of the roasted nut fragrance—the candy and nut counter—came up shortly after she entered, and she wished she had time to stop for a snack.

Further along, women in winter coats browsed the bargain tables on the Locust Street side of the floor, sifting through gloves, handbags, hats, and more. Across from the women's accessories, old men and a few middle-aged businessmen on lunch break wandered through the men's furnishings area, picking through socks, t-shirts, underwear, and ties.

Emily waved at salespeople she knew but didn't stop to chat; she couldn't, with the president waiting for her. A good friend who worked for a downtown bank was coming down the escalator from the second floor, but Emily ducked her head and kept going, avoiding an encounter.

Finally, she made it to the elevator bank along the side of the store facing Locust Street and Central Park. She punched the button for the upper floors, and a car arrived a moment later. After a woman with two small children got off, Emily boarded the car and hit the button for the fourth floor, where the corporate management offices were located.

The elevator dinged, the door slid open, and she stepped out onto the fourth floor. Passing the home furnishings and housewares departments, she reached her destination—the office of the president of the company, who had summoned her from Gee Bee in Richland.

Opening the door, she saw the secretary in the outer office was away from her desk...but the inner office wasn't empty at all.

"Hello? Who's there?"

"Emily Bradley." Nervous, she peeked around the corner of the inner office.

President Leonard Black smiled back at her from behind his big desk. "Come in, come in." He patted his silver hair and got to his feet. "Thank you for stopping down, Miss Bradley."

"Thank you, sir." Emily stepped inside, her heart pounding as she wondered about the object of the meeting.

It was only then that she saw someone else was in the room, standing just inside the doorway. It was a young man she didn't recognize, with curly black hair and a wide, dimpled grin. She could see, from the way his navy-blue leisure suit hung from his body, that he was athletic, with broad, muscular shoulders, beefy arms, and a lean, tapered midriff.

"Emily Bradley—Miss Gee Bee—I'd like you to meet Ryan Morgan." President Black gestured at the dark-haired man and smiled. "Otherwise known as Glossy the Glosser Boy."

"Nice to meet you, Emily." Ryan nodded and reached for a handshake.

Emily returned it, though she was confused. "Glossy the Glosser Boy?" She'd never heard the name before.

"Our brand-new mascot." President Black nodded. "Like Miss Gee Bee for the Glosser Bros. store."

"Right." Emily almost always made it a point to agree with the boss. "Nice to meet you, Ryan."

"We're phasing in the character." President Black held up a sheet of paper with "Glossy the Glosser Boy" printed alongside a drawing of a young man's smiling face—identical to Miss Gee Bee except for the shorter hair. "Eventually, he'll be in ads, on shopping bags, on billboards, just like you."

"That's neat," said Emily, though she didn't really think it was neat.

"And we'll start with the two of you together," said President Black. "Judging the Valentine's contest."

"Okay." Emily was becoming less thrilled by the minute.

"We've started telling people they can send poems to one or the other of you," explained President Black. "If the winning entry is written for you, Emily, the Sweetheart Shopping Spree will happen at Gee Bee in Richland. But if Ryan gets the winner, the spree will happen right here at Glosser Bros."

"Nothing like a little friendly competition." Ryan smiled. "Am I right, Emily?"

"So, wait." Emily frowned. "The *two* of us are supposed to judge the contest entries *together*?"

"Correct." President Black walked over to stand between them, putting his hands on their shoulders. "And to keep it fair, I want you to work here at Glosser's one day and up at Gee Bee the next. How does that strike you?"

"Just fine," said Emily, though it didn't strike her well at all. She worked at Gee Bee in Richland and lived just a few miles away in Geistown; running to downtown Johnstown every other day would be a pain.

"What a great idea," said Ryan. "Miss Gee Bee and Glossy the Glosser Boy, working together! People should really get a kick out of it."

"Can't hurt to give it a try," said President Black. "The folks in marketing think it has legs, so we'll see."

"I'll keep my fingers crossed," said Emily, though she didn't mean it.

"Now get downstairs on the sales floor, you two," said President Black. "I want you to judge the contest so everyone can see you. That'll really get 'em in the mood."

"Yes, sir," said Emily.

"And no romance between the two of *you*." President Black tousled their hair. "Remember, Glossy and Miss Gee Bee are practically brother and sister."

THE MAINTENANCE CREW set up one of the bargain tables in the middle of the first floor as contest central, cordoning it off with red velvet ropes. Then, the men dumped two full bags of mail on the table, creating a mountain of cards and letters in need of sorting.

It was enough to make the shoppers curious, especially until Judy from display advertising brought down a sign on a silver pedestal and set it up nearby.

Sweetheart Shopping Spree! Below that, in the big heart in the middle of the sign, it said, *Miss Gee Bee* and *Glossy the Glosser Boy Pick the Winning Poem.* Along the bottom, it said, *Winner Announced on Valentine's Day!*

Just like that, Emily found herself reading love poems in the middle of the Glosser Bros. Department Store with some guy she didn't know.

Named Glossy.

It wasn't exactly how she'd thought her day would go when she'd woken up that morning.

"Here's a good one!" Ryan was reading poems addressed to Miss Gee Bee since there were only a few addressed to Glossy so far. "'Violets are red, roses are blue. In the department store of love, the best bargain is you.'"

Emily groaned and let her head fall forward on the table. "Not again."

"What do you mean, not again?" asked Ryan.

"I mean I've seen *dozens* of versions of that poem in this contest." She rolled her head back and forth, crinkling letters underneath it. "*Hundreds,* even."

"No kidding." Ryan chuckled as he rummaged through the pile. "I wonder if...hey, you're right!" He pulled out a postcard and read it aloud. "'Roses are violets, red is blue. If I couldn't shop at Gee Bee, I don't know what I'd do.'"

Emily raised her head. "I swear, it's like every other poem is roses and violets. Where's the originality, man?"

Ryan read another one. "'Roses are red, violets are blue. Dear Miss Gee Bee, I love you.'"

An elderly woman was walking by just as he read it and smiled. "That's so sweet, young man. Miss Gee Bee's a lucky woman."

"Thank you, ma'am." Ryan nodded graciously. "And I'm a *very* lucky man."

As the old woman walked away from the table, Ryan and Emily both laughed quietly, into the pile. Another old lady happened by at that exact moment and gave them a cross look, which only made them laugh harder.

When the laughter finally faded, Emily grabbed a postcard and flicked it at him. "So have you done much poetry critiquing before this?"

"Oh my, yes," Ryan answered, putting on a snobbish voice. "I'm a *professional,* actually. I started out critiquing nursery rhymes and moved on from there to commercial jingles."

"You don't say!"

"Oh, but I do," said Ryan. "Sometimes, I even critique people's conversations for the fun of it. You'd never believe how many times the average person says things that are inadequate in one way or another."

"Fascinating." Emily ripped open an envelope and slid out the letter inside. "And how would you rate *my* conversation skills?"

"Pretty good. Especially the part where you called me a real looker with a dynamite personality and charm that won't quit."

"Hmmm." Emily tapped her chin with a fingertip. "You didn't *tell* me the conversations you critique are in your *imagination.*"

"I didn't think they were." Ryan laughed. "I guess I misheard what you said. Though it's also true I read minds from time to time. You might have been *thinking* those things, though you didn't say them out loud."

"Let's test that interesting theory." Emily narrowed her eyes and leaned toward him. "Can you read what I'm thinking right now?"

"That I'm a really wonderful guy in every possible way?"

Emily shook her head slowly. "Not even close, Glossy."

Just then, Judy returned from the display department, carrying a hatbox. "Hey, guys." She was a few years older than either of them, with blonde hair tied in a ponytail. She wore wire-framed granny glasses like the ones John Lennon had made famous. "I have something for you."

"Ah, you shouldn't have," said Ryan. "Unless it's cash."

"Or candy," said Emily. "I'm starving."

"Even better." Judy opened the box and tipped it toward them. "We just finished these this morning."

It only took a second for Emily to realize what was in the box. "You didn't. Please tell me you didn't."

"I did," said Judy.

"Oh, cool!" Ryan reached into the box and pulled out a black plastic bowler hat. The brim was wide and flat; the crown was printed with a jumble of op art hearts and curlicues. "Just like Miss Gee Bee's hat in the newspaper ads!"

"That's right." Judy reached in and pulled out a second plastic hat—identical except for the brim, which was more of a bill extending from one side. "And for Glossy, we have a *baseball* style hat with the same designs as Miss Gee Bee."

"I love it!" Grinning, Ryan took the hat and stuck it on his head—backwards. "This is perfect for my character!"

Judy turned the hat around so the bill faced forward as it should. "*Now* it's perfect."

Emily put her own hat on and smiled. "How do I look?"

"Very cute," said Judy. "Like Miss Gee Bee come to life."

Ryan reached over and tipped her hat to one side, then did the same for his own. "We match."

He met her gaze then and held it...just for a moment. Just long enough for her to notice something for the first time. A flicker of appreciation? Or was it just her imagination?

And then it was gone.

"So the hats were ordered by President Black." Judy put the lid back on the hat box and pushed it under her right arm. "He wants you to wear them while you're judging the contest or anytime you appear in public as Miss Gee Bee or Glossy."

"Can do," said Ryan. "But can we take them off when we go to the can?"

Judy laughed. "Up to you, Glossy. Just take care of the darn things. They took forever to work up, and we only have two."

"So no hat frisbee, then?" asked Ryan. "No hat horseshoes?"

"Correct," said Judy.

"But hat tackle football is okay," said Emily.

"Why wouldn't it be?" Judy chuckled.

It was then that a little old lady in a red coat stopped by the velvet rope, beaming. "Oh, heavens! Don't the two of you look wonderful? Just like the Gee Bee lady in the ads!"

"Thank you, ma'am," said Emily.

"Such adorable hats," said the old lady. "I just love all the little hearts on them! Glosser's and Gee Bee really are all about Valentine's Day, aren't they?"

"They sure are, ma'am," said Ryan.

The old lady leaned closer. "And you two make *just* the perfect couple. I wish you *all* the happiness."

Ryan flashed Emily a look. She suddenly realized she was blushing and looked away.

AFTER A FEW HOURS of going through love poems on the sales floor, Emily and Ryan went to Glosser's Cafeteria in the Annex for a break. They quickly discovered they had something in common: the soda fountain was their favorite place to eat in the store.

And they both knew the Shaffer twins who worked there, though they couldn't tell them apart.

"Hi, Ruby!" said Ryan as he bounded up to the counter and shook his hat in the air. "What kind of discount do we get if we're wearing these hats?"

"Oh, that's cute," said the twin at the counter. "But I'm Ruth."

"Whoops." Ryan shook the hat again. "So what's the special discount for Glossy the Glosser Boy and Miss Gee Bee?"

Ruth smiled, turned, and called out to her sister, who was just walking out of the kitchen with a tub of ice cream. "What's the special discount for Glossy and Miss Gee Bee?"

Ruby shrugged. "Just the usual employee discount, as far as I know. I could ask the manager, though."

"Or President Black," said Ruth.

"That's okay." Ryan tapped the hat down on his head with an index finger. "The usual employee discount is fine."

"So what would you like?" asked Ruth.

"One hot fudge sundae." Ryan glanced at Emily. "What about you?"

"I'll have the same," said Emily.

"And what else?" asked Ruth and Ruby at the same time.

"That's all, thanks," said Ryan.

"Okay," said Ruth. "And Ruby, how about throwing in some extra fudge sauce for these two since they missed out on the special discount?"

"You got it." Ruby winked.

It was then Emily realized the Shaffer twins had been teasing them all along.

"Oh my God." Emily put another spoonful of chocolate sauce and vanilla ice cream in her mouth and let it slide down her throat. "I *love* the sundaes here. *And* the banana splits *and* the milkshakes."

"Join the club." Ryan had another scoop of his own sundae and smiled blissfully. "Though I'm a little shocked to hear Miss Gee Bee say that. Aren't you supposed to love the snack bar at Gee Bee more?"

"Glosser's cafeteria is better." Emily leaned toward him and dropped her voice to a whisper. "Don't tell anyone."

"I promise not to tell." Ryan smirked. "Unless I think it will benefit me in some way."

"Just remember, two can play at that game." Emily nodded. "I can always tell on you for liking the restaurant at *Penn Traffic* better."

"But that's a lie!"

"Is it, Ryan? Is it?" Giggling, she spooned more sundae into her mouth, savoring the cold, chocolatey sweetness.

"You're a tough customer, you know that?" said Ryan. "Is that what happens when you grow up on the mean streets of...of..."

"Geistown."

"Ohhh. That *is* mean." It wasn't, not even a little. "That explains a lot about you, Miss Gee Bee."

"Like what?" asked Emily.

"Your hard-bitten attitude." Ryan scowled and shook a fist. "Your intimidating nastiness. Your quick, explosive temper."

"What about the foul language I use every other word?"

"That, too," said Ryan. "Though it *is* hard to be *too* scary when you've got a hot fudge sundae mustache."

Emily laughed, grabbed a napkin, and wiped her mouth. "What about you? What side of the tracks are you from?"

"Kernville," said Ryan. "The mellow part of town."

Kernville, a neighborhood in downtown Johnstown, wasn't mellow at all. "Are you serious?" asked Emily.

"Lived there all my life." Ryan nodded and dug more

fudge out of the sundae dish. "Why do you think I'm such a creampuff?"

Emily laughed. She doubted he was any kind of creampuff at all, coming from that tough neighborhood. "So whereabouts in Kernville do you live?"

"That's confidential information." Ryan narrowed his eyes. "But I *can* tell you it's not far from a great little sub and pizza place."

"Do you mean Brownie's?" Emily grinned. "They're the best in town!"

Ryan shrugged. "Maybe."

"Man of mystery, huh?" She ate a little more fudge from the sundae. "So can you at least tell me about your family? Do you have any brothers or sisters?"

"Let's see." He flicked his spoon as he counted them out loud. "There's Rossy, Bossy, and Mossy. Then my sisters Flossy, Tossy, Hossy, and Lossy. Nice big Catholic family."

"So Glossy is your *real* name." Emily chuckled. "No wonder you were perfect for the job!"

"I'm not surprised you never guessed 'Ryan' is just a nickname. I have *multiple* nicknames, actually: Joe, John, Tom, Ted, Frank, Rob, and Bob...though *most* folks know me as *Rubber Chicken*."

Emily laughed some more; she did that a lot with Ryan around. There could be *less* fun things than working with him on the contest, she realized.

"I guess we should get back downstairs and keep reading poems." She clinked her spoon in the sundae dish and got up from the table.

"*Or* we could just pick a winner at random and spend the rest of the time goofing around," suggested Ryan.

"And miss out on all the wonderful entries we haven't read yet? Not a chance!"

Ryan shrugged. "Who could stand missing out on all that?"

"Hey, maybe we'll find some great poems yet," said Emily.

"Maybe we will." Ryan smiled. "You never know."

THE NEXT DAY, the judging moved from Glosser Bros. downtown to Gee Bee in Richland. Emily got there bright and early at 8:45, expecting to arrive ahead of Ryan.

But by the time she walked onto the sales floor, he was already there and set up. Wearing his Glossy ball cap, he grinned and waved from behind a product table near the front of the store, just inside the big glass front doors. A sign promoting the contest rose from the middle of the table, mounted in a silver pedestal frame, with a mountain of mail heaped around it.

"Good morning, Miss Gee Bee!" With a flourish, Ryan dropped an envelope into a white mailsack on the floor. "I hope you don't mind that I took the liberty of getting a head start before you got here."

"How dare you?" she snapped with mock indignation. "What if I missed out on some great poems in the batch you judged on your own?"

"Trust me, you didn't." Ryan opened another envelope, glanced at the letter inside for a heartbeat, and tossed it in the sack. "You *really* didn't."

Emily joined him at the table and started scanning entries. "You do realize we might have to settle for something that's *the least bad,* right?"

"Have faith, Miss Gee Bee." Ryan deepened his voice, sounding like a hero on TV. "We may yet locate a work of highest quality among all this inferior slush."

"You haven't been doing this as long as I have," said Emily as she dumped the latest letter in the sack. "Believe me, you'll lose that silly optimism soon enough."

"Until then, I choose to look on the bright side." Ryan tipped his hat at a passing customer—a middle-aged woman with brown hair.

The move reminded Emily that she'd left her hat in the car. "Cover for me! I'll be right back!"

She darted out of the store, got the bowler hat from her bright green VW Beetle in the parking lot, and scurried back in, teeth chattering. Running to the car without her coat had been quick, but it was only in the 20s out there.

"I don't believe it," said Ryan when she got back to the sorting table.

Breathless, Emily tugged the plastic bowler hat on her head. "I know! I can't believe I forgot this, either!"

"No, no," said Ryan. "I mean I can't believe *this.*"

In his right hand, he waved a red envelope and a Valentine's Day card with a red heart on the front.

"What?" asked Emily. "Another contest entry?"

"I wouldn't call it *just* another entry." Ryan cleared his throat, opened the card wide, and read what was written inside. "'The stream flows fast from the mountain so vast. The sun shines bright and imbues us with light. The wind blows strong and accomp'nies birds' song. All the world's like a dream, every silver moonbeam, every heart full of love, shines like Heaven above. I just pray you'll soon see, sweet and soft Miss Gee Bee, how you make my soul soar, and embrace me for more.'"

For a moment after he'd finished, neither of them spoke. Then, Emily shook her head slowly, in a daze, and pointed at the card in his hand. "Wow," she said simply. "That's...that's actually..."

"I know." Ryan widened his eyes and nodded. "It's the first good one I've seen so far."

"Yeah, for sure." Emily frowned. "So don't keep me in suspense. Who *wrote* it?"

"Beats the heck outta me." Ryan flapped the envelope in his hand. "No return address. No identification whatsoever. Miss Gee Bee has a *secret admirer*."

"Huh." Emily thought for a moment, then took the envelope from him. "No stamp or postmark, either. Whoever submitted this must have dropped it off at the store."

"It was in the mail bag this morning." Ryan shrugged. "That's all I know."

Emily took the card from him next and scanned the poem. It read as well on paper as it had sounded out loud. "Do you know what else this means?"

"The contest is over?"

"It means we have to find out *who* this person is," said Emily. "Because he's the only actual poet we've found so far out of hundreds of entries."

"What if he—or she—doesn't *want* to be found?"

"He *does,* trust me," said Emily. "Why else would he send this to Miss Gee Bee?"

"Because he's too shy to come forward?"

"No way." Emily shook the card and envelope in her hand. "He *will.* We haven't heard the last of the *unknown poet.*"

THE HUNT WAS ON. Emily and Ryan combed through the rest of the entries in the mail bag but didn't find another card like the first. They asked around the staff, but none of them remembered seeing anyone dropping off the card that day or the day before. No surprise there; people dropped off entries in a cardboard contest box at the front of the store all the time.

The only clue came when Beth, a salesgirl, recognized the card as one sold in Gee Bee's greeting card department—though narrowing it down from there was next to impossible. Dozens of that same card had been purchased over the Valentine's Day shopping season.

The search was going nowhere fast. Emily and Ryan decided to talk about it over lunch at the Howard Johnson's restaurant located across the parking lot from Gee Bee.

"It's just so frustrating." Emily grabbed a French fry from her plate and popped it into her mouth. "We finally find someone who can write great poems, and we don't know who it *is*."

"It's enough to drive you crazy, all right." Ryan took a bite of his cheeseburger and chewed thoughtfully.

"What about the security cameras?"

Ryan swallowed and had a sip of cola. "People drop entries in the box all day. Even if we spotted the one who dropped in that particular card, how could we ever actually *identify* him?"

"You're right." Emily sighed and had another fry. "What about fingerprints? Do you have a cop in the family?"

Ryan laughed. "Sorry, my dad and brother both work at the mill."

"Really?" Emily brightened. "Which one?"

"Bethlehem," said Ryan. "The car shop."

"My dad works at Bethlehem, too! He's in the bar, rod, and wire mill." He was also a boss, though she didn't mention that part.

"Just about everybody works in the mills around here," said Ryan. "Bethlehem, U.S. Steel, whatever."

Emily tipped her head to one side as she watched him. "What about you? Are you waiting to get in?"

Ryan shook his head. "Get *out*, is more like it. I don't want anything to do with working at the mill. I want to move away and live a *different* life."

"Doing what?" asked Emily.

Ryan shrugged. "What about you? What do *you* want to do?"

"I don't know." Emily picked up another fry and twirled it between her thumb and forefinger. "I went to college for a while...UPJ. But then I sort of stopped going. It just wasn't doing it for me, y'know?"

"Have you thought about moving away?"

Emily nodded. "I just can't seem to make up my mind, though. At least being Miss Gee Bee's kind of fun."

"Maybe you should consider being a detective," said Ryan. "If you can solve the mystery of the unknown poet, at least."

Emily sighed. "I keep feeling like I'm *missing* something. Like if I could just put my finger on it, I could crack the case."

"I know exactly what you mean." Ryan raised his soda cup in a toast. "Maybe the two of us working together will get to the truth."

Emily smiled and raised her cup, too. "Here, here." Then, the two of them tapped their cups together, completing the toast.

THE NEXT DAY, Sunday, Glosser's and Gee Bee were closed —but Emily and Ryan couldn't wait to continue their investigation. They met at Glosser Bros. downtown and talked the security guard into letting them in so they could check the latest deposits in the contest box.

Sure enough, they found a red envelope near the top of the box, addressed with familiar handwriting, with no return address or other form of identification. The card inside wasn't identical to the previous one; it featured a cupid with bow and arrow instead of a big red heart.

But the poem written inside certainly had a familiar style and quality. Reading it aloud, Emily had no doubt in her mind that it was from the same person who'd written the first.

"'Tell me there's no tomorrow, and I might cry. Say I'm due for prison, and I might lie. Give me cause for battle, and I might try. But tell me there's no Miss Gee Bee, and I will die.'"

"Nice," said Lou the security guard. "Very romantic."

"There's more," said Emily. "'If the world in all its turning stops, and every flower wilts...if the stars turn all the seas to steam, and every mountain tilts...if every dream of every joy turns nightmare through and through...I still with every breath and pulse turn every thought to you.'"

"Can I borrow that for my wife?" asked Lou.

"That's him, all right," said Emily. "That's our man."

"Hey, Lou," said Ryan. "You didn't happen to see whoever put that card in the box, did you?"

Lou, a scrawny old man with gray hair and blotchy, reddish complexion, shook his head. "Nobody's in the store overnight during my shift. Whoever puts in those cards and letters—I don't ever see them."

"Damn," said Ryan. "I wish there was some way to monitor the entries as they come in."

"I can't think of any," said Lou. "It's a busy store during the day."

"Plus, he doesn't always drop them off here," said Emily. "He takes them to Gee Bee, too."

Ryan rummaged through the other mail on the contest table. "Let's see if he left us any others while we're here."

"Then I'm gonna have to show you out," said Lou. "The Glossers come in to work on Sunday sometimes, you know."

"WHAT DO WE DO NEXT?" asked Emily as Lou locked the doors behind them.

"Go for a walk in the park?" Ryan bowed and gestured at Johnstown's little Central Park across the street.

Emily shrugged, smiled, and went with him.

It was a cold day with gray, cloudy skies, but at least no snow was falling. As the two of them entered the park, the frosty puffs of their breath in the air were their only company.

"Do you think we'll ever find the unknown poet?" asked Emily.

"I honestly don't know," said Ryan.

"But we *have* to. We can't give up!"

"I knew you'd say that." Ryan smiled.

"Really?" Emily laughed. "But we've only known each other a few days."

“Sometimes that’s all it takes.” Ryan met her gaze. “Sometimes, you just *know* somebody from the start.”

Emily looked away. What was it about him that made her blush sometimes?

“You think we should just give up trying to find him?” she asked. “Do you think it’s a waste of time?”

“Not at all.” His voice changed a little, grew steadier and warmer. “As long as I’m spending time with you, it’s never a waste.”

Startled, Emily looked back over at him. Was he saying what she *thought* he was? Until now, she’d only considered the possibility in the abstract, in the back of her mind.

“Thanks,” she said simply.

“It’s been fun, hasn’t it?” said Ryan. “Working together, solving the mystery. We, uh...we make a good team, don’t we?”

She only had to think for a second. “Sure.” She couldn’t deny it. “We do.”

“Just like when two people are solving a crime in a movie,” said Ryan. “They investigate and find clues, and the mystery deepens.” He stopped in front of the gazebo and turned to face her. “Then they have a moment where he takes her hand.” He reached for her hand, and she didn’t pull it away. “Then the music swells, and he tells her how he really feels.”

Emily’s heart pounded. She was caught up in the magic of the moment, the feel of his hand, the sparkle in his eyes...the wondering what would come next.

Ryan leaned closer. The mist of his breath mingled with hers as he spoke.

"Then he tells her he's come to care for her, and he can't stop thinking about her, and he can't bear to be without her." He smiled.

Emily thought he might kiss her. If he'd tried, would she have pulled away?

She didn't get to find out.

Ryan was the one to pull away and let go of her hand. "Do you know the movies I'm talking about?" he asked.

Emily nodded.

"I love those movies," said Ryan, and then he kept walking.

Her legs were only a little bit shaky as she caught up to him and walked along the winding path by his side.

IT WAS STARTING to look like the unknown poet would not be revealed in time to win the contest.

Another of his poems arrived Monday, as good as the first two, but again no clues to his identity could be found. None of the other entries came close to that quality, either; no one else was worthy of being declared the winner.

By Tuesday morning, the day before Valentine's Day, Emily was on the verge of losing hope. It was the last day entries would be accepted. If she didn't unmask the poet then, it seemed to her the odds of *ever* unmasking him would be much lower.

Either way, the contest would soon be over. So would

her work with Ryan—at least until another promotion came around that required them to reunite. Thinking about that upset her almost as much as thinking about never solving the unknown poet mystery.

With so much on her mind, she hadn't slept well the night before, and she'd gotten up much too early. Rather than sit around and stew, she decided to drive to Gee Bee early and get started with her day.

The store didn't open until ten that day, but Emily was able to get in through the employee entrance around the back of the place. Hurrying through the store, she smiled at the thought of beating Ryan to work for a change. At least *that* little victory would give her a boost.

But even arriving an hour early wasn't enough, it turned out. Emily charged out of the employee locker room and headed for the front of the store, ready for an early start though Gee Bee wasn't open for the day yet.

Just as she rushed past a cluster of clothing racks, however, she caught sight of Ryan already stationed at the contest table, bent over his work.

Emily shook her head, wondering how early she had to be to beat him. At least she had the element of surprise in her favor, though, if revenge was on her mind.

Which it was.

Slowly, she sneaked through the women's clothing racks behind him, holding her breath. She came up close, crouched and ready to spring with a shout.

It was then that she saw what he was doing, and she froze. Her eyes shot wide open, and her heart raced even faster.

As Emily watched, he wrote something in a Valentine's card, then slipped it into a red envelope, licked the flap, and sealed it. Then, he placed the envelope with the card inside on top of the pile of mail on the table in front of him.

Emily was so stunned, she dropped the Miss Gee Bee hat she'd been carrying. Ryan heard it hit the floor and looked her way instantly.

"Good morning!" He grinned and waved as if she hadn't caught him red-handed. As if she hadn't fully understood what he'd just been up to. "You're here early! What's the occasion?"

Frowning, Emily picked up her hat but didn't put it on. Then, she walked up to the table and stared at the red envelope on top of the pile.

Ryan saw what she was looking at and grabbed it. "Oh, hey! Looks like we got another card from that poet, huh?"

Emily nodded.

"Why don't you go ahead and read it?" Ryan offered her the card. "The contest ends today, so this should be the last one we get."

She accepted the envelope from him and slit open the flap with a fingernail. The card, when she pulled it out, bore the image of a heart-shaped box of candy and a single red rose on a candlelit table, as if in preparation for a romantic dinner.

Opening the card, she saw another poem inside.

"Go ahead and read it out loud," said Ryan.

"I know it was you," said Emily. "I saw you writing the card."

"Just read it," said Ryan. "Please."

She took another look at the card, and her eyes were drawn to the few lines at the bottom, after the poem. "You signed it. Your put your name and address on it."

"Right. It's time to come clean."

"Why bother?" Emily glared at him. "You're a *judge.* You can't *win* the *contest.*"

"That's not why I did it. Why I did *any* of it. I don't *want* the money."

"Then why *did* you do it?"

"Because of how I feel about *you,*" said Ryan. "You *inspire* me. I *care* about you, Emily."

"You show you care for someone by *lying* to them? *Pretending* you don't know who's writing the poems?"

He looked rattled as he tried to explain. "But the *poems* don't lie. I mean, at first, I was hoping to get the bonus, but then I *fell* for you. My poems are all about how I truly *feel* about you, and..."

"What bonus?" Emily felt herself inching toward a terrible storm, a hurricane the likes of which she'd never known before.

"The *bonus,*" Ryan said matter-of-factly. "*You* know. For having the winning poem written in your honor."

Emily still couldn't believe what she was hearing. "There's a *bonus?*"

"I was originally going to write poems to *myself,*" explained Ryan. "I figured that even if the winning writer remained anonymous and didn't get the shopping spree, I could still at least get the bonus for being the subject of the winning poem. But when I met *you,* I wanted *you* to have the bonus. And I wanted you to know how I *felt* about you."

"No one *told* me about a *bonus*," snapped Emily.

"But the bonus doesn't matter," said Ryan. "All that matters are the *poems* and how I *feel* about..."

"Maybe the bonus would have *mattered* if I'd known it *existed*." Emily was furious. All her good feelings about the poems, about Ryan, were out the window. She was so upset, nothing made sense to her anymore; everything seemed like a blur of betrayal, lies, and secrets.

"Look, I didn't know you didn't know about that," said Ryan. "I *swear*."

"Oh my God." She backed away from him. "How could I have been so *wrong* about you? About *everything*?"

"Emily, please..."

"I can't *look* at you right now. I can't *stand* you." She turned and ran off through the store. "I need to get *away* from you!"

With that, she left him standing by the contest table with its mountain of cards and letters, watching her go with the saddest look on his face. Atop his head, he wore his plastic Glossy ball cap, its happy pattern of stylized hearts and curlicues the opposite of the true feelings swirling in his head at that moment.

EMILY FOUND herself wandering through the produce department of the Gee Bee supermarket, which was located next-door to the department store. By then, the anger had let up a little, at least enough that she could finally think clearly again. But that didn't mean she was any happier about the situation.

She still couldn't believe what Ryan had told her—not only that he'd never mentioned the bonus, but that he'd been trying to get it for himself.

Why had no one mentioned the bonus to her until now? For that matter, how could he have just stood there, day after day, and gone through those poems with her, never mentioning that he was the unknown poet? It bothered her on every level, especially because she'd started to think fondly of him.

She thought of the day when they'd gone walking in Central Park and he'd taken her hand and looked into her eyes. There had been a feeling there, something she hadn't wanted to turn away from. Even before then, she'd noticed he was different from other guys and that there might be some kind of connection between them. It was one of the reasons she'd enjoyed going through the contest entries and trying to pick a winner, even though it was kind of a tedious task.

Now here she was, having been lied to, having been fooled by someone whom she thought she might have been developing positive feelings for.

Here she was in the produce department, watching the housewives pick out potatoes, onions, lettuce, and other vegetables, while her heart raced from the stress of the day.

What was she going to do next? Give up on her job

at Gee Bee? To what end? To prove a point, that a woman had as much right as a man to know about bonuses and to be paid equal to a man for the same work? Or should she just move on and look for a better situation elsewhere? Should she look for a better workplace where she might be better appreciated, and even another co-worker who might be a better friend to her...or more?

Even as she was embroiled in these troubling thoughts, a friendly voice popped up behind her. "Hey Emily!" Tina Fontana stepped in front of her, smiled, and waved. "What's up? How's the contest going, Miss Gee Bee?"

"Not so great," said Emily. "To be honest, it's pretty awful right now."

"What do you mean?" asked Tina. "It looked like you and Ryan were having a good time out there, going through those cards and letters."

"It wasn't as much fun as I thought," said Emily. "*He* wasn't as much fun as I thought at first, either."

"Why?" asked Tina. "What happened?"

"It's a long story," said Emily. "Basically, there was bonus money involved, and nobody bothered to tell me about it. Ryan wasn't being up front with me about a *lot* of things."

"Like what?" asked Tina.

"*He* was writing some of the poems," said Emily, "and he let me think it was someone else. We were both working to try to figure out who the mystery poet was, and the whole time, it was him!"

"You gotta be kidding me." Tina's long blonde hair

swayed as she shook her head in disgust. "Well, at least you won't have to worry about *him* anymore, the jerk!"

Emily frowned. "Why do you say that?"

"He just *quit,*" said Tina. "No explanation, either, according to Mr. Shepherd...at least until now."

The information caught Emily off guard. Her first instinct was to say *good riddance*...but then she didn't. Something made her hold back.

"Aren't you gonna thank me for the good news?" asked Tina. "At least you won't have to deal with that idiot anymore."

"Yeah, thanks." Suddenly, unexpectedly, Emily felt adrift. The rage that had boiled over in her earlier was just gone.

"Why aren't you happier about this, hon? Miss Gee Bee is victorious! Glossy the Glosser Boy is history! That's a *good* thing, right?"

Why did Emily hesitate? "I don't know." Why wasn't she jumping for joy?

"Aw, you're just a little wired." Tina put an arm around her shoulders and gave her a squeeze. "It'll be okay, don't worry. Let's celebrate tonight at Freddie's or Mynderbinders, and you'll feel better."

Just then, a deep voice spoke up behind them, one they knew all too well. "Celebrate what?"

Turning, they saw the store manager, Jack Shepherd, staring back at them. The middle-aged man with thinning brown hair, a thick brown mustache, and a pot belly under his short-sleeved white button-down shirt did not look amused.

"Nothing in particular," Tina said flippantly.

Mr. Shepherd folded his arms over his chest. "It wouldn't have anything to do with Ryan leaving Glosser Bros., would it?"

"Absolutely not," said Tina.

Emily shook her head.

"Did something happen between you two?" asked Mr. Shepherd.

Again, Emily shook her head.

Mr. Shepherd scowled as if he knew she was holding back, but he didn't press it. "So who won the contest? Ryan said you picked the winner."

"He did?" Emily was confused.

"Yep. He also said the winning poem was written for Miss Gee Bee, so you get the bonus."

"What bonus?" asked Emily.

"Didn't I tell you?" Mr. Shepherd unfolded his arms and stuck his hands in his pants pockets. "I guess I must've forgotten." He looked a little sheepish.

"Huh." Tina gave Emily a meaningful glance. "Imagine that."

"Anyway, it's just fifty bucks," said Mr. Shepherd. "Ryan wanted to make sure you got it."

Emily stood there for a long moment, processing what she's heard. The rage that had been roaring through her was transforming, becoming another emotion altogether.

Apparently, things weren't as cut and dried as she'd at first thought. Maybe it was time for her to write a new draft of her reaction to the situation.

"Mr. Shepherd?" she said. "May I have the rest of the day off, please?"

"Sure, why not?" Mr. Shepherd pursed his lips and stuck his hands on his hips. "You're not exactly getting any work done right now anyway, are you?"

"I have one more favor to ask," said Emily. "Could you give me Ryan's home address? He forgot something when he left."

EMILY HAD to double-check the address on Franklin Street in Kernville when she got there.

Then, she laughed out loud.

As she got out of her car and headed for the front door, she shook her head. Leave it to Ryan, with his crazy sense of humor, to give *this* as his home address.

But sure enough, he was there when she walked in the place, sitting at a table across the room. He was reading a thick book with a tattered green cover and the title "Shakespearean Sonnets" in faded gold leaf on the spine.

When he looked up, she could tell he was surprised to see her. Worried, too. "Emily?"

"You *said* you lived near a great sub and pizza place," she told him. "But I never would've *guessed* you lived *in* Brownie's Bar!"

The surprise faded from his eyes, though the worry lingered. "Be it ever so humble." He shrugged.

"Not so humble at all, if you ask me. My stomach is growling just standing here!"

"I have found no sweeter perfume in all of Johnstown." He closed his eyes and inhaled deeply. "Hot Italian sub number five."

Emily felt a little awkward standing there and sat down across from him. "So where do you *really* live?"

"Across the street, I think." He frowned. "Or is that up the block and over the bridge? I can't keep track."

"Well, I'm glad I found you." Emily took a deep breath to calm her nerves. "There's something I wanted to talk to you about."

Ryan looked like he thought about leaving, but he didn't. "If it's about the contest, I..."

Emily held up a hand. "Just listen."

He opened his mouth to say something, then closed it.

"I just wanted to say...I know you're not the reason I didn't know about the bonus. Mr. Shepherd forgot to mention it, and I guess President Black must've assumed I already knew."

Ryan shifted restlessly on his chair. "Okay."

Emily took another deep breath and let it out slowly. "I also wanted to thank you for the poems. I mean, you could've just told me they were yours to begin with..."

"I know," said Ryan. "I'm sorry."

"...but they were still very sweet." She met his gaze. "Very romantic."

Again, he looked surprised. "You still like them?"

"Good question." Emily reached into the pocket of her coat and pulled out a red envelope. "Maybe this will shed some light on the matter." She slid the envelope across the table to him.

Frowning, he opened it and took out the card inside. This one had two swans on the front, beaks touching, their heads and necks forming the shape of a heart.

As he read it silently, eyes scanning each line she had written. Emily didn't need to hear it aloud to remember each heartfelt word:

Roses are red,

Violets are blue,

Gee Bee goes with Glosser's

Like I go with you.

It was enough to make Ryan laugh out loud. Emily laughed along with him, then reached over and covered his hand with her own.

"Glossy, will you split a Brownie's pizza with me?" she asked.

"Only if we can get a Shaffer twins sundae at Glosser's Cafeteria for dessert, Miss Gee Bee," said Ryan.

Then he leaned toward her, impulsively going in for a kiss.

Impulsively, she kissed him back.

LOSSER BROS
GLOSSER BROS

SAINT PATRICK'S DAY AT GLOSSER'S

Johnstown, Pennsylvania: Tuesday, March 17, 1936.

"Begorra!" Murphy the security guard grinned when he saw the outfit Betty Flanagan wore at the ladies' accessories counter of the Glosser Bros. Department Store. "I see you remembered the wearin' o' the green today!"

Betty, one of the younger girls working the sales floor at Glosser's, patted the bright green sleeves of the dress she wore under her standard issue brown smock. "I'd never dream of forgetting, Murphy. My wee Irish aunty would never forgive me."

"Nor should she." Murphy, a notorious talker, leaned on the accessories counter, pausing from his rounds for a bit of conversation. "And well done, you. Good to see a young person settin' an example."

"Thanks," said Betty, though she doubted such an

example was needed. Looking around the busy first floor of the store, she saw plenty of green on display.

Most of the salespeople and many of the customers in the store were wearing something—or everything—green that day, whether they were Irish or not. It was all in keeping with the spirit of Saint Patrick's Day—March 17, 1936—marking the heritage of those like Betty's grandparents who'd come from the Emerald Isle to live in the industrial city of Johnstown, Pennsylvania.

"It's always a fun day, ain't it?" Murphy smiled...then scowled as he looked around. "Not sure there'll be much *celebratin'*, though, if this *rain* don't let up."

Betty nodded, watching as customers shook out their soaked umbrellas in the main entrance foyer of the Franklin Building in which the store was located, at the corner of Franklin and Locust streets. This was the fourth straight day of rain, with no end in sight; it was a lot, even for Johnstown, which was known for rainy weather.

"At least it ain't freezin', or we'd have a real mess on our hands." Murphy stared out one of the big display windows at the scene across Locust Street in Central Park. There was plenty of old snow on the ground, but the temperature had been warm enough lately to melt much of it and ensure the latest precipitation was of the non-frozen variety. "I guess we'll take the good luck with the bad and be happy about it, eh?"

"Just like always." Betty patted her short red hair as a customer approached. It was true, she thought. As rough as times were—and they were *rough* in the heart of the

Great Depression—people always seemed to find a way to count their blessings and keep going.

Sometimes, though, she had to admit, she wished things could be different. Sometimes, as hour after hour plodded past in exactly the same way—with her at the accessories counter or in another department, dealing with one customer after another—she realized she wanted more out of life.

Not that she was likely to get it, poor girl that she was, with nothing but a high school diploma to her name, no parents, and hardly a pot to piss in.

Sometimes, her future seemed so hopeless, she wished she could be anyone but herself, and anywhere but Glosser's.

"Well, that's my cue." Murphy tipped his hat and wandered off, whistling the song "Pennies from Heaven." The latest customer—who wasn't wearing green, by the way—stepped up to the counter, inspecting the selection of ladies' gloves that were fanned out there.

Moments later, she moved on without a word, leaving the gloves in a sloppy pile for Betty to sort and straighten. If this was how Betty's whole day was going to go, it would be a long one…and the Saint Paddy's Day party she'd been invited to that night in Old Conemaugh Borough, the neighborhood where she and her aunty lived, would take an eternity to arrive.

"Hey, toots!" Just then, her pal Dorothy Fontina from cosmetics marched over and set to work helping rearrange the gloves. "How's it shakin'?"

"Not so hot," said Betty, but she was smiling. Dark-haired, brown-eyed Dorothy, who was five years older, had an upbeat personality and always made her laugh. "How about you?"

"Dying to fly the coop, of course." Dorothy winked. "Can't wait for that boring old party, can you?"

Betty shook her head. "It'll be sooo boring...but any port in a storm, I always say."

Dorothy laughed. "It's not like that good-looking lover boy of yours will be there, making life miserable."

"Heavens, no." Betty laughed, too, though Rick Merritt was far from her lover boy at that point. She hadn't kissed or danced with him even once...though hope sprang eternal. Perhaps the magic of Saint Patrick's Day would turn his heart in her direction.

"I hear there'll be some *alcohol* served," said Dorothy. "Maybe a little booze will be enough to loosen up ol' Ricky boy."

Betty blushed and giggled. Prohibition had ended three years ago, so the serving of alcohol was no longer illegal, but it still felt a bit scandalous to her to attend a gathering where it would be present.

"At least you're finally old enough to chug some hooch," said Dorothy. "Talk about perfect timing."

Betty laughed. "I can't wait to see what all the fuss is about." She'd just turned 21 yesterday, it was true, but her first taste of alcohol had happened long ago. She wasn't a wild girl by any stretch, but she liked to go to parties and have fun with Dorothy and other pals when possible.

"So let me know if you can't leave right at five," said

Dorothy. "Otherwise, we'll meet at the door and walk out together."

"Don't worry, hon. I'll be there at five, come hell or high water."

Just as Betty said that, a woman sneezed loudly from across the sales floor. Looking in that direction, Betty saw the sneezer was Mary Brandle, one of Glosser's cleaning ladies—a middle-aged woman with gray hair, a squat build, and a sweet disposition.

As Mary boarded an elevator with her mop and bucket of water, she let loose a second sneeze. Just as the operator slid the door shut, a third sneeze burst out of her—the loudest yet—and then a fourth.

Was it the power of suggestion or the effect of a rainy day that two other women on the sales floor blasted out sneezes of their own at that precise moment?

"Five o'clock will be here before you know it, toots." Dorothy fluttered the last two gloves like butterfly wings before arranging them on the counter with the rest. "We just have to stay out of trouble until then, and we'll be off to the races."

"I think I can manage," Betty said with a grin.

"Don't be so sure of that." Something caught Dorothy's eye, and she looked in the direction of the corner foyer. "Who is *he,* I wonder?"

Following Dorothy's gaze, Betty saw a young man entering the store, soaking wet, wearing a Glosser Bros. smock and black trousers. He was slim, with wavy black hair and dark eyes, and stood out as handsome even at a distance.

"Looks like new help," Dorothy said with a salacious smirk. "Well, he can help *me* any time he likes."

The young man looked their way, and Betty blushed... but then he quickly looked away again.

"Ian Sullivan," said Dorothy, who had just zipped off and back to find out his name from another salesgirl. "He just started working here a few days ago."

"He did, did he?" Betty nodded, captivated...then broke her stare and resumed straightening the accessories counter. "Well, good for him."

"Good for *you*, too, maybe." Dorothy elbowed her in the side. "I wonder if he's going to the shindig tonight?"

"I guess we'll find out, won't we?" Betty had to fight to keep from looking at him again. "He doesn't look Irish, though, so maybe we shouldn't expect him."

"Oh, but he *is*, I heard." Dorothy leaned in and whispered conspiratorially. "*Black* Irish, that is."

This time, Betty didn't deny herself another look. Dark hair and dark eyes were indeed characteristic of the Black Irish strain, supposedly descended from survivors of the Spanish Armada shipwrecked on the west coast of Ireland.

"*Now* you're interested." Dorothy chuckled. "I can always tell, toots."

Betty blushed again and laughed. Dorothy had a way of seeing right through her.

"Looks like this could be an interesting night," said Dorothy. "I can't wait to see how it all works out. Saint Paddy's Day bash, here we come!" Grabbing Betty's hands, she gave them a gleeful shake, then let go and headed back to Cosmetics with a bounce in her step.

Watching her go, Betty felt a burst of fresh enthusiasm. Her shift suddenly seemed a lot more bearable; she could get through it standing on her head with her hands tied behind her back, she thought.

Though it was true, if she had known exactly what lay in store for her that night, she wouldn't have hesitated to tell her boss she was sick and had to leave early...just as Mary Brandle—the cleaning lady--was about to do.

"ONE BOWL of corned beef and cabbage, please," said Betty. "And a slice of Irish soda bread to go with it."

"Happy Saint Paddy's Day!" The waitress at the lunch counter smiled as she wrote the order on her pad, then hurried off to fill it. Though her uniform was white, she wore a green shamrock pin on her collar in honor of the holiday.

Glosser's Cafeteria, on the second floor of the Franklin Street Annex building, was filled with employees and customers alike grabbing a quick lunchtime bite. As Betty sat at the U-shaped lunch counter and took in the scene, she noticed a lot of folks eating the Saint Paddy's Day specials—the Irish stew and corned beef and cabbage, especially. She also noticed a few of them were having sneezing jags.

"Here you go, hon," said the waitress when she

returned, though she didn't look much older than Betty. "Enjoy your lunch." She set down the bowl of corned beef and cabbage, followed that with the soda bread and a pat of butter on a small plate, then tore the check off her pad and put it on the counter, as well.

"Thanks." Betty had only a half-hour for lunch, so she dug in right away. The corned beef and cabbage wasn't bad, she thought, though not quite up to Aunty Ginny's standards. Adding a bit of salt and pepper helped.

Unfortunately, her appetite was soon spoiled.

"Hello, Miss Flanagan." The voice of her boss, Mr. Packer, caught her in mid-slurp. "Sorry to interrupt your lunch."

Betty had a sinking feeling in her stomach as she lowered her spoon into the bowl. "Hello, Mr. Packer."

Joe Packer, a genial, chubby man in his 40s, smiled from behind his dark-rimmed glasses. He wore nothing in honor of Saint Patrick's Day—just his usual dark suit, white Oxford shirt, and red tie. "How would you like to make some extra money, Miss Flanagan?"

"Sure, Mr. Packer." This being the Depression, money was always of great concern to Betty. Between what little she made at Glosser's and what Aunty Ginny made taking in laundry, they barely made ends meet these days.

"Great, that's great." Packer smiled and smoothed his thinning salt-and-pepper hair with a swipe of his thick-fingered hand. "We have some extra hours for you tonight, filling in for someone who's sick."

"Who's that?" asked Betty.

"Mary Brandle," said Packer.

The sinking feeling intensified as Betty glimpsed the outlines of where the conversation was headed. "You want me to fill in for Mary?"

"Yes, please."

The sound of Mary's sneezes echoed in Betty's memory. Little had she known they were signs of a real disaster in the offing. "Tonight, you said?"

"Starting this afternoon, actually." Packer eyed her soda bread like he wanted a taste. "The good news is, it's a *lot* of hours. Mary was already scheduled to work a double, covering for Justine, who had a family emergency. You'll pick up most of that time."

Betty didn't like the future that was taking shape, not one bit. Packer was asking her to work the remainder of her scheduled shift, then cover most of a double, missing out on the Saint Paddy's party with best friend Dorothy and prospective love interest Rick. As for having a choice in the matter, she didn't think it was an option.

Not that she let that stop her from inquiring further. "Have you asked anyone else?"

"Oh, yes." Packer nodded vigorously. "No one's available. Why? Is there a problem?"

During the Depression, having a "problem" on the job was never a good thing. There were always plenty of desperate people willing to replace you if given the chance.

That didn't mean she had to like it as she said those awful words: "All right, Mr. Packer. I'll do it."

"Excellent." He pocketed his watch, took another longing look at the bread, and headed for the door connecting the cafeteria to the main Glosser Bros. building. "Much appreciated, Miss Flanagan. Please start on your cleaning duties when you've finished lunch. No need to finish your shift on the sales floor."

"Yes, Mr. Packer." Appetite gone, Betty pushed away the corned beef and cabbage, wrapped the bread in a napkin, and put it in her pocket. Then, she put down the right number of coins to pay for lunch and got up from her stool, dejected...though even then, she had no idea whatsoever just how bad that night was going to be.

The Saint Patrick's Day from Hell had her firmly in its clutches.

Maybe you can still make it to the party. That was Dorothy's theory when Betty told her she'd be working a double. *There's nothing like being fashionably late to get all the right attention.*

Betty played along, promising to work extra fast to get out of there early...but she didn't share Dorothy's optimism. Glosser Bros. Department Store was vast; she knew from pitching in occasionally to help Mary that cleaning its five floors wasn't a task she could finish on her own in a hurry.

She told Dorothy what she wanted to hear anyway, just to end the cajoling and get on about her business. The less time she spent discussing the turn of events, the better her chances of getting out at a decent hour.

Heading to the basement, she met briefly with Mary, going over the rundown of her duties. The whole time, she took care not to get too close to Mary, who indeed was sneezing up a storm.

It was almost 2:00 when Mary left for the day—too early to mop floors, but there were plenty of other things to do. Since Betty was already near the janitor's closet in the basement, she made that her first stop, planning to gather some supplies to use when making her rounds of the store.

In spite of everything, she tried to keep a positive attitude as she pulled together rags, a broom, a dustpan, and more. She'd had a lot of misfortune in her life, and she was determined never to let it keep her down for long. Besides, having to work extra hours instead of going to a party wasn't really much of a hardship, was it? Especially when work hours and money were so often hard to come by.

She was nearly ready to head out and start her chores when she slipped on a spot of soapy water on the floor. She flailed, trying to keep her balance, and went over backward anyway, her head hitting the lip of the janitor's sink built into the floor.

The impact was hard enough to switch her lights off. She lay sprawled over the edge of the sink, unconscious and alone.

Meanwhile, events were moving fast in Glosser's Department Store. It would be a different situation indeed when she finally came around...*if* she came around.

All because the rain kept falling, as it so often did in Johnstown, Pennsylvania.

"BETTY? ARE YOU ALL RIGHT, BETTY?"

The sound of a young man's voice tugged Betty out of the darkness, pulling her back to a state of consciousness. Her eyes flickered open, though all she saw at first was a blur.

Closing her eyes and opening them again cleared enough of the haze, though, for her to see the face that went with the voice.

She recognized him instantly as Ian Sullivan, the Black Irish boy…the one she'd seen earlier that day from a distance and instantly liked. He was even more handsome close-up, with high, chiseled cheekbones, a strong, square jaw, and a gleam in his deep, dark eyes.

"Thank God." He made the sign of the cross as he gazed at her. "I thought maybe you were dead."

Betty blinked up at him, feeling incredibly weak. "How did you know my name?"

Ian smiled and pointed in the direction of her heart. "Your name tag, of course." He wore one, too, on his own brown smock, and patted it with the flat of hand. "Pleased to meet you."

Looking around, Betty realized where she was, though the details of her current situation were murky. "What happened? What are you doing here?"

"I was making sure everyone got out," said Ian. "I had a feeling I should check this room, and sure enough, I found you in here like that."

"Like what?" Betty's head hammered as she tried to sit up, and she hissed out a breath in pain.

Ian took her by the shoulders and helped her up. "In the janitor's sink, like you'd just taken a fall."

"I slipped." She felt dizzy at first, but her head stopped spinning after a moment. "Must've brained myself on the way down."

"Well, that explains a few things," said Ian. "Like why you're still *here* when the whole building's been *evacuated*."

Betty frowned. "Evacuated? Since when?"

Ian nodded. "Since three o'clock this afternoon. Seems you've missed out on a few things since you took your little nap, Betty van Winkle."

"What things?"

"I'll catch you up later." Ian got to his feet and helped her get to hers as well. "We've got bigger fish to fry just now, my friend."

"What fish?" Betty realized, as she steadied herself, that she was still a little shaky.

"Just stick with me, all right?" He reached for the doorknob. "Hold on tight if you need to."

Betty had a thousand questions, and lots more came to mind when Ian opened the door. Beyond the closet's threshold, trickles of water ran over the basement's cement floor, crisscrossing and joining together to form larger rivulets.

"We need to hurry." Ian's work-booted feet splashed in

the water as he crossed the threshold. "We have to get upstairs."

"Why?" Betty followed him, gaping at the widespread runoff in confusion. "What's happening?"

"More water's coming," Ian said grimly. "We're having a *flood*."

His words were enough to freeze the blood solid in her veins, even as her heart pounded a staccato tattoo in her chest.

For *this* was the worst thing that could have happened to her. *This* was what she'd been afraid of all her life.

"A FLOOD?" Halfway to the stairs, Betty froze. "There's a *flood*?"

Ian took her hand and tried to pull her along, but she wouldn't budge. "Come on, Betty." He looked nervous. "I'll tell you everything after we get upstairs."

"I can't." She pulled away from him without thinking. "Not a *flood*."

"Listen to me." Ian ran over and grabbed her shoulders. "We'll be *fine*…but only if you *trust* me."

Looking down, she saw the water running around their feet. She was caught in the throes of panic, locked in place…

And then he gave her a shake. "Betty, come on!" He did it again. "We need to get *upstairs*."

He jarred her just enough to snap her out of the state

of pure panic. She nodded and let him pull her along without another word, leading her to the steps.

That, she realized, was where much of the water was entering the basement. Each step was a waterfall, feeding a growing cascade.

Following Ian, she controlled her terror just enough to splash her way up the steps. The current wasn't strong enough yet to push her back down, though she realized it might not take long to reach that level of force. It was a good thing Ian had insisted on getting through it while they still could.

When they got to the ground floor, the water was up over their ankles, and the current was stronger, but what alarmed Betty the most was the view outside. The murky water was halfway up the windows out there, the ground and street fully submerged.

And the rain was still blasting down in sheets, its pounding punctuated by roars of thunder and flares of lightning.

"What do we do?" she asked, fighting the panic rising inside her.

"Well, we're not going out *there,* that's for sure." He gestured at the windows and the churning water beyond them.

"But the water's coming in here, too!"

"And we're got four more floors above us to keep away from it. Now come on!" Holding her hand tightly, Ian led her away from the windows, headed for the rear of the store. They passed the elevators and kept going, sloshing toward the glowing EXIT sign in the far back corner.

Ian hurled the door open, pulled her through, and started leading her up the cement stairs. They were a huge improvement over the steps from the basement, dry as a bone except for Ian and Betty's wet shoeprints.

Still, the two of them didn't stop until they'd reached the top and pushed through the door to the second floor. Only then did they dare rest from their narrow escape.

"Just another boring Saint Paddy's Day, huh?" Ian let out a loud, nervous laugh. "Nothin' exciting ever happens in this town."

"You can say that again." Betty slumped against the wall, slowly recovering…but she could only relax so much as long as the floodwaters kept rising on the level below her.

"How do you take your coffee?" asked Ian from behind the snack bar counter. "Black?"

Betty stood by a wall panel where she'd just flipped a few switches, lighting up the snack bar. "Cream and sugar, please." She sounded calm, but she wasn't. She and Ian had crossed the walkway from Glosser's second floor to level two of the cafeteria annex, but their dire situation was still the same. It would only be a matter of time till the floodwaters climbed to the second story of both buildings.

It was a good thing there were still three floors to retreat to in the main building, assuming a flood-related accident didn't claim their lives first.

"Coffee's brewing!" Ian shouted from the kitchen. "Should be just a few more minutes."

"We should call for help," said Betty as she switched on more lights. "Maybe someone could come rescue us."

"Sorry, but no can do," said Ian. "I just tried the kitchen phone, and it was dead."

"There are other phones in the building."

"Sure, but when one's down, they're probably *all* down. Anyway, how would someone even get here to save us? Swim?"

Betty shivered as thunder boomed nearby. "I need to call my Aunt Ginny, at least. She was going to visit friends up in Westmont for Saint Paddy's tonight."

"I'm sure she'll be fine, up on the hill like that," said Ian.

"I know, but...I still wish I could be sure she's safe." She dropped onto a stool at the lunch counter—the same stool where she'd sat earlier to eat her corned beef and cabbage. "My family does *not* have good luck when it comes to floods."

Looking around at the big, empty dining area, she felt a swell of hopelessness work its way through her, threatening to overwhelm her.

It didn't help that she was still in a state of shock, fighting to fill in the blanks. The questions she'd been suppressing since regaining consciousness were fighting their way to the surface, demanding answers.

"So the store was evacuated because of the flooding," she said when Ian brought two white mugs of steaming coffee to the counter. "Is that right?"

"Yes indeed." Ian smiled and sipped from his mug.

"If that's true, then why are *you* still here?"

Ian shrugged. "Does it matter?"

"I'm sure you weren't *told* to stay behind," said Betty.

Ian leaned against the lunch counter and sipped his coffee. "*Somebody* has to watch out for looters, don't they?"

"The Glossers wouldn't risk your life like that." Betty narrowed her eyes and leaned forward, sizing him up. "Which means staying behind was *your* idea, not theirs."

"Sounds sensible, when you say it like that."

Betty was starting to feel frustrated at his evasions. "But *why*, Ian? If it was your idea to stay behind, why did you do it?"

"Why were *you* down in the janitor's closet?" asked Ian. "I've only ever seen you working the sales floor."

"Mary the cleaning lady went home sick," said Betty. "Mr. Packer asked me to cover her shift."

Ian smirked. "Well, you sure picked a bad night for it."

"I sure did." Thunder boomed ominously when she said it. "But I needed the money."

"Tell me about it." Ian nodded. "At least *you're* getting paid for being here."

"And you're not?" She frowned. "Why is that?"

Sipping his coffee, Ian pushed away from the counter and wandered across the dining room. His form was silhouetted by the streetlamps outside as he sipped his coffee and watched the rain hammer away at the windows.

"Did you miss out on a Saint Paddy's Day party tonight?" he asked.

Betty's eyes widened in surprise. "How did you know?"

"Lucky guess." Ian walked to the windows and gazed down at the torrent of muddy water rushing down Franklin Street. "Something tells me you're not missing out on much, though. Pretty sure the parties all ended early tonight."

Betty got up and joined him at the window. "You're probably right."

"I'll bet everyone headed for home or higher ground," said Ian. "I don't see any lights on across the street."

She didn't, either. The streetlights still glowed in the storm, but none of the windows in the buildings across Franklin Street from Glosser's were lit from within.

She and Ian were alone on the block, on their own—and things were getting worse by the minute. Looking down at the raging, newborn river in the street, she saw a car float by—a black Studebaker—and her heart started pounding again.

Just then, the rain suddenly intensified, blasting the glass with hammer-blow impacts. Inhaling sharply, Betty took a step back from the glass.

"Scared of the water?" There was no cruelty in Ian's voice. "Don't like swimming?"

"Don't like *drowning*, is more like it." She stepped forward again, resting her right hand on the cold, thick pane. "I lost some people once in a flood in this town…the one in 1889."

Ian nodded respectfully. "The big one."

"Biggest so far." Betty shivered. "Unless this one turns out to be bigger."

They stood there for a moment, listening to the

pummeling rain and rolling thunder . The streetlamps flickered and brightened, and so did the lights in the cafeteria.

"Who were the people you lost?" he asked finally. "In the 1889 flood?"

Her eyes burned, and she hesitated to answer. She hadn't known those people, hadn't even been alive back then, but that didn't make the loss any less terrible. It didn't mean the wound would ever heal.

"My grandparents," she said.

"Which ones?" asked Ian.

"All of them," said Betty. "All four of them."

Ian shook his head sympathetically. "That's awful, Betty. That's just awful."

"I'll be going the same way," she told him darkly. "I've always known it."

He scowled. "In a flood?"

"Yes." She found she couldn't tear her eyes from the rushing, roiling water down below. "I've always known... and now here I am. It's all coming true."

"You don't know that. Just because people in your family died that way doesn't mean *you* will."

"That's probably what they told my Ma and Pa," said Betty. "And look what happened to *them*."

Ian's jaw dropped as he gaped at her. "Why? What happened to 'em?"

Just as Betty was about to answer, the lights outside flickered and died, and the lights in the cafeteria went dark, too.

When Betty first noticed the splashing sound her shoes were making, her heart raced so hard, she thought it might break free of her body. The sound of water underfoot as she and Ian crossed the second floor of the Franklin Building could mean only one thing, and it terrified her:

The floodwaters were rising above the ground level's ceiling.

She didn't say it out loud, though, and neither did he. Instead, they both stayed focused on working their way to the Notions department, which was located on the far side of the second floor from the cafeteria passageway.

It wasn't an easy hike, as all the lights in the store were out. There wasn't any light from the many windows along the walls, either, as the power outage had turned the downtown area pitch black.

At least Betty and Ian had stuffed their pockets with matchbooks in the cafeteria before setting out. Each match, once struck, didn't last long, but it gave them enough dim illumination to keep moving in the right direction and avoid the biggest obstacles.

Of course, they still had to make sure they didn't split up en route...but that part of it was working out okay. Betty was only too happy to hold on to his shoulders every step of the way, feeling the muscles shifting under his shirt with each movement he made.

Eventually, they reached their destination and found

what they were looking for—a shelf full of candles and candleholders.

"Good thing you remembered these were here," said Ian as he lit the wick of a footlong white taper with another match. "These darn matches have been burning the *heck* out of my fingers!"

"We should grab as many as we can." Betty filled the pockets of her smock with candles on top of the matchbooks. With the water infiltrating the second floor, this might be their only chance to stock up on such things... and they would need them to get through the night without electrical power.

"Is there anything else we need before we head for higher ground?" Ian stuck the lit candle in a tin holder and handed it to her.

"Maybe we should go back and grab some food from the cafeteria, now that we can see where we're going again."

"No!" snapped Betty. "Let's just go!"

Calmly, Ian lit another candle from Betty's burning wick. "Hold on. I almost forgot something." He walked around to the other side of the shelves, where office supplies were stocked, and grabbed a pocket-sized notebook and three pencils. "Now we're ready."

Betty stared down at the water around her feet. She could have sworn she felt it rising as she stood there. "Please, Ian. We need to *leave*."

"Okay, then." His dark-eyed gaze met hers in the candlelight, projecting waves of strength and tenderness. "But trust me, we're going to be okay."

Betty wanted to believe him, but the pain of the past loomed large, and the evidence of the curse she'd always dreaded was impossible to ignore. She was trapped on the second floor of a department store, and the floodwaters were rising around her; how could she not believe that her greatest fear was about to pull her under?

"Just remember, you're not alone," said Ian. "We're in this together."

"I just hope you don't regret that," she told him. "Having other people around didn't do my grandparents or parents any good."

"Well, this time will be different." He leaned closer as he said it, as if by force of will alone he could get her to believe. "For one thing, it's *us*, and we're *survivors*."

"And what's the other thing?" she asked.

"This is Glosser Bros. Department Store." He grinned. "Everybody *knows* only good things happen at *Glosser's*."

THE WATER WAS around their ankles as they headed for the third floor, the flames of their candles dancing in the updraft in the stairwell. Betty's candle actually blew out, and her heart skipped a beat...but she could still see just enough by the glow of Ian's candle to make it the rest of the way.

"Third floor," he said as he pushed open the door. "Women's and girls' dresses and coats, lingerie, layaway... and best of all, no flood waters of any kind."

Yet, Betty thought darkly as she emerged from the stairwell.

Ian followed, letting the door fall shut behind him. "Light 'em up." He tipped his candle toward hers, engulfing her wick with his still-burning flame…and it caught. "Two are better than one, I always say."

"Spooky," she said as she looked around at the shadowy space. "Maybe we should skip this floor and go straight up to four."

"No need to hurry." Ian started forward between racks of dresses, moving his candle from side to side to light the way. "Maybe we'll find something useful…like *life preservers*."

Betty's stomach growled, and she wished she'd grabbed some cafeteria food for the road after all. "Or a *boat*," she said as she followed Ian down the aisle.

Ian laughed. "I wonder if we could use our store discount to pay for it?"

Just then, Betty thought she heard something from the racks and froze. "Who's there?" She held up the lit candle, throwing as much light as she could on the mysterious shapes hulking in the darkness. "Is someone there?"

Ian saw where she was looking and marched over that way, throwing more light on the matter. Instead of a lurking menace, Betty now saw the shadows had been concealing a rack of dark fur coats.

"Nobody here but us chickens." Ian left the coats and returned to the path he'd been following from the rear of the store to the front windows.

She fell in behind him, relieved…but not for long.

There were just too many shadows all around in which her imagination could run wild.

Soon enough, though, Ian took her mind off imaginary things. "I'll bet everybody headed for higher ground before it got bad," he said. "I'm sure people like your aunt, who were already up in the hills, just stayed there."

"I hope you're right," said Betty. "God knows my family has never been very good at avoiding floods. They always end up in the middle of them."

"Like your grandparents and parents, you mean?"

"Exactly," said Betty. "None of them managed to escape when they still could."

"If you don't mind my asking," said Ian, "what exactly *happened* to your Mum and Dad?"

"They died," said Betty. "And I went to live with my Aunt Ginny."

"Sorry to hear that," said Ian. "Did you say they died the same way your grandparents did?"

"I didn't," said Betty. "And did *you* say how you ended up staying behind when everyone else evacuated the store because of the flooding?"

As she asked the question, lightning blazed from every window, illuminating the interior of the third floor...but only for an instant. She glimpsed the multitude of racks and displays arranged across the space, loaded with merchandise, but she and Ian were alone. The mannequins on their pedestals, attired in the latest styles, were the closest she saw to another living thing.

"Wow!" Ian stopped at one of the windows, put the

candle in its holder on the sill, and dug through his pockets. "That was *some* lightning bolt, wasn't it?"

Betty's hands trembled as she put her own candle and holder on the sill beside his. She tolerated lightning only slightly better than she did floodwaters. "It's a terrible storm, that's for sure." Thunder rumbled as she watched the rain slash the window, taking care not to look down at the rising, churning waters in the street below. It was a view, she knew, that would likely make her head spin; things were only getting worse out there.

"It seems like the rain will never stop," she said.

"But it will. It always does." Ian fished out a pocketknife and one of the pencils he'd grabbed in the Notions department. Unfolding the knife, he used it to whittle the end of the pencil, exposing the gray lead inside.

"I wonder if this is what they felt like," said Betty. "My grandparents, that night in 1889."

"I don't think so." Ian carved the pencil tip to a sharp point, blowing the shavings onto the floor. "I've heard it was very sudden, down here in the valley."

"Maybe that was a good thing." Lightning flashed, thunder rumbled, and Betty trembled. "Maybe it's better than this waiting."

"I already told you, we're going to get through this."

"And you said nobody's coming to *rescue* us."

"Doesn't matter, we'll survive." Ian stuck the sharpened pencil behind his ear, folded the knife, and slipped it into his pants pocket. Reaching into another pocket, then, he pulled out the notebook he'd found in Notions. "I know it for a fact."

She scowled at him. "That's impossible."

Ian opened the notebook, pulled the pencil from behind his ear, and started to write. "When I was a kid in Ohio, living on my grandpa's farm, I came across an old man once. Said he was lost and broke and hungry."

"A hobo?" asked Betty. Such destitute wanderers were common in the days of the Great Depression. They often turned up at Glosser Bros., and the store owners fed and clothed them as an act of mercy.

"I took him home, and my grandparents took him in for a few days," said Ian, still scribbling in the notebook. "They gave him food and a bed and a little money, though they couldn't spare much. Then, when he was ready to leave, they gave him directions to where he wanted to go."

"Good for them," said Betty.

Ian lifted the pencil from the page. "Do you know what he did then? He *blessed* us...the whole family. Said none of us would ever perish because we had too much or not enough water."

Again, lightning flashed. The hammering of the rain, which Betty hadn't thought could get any harder, suddenly intensified. "So much for that blessing, I guess."

"I *believe* him." Ian gestured with the pencil for emphasis. "He called himself Mr. Showers, and I'm here to tell you, that man could make it *rain* when he liked. I swear, I even saw him make the water jump out of a glass and swirl around in midair once!" Ian nodded, perfectly serious and sincere. "So you're in luck, Betty."

"I am?" She couldn't quite keep the tinge of sarcasm from her tone.

"You couldn't have picked a better person to be trapped in a flood with." Ian grinned. "I'm your lucky charm."

With that, he went back to writing in the notebook.

Betty glanced at the page but couldn't quite make out what he was writing by the dim candlelight. Instead, she found her gaze drifting up to his handsome profile—the dark eyes, dark hair, chiseled cheekbones, square jawline. Dark stubble peppered his cheeks, chin, and throat, the shadow of a shave too long deferred.

Her heart beat faster again—not from fear, but affection. Though she didn't put much stock in his story of Mr. Showers, she loved that he'd gone to the trouble to tell it… that he cared enough to try to make her feel better. She loved that he was doing his best to help her get through this disastrous night…starting with saving her life by getting her out of the janitor's closet before the water could drown her.

She had read enough stories about knights in shining armor to know one now that she'd finally come across him.

FOR A LITTLE WHILE, the two of them stood there by the windows—Betty watching the rain, Ian writing in the notebook. The scratching of the pencil and the flipping of pages accompanied the sound of the rain battering the glass and the rushing of the Franklin Street River as it carried cars, branches, siding, and all manner of junk past the building. At least there weren't any screams from out there, and she hadn't seen any bodies in the flashes of lightning...but she'd still rather concentrate on Ian's scribblings than the nightmarish floodscape on the other side of the glass.

Eventually, her curiosity got the better of her, and she asked the question that had been on her mind. "What are you writing?"

"Just taking notes," said Ian. "Jotting some things down."

"What kind of things?"

Candlelight shadowed the angles of Ian's face as he paused in his writing and gazed thoughtfully out the window. "Details. The sights and sounds of what's happening."

Betty frowned. "Why?"

"So I can write about it later." He smiled. "A newspaper story. A true, eyewitness account of the latest disaster to strike Johnstown."

"You write newspaper stories?"

"I *want* to. I want to be a *reporter*." He sounded energized at the mention of it. "I love stories—reading them, writing them, thinking about them. It's what I've always wanted to do."

Betty smiled. "I think you'll be good at it. You definitely have a flair for telling stories."

"Thank you." He turned, his dark eyes meeting her gaze in the candlelight. "What about you? What have you always wanted to do?"

"I don't know." Suddenly, she felt self-conscious, exposed. "I haven't thought about it much."

"Well, this is as good a time as any," he said, "now that you know you're safe from the flood."

Betty thought about it for a moment. As often as she'd longed for more out of life, more than a job at Glosser's and a drab little future, she'd never really decided on what exactly that would look like. She'd never envisioned the details of the life she'd rather lead or the path she'd have to take to get there.

What had she always wanted to do? The answer was as elusive as the deepest secrets at the heart of the mystery of life itself.

"Sorry." She shrugged. "I don't know what to tell you."

"Don't worry. It'll come to you." He smiled and jotted something in his notebook. "Everyone has a dream. Sometimes, it just takes a little time to work it out."

Something came to her then, and she blurted it out. "My mother was a nurse."

He looked up from his writing with interest. "She was?"

"When she died…she was volunteering with the Red Cross. She and my dad went to Arkansas in '27, helping victims of the Great Mississippi River Flood. They went there to *help*…and they ended up drowning themselves when a big levee suddenly broke."

"That's terrible," said Ian.

Tears rolled down her cheeks as she remembered the loss. "It wasn't fair. They were inspired by losing their own parents in the '89 flood, and then they died in exactly the same way."

"They died helping others, though. That's pretty great." Ian stuck the pencil behind his ear and closed the notebook. "So what kind of work did your dad do?"

"He worked at Bethlehem." A memory of her father's face came to her, and a small smile drifted onto her face. "He was a millwright. Had to take time off to go with Mom, but he didn't hesitate."

"You're lucky you had parents like that, even for a little while," said Ian. "Not everyone does."

"I know," said Betty, "but I wish they were here right now."

"Still, that is truly an amazing story." Ian shook the notebook in his hand and sighed. "Sort of like the one I was hoping to get tonight."

Betty nodded. "The eyewitness account you mentioned."

"I wanted to report from the heart of the disaster," explained Ian. "That's why, when the bosses evacuated everyone today, I stayed behind. I hid in a basement stockroom until everyone left...and then, when I came out to start witnessing the flood, I happened to check the janitor's closet and found you."

"And this story might help you become a newspaper reporter?"

"Maybe," said Ian. "The editor at the *Democrat* said he'd give me a reporter job if I came up with a big enough *scoop*. I'm hoping my eyewitness account of the flood will do the trick."

"It will," said Betty. "I think you've already got the scoop you were looking for."

"You do?"

"'Reporter saves girl employee's life.'" As she said it, Betty waved a hand as if tracing the words of a headline in midair. "It's the best story ever, if you ask me."

"Thanks." He smiled, looking a little bashful. "I just hope I do it justice when I write it up."

"Trust me, you will." Gazing into his eyes by the flickering candlelight, Betty felt a surge of affection wash over her. "All you need is a little inspiration."

"That's what I'm hoping for," he said, looking dead serious. "That's why I'm here, to experience all this."

Betty smiled. "Well, here's something else for you to experience." Impulsively, she leaned toward him, closing her eyes.

And their lips met, pressing together softly as the rain continued to drum against the glass.

He kissed her back, lovingly, and wrapped his arms around her, pulling her close. They stayed like that for a while, lips fused together, senses focused on every movement, sound, and feeling.

At least until a big drop of water fell from above and landed between them, running down their faces and off the tips of their pressed-together chins.

BETTY AND IAN ended the kiss and pulled apart. Just as they looked up, another fat drop fell between them and landed on the floor.

"Well, that shouldn't be there," said Ian.

Betty's every nerve and muscle tensed. She'd been so focused on the rising flood below, she hadn't expected problems with water from the *upper* parts of the building.

"Let's go look around." Ian gathered up his candle in its holder. "Maybe this is the only leak."

Betty picked up her candle and holder and followed him. "Where could it be coming in at?"

"Who knows? Maybe a window blew open." Holding up the candle, he inspected the ceiling along the windows. "Maybe the plumbing backed up and overflowed."

Following his lead, Betty raised her candle and stared at the ceiling. She saw no visible drops of water beading and falling, nothing to suggest a wider problem…

…and then a drop hit her smack on the top of her head.

"There!" She quickly swung her candle around to light the ceiling directly above her. A wet spot darkened the plaster, with a fresh drop bulging in its heart, ready to plunge.

Ian added his candlelight to hers, gazed at the spot, and nodded. "We need to find out what's causing this and stop it if we can."

With that, he spun and hurried toward the stairs, and Betty followed.

When he pulled open the door and held it for her,

though, she hesitated. “Maybe we shouldn’t go up,” she said. “Maybe it’s safer here on the third floor.”

“If it is, it might not be for long,” said Ian. “This might be our best chance to stop the leak before it gets worse.”

Betty swallowed hard, fighting her fear. “But what if…”

“Hey, come on.” Smiling, he took her hand. “Remember who you’re with. Mr. Showers won’t let anything happen to either of us.”

Gazing into his dark eyes in the candlelight gave her strength. So did the feeling of his lips against hers when he leaned closer and gave her an encouraging kiss.

“Let’s go.” He guided her into the stairwell. “Stick with me, and we’ll be hunky-dory.”

“Okay then.” She started up the steps behind him, trying her best to block out the sound of the floodwaters sloshing below them.

IT DIDN’T TAKE LONG to realize the problem wasn’t on the fourth floor.

At first, everything looked normal to Ian and Betty—normal for a department store with no lights or power, that is. Candles held high, they made their way from the stairwell through the home furnishings department, then on to Hardware, without incident.

In Hardware, they were finally able to abandon their candles, grabbing flashlights and batteries from the shelves. The brighter beams of the flashlights provided superior illumination, confirming the lack of leaks or wet spots on the ceiling over the furniture and housewares departments.

When they got to the paint and wallpaper department, however, Betty heard what she thought was a steady dripping sound. Moving closer, she realized it was coming from one of the row of offices beyond that department, along the windows.

Trying the door of the office, she found it was unlocked and swung it wide. Breathing fast, she swept the beam of the flashlight over the ceiling inside…and quickly found the source of the dripping.

Ian joined the beam of his light with hers, making the scene even brighter. "It's running down from the next floor, all right," he said. "And this is above where it's coming through on the third floor."

As he said it, drops fattened and fell from multiple dark spots in the plaster, splashing onto the hardwood floor below.

"I think it might also be coming in other places." Betty aimed her flashlight at the wall separating the office from the one next-door. "I hear dripping in there, too."

They took a quick look in the next office to confirm it…and then some. There were at least twice as many drops forming and falling, maybe three times as many.

"Now we know." Ian whirled and rushed to the stairwell. "Nowhere to go but up."

Stomach twisting, Betty followed. Going up was better than going down, but maybe not by much in the long run.

She hesitated again at the stairwell door, but his smile

convinced her to continue. Even if there'd been no real-life Mr. Showers, just a made-up story to soothe her fears, he still made her feel less afraid in the heart of the storm.

Halfway up to the fifth floor, thunder echoed through the stairwell, its mighty boom amplified like the crack of a gunshot down the barrel of a rifle. It was loud enough to make her stop and cover her ears as best she could without letting go of the flashlight.

When it had passed, though, she noticed Ian had stopped above her. He stood on the fifth-floor landing but didn't reach for the door; instead, he combed the space above him with the beam of his flashlight.

"Ian, what?" she said.

"Listen!" Looking down, he pressed a finger to his lips, signaling for her to be quiet.

Betty fell silent, wondering what he was getting at. What could he possibly be hearing over the sloshing of the water below and the hammering of the rain on the roof above?

"I don't..." Before she could finish her sentence, she finally heard it...faint at first, then with seemingly increased volume as she focused in on it. She knew exactly what he was calling her attention to, the one thing she hadn't expected to hear from above, not tonight.

Help! Oh God, help me!

A *voice.* A man's *voice,* coming from above, coming from the roof of the Glosser Building.

"Come on." Ian sounded grimly determined as he continued up the stairs, waving for her to follow. "We need to get up there *now.*"

As soon as Ian threw open the door at the top of the stairwell, water poured down the steps, and rain slashed in on powerful gusts of wind. He leaned into it, waving the beam of his flashlight over the roof, seeking the source of the human voice.

Betty crowded behind him, terrified of being atop the building in the midst of the spectacular storm. Everywhere she looked, she saw torrents of rain in the beam of her own flashlight, leaping out of the darkness…but she couldn't see whoever had shouted for help.

That changed suddenly, as a long, lingering flare of lightning blazed across the night sky. The whole roof lit up as if broad daylight had exploded overhead, and she saw him, near the far edge.

Murphy.

The security guard was there, soaked to the skin, but only the upper half of his body was visible. The rest was sunk in a hole with water rushing in around it from all sides.

He waved frantically as the lightning faded. "Thank God! Oh, thank God! Get me outta here, you two!"

Ian shouted something, but his voice was drowned out by thunder.

"Be careful, though!" shouted Murphy. "The roof has a weak spot over here, and you don't wanna break through it like I did!"

Ian cast the beam of his flashlight on the broken

roofing around Murphy, then turned to Betty. "Stay here!" he told her. "I'll be right back!"

Betty's eyes widened at the thought of being up there alone in the storm with the beleaguered Murphy. More than anything, she wanted to stay close to Ian, who'd kept her safe and sane so far.

But when he pushed past her and charged down the stairs, she let him go, determined to do as he'd asked in spite of her terror.

"Where'd he run off to, lass?" asked Murphy.

"He said he'll be right back," she shouted over the roar of the rain and wind.

"Well, I hope he hurries," said Murphy. "It feels like more of this roofing is giving way around me!"

Again, lightning flamed across the sky. Betty tried not to think about what would happen if the next bolt hit the roof, where she was standing in water over her feet.

As the rain pelted her like needles and the thunder barreled through, so loud it seemed to thump deep in her chest, she felt as if she were living a nightmare she'd dreamed all of her life...only different. Time and again, she'd imagined dying in a terrible flood like her parents and grandparents, perishing in the teeth of a savage storm. How could she have known that when it finally became a reality, she wouldn't be down in the floodwaters at all?

How could she have known, when it finally happened, that she'd be more than five stories above street level?

Just then, in the lee of the latest volley of thunder,

Murphy hollered to her again. "Some Saint Paddy's Day, eh?"

Shivering against the sheets of driving rain, she forced herself to push aside the fear and answer. "Worst ever, Murphy!"

"Oh, I don't know about *that*." Murphy laughed. "I could tell you *stories*, lass."

Sirens wailed in the distance then, intermingled with human screams and the howling of dogs. Overlaying it all, the crashing of the rain and the rush of the river in the street seemed louder than they'd ever been.

In the midst of all that clamor, Betty thought that maybe she heard Ian's footsteps and leaned into the stairwell, listening...but she was wrong. He hadn't returned from wherever he'd gone just yet.

"Tell me, lass," said Murphy. "Why are you and the lad still here tonight? They had an evacuation, you know."

"Why are *you* still here?" she asked.

"Doin' my job, a' course!" He laughed through another round of thunder. "I was lockin' the place up, makin' my final rounds, and I came to the roof for one last check. Lo and behold, there was a *drain* blocked with *birds' nests,* and the water was collectin' up here, on its way to collapsin' the top of the building. I was kickin' away the blockage, and *wham*...the roof broke through right under me."

"That's some bad luck, Murphy."

"But *good* luck that you and the lad stayed behind too and found me," said Murphy. "Take the good luck with the bad and be happy about it, I always say."

"That you do." Betty took another look down the stairwell, but Ian wasn't there. For an instant, she had a flash of fear that he might not come back at all—whether by choice or because something had happened to him—but she pushed it aside and returned to Murphy, squinting and shielding her face with her arms against the punishing downpour. "I'll tell you why I stayed behind if you promise not to tell anyone."

"So tell me!" said Murphy.

"I fell in the janitor's closet and hit my head," said Betty. "Knocked myself out cold."

Murphy howled with laughter as gales of wind slashed across the roof, nearly drowning out his voice. "Oh, that's a *good* one! Pure *comedy*!"

"Not if you're the one getting knocked out!"

"Oh, lass! So funny!" He kept shaking and rocking with laughter, clapping his hands. "I'm sorry! I'm *so* sorry!"

"For what?"

"For breaking my *promise*! There's *no way* on God's green Earth I can resist telling *that* story again!"

Just as he said it, something gave way under him, and he jolted further down the hole. He stopped just as suddenly, now stuck up to his chest in the cavity.

"Murphy!" Forgetting her terror, she splashed across the roof through the pounding rain, stopping short of where he'd sunk. "Try not to move!"

"What's the use, lassie? We both know I'm done for." He blinked at her, managing a mischievous grin in spite of everything. "Don't suppose you've got a *flask* on you now, do ya?"

Another blaze of lightning lashed the sky. Betty fell to

her knees and reached out, stretching as far as she could toward the man in the hole. "Take my hand!" she shouted as thunder boomed.

"Stop it, lass," said Murphy. "I'll just pull you down with me."

"Take it!" she repeated, her only thought rescuing the doomed man at any cost.

She inched toward him, still reaching while holding on to the flashlight with her other hand…feeling the give of the roof under her knees through the inches of water. He refused to accept the help she offered, leaning back away from her…

And then, suddenly, his eyes flashed up, catching sight of something behind her…*someone* behind her.

Looking over her shoulder, she saw Ian running toward them, carrying a coil of rope. Somewhere behind him, it was tied off, so it unspooled as he approached.

Betty's heart jumped with love and relief when she saw him. They weren't in the clear, not even close…but they had hope. Ian had come through.

"Sorry for the delay," he shouted. "I had to pick up a little something down in Hardware."

"No problem at all, lad," said Murphy. "We didn't even notice you were gone."

"Catch!" Ian tossed the remaining coil to Murphy. "Hurry and tie that under your arms as best you can, then hold on tight!"

"With pleasure!" Murphy did as instructed, wrapping the rope around behind him and tying a fat knot at his chest. "Don't suppose you've got a *flask,* in the meantime?"

A blaze of lightning and boom of thunder were his only answer.

Between the two of them, Ian and Betty managed to haul Murphy out of the hole with the rope. Once his legs were free, he was able to do his part to make it the rest of the way, crawling on his belly until he was clear of the weakened section. From there, they helped him to his feet and hurried him into the stairwell, slamming the door decisively behind them.

Thunder rumbled as they started down the stairs, as if enraged that they'd freed him from the grip of the storm.

They weren't out of the woods yet, though. Getting Murphy down the stairs was no easy task, as he'd hurt his left leg badly in the fall. Ian and Betty had to support him on either side, easing him down one step at a time while steadying him so he didn't topple forward.

They stopped at the door to the fifth floor, rested a moment, but decided to keep going. The fifth floor of Glosser's included the receiving and shipping departments, the display department, and the stockrooms—in other words, not much they could use for survival or comfort.

By the time they'd fought their way to the fourth floor landing, they were more than ready to get off the stairs. Making their way to the furniture department, they set up Murphy on one of the beds. Then, as Ian rummaged through the offices in search of food, drink, or other necessities, Betty set off on her own to visit the third floor.

She came back a few minutes later with supplies from the nurse's office on three, including antiseptic liquid, bandages, tape, and aspirin—all things she thought would be useful in treating Murphy.

As she cleaned the wound on his leg, a nasty gash, with antiseptic, then wrapped it with a bandage and tape, Betty felt as if she were channeling her mother's spirit. As she fed Murphy aspirin and made him as comfortable as she could, she felt good about what she was doing, felt happy to help someone and proud of herself for following in her mother's footsteps.

Ian was proud of her, too, for all that and more. He took her aside and told her so, then showed her how he felt by wrapping her in his arms and kissing her.

Sometime in the middle of that kiss, Betty forgot about the flood, and the rain, and the fear. She forgot about the pressure of the deadly destiny that had haunted her for so long, and the loss that had come to define her life.

All that mattered was the moment, and the kiss, and the possibilities it brought with it. All that mattered was the future and its potential to be better than she'd ever dared imagine.

All they had to do was make it to the end of the storm, whenever that might be.

"Is it my imagination, or is the rain finally letting up?"

When Ian asked the question, he and Betty were in one of the offices, kissing by candlelight. As for Murphy, he was still resting on a bed in the furniture department, nipping from a bottle of whiskey that Ian had found in a desk drawer.

Betty gazed at the rain streaking the window's glass pane, running in rivulets that constantly merged and wavered. The downpour seemed to be just as hard as ever, in spite of what Ian said and what she wanted to believe—coming down in the same ceaseless torrent.

But after a moment, she thought she detected a change…a lessening, ever so slight. Was it just wishful thinking, she wondered, or was the storm finally diminishing, relenting in its fitful, celestial frenzy?

"Not my imagination," said Ian, and then he kissed her again. "It's definitely slowing down out there."

"I can't believe it." Betty's eyes burned with tears of fierce joy. "It seemed like it would *never* end."

"O ye of little faith." Ian chuckled, wiping the teardrops from her cheeks with his thumbs. "I told you Mr. Showers was watching out for us. I knew we'd be okay."

"I guess your story will have a happy ending after all," said Betty. "The readers will like that, I'm sure."

He shrugged. "*If* anyone reads it. *If* it gets published at all."

"It will," she told him. "I *know* it will."

"But what if it doesn't? I want to be a reporter so *bad,* but what if I blow my big chance?"

Smiling, she cupped his face in her hands. "*Now* who's

the one with little faith?" Leaning forward, she tipped her forehead against his. "If you can believe in Mr. Showers, you sure as heck can believe in *yourself,* too."

"I believe in *you,*" he whispered.

"And *I* believe in *us.*" She kissed him, long and lovingly, lips moving against his with exquisite tenderness. After everything they'd been through together, and the incredible relief now that the rain had finally stopped, the embrace felt heavenly, like the most amazing bliss she'd ever experienced.

That was why it was doubly hard for her to end the kiss…but she knew she had to. The fulfillment of his dream meant as much to her as the fulfillment of her own—though it was a dream she'd never known she had until that very night. There would be a lot of struggle ahead—just getting out of Glosser's after the water went down could be a challenge—but at least she had an idea for how to make her life better. Following his lead, she would put her mind to the challenge and do everything she could to achieve it.

But first, she had to get him back on track.

Reaching for the front pocket of his smock, she pulled out the notebook in which he'd been scribbling all evening. She held it up, flapping the pages back and forth, and raised her eyebrows.

"Time to get writing, don't you think?" She smacked the notebook against his chest. "Or don't you *want* your story on the front page of tomorrow's paper?"

He took the notebook from her and nodded. "You know I do."

"Then get crackin'." She grabbed the pencil from behind his ear and held it out to him with a serious smile. "I've got a patient to attend to."

"You editor dames can sure be bossy," he said with a smirk.

"Yes, we can." She kissed him quick on the cheek, then headed out of the office to find Murphy and make sure he was okay. "And don't call me a dame *again* if you know what's *good* for you."

FIVE MONTHS LATER: *Thursday, August 13, 1936.*

Roxbury Park was dry as a bone that day, free of rain... and thousands of people packed the sprawling grounds for a very special occasion. Betty and Aunt Ginny were among them, in the thick of the excitement, getting bumped and thumped and jostled but determined to make the best of it anyway, come what may.

After all, it wasn't every day the President of the United States came to visit.

"I can't believe he's here!" Beaming with joyful anticipation, Ginny straightened her hat and fixed the collar of her dress. "I wonder if we'll get to shake his hand?"

"I don't know, Aunt Ginny," said Betty. "It could take an awful long time to shake *everyone's* hands in this crowd."

"I'll still give it the old college try." Ginny, a slight, slender woman in her fifties, rubbed her hands together, fairly quivering with energy—then shot a smile in Betty's direction. "Just promise you won't be angry if I go on without you, dear."

Betty grinned. "I promise."

As she said it, police car sirens wailed in the distance, signaling the approach of the motorcade bearing the main attraction. Franklin Delano Roosevelt himself had been touring Johnstown that day, taking in the view of what remained in the wake of the Saint Patrick's Day flood; now, he was en route to Roxbury Park for a speech about the flood and the federal government's response to it.

Five months after the disaster, Johnstown was still reeling. Much work had been done to help the city recover, with major projects mounted by volunteers and

government workers alike. Some 7,000 men from the WPA alone had aided the cleanup…but more assistance was needed.

Enter FDR. If anyone could breathe new life into the battered city, it was the man who was pulling America out of the Depression. People's expectations of the magic he might work were ridiculously high.

That was why, at the sound of the sirens, many of the thousands of supporters who were milling around the park ran for the street. Aunt Ginny joined them, with Betty not far behind.

Her progress was halted, however, by a hand grabbing hold of her shoulder and the sound of a familiar voice. "Hey, toots! How's it shakin'?"

Turning, Betty saw her friend, Dorothy Fontina, smiling back at her. She looked pretty as always in a summery floral frock, her features enhanced by makeup samples from Glosser's cosmetics counter.

"Just so you know, the President is mine." Dorothy chuckled. "He won't be able to resist my feminine wiles, will he?"

"Eleanor can't hold a candle to you." Betty cast her gaze at the crowd, spotting Ginny some distance away, heading for the edge of the park. "Speaking of FDR, you might have to fight for a front-row seat."

"Not a problem, kid." Dorothy bobbed her fists in front of her face like a prizefighter. "They won't know what hit 'em."

With that, they headed for the street, where the sirens were getting louder by the minute. Betty could just barely see the top of Ginny's head in the densest part of the crowd, and she aimed in that general direction.

"Taking the afternoon off, I guess?" asked Betty.

"Yeah, I called in sick," said Dorothy. "Turns out fresh air's the best thing for it, though."

"Lucky you."

"Luck has nothin' to do with it, honey." Dorothy laughed and elbowed her in the side. "What about you? Shouldn't you be in *class* or something?"

"I guess I'm playing hooky, too." The truth was, it was the first class Betty had missed since starting nursing school at Mercy Hospital that summer. She loved her studies so much, she hated to miss a single detail…though coming to see FDR was a big enough deal to warrant her making an exception this one time.

"Happens to the best of us, toots," said Dorothy. "Don't

they say the occasional hooky contributes to health and well-being?"

"Do they?"

"You tell me!" Dorothy laughed. "You're the nurse-in-training!"

Betty liked the sound of that. The idea of being a nurse had felt right to her since Saint Patrick's Day, when she'd tried to help Murphy on the roof and treated his injured leg. For the first time, she had a career goal, a vision of the kind of work she'd like to do for the rest of her life. She wasn't just expecting to work at Glosser's day in and day out, sorting gloves and scarves at the accessories counter (though she was still working there part-time for the money to supplement the Sisters of Mercy scholarship she'd received). She finally had a *plan*, a *dream*.

Just like a certain Black Irish boy she knew.

"I was wrong," said Dorothy as the crowd got so thick, it was almost impossible to advance. "I can't fight my way through all these bums, after all."

"Don't worry about it." Betty grinned as the motorcade rolled off Franklin Street onto the park access road and the crowd went wild. "I've got a feeling this is going to work out for us."

"How do you figure, toots?" Dorothy shouted over the roar of the crowd...though of course she knew darn well what Betty had meant. There were no secrets between best friends, at least when it came to love lives and the like.

Betty backtracked from the heaviest concentration of people, dragging Dorothy along with her. She made her way to a less-populated stretch of the road, where they were actually able to take up position right next to the pavement.

In the distance, she saw the President's limousine roll slowly forward with the top down. FDR, in the back seat, shook every hand that came his way, even as the car continued its gradual progress.

In the front seat, next to the driver, was a young man with curly black hair and dark eyes, dressed in a tweed suit, wearing a cap and tie. He was a reporter, whose eyewitness account of spending a night in Glosser's Department Store during the Saint Patrick's Day flood had in part inspired FDR to come to Johnstown to try to help. He was a writer whose words had made a difference...and who had many more words yet to write in what was sure to be an acclaimed career.

Even from a distance, his eyes found hers, and he grinned. Even at a distance, the thread of affection between them remained powerful, strengthened by their shared experience and survival.

Ian Sullivan was his name, of course, and he wasn't about to forget the girl he loved on such an auspicious occasion.

"Are you sure about this, toots?" Dorothy asked teasingly. "I mean, for the *life* of me, I can't figure out how you intend to get us to meet President Roosevelt."

"Relax, toots." Betty waved, and Ian waved back, then blew her a kiss. "Let's just say I *know* somebody."

GLOSSER BROS

EASTER AT GLOSSER'S

"SORRY, NO AUTOGRAPHS." The old man shook his head sadly. "I don't do that sort of thing anymore."

"C'mon, please?" The twentysomething woman who'd asked for the autograph pressed a pen and folded-up white envelope at the old man. "I've loved your work since I was a kid, Mr. Talisman. And I'm only in Johnstown for the day."

Owen Talisman, a tall man in a long black overcoat and black fedora hat, shook his head again, keeping his hands stuffed in his coat pockets. "I'm sorry." Then he kept walking up Somerset Street along the Stonycreek River.

The young man who'd been walking with him—his 17-year-old great-grandson, Ethan—shrugged apologetically at the autograph seeker. "Sorry."

"No worries." The autograph seeker smiled and gave her long blonde hair a toss. "I'm just glad I finally got to meet *Owen Talisman* in the flesh."

Ethan smiled back, charming as ever with his curly brown hair, brown eyes, and dimples. Then, he turned and jogged to catch up with his 89-year-old great-grandfather.

Some things never changed. People of all ages still loved Owen Talisman's books, especially the *Bunnyburg* series. They still recognized him from his photos on the books' covers and approached him on the street (or in the grocery store or doctor's office or bank) in search of autographs.

But other things *did* change. Owen never gave out those autographs anymore, not since that fateful day three and a half months ago. Not since Christmas, when he'd lost his partner, the illustrator of his books.

The woman who had also been his wife.

"She isn't following us, is she?" Owen didn't look back or stop walking up the sidewalk when he asked the question.

"Nope." Ethan fell in step beside him. "She's gone, Pap." That was what he'd called Owen as far back as he could remember—just "Pap," because it was easier than "Great-Grandfather" or "Great-Grandpa."

Owen had a nickname for Ethan, too: Chip, as in "chip off the old block." He said it was because Ethan reminded him of himself as a boy, especially because Ethan was the first family member who seemed to share Owen's writing talent and interest. Owen liked to say he saw that special "spark" in Ethan, the same one that had given Owen such a long and successful writing career.

Though it was true, Owen hadn't said anything like

that in quite a while. Losing his wife, Melinda, had taken his own special spark right out of him.

"I just want to be left alone." Owen looked over at Ethan with a scowl. "I shouldn't have let you drag me out today."

"It's *Easter,* Pap," said Ethan. "You had to get to *church,* didn't you?"

"Is that so?" Owen stopped and leaned on a waist-high brick wall along the sidewalk, meant to keep people from falling in the Stonycreek River below. "Then tell me." He gestured at the clustered buildings of downtown Johnstown on the other side of the river. "If church is *over there,* why the hell are we *over here?*"

Ethan had a very good explanation, an excellent reason for parking on the other side of the river from church...but he wasn't about to tell Owen. Not yet, anyway. "I thought you could use a little exercise and some fresh air," he lied.

"What're you? My *keeper?*" Owen's scowl deepened. "I've got a 17-year-old *babysitter* now?"

Ethan kept his cool and shook his head. "Just a 17-year-old great-grandson. A 17-year-old friend."

Owen brushed a hand through the air in dismissal. "This is your father's doing, isn't it? He put you up to this."

"Nope." Ethan leaned on the wall beside Owen and looked down at the river. The water was brown as mud, rushing from the heavy March rains they'd been having...glittering in the light of the first sunny day in two full weeks. "Just me, Pap. It's all good."

"Good?" Owen snorted. "*Nothing's* good anymore."

Ethan looked at Owen, then followed his gaze back to the river. The current swept between sloping gray concrete walls that formed a flat-bottomed "V." Erected after the flood of 1936, the walls were meant to prevent overflows in the flood-prone city. Their effectiveness was questionable, though; they hadn't seemed to do much good during the last flood in 1977.

"Enough of this." Owen pushed away from the wall. "I'm tired. Take me home."

Ethan felt a shot of panic in his belly. "We haven't gone to church yet," he said, though church wasn't what he was worried about.

"I don't care." Owen stuffed his hands back in his overcoat pockets. "I just want to go home."

Ethan's heart pounded. He had a secret plan, and taking Owen home wasn't part of it. He had to get him to a certain place at a certain time; the place was just a few blocks away, and the time was fifteen minutes from now.

Without arousing Owen's suspicions, he had to keep him downtown for another fifteen minutes.

Thinking it over, Ethan came up with the perfect delaying tactic, one that tied right in with the reason they were there in the first place. "Tell me the story, Pap," he said.

Owen frowned. "What story?"

"You know," said Ethan. "The one about Easter at Glosser Bros."

"Forget it." Owen glared across the river, in the direction not only of downtown Johnstown but Glosser Bros. Department Store. At least it *had been* Glosser's Department Store until 25 years ago, when it had closed its doors for good.

"Then *I'll* tell it," said Ethan. "I've heard it so many times, I think I know it by heart anyway."

Owen sighed. "I'm walking back to the car."

"Be my guest." Ethan shrugged. "But you'll have a long wait while I finish the story, since I have the keys."

Owen slumped, looking disgusted. But he didn't storm off to the car and leave Ethan standing there alone.

"Good." Ethan cleared his throat. "It all started three days before Easter in 1935..."

EIGHT-YEAR-OLD OWEN TALISMAN had to fight his way through the crowd to get a look at the day's main attraction on the first floor of the Glosser Bros. Department Store. It seemed like every kid in the place—and every parent, too—was mobbing the area near the base of the stairway to the second floor and the top of the stairs leading to the grocery department in the basement.

They all wanted to get closer to the incubator, just like Owen.

Though Owen was small for his age and on the scrawny side, he wasn't about to give up. He pushed and twisted his way through the mob, drawn by the siren song emanating from the incubator...the irresistible chirping of hundreds of tiny creatures.

Grunting, Owen struggled to squeeze between a tubby

girl and a stocky boy, the last obstacles separating him from his goal. He finally made it through, and the spectacle unveiled before him.

The incubator was four feet wide on each side and six feet high. It had four levels, each filled with a rainbow of multicolored chicks, their downy feathers dyed pink or blue or green or left a natural bright yellow.

Each level had an open front section where the chicks hopped around, eating and drinking from little metal troughs. Each of these front sections had a metal screen around it to keep the chicks from getting out while still letting Glosser's shoppers watch their antics.

The rear section of each level was enclosed with metal walls, floors, and ceilings. These boxed-in rear sections provided a refuge where the chicks could rest away from prying eyes, staying warm in the glow of heating bulbs mounted in the ceiling.

Front to back, top to bottom, the incubator was something to see...especially set up in the middle of the Glosser Bros. Department Store like that. Shoppers—adults as much as children—couldn't seem to get enough of watching the colorful chicks frolic while money changed hands and the smell of roasting nuts (a Glosser's trademark) wafted around them.

As for Owen, he had seen it before, in previous Easter seasons, but he never tired of it. His family had a few chickens; sometimes, there were peeps in the coop. But only at Glosser's at Easter time did he see *this many* peeps at once, all bouncing and chirping—a small army of adorable baby birds, crying out to be picked up and played with.

And that was exactly what he was going to do before leaving Glosser's and taking the streetcar back to Moxham Borough that day. One of those peeps would be *his,* no matter what happened.

Mesmerized, he reached toward the incubator, intending to press a fingertip against the screen and see if any of the chicks responded. Then, suddenly, a hand grabbed hold of his left upper arm. He resisted, hoping the hand would let him go...but it didn't.

Instead, it jerked him back out of the crowd and spun him around. Just like that, he stood facing his mother, who didn't look happy at all. "Owen Talisman! Who do you think you are, running off like that?"

"But the *peeps*!" Owen threw back his free arm and pointed at the incubator. "What if they *run out* before we get one?"

"Then we'll just have to *run after* them, I suppose." Owen's mother was making a joke. Her dark eyes twinkled when she said it.

"No!" Owen's face wrinkled with anger. "I mean what if they give them all *away*?"

"Don't worry, honey." Mom smiled reassuringly. "They have plenty to go around."

With that, she turned and headed for the elevators in the middle of the store, pulling Owen along after her. In spite of what she'd said, he couldn't help looking back over his shoulder at the crowd around the incubator.

It was a Glosser Bros. tradition, giving away a peep to

every child who entered the store at Easter time with a parent. And it was true, they had always had enough that Owen had never left empty-handed.

But still...who could say they wouldn't run out *this* year? Especially by the time Owen got done with his trip to the second floor and the major project that always seemed to him to take an eternity.

Though it was true, another wonderful prize awaited if he could just get through it. All he had to do was survive the torture without cracking...which he knew from experience would be no mean feat.

Just thinking about it made him gulp as he reluctantly stepped into the right-hand elevator car with Mom. As the doors closed, he even considered bolting and making a run for it.

But to get the reward, he knew he would have to tough it out, no matter how terrible it would be.

"What floor please?" asked the elevator operator, a pleasant, dark-skinned woman who knew Owen by name.

"Two, please." Mom smiled and patted Owen's head.

"Let me guess." The elevator operator raised an eyebrow at Owen. "Time for some new clothes, child?"

"*Special* clothes," said Mom. "We have to get him ready for *Easter*."

"Time for a new suit?" The elevator operator pulled the lever on the wall beside her, and the car climbed upward. "A new *church* suit?"

"And *shoes*," said Mom. "Isn't that right, Owen?"

"Yes, ma'am." Owen's voice was full of despair. "That's right."

The women laughed, and the elevator car stopped moving. Owen shivered with dread.

"Second floor." As the outer gate slid open, the elevator operator pulled the inner gate open, too. "Boys' suits and shoes. I hope you find some nice ones, Owen."

"Thanks." Owen didn't sound especially grateful.

The elevator operator leaned down and whispered confidentially. "Don't forget to ask about the *giveaway,* honey. One free *bunny rabbit* with every new suit."

Owen's frown became a small smile. It was exactly the reward he'd been anticipating.

"HERE." The salesman, a man in his late twenties or early thirties with dark hair, tugged a navy blue suit coat off a hanger and handed it to Owen. "Give this one a try."

Owen pulled the coat on quickly, without worrying about how it hung. His goal was to get done as fast as possible, so he could get to the prize at the end, then get his peep from the incubator downstairs and go home.

To say he hated trying on clothes would be the understatement of the decade. He'd only tried on three suit coats so far, but he felt like he'd tried on three dozen.

"Hmm." Mom leaned back and stared at him with narrowed eyes, tapping her bottom lip with a fingertip. "I don't like the cut of that one, do you?"

The salesman, whose name was Mr. Strump, straightened the coat on Owen's shoulders. "It's one of our top sellers." He stepped around Owen and fixed his lapels, which were folded inside the breast of the coat. Then, he stepped back beside Mom and joined her in staring. "Turn around, young man. Slowly, if you please."

As Owen turned in a slow circle, his eyes went straight to the big metal cage on the floor in the middle of the boys' department. Other children milled around it, gaping at what was inside and poking fingers through the bars, eager to touch and play with the occupants.

As for the rabbits inside the cage, they just huddled together and nibbled lettuce and bits of carrot. Owen's heart beat fast as he watched and wondered which animal he would get to take home as his very own personal Easter bunny.

"I don't think so." Mr. Strump helped him out of the navy blue coat and draped it over its hanger. "Let's try another. Something in brown, perhaps?"

Another. Owen winced, fighting the impulse to stomp his foot in anger. He hated the thought of trying on one more coat, but he hated the thought of not getting a free bunny even more.

Mom walked around a circular rack, running her hand along the suits hanging there. "Wait." Her hand stopped, and she pulled a light brown suit off the rack. "What about this one?"

Owen clenched his teeth as Mr. Strump reached for the suit. But then, when he put on the coat, a funny thing happened.

He didn't hate it.

It fit him perfectly. When he walked over to have a look in the mirror on the wall, he liked what he saw.

Mom seemed to be right in tune with him. "There we go." She sounded pleased. "Very nice."

"Good, good," said Mr. Strump.

Without being told, Owen turned slowly to look at the back and sides of the coat in the mirror. He was happy, because he'd found the right suit coat at last...and because now he could get to the *good* part.

Or so he thought.

"Now let's try on the *pants* as well." Mr. Strump held out the hanger with the matching trousers folded over the cross bar.

As much as he liked the suit, Owen still slumped as he took the pants and headed into the dressing room. Was he *ever* going to get that bunny?

LUCKILY, the pants fit fine. So did the first pair of brown dress shoes that Owen tried on with them.

Mr. Strump wrote up a sales slip for the purchases—including a dark brown tie that Mom had picked out—then walked it over to the cashier's desk for the boys' department. The young woman working there had short dark hair, brown eyes, and a pretty smile. She took the slip from Mr. Strump, told Mom how much she owed, then waited as Mom counted out the money from her pocketbook.

Mom had enough money to buy new clothes for Owen now that his father was back to work at Bethlehem Steel. Things had been tough for a few months before that, when Dad had been laid off...but things were better now. Mom had even paid back the credit she'd gotten from Glosser's, the "Glosser bucks" scrip vouchers that had helped her buy groceries during the layoff.

So Owen would have a new outfit for Easter that year...and a new rabbit, of course, which was something he wanted much more.

The cashier put the money and sales slip in a metal capsule about a foot long. Turning, she opened a door in the metal tube behind her, which ran straight up to the ceiling. She placed the capsule in the tube, then shut the door and pressed a button on the wall. The tube made a whooshing sound, and the capsule shot away through the store.

It was all part of what they called a pneumatic tube system, which used air pressure to transport sales slips and cash to the money office on the fourth floor and back again. Owen always loved to see it in action; once, a salesperson had even arranged for him to visit the money office and watch firsthand as the capsules flew up from the lower floors, then were cracked open, fed the correct change, and sent back down again.

This time, it took only a few minutes for the capsule to return to the cashier's desk. As she waited, the cashier packed Owen's new shoes in a box, then wrapped the suit in a paper sleeve with a hole at the top that fit over the hooked tip of the suit's wire hanger.

She had just finished packaging the purchases when the capsule whooshed back into the tube. "Here we are," she said, opening the tube and capsule and pulling out a receipt and change.

The cashier counted the change into Mom's hand, gave her the receipt, and thanked her for shopping at Glosser's.

"Thank you." Mom smiled and turned to go. "Happy Easter to you, too."

At which point, Owen started to panic. Heart hammering in his chest, he looked at Mom, then at the rabbit cage, wondering what he should do next.

They *couldn't* just walk out of there without the most important thing, could they?

"Oh, wait." Mom turned back to the cashier. "What about our complimentary rabbit?"

"Don't worry." Mr. Strump zipped past on his way to the bunny cage. "I wasn't going to let you forget *that*." He shot Owen a knowing wink.

And Owen's mood instantly shifted from worry to excitement.

With his back to Owen and Mom, Mr. Strump opened a door atop the cage and lifted something out. At first, Owen couldn't see what he held; then, after closing the cage door, Mr. Strump turned to face him.

"Perfect." Mr. Strump nodded and smiled at the fat white rabbit in the crook of his arm.

Owen's eyes widened. The other rabbits were brown or gray or black or white with spots and patches of other colors—but this one was pure, snowball white. He'd noticed him before, when he'd first sized up the cage; this was the only pure white rabbit of the lot.

And he was going to be Owen's personal pet.

"He's all yours, son." Mr. Strump grinned as he walked over with the white rabbit. "Any Glosser Bros. customer who buys a boys' suit at Easter time gets one of these at no additional cost. Though I have to say, you've gotten an exceptional value with *this* one." He winked as he handed the rabbit over to Owen. "He's an actual direct descendant of Peter Cottontail himself, I'm told."

"Really?" A shiver of delight tickled the back of Owen's neck as he took the bunny from Mr. Strump. The rabbit's white fur was softer and fluffier than anything he'd ever touched in his life. "He's related to *Peter*?"

Mr. Strump shrugged. "That's what I was told."

"*Wow.*" Owen held the rabbit up by its shoulders and gazed at its white-furred face. Its pink nose twitched constantly, and its long ears stood up straight. Its eyes were like glossy black marbles, staring directly at Owen.

"You're a lucky boy," said Mr. Strump. "True Cottontail rabbits are hard to come by."

"They are?" said Owen.

"Oh, yes," said Mr. Strump. "You'll have to take extra good care of him, so someday he can take Peter's place on the bunny trail."

Owen looked up at him in alarm. "Someday when?"

"Many years from now," said Mom. "Don't worry, you'll have lots of time together before then."

"Good." Owen pulled the rabbit against his side and cradled him in his left arm as Mr. Strump had done. He could feel the rabbit's little heart fluttering wildly inside its warm, fluffy body, like the wings of a hummingbird...and that gave him an idea. "I think I'll call him *Flutter.*"

"Fine by me." Mr. Strump winked. "I'll let the Bunny Brotherhood know as soon as you leave."

Owen gaped at him. There was a *Bunny Brotherhood?*

"Thank you so much, Mr. Strump." Mom waved and nudged Owen in the direction of the elevator. "We always love coming to Glosser's at Easter."

"Where else could you find the one-and-only Flutter Cottontail?" asked Mr. Strump. "And those adorable *peeps,* of course."

"The peeps!" Owen's head shot up from staring at the rabbit. "We need to get our *peep*!"

"We will, honey." The paper sleeve over the suit crumpled as Mom draped it over her arm.

"We need to *hurry*!" The rabbit bounced in Owen's arms as he ran toward the elevator doors in the middle of the second floor.

"No, you need to slow down!" shouted Mom. "You'll get your free peep, Owen...*won't* he, Mr. Strump?"

"Of course you'll get your peep," said Mr. Strump. "Cottontail rabbits are *magic,* aren't they?"

Owen stopped running and grinned down at Flutter. As a descendant of Peter Cottontail himself, he *had* to be magic.

"Cottontails make good things happen," said Mr. Strump. "They'll change your life for the *better,* son. *Believe* it!"

Bunnyburg. That was what the sign said, the one that Owen's dad had carved with his woodworking tools. It was the name of Flutter Cottontail's new home.

It was also the last piece of that home, a hutch that Dad had built in the back yard of the family's house in Moxham Borough with a little help from Owen. Dad even let Owen hammer in the last nail to fix the sign in place over the door of the hutch. Then, the two of them stood back and admired their handiwork.

The sturdy wood frame formed a box that was open to the air on all sides. Flutter wouldn't be able to get out, though; chicken wire lined every opening.

"What do you say, Owen?" asked Dad. "Will it do the trick?"

Owen grinned and nodded. "He'll love it, Dad."

"Did we put in enough straw, do you think?"

Owen cocked his head to one side and tapped his lower lip with a fingertip. "Maybe just a little more, Dad."

They added more straw in the bottom of the hutch, spreading it around and patting it down. Then, Owen fetched Flutter from the deep cardboard box where he'd been living for the past two days since his arrival from Glosser's.

"Home sweet home, Flutter Cottontail," said Owen as he lifted the white rabbit through the open door of the hutch. "Welcome to Bunnyburg."

Once Flutter was inside, Owen placed a little dish of

water in the corner closest to the door. Dad put in a handful of bright green lettuce, and Flutter started nibbling on it right away.

"He looks pretty comfy in there." Dad tipped back his brown fedora and folded his arms across his chest. "Looks like a happy rabbit, if you ask me."

Owen reached in and stroked Flutter's soft fur. "Blondie's happy, too, Dad." He was talking about the peep from Glosser's; he'd named her Blondie. She had her own box full of straw in the chicken coop, and he played with her often, though not as often as he played with Flutter. He loved both animals, but Flutter was more special to him...maybe because he was a direct descendant of Peter Cottontail and all.

"I'm proud of you, son." Dad reached down and tousled Owen's hair. "Being kind to animals is the mark of a good person."

Owen felt a surge of happiness...but then something he'd been worrying about came up over him. "Do you think the Bunny Brotherhood will ever take him away?" he asked.

"The Bunny Brotherhood?"

"Yeah," said Owen. "Mr. Strump said there's a Bunny Brotherhood. And he said Flutter will have to take Peter's place on the bunny trail someday. What if the Bunny Brotherhood takes him away to take Peter's place?"

Dad narrowed his eyes thoughtfully. "I don't think that will happen, as long as you take good enough care of him. Keep him happy enough that he'll never want to leave."

"You really think that'll work?"

Dad nodded. "It worked for me. Why do you think I never hopped away from *this* place?"

Owen shrugged. "Because you're happy?"

"That's right," said Dad. "You and your mother always keep me so happy, I never want to leave." With a smile, he rapped on the frame of the hutch. "Just do the same for Flutter here, and things ought to work out just fine."

BUT THINGS DIDN'T WORK out so fine after all.

On a sunny May morning two weeks after Easter, Owen walked out to feed and water Flutter. When he saw the open door of the hutch, he dropped the lettuce and dish of water on the ground and cried out in alarm.

Running to the hutch, he saw that Flutter was gone. All that remained were some tufts of white fur and little round pellets of poop in the mashed-down straw.

The rabbit had disappeared, but Owen grabbed the hutch and shook it anyway. Nothing moved inside except the rattling straw and pellets.

Just then, Mom ran out of the house behind him. "What happened? What's going on?"

Tears streamed down Owen's face as he dropped the hutch on its wooden stand. "Flutter's gone!"

Mom looked around. "Maybe he just got out. Are you sure you didn't leave the door unlatched?"

"I'm *sure* of it! I *never* leave it unlatched!"

"All right." Mom clapped her hands together. "So

however he got out, he might be somewhere nearby. Let's start searching."

"But what if it was the Bunny Brotherhood? What if they came and took him to take the place of Peter?"

"Let's hope for the best." Mom gestured at the left side of the yard. "You look that way, and I'll look over here." She gestured at the right side of the yard. "Maybe he'll turn up."

But he never turned up. The fluffy white rabbit would have been tough to miss among the greens in the vegetable garden or the berry bushes and weeds around the edge of the yard...but Mom and Owen never caught a glimpse of him.

Neither did Dad, when he got home from work that afternoon and joined the search. Neither did any of the neighbors, when Dad asked them to look around for a trace of the rabbit.

Flutter Cottontail was gone for good.

Mrs. Malonek next door had a theory about the disappearance. She thought that someone had taken Flutter, all right...but not the Bunny Brotherhood. It was the Great Depression, after all, and times were tough; she wouldn't put it past someone, she said, to have stolen Flutter for the cookpot.

As true as that might have been, it wasn't something Owen needed to hear. It made him all the more downcast in days to come, as his parents gave up searching, and the reality of life without Flutter set in.

All he could think about, day and night, was the missing rabbit. He slogged through school, barely able to focus on a word the teacher was saying. He walked home in a daze, not stopping to play stickball or marbles or cowboys and Indians with his friends. And when he got home, he went straight to his room and moped, lying on his bed and staring up at the ceiling.

He was miserable.

"Why don't you go play with Blondie?" asked Mom, trying to take his mind off Flutter. "She's probably starting to feel lonely, don't you think?"

"I don't care," said Owen. "I want Flutter back."

"Honey." Mom sat beside him on the bed. "I'm sorry, but I don't think he's *coming* back. I think you're going to have to let him go."

"I won't. I *can't*." With that, Owen rolled over, turning his back to her. "I miss him *too much*."

"Don't worry," said Mom. "This too shall pass."

"No it won't," said Owen. "It'll *never* pass."

"It will," Mom said reassuringly. "You'll see. Somehow, things will get better."

Owen didn't believe her. In the days that followed, he just felt worse and worse. He couldn't imagine ever feeling better again in his life, no matter what happened.

Not unless Flutter came back to him.

A MONTH AFTER EASTER, Owen was still depressed about Flutter. His parents were more worried about him than ever, but nothing they tried could snap him out of his despair.

He just couldn't accept that Flutter was gone. Whether the rabbit had been stolen and eaten or taken away to replace Peter Cottontail, Owen couldn't seem to move on without him.

Then, one Saturday morning, there was a loud knock at the front door. A moment later, Mom called for Owen, who was reading a book in his bedroom.

Reluctantly, Owen put the book down and walked to the parlor. When he got there, he saw that Mom was standing in the doorway, holding the front screen door open. She was looking down at a little brown basket on the porch floorboards outside.

"What is it?" asked Owen.

"You tell me." Mom nodded at the basket. "It has your name in it."

Frowning, Owen stepped out for a closer look. Inside the basket was a folded piece of white paper with two words printed on it: OWEN TALISMAN.

There was something else in the basket, too. When Owen bent down and pulled out the folded paper, he saw a tiny tuft of white fur stuck underneath it.

White fur. Suddenly, his heart started pounding.

"Is that what I think it is?" asked Mom.

Owen didn't answer. Instead, he unfolded the paper and read the note that was printed inside.

He couldn't keep his hands from shaking with excitement. He read the note three times before Mom insisted he read it aloud to her.

"'Special message arriving tonight. Meet at the big apple tree on the edge of the woods at the top of the hill at sunset.'"

"Wow," said Mom. "What do you think that's about?"

Owen couldn't take his eyes off the paper. He just kept staring at the words...and what was below them, on the bottom half of the page.

"Are you going to the apple tree tonight?" Mom's eyes were wide, and she was smiling. "Are you going to find out what the special message is?"

"I guess I'd better." Owen pointed at the marks on the bottom of the page. They looked like a bunny's paw print, stamped in ink. "He *signed* it. I think Flutter *signed* it."

IT WAS after eight o'clock when Owen and Dad set out for the woods. The sun was lowering in the sky, slowly drifting toward the rooftops of the neighborhood.

The air was cool and smelled of sweet spring blossoms and new-mown grass. The laughter of children and the barking of dogs abounded, though the end of daylight and playtime was fast approaching. Lamps flicked on in windows, one by one, lighting up parlors and dining rooms from within for passersby to see in bright relief against the coming of night's darkness.

All these details made stronger impressions than

usual on Owen's young mind. Normally, they were background noise, part of his everyday world...but tonight, they were part of something infinitely more thrilling. He was on his way to a secret meeting, one that might bring him face to face with something magical and extraordinary. In the course of this meeting, he would receive some kind of "special message" that might provide the answer to the biggest mystery of his life so far.

Namely, what had become of Flutter Cottontail?

"Are you nervous?" asked Dad as they turned the corner from Linden Avenue onto Bond Street and headed up the hill.

"A little," said Owen. "What do you think the special message will be?"

"Who knows?" Dad was holding Owen's hand and gave it a squeeze. "I guess we'll find out soon enough."

Near the top of the hill, Owen stopped, and Dad stopped with him. From where they stood, Owen could see the big old apple tree at the edge of the woods.

Squinting, he looked for some sign of whomever he was going to meet. Mostly, he looked for a glimpse of Flutter's white fur, because that was what he secretly expected to see.

But there wasn't any white fur in sight. Around the base of the apple tree, Owen saw nothing but shadows.

"This is it." Dad gave Owen's hand a shake. "So do you want me to go with you the rest of the way?"

Owen swallowed hard and pulled his hand free of Dad's. He was getting more nervous as the big moment approached, but he was determined to act like a big boy. "I'll go myself."

"Good luck then," said Dad. "I'll be right here if you need me."

Owen had twenty feet to go to get to the apple tree. Halfway there, he stopped, frozen in place with fearful shivering.

Then, he heard footsteps behind him. He felt a familiar hand on his shoulder and instantly felt at ease.

It was Dad, of course. "Can I come with you after all?" he asked. "I can't wait to see who shows up and find out what the message is."

Owen nodded, and they continued on together.

When they finally reached the tree, Owen heard a rustling noise that made him jump. Instinctively, he grabbed Dad's hand and held it tight.

"Hello?" said Dad. "Who's there?"

Owen heard more rustling from the brush around the tree. Then, suddenly, a figure emerged from behind the broad trunk.

Owen felt a pang of disappointment, because the figure was human. He'd been hoping for Flutter Cotton-tail, but instead, he saw a man looking back at him from the shadows.

"Greetings." The man was old, with a full gray beard and a big, round face. He wore ragged, mismatched clothes: a rumpled top hat, a tattered blue jacket, a gray work shirt, and faded jeans. The hodge-podge outfit put Owen in mind of the hobos he saw passing through town, the ones who sometimes went to Glosser's and were given a free meal by the Glosser family to sustain them. "Are you Owen Talisman?" The man's voice was deep and gravelly.

"Y-yes." Owen nodded. The man had made no hostile moves, but Owen was still glad that Dad had come with him.

"Very good." The man tipped his hat and smiled. "My name is Lightfoot. Flutter Cottontail sent me."

"He did?" Owen's eyes grew wide as softballs.

Lightfoot reached into a pocket of his jacket and pulled out a tuft of white fur, which he handed to Owen. "Indeed he did."

Owen marveled at the tuft and showed it to Dad, who grinned and nodded.

"Very good to meet you." Lightfoot reached out and shook Owen's hand, then cast a suspicious look in Dad's direction. "And I suppose you can vouch for *him?*"

Owen nodded. "That's my Dad. He's okay."

"All right then." Lightfoot shook Dad's hand. "Now let's get down to business. I have a special message from Flutter." Opening his jacket wide, he pointed at a badge pinned to the left chest of his work shirt. The badge was silver and simply designed, with the letters "BB" printed in white in the middle of it. "Y'see, I'm a representative of the Bunny Brotherhood."

"Really?" said Owen.

"Absolutely." Lightfoot stuck up the index and middle fingers of his right hand and wiggled them back and forth like rabbit ears. "There's the high sign for you, Owen. Any time you see it, you'll know for sure it's one of us."

Owen nodded slowly.

Lightfoot ended the salute and lowered his hand. "Flutter sends his apologies. He wished he could make it himself, but he's just too busy. It isn't easy stepping into the shoes of Peter Cottontail, the most famous rabbit who ever lived."

"Flutter's okay?" asked Owen. "He didn't get thrown in a cookpot and eaten?"

Lightfoot laughed. "Of course not! He's just fine! He's a magical *Cottontail,* isn't he?"

Owen felt a deep relief at hearing the news. The shadow that had been hanging over him for weeks suddenly lifted.

"Flutter's better than ever, actually," said Lightfoot. "He's the new king of Bunnyburg, and he's really making the place shine."

"Is he ever coming back?" asked Owen.

Lightfoot squinted his left eye and shook his head. "I doubt it," he said. "I mean, he might pass through on Easter morning, but he'll be too busy to stop off and chew the fat with you. Understand?"

"Well, can *I* go and visit *him* in Bunnyburg, then?" asked Owen.

Lightfoot met Dad's gaze, then cleared his throat. "Sorry, but no. No humans allowed. Not even the Bunny Brotherhood."

"But that's not fair!" Owen felt the pressure of tears building up in his eyes, getting ready to burst forth. "I miss him so *much.*"

"Which is exactly why I'm here." Lightfoot raised his hand and wiggled his two fingers again. "To report the latest news so you'll know exactly what's going on in Flutter's life. He said that's the least we could do, after you took care of him so well."

Owen swallowed hard, holding back tears.

"There's just one catch, Owen," said Lightfoot. "I need you to do one thing before I tell you the latest."

"What's that?" asked Owen.

"What I'm about to tell you is confidential information," said Lightfoot. "It can only be shared with trusted members of the Bunny Brotherhood."

Owen frowned. "But I'm not..."

"Which is why you need to join the Bunny Brotherhood before I tell you a single thing. You, too, big guy." Lightfoot wiggled his two fingers at Dad.

Dad shrugged. "Fair enough." He raised a hand and wiggled his fingers just like Lightfoot.

Owen did the same.

"Very good." Lightfoot grinned, revealing several gaps in his smile where teeth were missing. "Now repeat after me. In the name of the great carrot patch, I hereby swear to uphold the code of the Bunny Brotherhood."

Owen and Dad repeated the oath word-for-word.

"I swear always to help rabbits whenever I can," continued Lightfoot. "Setting out carrots and lettuce to feed them...keeping the bunny trails and burrows clear for them...chasing away the cats and dogs who hunt them...and doing everything in my power to keep all bunnies safe from harm."

Owen and Dad finished the oath, and everyone wiggled their fingers in the salute that Lightfoot had taught them. When Lightfoot wiggled his nose like a bunny, they did that, too.

"Congratulations," said Lightfoot. "You are now official members of the Bunny Brotherhood...and I may now tell you the story of Flutter Cottontail's adventures since returning to the magical land of Bunnyburg."

With that, he began to tell Flutter's story. Dad listened with interest, leaning a shoulder against the trunk of the apple tree.

And Owen hung on every word with attention so rapt, nothing could tear him away until the last word of the story had been spoken.

LATER, Owen walked back down the hill of Bond Street with Dad, talking about the amazing visit they'd had with Lightfoot. The messenger of the Bunny Brotherhood had told them so many wonderful things before he'd gone, all about Flutter and the kingdom of Bunnyburg.

Then, at the end, he'd told them the most wonderful thing of all. It was all Owen could think about, in fact.

"I regret to say I must go now," Lightfoot had said. "But have no fear. This won't be the last you hear of Flutter Cottontail."

"What do you mean?" Owen had asked breathlessly.

"I mean Flutter isn't going to leave you in the dark." Lightfoot had shaken his head slowly, emphatically. "From time to time, he will send a fellow member of the Bunny

Brotherhood to bring you the latest news report from Bunnyburg. You'll be notified of the time and meeting place just as you were today."

"*When?*" Owen had shouted, unable to contain his excitement. "When will I get the next report?"

"It depends," Lightfoot had told him. "You'll just have to wait and see."

"But I'll definitely *get* another report?"

"Now that you're part of the Brotherhood, you *have* to get one." Lightfoot had nodded and taken off his "BB" badge. "It's one of your rights and privileges."

Then, Lightfoot had pinned the badge to Owen's shirt and tousled his hair. Moments later, with one last wiggling fingers salute, he'd disappeared into the darkness of the woods as if he'd never been at the apple tree in the first place.

Now, on the way home with Dad, Owen couldn't stop looking at and touching the badge on his chest. And he couldn't stop thinking about the next news report from Bunnyburg.

"When do you think it will be?" he asked Dad. "When will I get the next message?"

Dad shrugged. "We'll have to wait and see, like Lightfoot said."

"But I *can't* wait," said Owen.

Dad chuckled. "Sure you can. After tonight's news report, you'll have plenty to keep you busy until then."

Owen frowned up at him. "What do you mean?"

"Don't you think you'd better write down the news you heard?" said Dad. "*Somebody* has to put the stories down on paper, for posterity's sake."

"Posterity?" Owen scowled at the word.

"History," said Dad. "You need to save the stories for future generations. Maybe even draw some pictures to go with them. Think you're up to the job?"

"Yeah!" Owen kicked a stone down the hill victoriously.

"It's a lot of responsibility," Dad said sternly. "Are you sure you can do it?"

"Yeah, Dad! I can do a *great* job at it!"

"Okay then." Dad smiled and patted his head.

"I'll start tonight, as soon as we get home!" said Owen.

"Isn't it already past your bedtime?"

"But I don't want to *forget* anything," said Owen.

"Maybe you can do a *little,* then," said Dad. "Just until you fall asleep."

"I *won't* fall asleep. I'll work all night and get all the stories and pictures on paper."

"Sounds good." Dad didn't seem too worried that Owen would manage to stay up all night. "I can't wait to see what you come up with."

"Do you think I can send a copy to Flutter Cottontail?" asked Owen.

"I don't see why not," said Dad. "Who knows? Other folks might want to read it, too."

"You think so?"

Dad grinned and reached for Owen's hand. "You never know."

LIGHTFOOT'S PROMISE CAME TRUE. One month after his visit, another note showed up in a basket on Owen's front porch, inviting him to return to the apple tree for another special message.

This time, a different man showed up, a young man with black hair and glasses. Like Lightfoot, he wore mismatched hobo-style clothes...and a top hat and Bunny Brotherhood badge. He said his name was Fencedigger, and he told stories of Flutter's adventures that were even more amazing than the stories Lightfoot had told.

A month after that, another invitation arrived, and another top-hatted representative of the Bunny Brotherhood arrived—this one an elderly woman with silver hair and bright green eyes. She nibbled a carrot the whole time she spoke and gave Owen a piece of hard candy when her stories were done.

More Bunny Brotherhood messengers came to see Owen in the months that followed. And Owen faithfully wrote down and drew every story they told him.

He kept everything that he wrote and drew in notebooks under his bed—a detailed record of events in Bunnyburg and the epic life and times of its king, Flutter Cottontail. Owen made copies that he gave to the Bunny Brotherhood messengers to give to Flutter...but he always kept the originals safe at home.

And over time, he added stories to them that he hadn't heard from the Brotherhood, stories that he had made up on his own. He had to, because he needed new stories, and the Brotherhood came less and less often over time; around Christmas, they stopped coming altogether, only reappearing at Easter time the next year.

By then, Owen had filled entire notebooks with new stories. He was much more interested in creating his own Bunnyburg stories than hearing the ones that the Brotherhood messengers told him at the apple tree.

And when he finally found out, as an adult, that the messengers had all been hobos after all, recruited and paid by Dad to help him get over Flutter's disappearance, it didn't trouble him at all. Because Owen recognized that Dad had kept the magic alive for him. He realized that those emissaries of Flutter Cottontail had given him hope and wonder and a gift that could change the direction of his life.

For those notebooks became the foundation of his writing career, the basis of the *Bunnyburg* series that would someday capture the imaginations of children around the world. It was a series that would bring him all the good things life had to offer: money, recognition, travel...and the love of a good woman who was also his artistic partner and number one supporter.

Though, ultimately, the books could not do one particular thing for him, one thing that mattered more than anything in the world.

They could not keep his wife alive when she got sick, and they could not bring her back when she died.

EASTER AT GLOSSER'S

ETHAN TALISMAN LEFT that last part out when he finished retelling the story on Easter morning along the bank of the Stonycreek River. Great-grandfather Owen didn't need another reminder of what had happened to the love of his life, Melinda.

Though, from the look on Owen's face, Ethan thought maybe he'd filled in that last part on his own.

"The end." Ethan smiled. "So how'd I do, Pap? Did I tell it right?"

Owen shrugged, looking grimmer than ever. "Can we finally go now?" He gestured in the general direction of Ethan's car. "I want to go home."

Ethan kept smiling. He was determined to carry out his secret plan in spite of Owen's resistance. "Right after church." Checking the watch on his wrist, he saw the storytelling had taken just long enough. There were five minutes left until he had to get Owen to where he needed to be for the surprise to occur.

"No church." Owen shook his head darkly. "Church does nothing for me anymore."

"So go through the motions. Humor me." Ethan took Owen by the arm and gestured toward the Franklin Street Bridge, which was less than half a block away and would take them to downtown proper. "Maybe I just want to have one more traditional Easter with my Pap."

A gust of wind swept up from the river, and Owen pulled the fedora tighter on his head. Otherwise, he didn't budge. His face, which once upon a time had been merry more often than not, was etched with the ingrained scowl of personal loss and endless misery.

"Please, Pap?" Ethan tugged Owen's arm. "Just this one more time?"

Owen seemed no more inclined to cooperate, and Ethan was starting to think his plan was doomed. The old man shrugged off Ethan's hand and glared at him with the same dark expression, lacking any trace of the spark he'd once had in such abundance. Owen steeled himself, expecting a nasty refusal that made his plan even less likely to succeed.

But then, without a word, Owen started walking toward the bridge.

Ethan cheered silently and fell in step beside him. As long as Owen kept moving and didn't pull a fast one of some kind, there was still time for everything to happen exactly as Ethan had planned.

A car beeped as it passed them, and Owen didn't react. Following the right turn of the sidewalk, he started across the bridge above the muddy, rushing water.

"You're more *her* chip than mine," said the old man.

Ethan frowned. "Huh?"

"Your great-grandmother," said Owen. "You're more like her than me. So stubborn. Always trying to get me to do the right thing." He nodded. "When I said you were a chip off the old block, I meant that you were a chip off *her* block more than *mine*."

Ethan was surprised. "Really?"

"Now you know my secret." Owen snorted. "One of them, anyway."

As they crossed the bridge together in the Easter morning sun, Ethan thought about his great-grandma, Melinda. He remembered her delicate features, her bright blue eyes, and the way she'd always tipped her head when she'd listened to what he said. Echoes of her sweet voice and girlish giggle rippled through his memory.

Owen could not have paid him a higher compliment, he decided, than saying that she was the block from which he'd been chipped the most.

"I miss her, too," said Ethan. "I miss her every day."

"Good." Owen didn't look up from the sidewalk when he said it.

A few more steps, and the bridge ended. Ethan and Owen continued past the Conrad Building, an ancient flatiron-style structure that had partially crumbled into the river.

When they got to the intersection of Franklin and Vine streets, they had to wait for a few cars to roll past. Then, the light changed, and the pedestrian signal on the opposite corner flashed the white outline of a walking man for their benefit.

The two of them proceeded down Franklin, then stopped for another light at the intersection with Main Street. At that point, Ethan couldn't help looking toward Central Park, where his plan would reach its culmination. He couldn't see anything out of the ordinary from where he was standing, which was good; he didn't want anything to tip off Owen before the time was right.

"I expect you to take me home the *instant* church is over," said Owen as they crossed Main. "No brunch nonsense and no unexpected stops or drives through the countryside. Capische?"

"Got it." Ethan slowed his pace fractionally, glancing across the street at Central Park. There was no way to know if everything was ready; he would just have to trust that his helpers had all done their jobs.

For his part, Owen seemed to have no inkling that anything unusual was in the wind. "Let's get this over with," he said, sparing not a single glance at the park as he stalked along the sidewalk.

He didn't look at the big brick building across Locust Street from the park, either, though it had once played a prominent role in his life. That building had once housed the Glosser Bros. Department Store; it looked much the same now as it had on that long-ago day in 1935 when Owen had gotten Blondie the chick and Flutter Cottontail...though the signage and awnings that had once adorned it were long gone.

Was it too painful for Owen to look at that building—now a county property full of offices and courtrooms—and remember the good times he'd once had there? Would it hurt too much to recall the experiences he'd shared at Glosser's with his loved ones, so many of whom were now gone?

It was probably best to leave those questions unspoken, Ethan thought.

Up ahead, at the end of the block, people were filing

into the Franklin Street United Methodist Church. For all Owen knew, he'd be filing inside the place, too.

Then, suddenly, his immediate destiny became less predictable.

"Pap, hold on." Ethan caught Owen's elbow and stopped him from merging with the flow of churchgoers. "Look over there." He pointed at Central Park across the street, at the bench closest to the corner of Franklin and Locust.

"What?" Owen looked annoyed.

"That little girl." Ethan took a step toward the curb. "She's sitting there alone, crying."

Owen looked where Ethan was pointing, then brushed a hand through the air dismissively. "Not our business."

"You don't think?" Ethan stood a moment more, watching the little blonde girl on the bench. She was clearly sobbing; her head was bowed, her shoulders were rising and falling. "But what if you're wrong? What if she needs help?"

Owen gestured toward the crowd filing into the church. "Plenty of other people around if she does."

"Come on." Ethan waited till the street was clear of traffic, then stepped down off the curb. "It can't hurt to make sure she's okay."

"Go ahead," said Owen. "I'll meet you inside." He turned to head for the entrance of the church.

At which point, Ethan hopped back up onto the curb and grabbed his arm. "Come on, Pap." He bobbed his head toward the park. "Just come with me for a minute, in case I need you."

Owen resisted, leaning toward the church. Then, with a grunt of disgust, he surrendered. "All right, all right." He let Ethan help him down from the curb. "As long as we don't miss church, now that we've decided to go."

"Don't worry, we won't." Ethan looked both ways, then led Owen across the street. His heart was pounding like a drummer on a rampage in his chest; the secret plan was about to be realized.

Bright pink blossoms hung from the trees around them as they made their way around the corner and up the walk that cut diagonally through that part of the park. When they approached the bench where the little girl sat, they could hear her sobbing softly amid the tweets and chirps of the robins, sparrows, and wrens.

Ethan stopped a few feet away, holding Owen there with him, and cleared his throat. "Excuse me."

The girl, who couldn't have been older than six or seven, looked up at him. "Yes?" She wore a white sweater over a colorful Easter dress—knee-length, printed with tulips and lilies and daffodils.

"Are you all right?" asked Ethan. "We thought you might need help."

The little girl shook her head, then turned her gaze to Owen. "Mister?" A pair of bright pink clips held her hair back at the temples. "What's your name?"

Frowning, Owen hesitated. "Owen," he said finally.

"Owen." The girl nodded, then pushed herself off the bench to her feet. "Owen what?"

Again, Owen hesitated. "Talisman. Owen Talisman."

Smiling, the girl reached into the pocket of her little

white sweater. "Then this is for you." She pulled out her hand, cupped her other hand over it, and reached up to Owen.

His frown *really* deepened at that. He leaned back, staring at her cupped hands as if they might contain a grenade.

Ethan put a reassuring arm around his shoulders. "Go ahead."

Owen shook his head. "But what if..."

"She's like six years old," said Ethan. "Go ahead, see what she's got for you."

Still, the old man hesitated.

"Please, Mister." The girl stepped closer and held her cupped hands higher. "It's an Easter present."

Owen scowled and tried to back away. "What kind of..."

Which was when he heard a sound from the little girl's hands. And his eyes shot wide open.

Then, he heard it again. It was a familiar sound, one he hadn't heard in ages but knew so well he could never forget it.

There it was again. A tiny, high-pitched chirp. *Peep.*

"Oh my God." Just as Owen said it, the girl opened her hands.

There between her little pink fingers was a fluffy yellow chick, a peep just like Blondie had once been.

"Here, Owen." She pressed it toward him.

Owen took the chick in his withered, shaking hands. He couldn't take his eyes off the baby bird as it chirped and squirmed in his grip.

Ethan, in turn, watched Owen's face closely. Was that a

trace of a smile he saw on that wrinkled visage he loved so well?

It didn't matter, because the secret plan wasn't done yet.

After giving Owen a moment to take in the chick, Ethan nodded at the little girl, giving her the cue to deliver her next lines.

"Greetings from the Bunny Brotherhood." The girl pulled one side of her sweater back, revealing the silver badge that was pinned to her dress. The letters "BB" were printed on the badge in white paint.

"The Brotherhood?" said Ethan. "You mean like with the high sign and everything?" He was prompting the girl, who'd forgotten to give the salute.

Nodding, she raised her right hand, then wiggled the index and middle fingers in the rabbit-ears salute. "A friend sends his regards," she said.

"Friend?" Owen frowned. "*What* friend?"

Just then, a boy stepped out from behind a nearby tree. He had red hair and freckles and looked about eight or nine years old. He was wearing a white button-down shirt, dark slacks, and a red tie with a Bunny Brotherhood badge pinned to it where the tie tack should have been. "He said to give you this." The boy walked over and held out a fist, then turned it palm up and uncurled his fingers. "He said you would know who he was."

Again, Owen's eyes widened. In the palm of the boy's hand, there was a tuft of white fur.

With the chick in one hand, Owen took the tuft of fur

in the other. He stared at them both, speechless, as the boy and girl looked on.

The boy cleared his throat. "He said it's been a long time since you heard from him. He said you'll want to catch up on all the news you've missed from Bunnyburg."

"But here's the thing." Another child emerged from behind another tree—a girl, a little older than the others, with short brown hair and a pale green dress. She wore a Bunny Brotherhood badge on the strap of her white vinyl purse. "It's been a *really* long time since you last heard from him. So there's *lots* of news. Much more than one or two or even three of us can tell."

"That's why he sent more of us." The fifth child's voice —the squeaky voice of a very young boy—came from somewhere nearby, though he couldn't be seen yet. "That's why he sent *lots* more."

Someone let loose a loud whistle, then, and children poured out from behind every tree in Central Park. They came from behind the statue of Joseph Johns (founder of Johnstown) and the twin cannons on either side of it. They came from behind the statue of a Civil War soldier from the 54th Pennsylvania Infantry. They marched from around the Pasquerilla Fountain, the gazebo, the war monument, and the memorial to the victims of the 1977 Johnstown Flood.

And all of them were dressed in their Easter finest, wearing Bunny Brotherhood badges.

There were dozens of them, all converging on Owen...all recruited from the actual Bunny Brotherhood fan club that supported his Bunnyburg books. Ethan had enlisted them for this special day, to remind Owen of what his work meant and that his life had meaning and could continue to do so. He could never take away Owen's pain for the loss of his wife and partner, but maybe he could take his mind off it for just a little while.

And maybe he could give him new purpose to boot.

"Every one of us has a story," said the still-unseen fifth child with the squeaky voice. "We bring them to catch you up on what you've missed. Could you help us bring them to the world in turn?"

As Owen gazed at the crowd of children surrounding him, he looked confused...perhaps overwhelmed. "I don't understand." He sounded flustered when he spoke. "Why do all this...for me?"

"To keep Bunnyburg alive," said the unseen child.

"But I can't," said Owen. "I don't...I don't have an *artist* anymore."

"Sure you do," said Ethan, and then he raised his voice for the crowd. "How many of you can *draw*?"

Every child in the park shot his or her hand in the air, fluttering their fingers in the Bunny Brotherhood high sign.

Owen sniffed. "This is too much." His lips quivered. "I don't deserve any of this."

"Sure you do." Ethan put his arm around his great-grandfather and squeezed his shoulders. "Just ask *him*."

With that, the unseen child finally made himself seen, stepping out from behind a nearby bush. He was a skinny kid with dark hair, and he wore a light brown suit and dark brown tie—a suit that resembled the one that Owen's mom had bought three days before Easter in 1935.

But the suit wasn't the most interesting thing about the kid. There was something else, something that caught everyone's eye, from the littlest child in the crowd to Owen Talisman himself.

The interesting thing was this: the kid was cradling a white-furred rabbit in his arms.

Ethan felt Owen relax against him. When he looked at Owen's face, he saw that for once, there wasn't a frown carved there.

As the kid carried the white rabbit forward, the crowd parted before him. Some of the children petted the bunny as it passed, and many of them giggled and whispered among themselves.

The kid stopped in front of Owen. "You already know each other, right?" The kid lifted the rabbit, turning its face toward Owen. "You remember *him,* don't you?" He put his ear near the rabbit's mouth, pretending to hear it talk. "That's right, he's Owen Talisman. And *you.*" He looked up at Owen. "You remember *him,* right?" He held up the rabbit for Owen to take.

Owen cradled the rabbit in the crook of his right arm while holding the peeping chick in his left hand. "Of course I do." For the first time in so long that Ethan couldn't remember, an actual smile flowed across Owen's face. "How could I forget *Flutter Cottontail?*"

At which point, all the children clapped. And so did Ethan.

"Can we tell you our stories now?" asked the little blonde girl from the bench. "Please?"

That was when Owen did something that made the whole secret plan worthwhile for Ethan, aka Chip, aka his great-grandson. He turned and gave him a wink, and there was a spark in his eye when he did it.

Then, Owen turned back to the kids. "Okay, one at a time," he said. "And somebody get me a pen and a notebook, so I can write everything down."

As soon as the words left his lips, the children of the Bunny Brotherhood swarmed around him, all telling their stories at once, all tugging his sleeves, all reaching for Flutter Cottontail, the once and future king of the kingdom of Bunnyburg.

HAPPY BICENTENNIAL
1776-1976
GLOSSER BROS
GLOSSER BROS

FOURTH OF JULY AT GLOSSER'S

"CAN WE LIGHT ONE *NOW*, Grandpa? *Can* we?"

Amy Lindsey's little redheaded brother ran out of the house first, leaving her and Mom in the dust. The kid was so worked up, Amy thought he might explode.

The heap of fireworks in the trunk of her grandpa's old Chevy was a dream come true for the seven-year-old, whose nickname, after all, was...

"Boom, no," said Grandpa. "You *know* these are for the Fourth of July."

"Just one!" Boom's hand snapped out, reaching for a bottle rocket. His actual name was Boone, but Boom fit him for obvious reasons. "Just a test fire!"

It was then that Mom intervened, grabbing his wrist. "I *think* you can wait *two nights*. We have to keep up the tradition, don't we, Amy?"

All eyes were on Amy, as if the 15-year-old with the short auburn hair had any great interest in the tradition...especially these days. Why bother trying to keep a family tradition going when the family itself was falling apart?

But Amy played along. "That's right." She nodded for Boom's benefit.

"And this has to be the biggest year yet," added Grandpa. "It'll be the Bicentennial, remember," he said, as if anyone could possibly forget. As if anyone in Johnstown, Pennsylvania could talk about anything else with July 4th, 1976 just two days away.

Especially now that Paul Newman the movie star had left town.

With one hand restrained by Mom, Boom grabbed with the other for a sphere wrapped in brown paper, but she jerked him back, and he missed it.

"Nooo!" squawked Boom. "I just wanna light *one*! Just *one*!"

"Just wait till Monday," Mom said firmly, pulling him away from the bed of the truck. "We'll have our very own Bicentennial spectacle."

Grandpa smiled. "You better believe it. I must've bought all the fireworks in the state of West Virginia!"

"More than Dad?" asked Boom.

At that, everyone got quiet all of a sudden. Dad was the one who had made the traditional fireworks run every year, driving south of the Pennsylvania border where buying fireworks wasn't breaking the law (though bringing them back over the border was). Dad was the one who had hauled the fireworks, set them up, and set them off on the Fourth, providing a free show that he claimed was better than the one sponsored by the Glosser Bros. Department Store. Dad was the one who'd done all that.

And now Dad wasn't around. He was no longer part of the family. He didn't live in the little white house on the wooded double lot on top of a hill in Roxbury with them anymore.

"You be the judge, Boom." Grandpa chuckled and tousled Boom's wild red hair. "I did the best I could, buying all this stuff and driving it here. You tell me Monday night if I did as well as your dad."

"I will! Don't worry!" Boom's eyes were drawn back to the heap of fireworks. His fingers twitched as if he were ready to snatch up handfuls and run.

"In the meantime, I better get these unloaded." Grandpa scooped up a bunch of rockets and headed for the shed in the back yard, giving Mom a look on the way past. "I just hope none are missing by the time I get back."

Mom nodded. "Boom, honey, I need you and Amy to come with me and pick up some decorations and picnic stuff. Let's go."

Boom's shoulders slumped. "Aw, Mom." He stared at the fireworks in the trunk a long time...but then he turned and followed Mom.

As for Amy, she fell in step, too. "Where are we going?"

"Glosser's." Mom smiled at her. "Where else?"

The Glosser Bros. Department Store in downtown Johnstown could not have been more patriotic. Everywhere Amy looked as she walked through the ground floor, there were red, white, and blue streamers, American flags, and images of fireworks, the Declaration of Independence, President George Washington, and the Liberty Bell. Mannequins were dressed in Colonial outfits, some armed with muskets and wearing tri-corner hats. The "Star-Spangled Banner" played over the P.A. system speakers, along with John Philip Sousa marches and other patriotic music.

Signs amid the racks and tables of merchandise announced the big fireworks show at Point Stadium on July Fourth, sponsored by Glosser Bros.—but seeing them made Amy feel sad. She couldn't help remembering what her dad had always said when he'd seen those signs and how it had made her laugh.

They need to update that sign. Change it to "The Don't-Bother Fourth of July So-Called Fireworks," as in "Nowhere near as good as the spectacular in the Lindsey family's backyard in Roxbury, so don't bother coming."

She'd loved hearing him say that, even if he'd had alcohol on his breath at the time. The alcohol had rarely bothered her, actually, except once in a while, when he'd had too much. Even then, it hadn't always been a problem—except when "silly Dad" turned into "angry Dad" and argued with Mom.

Would Amy ever hear him say those words again? She didn't think so. Dad wasn't coming back, according to Mom—and neither was Amy's older brother, Mark...fun-loving, loveable Mark. She'd always adored and looked up to him, and he'd always been there for her—until the 19-year-old had walked out the door after Dad, that is. Mark had gone to look after him, he'd insisted, because Dad didn't seem to be in his right mind...but the end result was the same whatever the reason. Dad and Mark were both gone.

And it was all because of that stupid Paul Newman.

"Hey, these are fun." Mom picked up boxes of sparklers from one of the tables. "Maybe I'll buy a few."

Boom sighed loudly and shook his head. "Waste of money, Mom. We won't need those with all the firepower we'll be setting off."

"Okay then." Mom put the sparklers down and moved to another table that was heaped with decorations. "I'll use my employee discount for something else."

Amy trailed after them, her hands idly drifting over items on the tables and in the bins. Mom worked at Glosser's, and Amy loved to go there—but the place wasn't lifting her spirits today.

As mean as Dad had been in moving away, it just didn't feel like the Fourth of July without him.

"These are perfect." Mom gathered up rolls of red, white, and blue crepe paper and dropped them in the wire basket she carried. She threw in some cardboard cutouts, too—images of American flags, hot dogs, hamburgers, apple pie, and fireworks. "We'll have a real Bicentennial blast, you guys."

Suddenly, Amy couldn't take it anymore. When Mom's back was turned, she darted away down the aisle and ducked into an open elevator as a young woman stepped out.

She hit the button for the second floor, and the door slid closed. When it opened again, she ran past racks of lingerie, dresses, and men's suits, and sprinted through the tunnel to the Cafeteria building next door, heading for her favorite place in her favorite department store.

"HELLO, AMY." Ruby Shaffer smiled and waved from behind the counter of the Glosser Bros. soda fountain. "So nice to see you, dear."

For the first time that day, Amy managed a genuine smile. Ruby—and her twin sister, Ruth, who also worked the soda fountain—had known Amy for as long as she could remember. They had a way of making her feel better no matter what...and the free samples of ice cream they gave her were just one small part of it.

"Hi, Ruby." Amy managed half a smile as she folded her arms on the counter.

"All ready for the Fourth?" asked Ruby.

Amy shook her head. "How about you?"

"Just the usual." The little brown-haired woman in the red Glosser Bros. smock shrugged. "Going to Point Stadium for Glosser's fireworks with Ruth." She hiked a thumb over her shoulder toward the kitchen door. "Plus watching the Bicentennial celebrations on TV, of course."

"I just wish it was over," said Amy.

Ruby frowned. "Now why do you say that?"

Amy shrugged. "Reminds me too much of how things used to be, I guess."

Ruby reached out and patted her arm. "With your dad, you mean. And your brother."

Amy nodded. "I hate how things are now. I just hate 'em."

"But you still have your mother and little brother," said Ruby. "And your grandpa. And me and Ruth."

"I wish Paul Newman had never come here." Amy felt tears welling in her eyes. "I wish he'd just stayed in stupid Hollywood."

Ruby frowned. She was just about to ask a question when Amy's mom rushed out of the tunnel from Glosser's second floor with Boom in tow.

"There you are!" Mom looked suddenly relieved. "I *thought* this was where I'd find you."

Amy wiped the tears from her eyes and turned to face her. "Uh-huh."

"Thanks, Ruby," said Mom.

"Any time, sweetie." Ruby still looked concerned. "No trouble at all."

Mom took a good look at Amy and seemed to catch on. "You know what? Could you fix us a couple hot fudge sundaes, Rube?"

"Well, sure." Ruby smiled. "One for each of the kids?"

Mom nodded, then shook her head. "You know what? Make it three. I think we could all use a treat today."

"And what else?" asked Ruby.

"Extra sprinkles!" shouted Boom.

"Will do." Ruby winked at Amy. "And extra fudge for you."

Amy nodded. She wouldn't turn it down.

WHEN MOM, Boom, and Amy got home, her best friend Kim Evans was sitting on the front steps, waiting for them.

"Hey!" Kim lived a street away. She and Amy had been friends since second grade. "What took you so long?" She grinned and got to her feet.

Amy plodded from the car to the steps, unable to summon much enthusiasm. Even a surprise visit from her best friend felt like an annoyance today.

"We were just picking up some decorations for our big Bicentennial party." Mom hefted her white Glosser Bros. shopping bag with the brown stripes down the side. "You're coming, aren't you, Kim?"

Kim patted her tightly braided cornrows. "Well, I'd *like* to." She winced. "That's kind of why I'm here, Mrs. Lindsey."

"Oh?" Mom tipped her head to one side, looking concerned.

"See, my family is going out of town." Kim folded her skinny brown arms over her pink t-shirt. "Tomorrow. I can't make it to the party."

"That's too bad, honey," said Mom.

"Where're you going?" asked Amy.

"Actually," said Kim, "the question is, where are *we* going?" A huge, bright smile spread over her face as her dark eyes fixed on Amy.

"Huh?" Amy frowned.

Kim grabbed her hands and shook them giddily. "*We* are going to *Washington, D.C.* for the big Bicentennial *fireworks* extravaganza!"

"We are?"

Kim looked in Mom's direction. "If it's *okay,* that is."

"Who's driving?" Mom seemed a little dazed.

"My dad," said Kim. "My mom and sisters are going, too, and we're staying with my cousins who live right in the city."

"Hmm." If Mom was thrilled with the idea, she didn't show it.

Amy, on the other hand, needed no persuading. Getting out of town would be the perfect way to put some distance between her and the bad feelings stirred up by the Fourth of July in Johnstown.

"Sounds great!" Amy squeezed Kim's hands back and beamed with delight. "Mom, can I go? Please?"

"What about the fireworks?" Mom nodded in the general direction of the shed where Grandpa had stowed his smuggled cargo. "Your grandfather says it'll be the best show yet."

"I know, but this is the *Bicentennial,*" said Amy. "In the nation's *capital.*"

"*Our* fireworks will be *better,*" said Boom.

Amy let go of Kim's hands. "*Please,* Mom?" She folded her hands as if in prayer. "I don't want to *miss* this!"

Mom stared at Amy for a long moment, then sighed. "Okay." She still didn't sound thrilled. "As long as you let me know you're all right."

Amy unfolded her hands, wrapped them into fists, and shook them excitedly. "You know I will! Thanks, Mom!"

It was then that Boom stormed over and angrily jabbed a finger at both of them. "You're ruining everything! The biggest night of the year, and you're ruining it!"

With that, he whirled and ran off into the house, slamming the front door behind him.

But none of that bothered Amy in the slightest. All that mattered was being away from home on what was becoming her least favorite night of the year.

Which had been her dad's *most* favorite night until Paul Newman had come along and talked him into leaving them all behind and taking her brother Mark with him.

Amy couldn't sleep that night, which made no sense. After all, she was getting out of being home for the Lindsey Family Fireworks Spectacular. She was going to Washington, D.C., where her family's breakup was bound to be the furthest thing from her mind.

She should have been relieved and sleeping soundly—so why was she wide awake at three in the morning? And why, every time she closed her eyes, did she see that actor on the ice of the local hockey rink, taking off his uniform a piece at a time while striptease music played from the loudspeakers?

Maybe because it had been the last time that she and her parents and brothers had been together, having fun?

It felt like she was being haunted by that moment, which was a scene from a movie. She and her family had been extras that day, along with several thousand other Johnstown residents—all cheering at the top of their lungs as the actor skated and stripped in the War Memorial Arena and the movie cameras rolled. It had seemed like so much fun at the time; how could she have known it would be the last fun her family would have together?

How could she have known that months later, she'd be haunted by the movie they were making? How could she have known that she'd be haunted by *Slap Shot*?

Pushing off the covers, Amy got out of bed and padded out of her room. The house was dark and quiet, with everyone sound asleep. That in itself was unsettling, not at all the way things had been before. With Dad and Mark in the house, there had always been snoring and tossing and turning. Neither of them had been passive or quiet sleepers, which used to drive Amy crazy, always waking her up.

But now, there was just quiet. Except for the stripper music she heard when she closed her eyes.

The film crew was long gone now, and so was the cast. They'd come to make a movie about small-town hockey, based on the true story of the local Johnstown Jets, who'd won the championship in '75. For a few short months, they had turned the town into a mini-Hollywood, using local landmarks as sets and backdrops, using local people in bit parts and as extras...giving them a taste of the movie business magic. Letting them rub elbows with stars like the great Paul Newman.

Then they'd moved on in June, leaving hopes and dreams in their wake—and in some cases, wreckage.

Mom had gotten plenty of both. After the filming, her husband had left her—but during it, she'd been luckier than most.

Entering the living room, Amy saw the proof of that luck propped on an end table by the couch. A black-and-white 8 by 10 photo occupied a wooden frame, an image that captured the excitement of what had promised to be the biggest and best break of Mom's life.

In the photo, Mom and three other women were all laughing and holding up hockey sticks. They surrounded two men in hockey uniforms with "Chiefs" printed in bold letters across the chest—Michael Ontkean (who'd done the stripping) and the biggest star of the movie, one of the biggest stars in the world, whose bright eyes twinkled as he grinned self-effacingly.

There he was, the one and only Paul Newman.

Amy turned on the lamp on the table, picked up the photo, and stared. She remembered how thrilled Mom had been to get a small speaking role in the movie, playing the wife of one of the hockey players. Her community theater experience had really paid off, helping her audition well enough to get the part.

It had been a dream come true. Every day, she'd had more great stories to tell when she got home. Several times, she'd even brought Amy or Mark or Boom to the set during filming.

And when Paul had told her how well she was doing, it had made her feel like a million bucks. And when he'd written an encouraging message on the 8x10 photo, it had sent her straight into the stratosphere.

You're the real deal, Kelly. That was what he'd written in black Sharpie marker across the lower right corner. *Don't let anyone tell you otherwise.*

See you in Hollywood, Paul Newman.

Who would have thought such a wonderful message—such a wonderful experience—could lead to so much pain?

Sometimes, Amy just wanted to throw that photo in the garbage and forget about what had happened. Tonight, she settled for putting it face down on the end table, then dropping herself face down on the sofa. She just wanted to put *Slap Shot* and what had happened to her family right out of her mind.

Instead, as soon as she started to doze, the striptease music rose unbidden within her. Again, she saw Michael Ontkean skating around the rink, taking off one article of clothing after another.

Her eyes popped open. She had only been an extra in one scene, had never seen the finished film (which wouldn't premiere until the following year), and yet she couldn't get it out of her mind. It wouldn't stop haunting her.

She could only hope the Bicentennial fireworks in

Washington, D.C. might finally drive it away...at least for a while. Paul Newman had done enough damage already.

She didn't want anything to do with him or his stupid movie, no matter what he'd written on Mom's picture.

No matter what he'd told Amy herself on his last day in town.

AFTER A NIGHT of very little sleep, Amy was dead on her feet the next day. If she hadn't already promised to help Mom on the job that morning, she never would have volunteered to go along and lend a hand.

"Thanks again, honey." Mom smiled as she drove the family car—a red '74 Ford Pinto—from Roxbury into town. "I really appreciate this."

"No problem." Amy blinked hard, clearing the sleepy haze from her eyes. She couldn't believe she was up and on the road at seven a.m. after sleeping maybe three hours thanks to visions of *Slap Shot*. All she wanted to do was roll over and drift off for the rest of the day.

"Well, the bosses will be glad to see you," said Mom. "It means a lot that my daughter is helping set up Point Stadium for the big show."

"Good." Amy yawned as the Pinto rolled down Franklin Street past Conemaugh Hospital and next-door Mercy Hospital. Lots of people were already crisscrossing the street, some in blue-green surgical scrubs, some in white lab coats.

"These fireworks are the Glosser company's chance to shine, especially this year," said Mom. "Everybody's in the patriotic spirit because of the Bicentennial."

Not everybody, thought Amy. "Just so there's no hockey tribute," she mumbled.

"What was that?" asked Mom. "I didn't hear you."

"Nothing." Amy yawned again. "Just thinking out loud."

"KELLY LINDSEY! THANKS FOR COMING!" Bill Glosser stood inside the gate of the stadium in his tweed suit and wire-framed glasses, grinning around the stem of his ever-present pipe. "And thank you for bringing along this lovely young assistant!"

Amy barely managed the slightest smile. She liked Bill, he was always wry and kind, but her lack of sleep continued to drag her down.

"As you can see, we have our work cut out for us." Bill turned and spread his arms to take in the stadium. Nothing had been done to decorate it, from what Amy could see. "And yet, I am confident we can make the magic happen in time. Do you know why?"

"Teamwork?" said Mom.

Bill chuckled, puffing pipe smoke over his shoulder. "The Bicentennial spirit!" he said. "I think we can all agree that it moves mountains."

Mom smiled at Amy. She, too, got a kick out of Bill. "Absolutely, we can all agree on that."

Amy just nodded and yawned.

"Let's get to it, shall we?" Bill navigated the cement walkway from the gate to the concession stand, and they followed. "Uncle Sam is depending on us."

The concession stand counter and the pavement in front of it were piled with cartons of decorations. Three twentysomething women in shorts and t-shirts were sorting through the contents, taking stock of what they had, and smiled when they saw Bill, Kelly, and Amy approach.

"Ladies," said Bill. "I bring you reinforcements."

The women all smiled and waved at Kelly and Amy, and they waved back.

"As for the plan, it is this," Bill said between smoky puffs. "Let your love of America guide your every move, in the name of Glosser Bros. and the hope that I will not hold up your efforts to relentless ridicule."

The women laughed and kept working. Kelly walked over to join them, and Amy started to follow.

But Bill caught her arm on the way past. "Not you, slugger." He pulled her along to a huge roll of white vinyl leaning against the wall of the concession stand. "There's a critical task with your name on it right here."

Pipe clamped firmly between his teeth, Bill picked up one end of the roll, and Amy got the other. Carrying the load between them, they crossed the field—set up as a baseball diamond for the summer—and climbed the steps up into the stands on the side opposite where they'd entered the park in the first place.

"Are you excited about the big show tomorrow night?"

The higher they climbed, the more out of breath Bill sounded.

"Well..."

"What if I told you the fun quotient would be through the *roof* for *you* in particular?" Five rows from the top, Bill paused to rest. "What if I said *you* would have the honor of a *lifetime?*"

Amy cleared her throat, not sure where this was going. "I'd say I can't be here because..."

He turned and smiled, looking as amused and fatherly as ever. "You will be our button-pusher. The starter of the show. Like Lady Liberty, you will light the flames of freedom in the skies overhead."

She frowned. "But I..."

"It's a very great honor, you know," said Bill. "*Especially* on such a historic occasion. No one else will ever be able to say they pushed the button that set off the fireworks in Johnstown for the nation's Bicentennial."

This time, Amy said it loud and clear. "No." She shook her head emphatically. "Thank you for the honor, but I can't accept it. I won't be here."

"You won't?" Smoke obscured Bill's face as he puffed harder on the pipe.

"I'm going to Washington, D.C. with my best friend's family," explained Amy. "To see the Bicentennial fireworks."

"I can't argue, that's a wonderful opportunity." Bill nodded. "But so is this. Are you sure I can't talk you into staying?"

"Thank you, Mr. Glosser, but no."

"It's Bill," he told her. "And if you change your mind, the offer still stands." Smiling, he hefted his end of the roll and climbed the rest of the steps with Amy close behind.

When they got to the top of the stands, they unrolled the vinyl to reveal a giant red, white, and blue banner. Then they hung it from the rails along the back side of Point Stadium, unfurling it over the curved brick wall so drivers on the elevated Johnstown expressway could see it clearly as they passed.

Happy Bicentennial from Glosser Bros.! That was what it said, with the instantly recognizable Glosser Bros. logo in flowing script lettering and the star-shaped Bicentennial logo on either end.

"Not bad," said Bill as he and Amy leaned over the railing to admire their work. "We know how to put on a show here in Johnstown, too, don't we?"

"Uh-huh," said Amy, though she still wanted nothing more than to get out of town on the Fourth of July.

HOURS LATER, Mom and Amy wrapped up their work and left Point Stadium, heading for home. Mom wasn't done for the day; she still had to put in some hours at the store that afternoon. But Amy had worked hard at the Point, and Kim had mentioned getting together later to prep for D.C., so Mom wasn't going to drag things out.

Lunchtime traffic was heavy that day, so the ride up Main Street was slow. Workers and shoppers hurried back and forth across the street, darting into restaurants like Johnnie's or stores like the Hello Shop or McCrory's.

Central Park was crowded, too, with people strolling along the sidewalks or sitting on benches among the trees and monuments to enjoy the midday sun and warmth.

Seeing all that, Amy remembered a scene from months ago, right there on that same street along that same park. Crowds had jammed every inch of the place, cheering and clapping as a parade passed between them—a fake victory parade staged by the film crew for the movie.

Actors playing hockey team members rode in convertibles up the street, waving and grinning as the crowd cheered their fictional victory. Paul Newman himself rode with Michael Ontkean and Lindsay Crouse (who played Michael's wife), flashing thumbs-ups as they slowly rolled past in a white Lincoln Continental draped with victory banners.

The scene was so vivid in Amy's mind, it was almost as if she'd traveled back in time to be a part of it all again. It was almost as if she were standing on the curb in front of the Embassy Theater, clapping as Mom rode by in one of the cars.

Closing her eyes, she fell instantly asleep and was lost in a dream of that moment...only this time, she was in the Continental with Paul Newman and Michael Ontkean instead of Lindsay Crouse. This time, she was waving at the crowd, drinking in the excitement.

And then Paul leaned over and whispered in her ear. The words were soft but plain as day, and she knew them very well.

They were the last words he'd said to her. As much as she hated him now, she always tried not to think about them...but there they were.

"Earth to Amy! Come in, Amy!"

Startled, Amy snapped her eyes open and was out of the dream. Mom, who'd said the words that had awakened her, gave her shoulder one last shake for good measure.

"Maybe you should take a nap when you get home, honey," said Mom. "You need to rest up if you're going to D.C. tomorrow."

Amy yawned, the memory of the parade echoing in her mind as Mom turned off Main Street. "I'm fine," she said. "Trust me, there's *no way* I'll sleep through those fireworks."

"KNOCK KNOCK. ANYONE HOME?"

An hour and a half later, Amy was awakened by another voice—that of her best friend. Blinking her eyes open, she saw Kim's face through the darkened lenses of her sunglasses, smiling down at her.

It was then she quickly remembered where she was and how she'd gotten there.

"You just missed the handsomest boy," said Kim. "I nudged you, but I couldn't get you to wake up."

Propping herself up on her elbows, Amy looked around. From her perch on a chaise lounge in the sun, she scanned the deck of the bright blue swimming pool, taking in the swimmers and sunbathers crowding the cement and water alike.

"Don't worry." Kim chuckled. "There are always plenty of good-looking guys at Bethco Pines."

"I can't argue with that," said Amy.

This, then, was their idea of packing and getting ready for the trip to D.C. Kim, who was old enough to drive, had borrowed her mom's car, picked up Amy, and driven to Bethco Pines in Somerset County.

It was their favorite place to hang out in the summer—a private club on the shore of the Quemahoning Reservoir, a half-hour drive from home. As the daughter of a boss at Bethlehem Steel in Johnstown, Kim was a member, and she borrowed her sister's pass to get Amy in without having to buy a guest pass.

What better way to spend a hot summer afternoon instead of staying home and packing suitcases indoors?

"You know we're going to see loads of cute guys in D.C., right?" Kim raised a half-empty bottle of Coke and had a sip.

"I thought we were going for the fireworks," said Amy.

"Oh, we'll see stars if they're cute enough." Kim laughed. "I can't *wait* to get there."

"Me, too."

Just then, the lifeguard blew his whistle and announced an adult swim. All the kids clambered out of the pool, whining every step of the way.

"This trip is going to be the best," said Kim. "I'm telling you, my cousins are *fun*."

"Thanks for rescuing me," said Amy. "Being stuck at

home with my dad gone is like the saddest possible way to spend the Fourth of July."

"That's me." Kim smiled. "Coming to the rescue is what I do."

Amy watched as the adult swim ran its course—a flock of mostly middle-aged women sedately paddling back and forth in the crystal blue waters. Meanwhile, the exiled kids lined the edge of the pool, staring furtively as they waited for the whistle to blow again, giving them the signal to dive-bomb back into the water as obnoxiously as possible.

"How's your dad doing, anyway?" asked Kim. "And your brother?"

"Beats me. I haven't talked to either of them since they left."

"By choice?"

Amy shrugged. "Maybe they don't have telephones where they went. Who knows?"

Kim sipped more Coke and put the bottle back down on the cement. "How long has it been, now? A month?"

"A little less, but it seems like a lot longer." Amy sighed. "I just wish things could go back to the way they were."

Kim swung her legs off the chaise and turned to face her. "What if he asked you to go live with him? Your dad, I mean. Would you go?"

Amy shook her head. "Not a chance, after what he did."

"What about Mark?"

"He just went along to watch out for Dad," said Amy. "It wasn't his idea."

"But you won't forgive your dad."

"Right," said Amy. "That'll never change."

"But what if it does? Maybe things won't seem so bad after a while."

"What if it was *your* dad?" asked Amy. "What if he just up and left one day? Could you forgive him?"

Kim frowned, thinking it over. She opened her mouth to answer—but before she got the words out, the lifeguard blew the whistle.

All at once, every kid in the pool area hurled themselves into the water, raising an unholy splash that drenched the adults before they could escape.

Amy and Kim both watched, smirking, and shook their heads. Not long ago, they had been among that wild number, causing mischief with the glorious waters of Quemahoning Reservoir rippling in the background. Now, at ages 15 and 16, it all looked different. Their concerns and obsessions had changed.

Though, sometimes, Amy secretly wished they had never changed at all.

"Damn kids," she said as a joke.

"Seriously," said Kim. "Somebody oughtta go dunk their asses."

"Sounds like a plan." Amy settled back on the chaise and closed her eyes. "Just as soon as I map out our moves on the backs of my eyelids."

"No, wait." Kim shook her by the shoulder. "You have *got* to see the new lifeguard!"

Amy opened her eyes, again denied the rest she craved, and she didn't get another wink of sleep the whole time they were there at Bethco.

THAT NIGHT, finally, Amy was able to sleep soundly. She went to bed early, not long after dinner, and fell instantly into the deepest of slumbers.

No dreams of *Slap Shot* disturbed her—no striptease music or visions of riding with Paul Newman in a Lincoln Continental in a victory parade. For once, her worried mind went blank, allowing her to completely relax and get the rest she needed for her busy day tomorrow in D.C.

But it didn't last.

Deep in the night, the peace and quiet was suddenly torn asunder by a thundering *boom*. It was so loud, it sounded like it was coming from right outside her window.

Instantly, Amy sprang awake and shot out of bed, half falling onto the floor. She pulled herself up and shook her head hard, trying to clear away the cobwebs clogging her mind.

Before she could get to her bedroom window to see what was happening, another boom rang out, followed by a series of short, chattering bursts. She dropped back onto her bed, stunned by the sudden cacophony, unable to think straight long enough to figure out what had caused it.

Then, without warning, something crashed through her window and flew across the room, shedding sparks along the way.

As Amy cried out, the object crashed into the wall and

exploded. Fiery pieces of debris showered her dresser and carpet, even landing on her bed.

Bottle rocket. That, she realized, was what had smashed through her window. And all the noise that had preceded it could only have come from one source—a source she knew was plentiful in the Lindsey family's back yard shed.

Fireworks.

Again, there were percussive booms and chattering cracks...then shrieking whistles and whooshing hisses one after another. Colorful lights flared through the broken window, playing on the walls, rug, and furniture, spraying over the spots of flame that were igniting all over the room from the bottle rocket.

The loudest blast yet went off next, shaking the floor under her feet. Another fiery missile flashed in through the window and blew against the wall, spreading more flames.

Eyes wide with fear, Amy leaped off the bed and ran out of her room while she still could. As she hurled open her door, she saw Mom running toward her, barefoot and wrapped in a red flannel bathrobe.

"Let's go!" Mom grabbed her hand and pulled her into the hall. "Come on, hurry!"

As they raced past open doorways, colored lights blazed across their path from within, cast from windows facing the back yard. The cascade of blasts continued, rattling glass and wood alike, roaring again and again in a terrible, deafening symphony.

Amy looked in every doorway they passed but saw no sign of her brother. "Where's Boom?" she shouted.

"I don't know!" yelled Mom. "He must be outside somewhere!"

As they sprinted toward the kitchen, something big smashed through a window and plowed through the hallway ahead of them. Mom flung herself back from the ball of flame, taking Amy down with her.

They heard the fireball collide with the living room wall and explode. Red and blue sparks showered in its wake, pulsing into the hall and kitchen like a fountain of hot, bright shrapnel.

"This way." Mom leaped to her feet and dragged Amy up with her. Without hesitation, she charged the rest of the way through the hall and hurtled across the kitchen.

Something whistled past behind them, but they made it through without being hit. Mom swung open the back door and barreled out onto the porch with Amy close behind.

They paused then and took in the scene...just long enough to see fireworks launching everywhere from the direction of the old wooden shed. The light show kept blasting away, seemingly inexhaustible, illuminating the yard in rainbow colors bright enough to be the middle of the day.

Bright enough, too, to see the lone human figure curled up in a fetal position on the ground—the figure of a red-headed child.

Without a word, Mom sprinted down the three steps from the porch and bolted across the yard. As fireworks shot randomly around her, she scooped up Boom and ran, heading for the corner of the house.

Amy fell in behind her, racing full-tilt through the fireworks barrage.

As they rounded the front of the house, finally out of the line of fire, sirens wailed in the distance, getting closer. Through the trees, Amy could see fire truck lights flashing in the sky, fast approaching.

Then, looking back, she saw flames leaping from the windows of the house, lashing angrily out of the empty sockets.

Still, the night echoed with booms and shrieks, pounding relentlessly from the backyard war zone.

ACCORDING TO THE PARAMEDICS, Boom was fine—just upset, as he should be. After all, the disaster was his fault.

Unable to wait another night to try the fireworks, he'd sneaked out to the shed when Mom and Amy were asleep, taking the key with him. He'd meant to set off a single bottle rocket, but he'd burned himself while lighting it and dropped the match in the shed. Another firework had blown instead and set off a chain reaction in the pile.

The rest was history.

"I'm sorry! I'm so sorry!" He bawled like a baby as the paramedics treated the burn on his hand. "I ruined everything!"

Mom didn't comfort him. She was too busy talking to police about all the illegal fireworks she'd been storing in her shed.

As for Amy, she stood and stared at the smoldering house, still stunned at what had happened. A firefighter had wrapped her in a blanket, and she held it tight around her, feeling like she was stuck in a bad dream.

"Oh my God." Grandpa walked up beside her, looking sadder than she'd ever seen him. "This is all my fault. My fault."

Amy said nothing. The fireworks had stopped long ago, but her ears still rang from the cacophony they'd caused.

"I just wanted this Fourth of July to be perfect for you kids," said Grandpa. "I wanted it to be perfect after what happened...but I just made things worse."

Firefighters stomped out of the house, pulling off their face masks. The fire was out, though it still wasn't clear to Amy how much damage had been done.

When Mom finally broke away from the cops and came over, Amy had a bad feeling about what she was going to say. Dread filled her like a cloud of smoke.

"So much for the fireworks spectacular," said Mom. "And so much for the house. I don't even know if the insurance will cover it."

"Oh God," said Grandpa.

"We'll be lucky if we don't get charged for stockpiling illegal fireworks," said Mom.

"I'll talk to the police," said Grandpa. "I'll tell them it was my fault, and..."

Mom chopped her hand through the air. "*No*. Please don't make this any *worse,* Dad."

"So what do we do?" asked Amy. "What's next?"

"As soon as they'll let me, I'm going to get in the house and see what I can salvage," said Mom. "You both can help with that, anyway."

"I don't think I can," said Amy. "I'm so tired, I can hardly stand up."

Just then, Kim approached from the street. "You can sleep at my house, if you'd like."

Amy looked expectantly at Mom. "Can I? Just for a few hours?"

"She'll need the rest before we go to Washington," said Kim.

Mom shook her head. "I'm sorry, but Washington's off the table."

Amy's feeling of dread blossomed into awful reality. "What?"

"After what just happened?" Mom was adamant. "We don't even know where we're going to *live*."

"You can stay with me," said Grandpa.

"Your house is tiny," said Mom.

"I'll do what it takes," said Grandpa. "We'll make it work."

"That's *not* our only problem." Mom folded her arms over her chest. "It might not even be our *biggest* problem."

"Please let me go to D.C.," said Amy. "*Please.*"

"No," Mom said firmly. "I need all of us here until I get this figured out."

"But it's just one day!" said Amy.

"Our *lives* have just been blown to *smithereens*," snapped Mom. "I need you *here*. End of story."

With that, she turned and marched off to the ambulance, where the paramedics had finished treating Boom.

"This is bad," said Kim. "This is really, really bad."

Amy just stood there and glared. Across the yard, she saw a female paramedic give Boom a lollipop as he hopped off the bumper of the ambulance, and her blood ran cold.

"It'll be okay, honey," said Grandpa. "Everything happens for a reason."

Amy didn't answer. She wasn't in the mood for platitudes, to say the least.

"I could ask my mom to talk to her," offered Kim. "Maybe she could convince her to let you go."

Amy thought for a moment, then shook her head. "Thanks anyway. That might just make things worse."

Kim reached out and touched her arm. "I'm so sorry, Amy. I wish none of this had happened. I really do."

"Thanks. Me, too." When she said it, Amy was thinking not just of that night, but of everything leading up to it. She was thinking of Paul Newman coming to town and Dad and Mark leaving and all the sadness and confusion in between.

Once again, she remembered Michael Ontkean skating at the War Memorial. The striptease music played in her mind: *Da da da...da DA da da...da da da...da DA da da...*

And it was then that the tears finally started rolling down her cheeks, glistening in the flashing red lights of the fire trucks and police cars.

"HERE YA GO, SWEETHEART." The burly, bald cook in the white t-shirt and smock stained with chili sauce banged a plate full of hot dogs on the counter in front of Amy. "Two with everything."

"Thanks." Amy slid the plate to the end of the counter, where Mom was paying for the food.

"Enjoy your picnic." The cook smirked and let out a little burp. "Happy Bicentennial."

So that was what it had come to. Instead of spending the Fourth of July in D.C. for the show of the century, she was stuck in Johnstown with Mom and Boom.

Whoop-de-doo.

"Here." Mom handed her a clear plastic cup full of water, then got an empty cup from the stack on the counter and filled it from a tap that was mounted there. It was a tradition at the Coney Island Lunch restaurant—a free glass of water with each purchase.

When she'd finished filling the cup, Mom headed for one of the orange tables along the wall, where Boom was already sitting. She put her tray on the table and lowered herself onto the bright green bench beside her son.

Amy sat across from them, staring at the hot dogs on her bright green plate. As much as she loved Coney Island's food, she wished she were anywhere but there at that moment—as far away as possible.

But that just wasn't in the cards for her.

"Eat up, guys." Mom handed Boom a hot dog—plain, on a bun, which was practically sacrilege in that place—and picked up one of her own. "I know it's not our usual cookout food, but it'll have to do."

There were so many things Amy wanted to say to her, to both of them, none of them good...but she held back the words. Instead, she grabbed one of the hot dogs on her plate and took a bite.

As usual, it was delicious—not that she was going to admit it. The mix of hot dog, chili, onions, mustard, and salt and pepper on a perfectly toasted bun was heavenly. It was the one bright spot in an otherwise lousy day.

It brought back good memories of Dad, too. He'd always loved Coney Island hot dogs, especially when he'd been drinking. He'd often brought her there for a late-night treat after he'd returned from making the rounds of his favorite bars. She'd loved spending time with him, even with his voice a little too loud and the alcohol strong on his breath.

"At least we salvaged some things at the house," Mom said between bites. "Some clothes and belongings. It wasn't a *total* loss."

Amy didn't answer. For one thing, she was in the worst mood ever over missing D.C. For another, she was utterly exhausted after spending the whole day digging for possessions in the rubble from the fire.

It was evening now, just after seven, and she was ready to collapse. Falling into a deep sleep and waking up the next morning seemed like the perfect way to put this god-awful day behind her.

There was just one small problem with that plan. She still didn't know where she was going to sleep that night.

"So where are we staying?" she asked.

"Grandpa's," said Mom. "But just for tonight."

"What about after that?" Boom actually sounded meek for a change. He hadn't been himself since he'd burned down the house.

"Well, I didn't want to say anything until it was definite," said Mom, "but I think we're going to stay with my friend Bonnie for a while."

Amy's shoulders slumped. Bonnie was nice, but her kids were rotten, and she lived in a neighborhood on the far side of Johnstown from Roxbury. It was nowhere near Kim, Roxbury Park, or anything else that Amy enjoyed.

"I have to call her tomorrow to find out for sure," said Mom. "But I can't imagine she'll say no."

Amy's next bite of the hot dog didn't taste as good as the last. The thought of moving in with Bonnie and her nasty kids made her heart sink...though she intended to keep it to herself, given the circumstances.

But Boom, for once, said exactly what she was thinking.

"I don't wanna stay with Bonnie."

Mom frowned. "But you always have fun when we visit her."

"No." Boom shook his head forcefully. "I don't wanna do it."

"It'll be fine." Mom looked at Amy for support. "Won't it, honey?"

But Amy didn't back her up. She just finished her first hot dog and washed it down with lukewarm water.

"I wish you never got that part in the movie," said Boom. "I wish Paul Newman never told Dad to leave."

"Well, he didn't," said Mom. "Dad just took what he said

the wrong way."

"I was there!" snapped Boom. "I heard it! So did she!"

He pointed a finger at Amy.

And he was right. She thought back to that moment, just after the big parade, when she and Boom had run over to see Mom with Dad close behind. Mom had been standing by the white Lincoln Continental, chatting with Paul Newman in his hockey uniform.

And Dad, who'd been drunk, had pushed between them, face to face with Paul himself.

Dad had told Paul to leave his wife alone or he'd let him have it. Paul had told him to back off, there was nothing going on and never had been.

Then Dad had said that was the only reason she'd gotten a part in the movie, because she'd been running around with Paul behind Dad's back.

Again, Paul had denied the accusations. After that, Dad had taken a swing, but Paul had ducked and thrown him against the hood of the car. He'd gotten Dad in a hold, keeping his arm locked tight against his back.

Then he'd said it, loud enough for all of us to hear. He'd said the words that had broken up our family—even though he hadn't meant for that to happen.

"Do yourself a favor, buddy," he'd said. "Focus in on this great family you've got here and give the booze a rest."

Which, it turned out, had been the absolute wrong thing to say to Dad.

"Tell *me* to focus in?" he'd howled as a cop had dragged him away. "How about if I *focus in* on living my own *life* for a change!"

And he'd never looked back.

And Amy had never stopped looking back to that moment.

"Remember, Amy?" said Boom. "You remember what he told Dad, don't you?"

Amy pushed away her second hot dog. She wasn't hungry anymore.

"Yeah," she said. "And Mom's right."

Boom pounded the table with his fist. "No! That's not what you're supposed to—"

"Dad *did* take it the wrong way," said Amy, and then she got up and went to the counter for another cup of water.

"Hey, kid," said the burly counterman as she reached for a fresh cup. "What's a Fourth of July picnic without this?" He pulled out a cigarette lighter, flipped it open, and flicked the switch, raising a flame from the nozzle.

Then he laughed. "Just for you, kid! Enjoy the fireworks!"

BLAM!

Amy jumped as two bratty little boys set off a firecracker on the sidewalk outside Point Stadium. Though she was going to see the fireworks display at the Point—coerced by Mom, who wanted to show the flag for her bosses at Glosser Bros.—she was still a little rattled from her explosive experience of the night before.

She hesitated on the threshold, nearly turning and

walking away...but Mom looked back and bobbed her head, summoning her inside. Though attending the Fourth of July production in downtown Johnstown was about the last thing Amy wanted to do, she rolled her eyes and followed.

She just had to get through this night, then deal with the rest of what was coming. It was just the way things were, given the circumstances.

"Well hello there!" Bill Glosser strode toward them, wearing a stars-and-stripes tie and a navy-blue pinstriped suit and carrying a thin sheaf of papers. As usual, plumes of smoke rolled out of his pipe, the stem clenched between his teeth as if attached there. "Good to see the Lindsey family won't let such a trivial thing as a house fire keep them from attending this soiree."

"Hello, Bill." Mom looked around at the stands, which were packed with people. "Looks like you've got a decent crowd tonight."

"Don't tell me that," said Bill. "You'll get me nervous before my big speech."

He chuckled, and so did Mom. Amy didn't react, though, and Boom just looked like he wanted to run wild —though Mom kept his hand clamped in her own.

Just then, the organist started playing "God Bless America," and the audience applauded.

"That's my cue." Bill straightened his tie, adjusted his pipe, and turned, starting toward the podium set up on the pitcher's mound. But then he paused and looked back at Amy. "Sorry you missed out on that big honor I told you about the other day, sweetheart. When you said you weren't going to be here, we found someone else to kick things off."

"That's all right." Amy wasn't in the mood anyway. "I understand."

"Maybe for the Tricentennial, yeah?" Bill flapped the sheaf of papers, then resumed his course toward the podium.

"Let's go grab a seat," said Mom.

They ended up sitting in the front row, in a special section reserved for Glosser's employees. They were right by the concession stand, which of course caught Boom's attention as soon as his butt hit the bleacher.

As for Amy, the clock was already ticking in her head. Mom had promised they wouldn't stay long, and she was going to hold her to it.

At least that was the plan. But as Bill made his opening remarks, and local singers led the crowd in one patriotic song after another, Mom gave no sign of leaving.

Even when they trotted out the Cambria County Junior Miss finalists in all their teenage glory, Mom stayed in place. She didn't evacuate during the endless introduction of the Bicentennial committee members or the speech by Mayor Herb Pfuhl, either.

The sky darkened, and the stadium lights flashed to life. Amy's impatience grew to the point where she actually jabbed Mom with an elbow—but Mom paid no attention. Were they *ever* going to get out of there?

Finally, Bill returned to the podium, and Mom jumped to her feet, clapping and cheering. So did the rest of the reserved section, and most of the crowd followed suit.

Bill's voice boomed from the P.A. system. "And now, ladies and gentlemen, the moment you've all been waiting for! The Bicentennial Fourth of July fireworks, sponsored by the Glosser Bros. and Gee Bee department stores!"

Everyone in the stadium applauded and cheered. This *was* what they'd all been waiting for.

"To start this spectacular event, we have a very special guest," said Bill. "She may have lost her home in a fire last night, but she's here tonight to launch the greatest fireworks display in Johnstown history!"

Amy's eyes widened. Had she heard him correctly?

The answer was yes, she had.

"Amy Lindsey, come on out here!" said Bill.

Amy was completely surprised. Everyone clapped and shouted her name...except Boom, who just slumped and gaped in dejected disbelief.

"Go ahead, honey." Mom grinned and pointed at the podium. "You heard the man."

Amy rose and started across the field—then stopped and turned. "Come on!" She gestured for Boom to join her.

And he didn't need convincing. Leaping to his feet, he charged out after her, grinning like a maniac.

"Stay with me." She gripped his arm tight. "Don't do *anything* till I tell you to."

"Okay okay okay!" Boom nodded excitedly.

And she led him to the podium where Bill was waiting.

"Good for you!" Bill said between puffs of pipe smoke. "You brought your little brother."

Amy and Boom just smiled.

"Right this way, then."

As Bill invited them to join him, Amy saw a wooden box with a big red button atop the podium. A thick bundle of wires ran out of it, snaking all the way across the field.

"All right, you two." Bill pulled his pipe out and gestured with the stem at the big red button. "We're all going to count down from ten. When we get to zero, hit that button. Got it?"

"Got it!" said Boom.

Amy just nodded.

"Here we go!" Bill waved his pipe in the air, and the stadium lights went out. Then he leaned over the podium and spoke into the mic again. "Count with me, folks!"

The crowd applauded.

"Ten!" said Bill. "Nine! Eight!"

Boom's hand shook as it hovered over the button. Amy held her hand just above, ready to grab him if he jumped the gun.

But he didn't. Not this time.

"Seven!" said Bill. "Six!"

The organist hit a dramatic chord each time Bill announced a number. The voices of everyone in the stadium joined together in a chorus of anticipation.

"Five!" said Bill. "Four! Three!"

The cords in Boom's hand flexed, and Amy thought he might hit the button early...but he didn't.

Her heart raced as the countdown neared its end.

"Two!" shouted Bill. "One!"

Amy and Boom's hands came down on the button at the same time.

For a moment, nothing happened...just long enough for Amy to wonder if something had gone wrong.

Then, she heard a loud hiss from behind her, in the direction of the Stonycreek River. She spun in time to see a smoky trail rise into the air.

And then it exploded in a burst of brilliant red.

Another one followed, hissing up and bursting into a sphere of cobalt blue...and another soared up after that and became a flare of bright white.

From that point on, the fireworks kept coming—shell after shell blazing to life above the stadium as a recording of "The Stars and Stripes Forever" blared over the P.A. Fireballs of every color blossomed in the night, casting the upturned faces of the spectators in mingled shades of green and gold and pink and red and blue.

When the biggest, most exciting blasts unfolded overhead, the crowd let out the usual oohs and aahs. Little kids jumped to their feet and shrieked with delight, pointing and describing the dazzling lights.

Meanwhile, Boom and Amy watched it all hand in hand from the field. He beamed and laughed and jounced as if nothing bad had happened in the past 24 hours—as if their family's future was not uncertain in the extreme.

Amy forgot it all, too, and just lost herself in the show. Smiling, she gazed at the flares and flashes, listened to the booms and whistles without flinching. Not once did she think of Dad or *Slap Shot* or the burned-out house or going to live at Bonnie's.

She just melted into the play of lights and sound, enjoying the show though it surely didn't measure up to the extravaganza in D.C. Though it didn't come close to any of the shows she'd seen with Dad at her side, back when her family was still whole.

All that mattered for a while were the *whumps* and the *wheees,* the whites and the yellows and reds, the warm breeze and the heat of her little brother's hand clasped in hers.

WHEN THE FIREWORKS ENDED, and the stadium lights came up, Bill Glosser grinned at Amy and Boom. "So what do you two think? Did we put on a good show for our nation's 200th birthday?"

Amy and Boom both nodded.

"I agree." Bill puffed on his pipe. "The founding fathers would have been proud."

"It was *great!"* said Boom.

"Well, you two certainly did your part." Bill looked past them, then, and raised his voice. "Wouldn't you fellas agree?"

Amy turned and saw three men approach, all of them Glosser VIPs.

"One hundred percent." A balding, cheerful cousin of Bill's, Fred Glosser was in charge of construction for the Gee Bee stores. "We couldn't have done it without them."

Fred's brother, Izzy, was a tall, athletic guy who also worked in the Gee Bee division. "You started that show like a couple of pros."

"I know talent when I see it," said bearded, dark-haired Paul, who ran the grocery division. "We'll have to keep them in mind, the next time we need a button pushed."

The four Glossers all laughed and patted Amy and Boom on the shoulders.

"Thanks again," said Bill, saluting with his smoldering pipe before turning away to chat with his family.

Amy realized it was time to go. "Come on, Boom. Let's go find Mom."

The rest of the crowd had the same idea, and they got separated in the rush for the gate. Amy got spun around once, then twice, and ended up falling when the kids who'd set off a firecracker earlier crashed past her.

Luckily, someone caught her from behind...and a pair of friendly faces leaned in to smile in front of her.

"Amy!" One was Ruby Shaffer from the soda fountain. She wore a red, white, and blue sweatshirt and a foam tiara like the Statue of Liberty's. "Just the girl we were looking for!"

"That's right." The other face, nearly identical, belonged to Ruby's twin sister, Ruth. She wore exactly the same outfit as Ruby. "We've been waiting for you since the show ended."

Amy was glad to see them but still unsteady on her feet and flustered. "Hi, guys."

"There's someone we want you to see," said Ruby.

"Someone *important*," said Ruth. "Are you ready to see him?"

"Well, I..." Amy frowned.

Ruby leaned closer and whispered in her ear. "He's

right behind you."

Puzzled, Amy looked back...and nearly fell again.

Her heart pounded, and she let out a cry of surprise and delight. Quickly regaining her footing, she whirled and threw her arms around the person who'd caught her —one of the last people she had expected to see on that night.

"I can't believe it!" Tears gushed from her eyes. "I can't believe you're here!"

"Of course I'm here," said her big brother, Mark, whom she hadn't seen in weeks. "You didn't think I'd miss out on the Point Stadium fireworks, did you?"

Ruth and Ruby waved and moved on with the crowd, but Amy was oblivious. Mark had her undivided attention.

"When did you...how did you...?" She didn't want to let go of him.

"I got in tonight, right before the fireworks," said Mark. "After what happened at the house, I had a feeling you'd be here."

"You know about the fire?"

"Boom called me," said Mark. "It sounded like you guys could use a hand."

"You drove all the way today?" asked Amy. "All the way from..." She stopped, because she didn't know where he and Dad had been living. They never called.

"All the way from Arlington." Mark nodded, stepped back, and pulled something from the front pocket of his jeans. "And I picked up a little something for you on my way out of D.C. today."

He laid a silver coin in her palm, a commemorative coin with the Bicentennial logo on one side and the American flag on the other. It gleamed in the glow of the stadium lights, flashing as she moved it around.

"Oh, Mark." Amy thought she might break down and cry on the spot. Had Boom told him she couldn't go to see the fireworks in D.C. as she'd planned? Was that why he'd brought her a souvenir?

In the end, it didn't matter. All she cared about was that he was there—though his presence put a question in her mind, a question she had to ask.

"Is Dad here, too? Did he come with you?"

Mark shook his head. "I don't even know where he is, to tell you the truth. He talked about going to Hollywood to find Paul Newman, but who knows? He took off a couple weeks ago."

Amy slumped. As much as she hated her father for what he'd done, a part of her had still hoped he'd come back with Mark.

But maybe the one surprise guest would be enough.

"So anyway," said Mark. "What would you say if I stuck around a while and helped get the house fixed up?"

Amy just stared at him, stunned.

"I've been working, so I've got some money," Mark continued. "And I could get some buddies of mine to lend a hand."

Still, Amy was speechless.

"Do you think Mom would go along with that?" asked Mark. "We could camp out and rebuild, get the place livable again. Then none of you would have to go stay at Bonnie's."

"Oh, Mark." Tears flowed from Amy's eyes.

"I mean, unless you *want* to live with those bratty kids of hers," said Mark, "way out there in Tanneryville."

Amy shook her head. "She'll go along with it," she said. "She *has* to."

"Well, good." Mark smiled and reeled her in for a hug. "We'll stick together and make this work."

It was then that Amy remembered what Paul Newman had said to her, the one thing he'd told her and her alone. She'd been so angry with him for so long, she'd kept herself from thinking about it—but now it came back to her.

She'd gone to Johnnie's Restaurant on Main Street for breakfast with Mom, Mark, and Boom, and Paul had been eating at the bar, about to leave town. Mom had thanked him for everything and said goodbye, and Paul had hugged her...and then, as she and Boom had headed for a table, Paul had caught Amy in a handshake and said one last thing.

"Take care of what you've got there, kid," he'd told her, nodding in the direction of Mom, Mark, and Boom. "They'll do the same for you."

The words echoed in her head as Mark held her tight, his embrace a promise that things would get better.

"Don't worry," he said. "I'll get you through this, I swear."

"Thanks," said Amy, smiling through her tears. "I swear I'll get *you* through this, too."

GLOSSER BROS
GLOSSER

OLD-FASHIONED BARGAIN DAYS AT GLOSSER'S

As Debbie Kaminski walked out of the dressing room for female employees of the Glosser Bros. Department Store, she adjusted her cowgirl costume—straightening her buckskin fringe jacket and tightening the braided leather drawstring on her broad-brimmed hat. The gunbelt kept sliding as the weight of the toy revolver in the holster bumped her hip, and she tightened that, too.

"Not bad!" Linda Yellovich looked over and grinned. In her own costume, a long suede dress and moccasins, she resembled a Native American princess right out of a movie or TV show. "Just one thing missing."

Linda—who, like Debbie, was 17 years old—hurried over to the pile of costumes and accessories on a nearby counter and pawed through them…then rushed back with a red-and-white polka-dot bandana in her hand. Reaching over, she arranged the bandana around Debbie's neck under her bright red hair and tied it at the side in a big knot, then pulled Debbie over in front of the mirror for a look.

"Am I right?" Linda tweaked the bandana, then patted Debbie's shoulder.

Debbie smiled and nodded. She had to admit, the bandana helped. The outfit looked slightly better—as good as it could, at least, on someone who would much rather be dressed as a princess...and *would* have been, if things had worked out differently.

But now that she was here like this, she would just have to get through it. As part of the Old-Fashioned Bargain Days sale, almost everyone working at the store that day would be dressed in the style of the Old West. To blend in, Debbie had to look as if she'd stepped out of 1880 instead of the present day of 1980.

The good news was, it wouldn't last long...and the reward would make it all worthwhile in the end. She just had to stay in character, get through her shift, and remember one all-important thing.

"Looking good!" Checking herself in the big three-panel mirror, Linda smoothed her braided ponytails, adjusted her beaded headband and the feathers in her hair, and spun around once. "Now let's go rope us some varmints, Beth girl!"

That was the all-important thing to remember. Debbie Kaminski wasn't Debbie Kaminski anymore. She was Beth Popchak.

At least until Old-Fashioned Bargain Days at Glosser Bros. were over.

"Good morning!" Leonard Black, president of Glosser Bros. Inc., held the door open for Debbie and Linda as they hauled cartons of ladies' accessories out of the store. Unlike most Glosser's employees, he wasn't wearing Old West attire...just his usual pinstriped business suit. "It's such a beautiful, sunny day, isn't it?"

"It sure it!" Linda grinned as she strolled past him. "Perfect weather for a sidewalk sale, Mr. Black!"

Debbie smiled, too, but she was nervous. To be the president of Glosser Bros., Mr. Black had to have a lot on the ball. What if he was sharp enough to realize that she was a fake employee?

"Thank you," Debbie said softly, averting her eyes as she passed...hoping nothing would give away her true identity.

"Just get out there and make it fun for the customers," said Mr. Black. "Make them feel at home even though they're outside the store."

"Yes sir, we will." Just as Debbie said it, he caught her by the shoulder, stopping her in the vestibule. She held her breath, wondering if he'd seen through her disguise.

The way she looked *should* have been enough to fool him...but maybe he'd noticed something she hadn't considered, something that had tipped him off.

"Hold on, Miss," said Mr. Black.

Debbie's heart hammered in her chest. If he realized

who she really was, her plan was dead in the water, and she was in big trouble.

"You shouldn't be doing this," said Mr. Black.

Debbie's hands shook, and she wondered if she ought to drop the box and run. There wasn't any reason for him to think she wasn't the real Beth Popchak, but it seemed he'd caught on to her game just the same.

Before she could take drastic action, however, she realized he was just reaching for her box.

"You shouldn't be carrying this heavy box by yourself," said Mr. Black as he turned and marched outside with the box in his arms. "Allow me to give you a hand."

Intensely relieved, Debbie followed him out into the bright June sunlight, hoping there would be no more close calls.

As Debbie stepped around the corner of the Glosser Building, she saw that folding card tables had been set up along the side of the store, one after another. Employees dressed in Old West costumes arranged merchandise and signage on each table, getting ready for the business day to begin—though some customers clearly thought it had started already and were grabbing items as soon as they hit the tables.

It was a sign of the action to come, and Debbie knew it. Though she was only masquerading as a Glosser Bros. employee, she'd lived in Johnstown her whole life and knew what a big deal Old-Fashioned Bargain Days were. While the sale was underway, shoppers flooded the downtown business district, hunting for deals and enjoying the carnival atmosphere.

Employees of the downtown merchants got into the spirit of things by dressing up in historical costumes and competing for prizes. This year, the Glosser Bros. team came as figures out of the Old West...and their biggest competition, the Penn Traffic Department Store team, had chosen knights, damsels, and other figures from medieval times.

Debbie knew all about Penn Traffic's plans, and with good reason. Until very recently, she'd had every reason to think she'd be dressing in medieval attire, as well.

"Where should I put this?" Mr. Black turned with the heavy box in his arms, eyeing nearby tables.

Debbie saw a clear spot on the corner of a table full of handbags and pointed at it. "Right here, thanks."

"Happy to help." Mr. Black grinned as he put down the box, then straightened his suit jacket. "Now the hard work is up to you. Keep those sales rolling today, pardner." Raising a thumb and extending a forefinger like the barrel of a gun, he pretended to fire a shot in the air. "Giddyap li'l dogies."

With that, he turned and ambled back into the building, greeting other employees and customers along the way.

"Must be nice, having the president of Glosser Bros. carry your stuff out for you." Linda bumped in next to her and reached into the box Mr. Black had delivered, pulling out ladies' scarves. "I guess your career is on the upswing, Beth."

"What can I say?" Debbie shrugged. "Looks like my ship has finally come in."

Secretly, though, she felt the opposite. She had no desire to work at Glosser's, a place she'd never liked much. According to her mom, Penn Traffic was the better store with better quality merchandise and overall service. Mom said Glosser's was more of a discount store with lower prices and inferior quality—a blue-collar place to shop, as opposed to white-collar Penn Traffic. *You get what you pay for,* Mom always said.

That wasn't to say Debbie and her family were wealthy snobs...but they weren't exactly poor, either. They lived in a nice house in Westmont, the well-to-do suburb on top of the hill above downtown. Debbie's dad was a boss at U.S. Steel, and he made enough money for the family to live comfortably, if not extravagantly. In spite of all that, Mom and Dad had always taught Debbie the value of hard work, which was why she'd gotten a job as a teenager in the first place.

But that job was at Penn Traffic, not Glosser Bros. She was only "working" at Glosser's today for one reason, in fact.

"Hey, Beth! Hey, Linda!"

And there he was now.

"How are you two doing?"

The sound of his voice alone was enough to make Debbie's heart jump. It had done the same since the first time she'd heard it on a visit to George's Song Shop.

Looking at him again was as wonderful as the first time, too. Tall, lean, and athletically muscular, he had a head of wavy, golden hair and a broad smile. His bright blue eyes glittered like the water at her favorite beach in Florida, so dazzling they positively blazed.

He looked even better in costume, like a natural-born cowboy. His brown hat was cocked slightly back, his matching brown vest parted over a black shirt open to the third button. His thumbs were hooked in his double-holstered gun belt as if he'd worn it all his life, and his faded jeans fit him like a glove. His brown boots, complete with spurs, looked worn and dusty, as if he'd been wearing them through many long cattle drives across the prairie.

It was like coming face to face with an angel, she thought...someone supernatural, giving off an irresistible magnetic force. Yet she'd only been in his presence once so far, and then only with other people around, in a situation where she hadn't managed to connect.

It was a condition she hoped to correct today. It was the whole reason she was pretending to work for Glosser Bros. at the Old-Fashioned Bargain Days Sale.

"We're doing great, Matt." Linda twirled a pale red scarf in the air. "Having so much fun, it shouldn't be legal."

Matt chuckled. "Good to hear, good to hear." He pulled one of the toy six-shooter revolvers from its holster and spun it around his index finger with practiced ease. "Y'all seen any of them there *Penn Traffic* desperadoes lurkin' around?"

"We haven't seen a single one of them," Debbie said without a trace of irony.

"Maybe they're afraid to show their faces." Matt smirked as he gave the gun another twirl, shifting into an accent straight out of a Western movie. "Reckon they know how bad we're gonna beat 'em in the costume contest this afternoon."

"Darn tootin'," said Linda. "Gonna beat the pants right off 'em!"

"They won't know what hit 'em." Matt twirled the gun again and smoothly slipped it back into its holster. "We'll teach 'em not to mess with the Glosser's gang, won't we?"

"We sure will!" Debbie would have agreed with just about anything Matt said, though she secretly had her doubts about the contest outcome. With access to higher quality materials and big city-level designers, Penn Traffic had won the competition every year for the past decade. It would take a miracle for Glosser's to triumph this time.

But as long as Debbie was able to bask in Matt's dazzling smile, she was willing to suspend her disbelief and hold out hope for the Glosser Bros. team.

Just then, Mrs. Martinelli, the manager of the shoe department, leaned out the store's front door and called Matt's name. She was dressed like a saloon girl, complete with a satiny red dress and feathery pink boa.

"Duty calls!" Matt gave the brim of his hat a tug for Linda, then Debbie. "But I will see the both of you soon, or my name ain't Mattie the Kid."

Both girls giggled as he sashayed down the sidewalk with spurs jingling, though Mrs. Martinelli didn't look at all amused.

"Could he *get* any *cuter?*" asked Linda as she watched him go.

Debbie didn't say, but the answer was clear. And she felt better than ever about the deal she'd made with the real Beth Popchak.

Masquerading as a Glosser's employee had gotten her closer to the man she adored. Now all she had to do was make the right move before her shift ended and she ran out of time.

"WHO WANTS *LEMONADE*?"

Debbie and Linda had just finished setting up the women's accessories table when the lemonade arrived. Two women dressed as settlers, complete with bonnets, white blouses, and long, black skirts strolled around the corner of Franklin and Locust streets, each carrying a stack of plastic cups and a clear plastic pitcher filled with yellow liquid.

"Oh, good!" Linda popped out from behind the table and headed straight for them. "The Shaffer Twins are here!"

Debbie frowned, wondering what was so special about the Shaffer Twins. Beth had never mentioned them before.

"Get your ice-cold lemonade here!" shouted one of the twins. "Straight from the Glosser Bros. Cafeteria!"

As Linda hurried over, the twin held out the stack of

plastic cups so she could grab one. Then, as Linda flipped and raised the cup, the twin filled it with lemonade from the pitcher.

As soon as the cup was full, Linda gulped the liquid with eyes closed. The look on her face when she finished that first big drink was blissful.

"Ruby, you're a lifesaver!" She lifted the cup for another long swallow. "This is the best lemonade *ever*."

"Glad to hear it, sweetie." Ruby grinned and nodded. "We thought you folks might be getting a little thirsty out here."

"You better believe it!" Linda swigged more of her drink, then held out the cup again. "Any chance you could top me off?"

"What do you say, Ruth?" asked Ruby. "Can she have a little more?"

"Of course she can," said the other twin, who was filling a cup for Debbie. "She's part of the Glosser's family, isn't she?"

Ruth handed Debbie her cup with a wink, and Debbie smiled weakly. Not only wasn't she part of the Glosser's family, but she had no desire to join it.

She was, however, fascinated by the Shaffer Twins, who were identical in nearly every way. They both had the same height and build (just over five feet, on the stocky side), and their voices were impossible to tell apart. Other than a slight difference in facial features, the two women were completely the same to Debbie's eyes and ears.

They reminded her of another set of identical people,

though these other people weren't twin sisters. They weren't even related, or if they were, Debbie didn't know how.

And their first meeting, just a few weeks ago, had led to Debbie standing there right now, sipping lemonade in a cowgirl costume outside Glosser Bros. Department Store.

IT HAD all started one Friday at Coney Island Lunch on Clinton Street in downtown Johnstown. Debbie had walked over on her break for one of their famous hot dogs, complete with chili sauce, mustard, and salt and pepper (but no onions, since she had to go back to work at Penn Traffic after lunch). The place had been busy with the lunchtime crowd—workers from Bethlehem Steel and the many downtown businesses—but Debbie had been lucky enough to find a seat. Just as she'd put down her tray on the bright orange table, however—complete with a cup of water from the tap at the end of the counter, free of charge—she'd realized someone was hovering beside her.

"Excuse me." The young woman who stood there had an expression midway between a frown and a smile. "Do I know you from somewhere?"

Debbie had just stared at her, mouth falling open with utter surprise.

"You look awfully familiar," the woman had said... which was putting it very mildly.

Because for Debbie, it had been just like looking in a mirror.

"I'm Beth." The woman had slid onto the bright green bench across the table and put her own tray of food down in front of her. "Beth Popchak."

Debbie had slid in across from her, arms framing the orange tray with her hot dog and water. "I'm Debbie Kaminski. And this is pretty wild."

"It is, isn't it?" From the start, Beth's laugh had struck her as warm and friendly, unpretentious. "A total shocker."

"I can't get over it," Debbie had said. "We're *identical*."

"Well, almost." Beth had gestured at the food on her tray, which wasn't a Coney Island hot dog like Debbie's. "I prefer the *Sundowner*."

Debbie had laughed. "I like that, too," she'd said, though the Sundowner—a hamburger patty topped with a fried egg, chili, and onions on a bun—wasn't really her favorite.

"As long as we both like Coney Island, I'd say that's close enough, right?" Beth had grabbed the Sundowner then and taken a bite, rolling her eyes with pleasure as she chewed.

Beth had liked her automatically, though maybe that had been partly because of the resemblance. "They say everyone has a twin somewhere, don't they?"

"Yeah," Beth had said, putting down her sandwich. "But what are the chances of us being in the same small town!"

"And we're only just now crossing paths," Debbie had said. "So how long have you lived here, anyway?"

"Well, my mom and I just moved to town recently." Beth had shrugged. "What about you?"

"I've lived here all my life."

"Isn't that something?" Beth had shaken her head slowly. "Fate finally brought us together after all this time."

Debbie had reached for her water, then replaced it on the tray without taking a sip. "But this can't just be a coincidence, can it?"

"Look, don't knock it." Beth had leaned over and taken her hand. "All that matters is that we *found* each other. And we can really have some *fun* with this."

Debbie had frowned. "What kind of fun?"

"We'll think of something." Beth had chuckled and squeezed her hand. "Give it time, 'sis.'"

And she'd been right. The two of them had thought of several interesting things to do that involved identical twin strangers.

One of which was getting Debbie closer to the man she wanted as her boyfriend.

UNFORTUNATELY, she wasn't getting many opportunities to seek him out today, with the sidewalk sale in full swing.

"Right this way, ma'am." Debbie guided another customer, merchandise in hand, from the women's accessories table to the front door of Glosser's. "That man over there at the register will ring you up."

Things were busier than ever now, just after 11 a.m., with customers pouring in from all directions to snatch up the bargains. Debbie hadn't had a chance to catch her breath since the lemonade break near the start of her shift; ever since the clock had struck 10, the shoppers had been out in force.

She'd been jumping between tables, in fact, to fill gaps as needed—mostly covering ladies' accessories but also menswear, children's clothes, housewares, hardware, and the bargain table (a kind of rummage sale assortment of odds and ends sold at deep discounts).

It was a good thing she had enough experience from working at Penn Traffic to cover the bases. Glosser's had its own unique way of doing things, but Debbie had picked it up well enough that none of the managers had objected so far. She seemed to be doing a decent job of convincing them she belonged there, though.

Still, none of this was what she'd come here for. None of this was why she'd gone to the trouble of switching places with Beth Popchak for the day.

She was there for Matt Harrigan, though the two of them couldn't seem to connect.

Every time she laid eyes on him, in fact, he seemed to be at least as busy as she was. The department managers had him running errands constantly, hauling merchandise from inside the store as needed to fill gaps on the rapidly emptying tables. The whole time, his pleasant disposition and handsome good looks never faded, and his cowboy costume never had a piece out of place.

Seeing him that way just made Debbie want to spend time with him even more.

Maybe she'd be able to get closer at lunchtime, she thought, assuming they could sync up their breaks.

To put her plan in motion, she started by cornering him on his way back into the store on yet another errand.

"Howdy." He smirked and brushed the brim of his hat with a thumb and index finger. "How's the old-fashioned sale treatin' ya, Missy?"

To Debbie, he was more adorable than ever. "To be honest, I could use a break soon. How about you?"

"The same, I reckon." Matt looked over his shoulder. "The way they've got me jumpin', I'm about plumb tuckered out."

Debbie nodded. "So when *is* your break? Noon, maybe?"

"I wish." Matt blew out his breath. "No one gets a break at noon 'round these parts. It's our busiest time, what with all the other downtown workers gettin' breaks of their own for lunch about then."

Debbie forced herself not to slump with disappointment. "When *will* you get a break, then?"

"One o'clock, dependin' on how crazy it is by then. If I need to push it later, I will."

"Right." Debbie winced to herself at the sound of Mrs. Martinelli's voice calling Matt from the store's front door. The time for a chat was over.

"Gotta go." Matt didn't look happy about it. "Trail boss has got my number."

"I'll see you later," Debbie said as he started to walk away, spurs jingling. "Hopefully during your break."

"Sounds good," said Matt. "Long as I don't get hogtied on my way outta the corral first."

OPERATION MATT HARRIGAN had come together soon after the first meeting between Debbie and Beth Popchak. The two had been hanging out in George's Song Shop on Market Street one afternoon during their lunch break, comparing their tastes in music, when Matt had walked in to talk to the cashier.

He hadn't seemed to notice either of them at the racks further back in the store...but their attention had zeroed in on him immediately.

"That guy is so hot," Debbie had whispered. "He's like... a young Robert Plant with short hair."

"Guess what?" Beth had whispered back. "I work with him at Glosser's!"

"Seriously?" Debbie's gaze had stayed locked on Matt instead of the vinyl 45 RPM singles in her hands. "You're so lucky!"

"He's all right," Beth had said. "Seems like a decent guy. Just about every girl working there has a crush on him, I think."

"It figures." As Debbie watched, Matt had given the cashier a flyer of some kind. From a distance, she hadn't been able to read what was printed on it. "Is he dating any of them?"

"Not at the moment, as far as I know." With that, Beth had bumped her shoulder and smiled. "Want me to set you up?"

Debbie had felt herself blush. "God, no. I mean, yes, but no. Definitely no."

"I could introduce you right now. Let me catch him before he leaves." Beth had started to move toward the front of the store.

"No, wait." Debbie had grabbed her by the arm and held her back. "Don't do it. Not yet. I don't know what I'd say to him..."

"Hey, don't tell me you're *shy*. You're not allowed to be! *I'm* not shy."

"Just a little, if I really like someone." Debbie had held up the 45 singles to hide her face from the front of the store. "I'm just not *ready* to talk to him right now!"

"Okay, okay!" Beth had stood there a moment as Matt and the cashier talked and laughed. "But what if there's another way?"

"What other way?"

"I've got an idea," Beth had told her. "The perfect way for you to get up close and personal with the hunk of your dreams."

Debbie had narrowed her eyes suspiciously. "For real?"

Beth had nodded emphatically. "Absolutely. It's guaranteed to work."

"Tell me more," Debbie had said.

"What's the one thing identical friends like us can do that no one else can?"

Debbie had shrugged, watching as Matt walked out of the store. "What's that?"

"Trade places," Beth had told her. "Just for a shift. You

pose as me and work at Glosser's for the day, and I'll pose as you and work at Penn Traffic."

Thinking it over as Matt passed the big front window of the store, Debbie had made her decision. "Let's do it."

"Awesome," Beth had said. "Let's plan for Old-Fashioned Bargain Days, which are always super-busy. You'll be less likely to get found out."

"Okay, cool." Something had occurred to Debbie then, and she'd frowned. "And you're sure you won't mind?"

"Nah, it'll be fun."

"But it's all about me getting closer to Matt. There's nothing in it for you."

With that, Beth had aimed a conspiratorial smirk in her direction. "Who says?"

IT WASN'T until 1:30 p.m. that Matt showed up and said he was finally taking his break. Luckily, business had slowed just enough by then that Debbie was able to take her break, too (with help from Linda, who agreed to wait till 2:00 to step away herself).

With just a half-hour of downtime ahead, Debbie and Matt hurried to the McDonald's on upper Main Street, where they grabbed burgers, fries, and sodas to go. Then they set out to stroll while they ate, meanwhile scoping out the costumes on other downtown employees working the sidewalk sale.

"Pilgrims?" Matt gestured with a French fry at the team

of four employees set up outside McCrory's Department Store on Main Street. "That's the best they could come up with? Dig out the costumes from Thanksgiving Day?"

"Pretty lame, all right." Debbie chuckled. "The Hello Shop's pretty good, though."

"I love Vikings!" Matt grinned. "Wish we'd picked that theme at Glosser's!"

"Me, too! I'd love to wear one of those horned helmets!"

"Look at the guy in front of City Hall, though," said Matt. "What's he supposed to be? A hobo from the Depression?"

Debbie bumped Matt's arm with her elbow...and the contact was electric. "He's not in costume, Matt. That's the mayor of Johnstown."

"Whoops." Matt made a loud gulping noise. "I was just gonna say, that's not a bad outfit, really."

They both laughed at that.

Crossing the street then, they passed the Embassy Theater and the little newsstand beside it, settling on a bench at the corner of Main and Market Streets. As they sat and ate their lunch, she was very aware of him, feeling the heat of his body next to hers. Between bites of her burger and fries, she sneaked glimpses of him...only getting caught once, though neither of them looked away when their gazes met.

"Do you mind if I ask you a question?" he said.

Debbie's heart pounded in her chest. "Go ahead." She had a feeling he was about to ask her out, which was exactly what she'd been hoping he'd do all along.

He cleared his throat. "I was just wondering if you'd like to…if the two of us could…"

Before he could finish his sentence, a guy dressed like a knight stomped over and interrupted. "Debbie? Is that you?"

Startled, Debbie gaped at him, not recognizing his voice at first. When he swung up the faceplate of his tin helmet, though, she got the picture.

He was Todd Filipovich, one of her co-workers from Penn Traffic.

Cursing him for showing up at the worst possible moment, she couldn't help looking annoyed. "Excuse me?"

"It's me, Todd!" He waved a silver-painted plastic lance in the air. "What the heck are you doing dressed like a *cowgirl?*"

"Sorry, my name's Beth Popchak," she said, staying in character. She wasn't ready yet for Matt to know her true identity…though she wasn't sure exactly when she *would* be ready for that. "You must be confusing me with somebody else."

Todd laughed. "Stop pulling my leg, Debbie. I just got done talking to you five minutes ago at Penn Traffic."

"Nope." She shook her head insistently. "I work at Glosser's."

"With me," said Matt. "She works at Glosser's with me."

"Okay, whatever." Todd rolled his eyes. "Well, maybe she wants to stay out of the line of fire at Penn Traffic, then."

Debbie scowled. "What are you talking about?"

"You of all people should know, Deb." Todd hiked a

thumb over his shoulder in the direction of Penn Traffic. "You're the one who told us about it at the store."

It was then that Debbie realized whom he must have been talking about—*Beth*—though no other details were clear to her yet. "What exactly did she...*I* tell you?"

Todd shifted, casting a wary gaze at Matt. "I'd rather not say in front of certain people...*Glosser's* people, that is."

Matt put the McDonald's bag down on the bench and got up, squaring his shoulders. "We're *both* Glosser's people, buddy."

"Just tell us," said Debbie. "I want to make sure you got the story straight."

"Yeah, right." Todd narrowed his eyes at Matt like he wanted to fight him.

Debbie got up from the bench, too, and pushed between them. "Matt's with me! If I say he's all right, he is. Now *tell* us. Why is Penn Traffic in the line of fire?"

Still, Todd hesitated...then finally leaned back and relaxed. "The big brawl, that's why. The fight between the department stores."

"Between Penn Traffic and Glosser's?" asked Matt.

Todd shook his head. "No, man. Between Penn Traffic and McCrory's! A real knock-down-drag-out!"

"Seriously?" said Matt. "Why would Penn Traffic guys pick a fight with McCrory's guys?"

"Guys *and* girls, apparently," said Todd. "A *bunch* of people are jumping in on this."

"And why is it happening?" asked Debbie. "Refresh my memory."

"Too much badmouthing," explained Todd. "McCrory's

people talking trash about Penn Traffic people…spreading the word about how bad we suck." He pointed at Debbie. "I'm just glad you found out and set us straight."

"Right," said Debbie. "Glad I could help out."

"When is this brawl supposed to happen?" asked Matt.

"Three o'clock in Central Park," said Todd.

"And everyone's who's planning to fight is just going to walk out of work in the middle of the day?" said Debbie. "They aren't worried about getting fired?"

"Some people finish their shifts by three, some have the day off anyway, and others don't seem to care if they get fired or not," said Todd. "Their philosophy is, whatever happens, happens. Sometimes, you have to stand up for yourself, no matter what the cost might be."

"Just so you don't get knocked down in the process," said Matt.

"Don't worry, we won't be." Todd smirked. "We're bringing our toughest guys, and we're gonna tear those McCrory's jerks a new one. We're gonna make them sorry they ever ran their fat mouths about us."

Just then, the bells of St. John Gualbert Cathedral near Coney Island rang out, signaling it was two o'clock in the afternoon. Debbie's heart pounded as she realized how precious little time there was until the big brawl was due to break out.

As the echoes of St. John's bells faded in the afternoon air, Debbie stood and fretted, wondering what to do next.

Wondering, also, why Beth had set the situation in motion in the first place.

At least it did her heart some good to see that Matt didn't seem thrilled about the fight. "This brawl could get ugly," he said. "A lot of folks could get hurt."

"Those McCrory dopes have it coming." Todd smirked and shook his lance. "Someone needs to teach them a lesson."

"What exactly did they say about the Penn Traffic people?" asked Debbie. "I mean, what did *I* tell you they said?"

Todd gave her an *Are you high?* look but kept talking. "All kinds of nasty crap! It's like they were begging for it!"

"And you're absolutely sure they said it?" asked Matt.

"Of course." Todd gestured at Debbie. "What possible reason could *she* have to lie?"

That was exactly what Debbie was wondering. Why would Beth spread lies at Penn Traffic and McCrory's? What could she possibly have to gain from starting a brawl between them?

Back at George's Song Shop, when she and Debbie had first planned to trade places, Debbie had suggested the deal was one-sided. "There's nothing in it for you," she'd said...to which Beth had replied, "Who says?"

Was this, then, what Beth had wanted out of the bargain all along? Had she planned from the start to set off a clash between Penn Traffic and McCrory's...and if so, why? It didn't seem to make sense, at least not yet.

But maybe that was beside the point. Maybe avoiding disaster should be Debbie's immediate goal...even if it meant ending her masquerade.

"Well, I'd better get going." Todd flipped his tin face-plate down and pointed himself in the direction of Central Park. "Doesn't look good if a knight in shining armor is late for a battle, you know."

"Hold on." Debbie grabbed his arm. "I need your help with something." She looked over her shoulder and met Matt's gaze. "And I need your help, too."

Matt checked his wristwatch and shook his head. "I'm already late getting back to work, Beth. Both of us are."

"Work can wait," Debbie said firmly. "This is important."

Matt fidgeted and looked toward Glosser's...but he stayed put. She'd persuaded him to hear her out.

If only that didn't mean revealing the secret that had brought them together.

Releasing Todd's arm, she cleared her throat. She didn't want to let the next words out of her mouth. "Guys, I have to tell you something. When I'm done, you'll see why the favor I'm about to ask for is so important."

Matt frowned. "Why? What's the favor?"

She took a deep breath, then let it out slowly. "To work together to stop the brawl before it's too late."

"Oh, is that all?" Matt tipped his cowboy hat back and grinned. "Here I was worried you might ask us to do something crazy."

DEBBIE SPENT the next few minutes coming clean about who she was...and who she wasn't. She explained the existence of her twin and the identity switch they'd made for the day—though Beth had since gone off the rails without explanation. She was the one who'd spread the rumors about trash talk between Penn Traffic and McCrory's, sparking the brawl that was set to commence in less than an hour. Why she was doing so, Debbie had no idea... though she believed strongly it should be stopped in its tracks.

The whole time Debbie said all this, she was keenly aware of every flicker of expression on Matt's face. She was terrified the truth would undo whatever bond had formed between them, and he'd walk away and leave her to fend for herself.

But the truth was, she couldn't tell what he was thinking from looking at him. His expression was calm and unreadable—not outright hostile, at least, but not overly approving, either. He wasn't showing her all his cards just yet.

Though she wouldn't have to wait long to see them. "So that's my story." She locked eyes with Matt, projecting as much sincerity as she possibly could. "I'm sorry for pretending to be someone I'm not...but I swear, I never wanted to hurt anyone."

"And now you expect us to trust you." Todd sniffed and shook his head. "You want our help stopping the brawl."

"Hey, don't do it for me," said Debbie. "Do it for your friends at Penn Traffic."

"I just don't see what the big deal is," said Todd. "What's the worst that can happen? Some folks get banged up in Central Park? Maybe the cops arrest some people?"

"I don't know." Debbie scowled in frustration. "Beth must have a reason for going to so much trouble to set it up, though."

"What if it's all about the timing?" asked Matt. "It'll make a bigger splash happening during the end of Old-Fashioned Bargain Days, that's for sure."

"Will it ever." Todd smirked. "Right before they hand out the best costume awards, too."

As soon as he said it, the little hairs jumped on the back of Debbie's neck. "That's it." Instantly, she recognized the insight she'd been reaching for, one that might reveal the truth behind the situation. "That's why she's doing this."

Matt smiled, understanding dawning in his glittering blue eyes. "The brawlers will be disqualified."

"She doesn't care who loses the fight," said Debbie. "As long as they *both* lose the *prize*."

DEBBIE and the boys ran across town in opposite directions—the boys up Main Street toward Central Park, Debbie down Market Street toward Penn Traffic. They all had the same end goal in mind, thwarting Beth's plan (though being away from work for so long might cost them their jobs) and they were all on the same tight timetable. Three o'clock, and the start of the brawl, were racing toward them at what felt like light speed.

When Debbie got to the intersection at Washington Street, she stopped and looked up, shading her eyes against the afternoon sunlight. What she saw on the roof of the department store—someone in a princess costume leaning over, working with something suspended from the edge—was enough to show her she'd come to the right place.

As she charged across Washington, darted past the Bargain Days tables arrayed along the sidewalk, and hurried through the corner door into Penn Traffic, a memory came back to her from something that had happened just days ago. She and Beth had been sharing a basket of French fries at the Fish Boat on Main Street, and the subject of the costume competition had come up.

I'd love to see Penn Traffic lose for once, Beth had told her. *Think you can make that happen?*

Not on my own. Debbie had laughed. *It would take a lot more people to ruin the whole store's chances.*

Maybe that could be arranged, Beth had said, and then she'd popped another fry in her mouth and chuckled wickedly.

Now, today, it was finally clear what Beth had had in mind when she'd said that.

As Debbie hurtled through the ground floor of the store, she noticed there weren't many employees around to watch her pass. Most had already headed across town to the brawl, she guessed, leaving a skeleton crew to man the various departments.

It was probably for the best, as there were fewer people to potentially trip her up. As it was, she was able to leap into an elevator and ride all the way to the fifth floor without stopping once along the way.

As soon as the door slid open on five, Debbie bolted out of the car on a beeline for the stairwell. Seconds later, she heaved open the heavy metal door that gave way to the roof, emerging near the shed that housed the building's air conditioning system.

She ran straight for the edge of the roof, where she'd seen the activity from below…then slammed on the brakes from a few yards away. The girl in the pale pink princess costume was there, letting something fall over the edge.

When the girl heard her and turned, Debbie saw it was Beth, as expected.

The twin friends were reunited—though what would happen next was anyone's guess.

"Funny meeting you here!" Grinning, Beth brushed off her hands. "Great minds really do think alike, don't they?"

"Looks that way," said Debbie.

"So how'd it go with Matt at Glosser's?" Beth winked. "Did you two hit it off?"

"He's a great guy, all right." Debbie nodded. "He didn't even tell me to get lost when I told him who I really was."

Beth's grin suddenly shifted to a frown. "You told him? Why the hell did you do that?"

"Because I needed a hand with something." Casually, Debbie walked over to join Beth at the edge. It was only then she saw that what Beth had thrown down over the wall of the store was a huge white cloth banner. It was secured to the roof by two metal spikes that she must have driven in with the wood-handled hammer at her feet.

"But wasn't the whole point of the job switch to keep your identity *secret?*" asked Beth. "Because you were too shy to meet him Matt on your own, as yourself?"

"I thought so," said Debbie. "But I thought wrong. It turns out there was a completely different point the whole time. I just didn't know about it."

Beth's frown deepened. "You're not making a lot of sense here, Deb."

"You just wanted to get inside Penn Traffic for a day so you could sabotage their chances of winning the costume contest again." Leaning out over the edge of the roof—but not too far, as there wasn't a railing—she got a look at what was painted on the giant banner.

Losers. That was what it said.

"Well, I wouldn't say that outcome isn't overdue, necessarily," said Beth. "But what kind of person do you think I am, that I'd trick you over something like a costume contest?"

"The *actual* loser, actually," said Debbie. "Because your plan just fell apart, thanks to me."

"What are you talking about?" snapped Beth.

"Might want to pull this banner back up." Debbie pointed at the banner draped over the side of the store.

"Why the hell would I do that?"

"Because it isn't true anymore." Debbie smirked. "Let's go for a walk, and I'll show you what I'm talking about."

"A walk? Where?"

"Central Park." Debbie drew a toy gun from its holster and aimed the barrel across town in the direction of the park. "Over thataway, pardner."

BETH DID NOT LOOK happy when she and Debbie approached Central Park by way of Locust Street. Was it because of the complete lack of a brawl on the premises?

Debbie thought that was a pretty good guess.

"Not what you expected to see, is it?" Debbie poked her in the side with an elbow. "Wasn't there supposed to be a big fight here right about now? That's what I heard on the grapevine."

Beth's only answer was to keep stewing.

"You know what else I heard?" asked Debbie. "A little bird told me that a couple of guys got together and talked the two sides out of it. They exposed the lies that a certain *undercover infiltrator* told to get them stirred up, and that did the trick. The employees of Penn Traffic and McCrory's decided to get mad at somebody *else* instead of each other.

"Guess who that somebody else is." Debbie leaned in closed and whispered in Beth's ear. "Want me to give you a clue?"

Beth gave her a look that was part angry glare and part panic.

"Hey, you figured it out." Debbie laughed.

Beth tried to turn around, but Debbie threw an arm around her shoulders and kept her moving up the sidewalk in front of Glosser's.

"I'll bet some folks are pretty ticked off at you," said Debbie. "Nobody likes being used, do they?"

Just then, a side door swung open, and Matt stepped out. "Well, well. If it isn't little Miss Troublemaker." He pulled a toy revolver from its holster and spun it around his index finger. "Just the person we've been looking for."

"Nice job, Matt!" Debbie grinned, as happy as ever to see him. "Not a brawl in sight, thanks to you and Todd!"

"Happy to oblige, ma'am." He tipped his cowboy hat and winked. "Nice work on your part, wranglin' the perpetrator herself."

"Yeah, but what are we gonna do with her?"

Matt spun the toy gun once more, then clapped it in the holster. "I got an idea about that, actually. See, I know some people who're lookin' for volunteers…and I hear volunteer work is good for the soul."

Beth scowled. "What kind of volunteer work?"

"The kind that keeps you from gettin' fired and havin' your ass kicked," said Matt, "unless you'd *prefer* the firin' and kickin'."

"Can you be more specific?" growled Beth.

"Let's just say, you should try and be a good sport," said Matt. "Which shouldn't be a problem, since that's the Glosser Bros. way."

DEBBIE AND BETH followed Matt through the first floor of the store, then down the steps into the Bargain Basement.

Halfway down, Debbie heard the excited shouts of a crowd of people from below. When she reached the last few steps, she saw the basement was filled with employees...but not all from the same store. Some were dressed in the style of the Old West, clearly from Glosser's, while others wore suits of armor, princess costumes, and other medieval attire—guests from Penn Traffic. Mixed in among them both were McCrory's employees dressed like pilgrims and Native Americans.

Employees of three downtown department stores were all together in the same place, all looking in the same direction—the far end of the room.

"What is this?" she asked Matt. "What's going on?"

"It's a real hoot, ain't it?" Matt laughed. "I helped get it set up this morning with the display people. It was supposed to be a Bargain Days wrap-up party to thank the employees of Glosser's for their hard work during the sale...but when the folks from Penn Traffic and McCrory's showed up in the park for the big fight, I came up with a better idea. I fast-talked the Glosser bosses into inviting all those folks to join the fun, instead...so now the party includes workers from a mess of downtown Johnstown department stores instead of just one."

"That's great!" said Debbie. "And the other stores are okay with it, too?"

"You're darn tootin'," said Matt. "The bosses at those other stores agreed to give most everyone the time off to attend. As long as they have enough people to keep the doors open during the party, nobody loses their jobs over this...including us." He spread his arms to indicate Beth and Debbie as well as himself. "We're free and clear, little dogies...other than that volunteer work I mentioned." He tipped his hat in Beth's direction.

The three of them continued to weave through the crowd, winding ever closer to the heart of the action. When they finally pushed into the front row, Debbie saw the focus of attention spread out before her in all its ramshackle glory...and she couldn't help smiling.

Silver foil letters stuck to the white plaster wall spelled out, "Fred's Old-Fashioned Honky-Tonk" just below the level of the ceiling. Below the text, cutouts of cowboy hats, horses, whiskey bottles, revolvers, cash, coins, and dice were arranged on the plaster, setting the scene. In front of all that, a guy from the shoe department with a bushy walrus mustache pasted on, his ample frame clad in a red-and-white striped shirt and white apron, was speaking to the audience.

"Ladies and gentlemen!" His deep voice rumbled through the big space, reaching far even without a mic. "The time has come! Do we have any volunteers to help run this gambling establishment?"

"Right here!" Matt gave Beth a shove, and she lurched out in front of the emcee. "She's here to pay off a debt to society!"

"Excellent!" The emcee guided her to one side of the big vertically mounted wheel. "We have our spinner!"

Most of the crowd booed, but Beth just took it and shrugged. Maybe Matt's advice about being a good sport had sunk in.

"All right, all right! This lovely lady is about to determine who wins some spectacular prizes, so don't you think you ought to stay on her *good* side?"

Some, but not all, of the boos changed to cheers.

Grinning, the emcee waved dramatically at the big wheel. "And now, a spin of our magnificent Wheel of Prizes will reveal the winner of a five-dollar gift certificate to Glosser's Hunt Room Restaurant! Let the wheel spin, my dear!"

Beth took hold of one of the pegs along the edge of the wheel and gave it a hard downward pull. Each wedge of the wheel's white surface had someone's name printed on it in a different color of ink; as the wheel spun, its pegs clicking past the bright orange pointer, the crowd rooted for whichever contestant was their favorite.

When the wheel stopped on the name "Cindy Lawson," a woman in the back cried out with excitement, and everyone applauded her win. They parted to let her through, congratulating her as she passed—and when she got to the front, they gave her the biggest cheer yet.

"That's right, everyone!" said the emcee. "The winner is

our own Deb Lawson from the candy counter! Way to go, Cindy!"

Just then, a tall man in a brown shirt and Western string tie stepped forward and handed a gift certificate to Cindy. The man was Fred Glosser, one of the higher-ups at the store. Debbie had met him earlier when he'd passed her table on the sidewalk, and she'd thought he seemed like a real sweetheart of a guy.

Beaming, Cindy thanked Fred as she took the prize and waved it overhead for the crowd to see.

"Next up, we add a name to the wheel!" The emcee wiped Cindy's name from the wheel with a cloth, then wrote in someone else. "And then we'll spin for our next prize—a ten-dollar gift certificate for the Gee Bee Supermarket on Walnut Street!"

Suddenly, Fred waved both his arms in the air and called out, his voice carrying as well as the host's. "We're throwing in a bag of our famous roasted cashews, too! Served warm, of course!"

Everyone applauded, cheered, and whistled at that.

Matt turned to Debbie, grinning. "I'm going to get your name up there next."

"Don't you dare," she said.

"Hey, it's not like there isn't a catch." Matt smiled. "Whatever you win, you'll have to split it with me."

Meeting his gaze, she smiled back. "It's a deal."

Just then, before Beth could spin the wheel again, a woman's voice called out from across the basement. "The Chamber of Commerce just called! They announced who won the costume contest!"

Everyone fell silent at once. Every cowboy, pilgrim, knight, princess, and Native American in the place swung around to look in her direction.

"It's Glosser's!" she shouted. "After all these years, it's Glosser's! Can you believe it?"

At which point, the crowd went wild. Even the people from Penn Traffic and McCrory's were cheering the news, because there was one thing Beth had been right about.

A Glosser Bros. victory had been long overdue.

"IT ALL WORKED out in the end, didn't it?" said Beth as she and Debbie left the employee dressing room on the fourth floor of Glosser's. "Penn Traffic and McCrory's didn't have to be disqualified for Glosser's to win the contest."

"Looks that way." Debbie laid her cowgirl outfit on top of a pile of costumes on the counter. She was finally back in her civilian clothes—a bright yellow top, blue jeans, and navy blue sneakers.

Beth was back in her own street clothes, too, a rainbow striped tank and jeans, but she didn't add her princess costume to the pile since it was Penn Traffic property. "If I'd known it would go like this, I could've saved myself a lot of trouble."

"Saved me a lot of trouble, too," muttered Debbie as they headed for the elevator.

"Hey, look," said Beth. "I'm really sorry, okay? I'm sorry I didn't tell you what was going on sooner."

Debbie hit the down button, and the door slid open. "You shouldn't've done it at all." She entered the car and pressed the button for the first floor. "It wasn't a cool thing to do, Beth."

"I know, I just..." Beth sighed. "I guess I thought I had it all figured out. I didn't think anyone would get hurt. I mean, I didn't think *you* would get hurt."

"Well, you were wrong." Debbie had put on a good front about everything, but she still felt betrayed and angry. Smoothing things over with the crowd to avoid Beth getting lynched had been one thing; actually forgiving her for what she'd done was quite another.

"Sorry," said Beth as the car stopped on the first floor. "I'm really, really sorry."

"Here." As the door opened, Debbie reached over and took the princess costume. "I'll return this to Penn Traffic tomorrow when I go in for my shift."

"Thanks," said Beth, and then the two of them left the elevator and headed for the corner exit.

"So what about Matt, though?" asked Beth as they stepped out into the warm summer evening. "That all turned out great, didn't it?"

Debbie couldn't deny it had, but she didn't want to give her too much satisfaction. "Yeah, we're going out Saturday night," she said.

"Great!" said Beth. "That has to count for something, right?"

Debbie didn't answer the question. "Well, maybe I'll see you around." She gestured at a burgundy Chrysler LeBaron that was parked along Franklin Street, catty-corner from the store. "There's my ride."

As she said it, her mother waved from the driver's side window, her short blonde hair and bright smile flashing. Mom never minded picking her up after work, which often coincided with the end of her own work day, and that was a good thing; parking downtown during the day was at a premium and expensive to boot.

"Yeah, my ride's here, too." Beth pointed at a dark blue AMC Gremlin parked along Locust Street. "Mom's taxi service, right?"

"Okay, then. See ya."

"Hold on." Beth caught her by the shoulder. "Look, I really am sorry, okay? I hope we can still get together sometime."

Debbie kept her expression as neutral as she could. "We'll see. Give it time, all right?"

Just then, her mother's voice rang out from the street. Looking over, Debbie saw Mom jog across Franklin, then Locust. She wore a short-sleeved white pullover, dress slacks, and heels, and she waved enthusiastically at her daughter the whole time.

"Hi honey," she said as she stepped up onto the curb... and then she froze, gaping at Beth. "Oh my God."

"Hi." Beth nodded.

Debbie's mom did a double take, absolutely stunned. "You're...you're..." She couldn't look away.

As the three of them stood there, the awkward moment playing out, someone else joined them—Beth's mother, who'd just gotten out of the dark blue Gremlin on

Locust. She, too, was stunned...but it wasn't Beth she was staring at...and it wasn't Debbie, either.

It was Debbie's mom. And Debbie's mom stared right back.

Beth's mom had shoulder-length blonde hair and wore a black blouse, faded jeans, and tennis shoes. Otherwise, she looked exactly like Debbie's mom in every way.

"Uh, Mom?" Beth's eyes were wide as she looked from her mother to Debbie's and back again. "What the hell?"

The four of them kept staring at each other, too stunned for words. The resemblance was undeniable: Debbie's mom looked like Beth's mom, just as Debbie looked identical to Beth. Other than their clothes and the way they wore their hair, they were absolute mirror images.

Seconds ticked away as the shock continued, holding them all in its grip. Then, suddenly, Debbie's and Beth's moms lunged into each other's arms and burst into tears.

"Oh my God." Debbie's mom gasped the words out between sobs. "I can't *believe* this. I can't believe it's *you*."

"Tell me about it!" said Beth's mom. "I gave up hoping a *long* time ago!"

"Hoping for what?" Beth frowned in confusion. "I don't *get* it."

"Hoping we'd ever *meet*." Beth's mom smiled through the tears flowing down her face. "It didn't seem *possible*."

"Yet here we are." Debbie's mom sobbed freely, her words muffled against Beth's mom's shoulder. "And it's *true*. It's all *true*."

"What?" asked Debbie. "What's true?"

"That I have a *sister*." Beth's mom stopped sobbing long enough to laugh. "A *twin sister*."

Beth scowled. "You had a twin sister all this time and never knew it?"

"I was adopted," said her mom.

"So was I," said Debbie's mom.

"My mother told me she thought I had a twin sister somewhere," said Beth's mom. "Something the woman at the adoption agency said made her think that was the case."

"But we were adopted by separate families, apparently." Debbie's mom nodded. "And the records were lost or something."

"I used to wonder, though." Beth's mom smiled warmly and reached over to touch her newfound sister's face. "I used to wish you were really out there somewhere, and we'd find each other someday."

"Now here we are." Debbie's mom touched Beth's mom's face in turn, gazing tenderly into her eyes. "Reunited out of the blue."

"And we have *so* much catching up to do." Beth's mom brushed a tear from her sister's cheek. "Where do we start?"

"How about with a cup of coffee?" said Debbie's mom. "I know a place that serves a great one, and it's not far."

"Where's that?"

"Glosser's Cafeteria." Debbie's mom gestured at Franklin Street, where the Cafeteria annex was located.

"Sounds good to me, sis," said Beth's mom.

It was then that Beth laughed and threw an arm around Debbie's shoulders. "Isn't this awesome, cuz? I guess we have more in common than we ever realized, huh?"

Brushing a tear from her own face, Debbie was too amazed to answer. She couldn't look away as the two moms beamed with pure joy, celebrating a miracle that had happened, like so many other magical moments in so many other people's lives, at the one and only original Glosser Bros. Department Store in downtown Johnstown, Pennsylvania.

HALLOWEEN AT GLOSSER'S

"Why not make the flower a meat-eater?" asked Mrs. Mulligan. "Give it some blood-drenched fangs. Maybe have a person's foot sticking out of its mouth. *That* would be scary, don't you think?"

Sixteen-year-old Erin Lewis just shrugged at the colorful picture she'd painted on the big front window of the Glosser Bros. Department Store in Johnstown, Pennsylvania. It was supposed to be an entry in the 1970 Halloween window painting contest sponsored by Glosser's, but somehow, it just wasn't shaping up to be winner material.

Happy flowers and beaming butterflies didn't exactly shout "Halloween." Neither did the other elements of Erin's painting.

"You need to do something about that sun up there, too." Mrs. Mulligan pointed one thick finger at the big, smiling orb in the top right corner of the painting. Its bright yellow color was almost the same as the yellow sweater dress clinging to the art teacher's pudgy body. "Instead of a smile, why not give it a gaping, jagged-toothed maw? Maybe give it some devil horns while you're at it, and some big, maniacal eyes."

Erin sighed and frowned. Her right hand fiddled with the military dog tags that hung from a chain at her throat, turning the cool metal chips between her fingers.

"Look, I'm just trying to help you." Mrs. Mulligan gave Erin's shoulder a squeeze. "You're the best artist at Johnstown High School, but you'll never win a prize if you don't paint something scary, or at least give it a Halloween theme."

Looking right and left, Erin saw other kids her age hard at work painting their own visions on Glosser's big windows. There were vampires, zombies, mummies, ghosts, werewolves, aliens, witches, demons, and all manner of monsters...the usual Halloween-type images. She knew how to draw all that stuff; it wasn't brain surgery.

But she didn't feel like it. It was the day before Halloween, but she wasn't in the mood to paint Halloweeny pictures.

"I know you can do it." Mrs. Mulligan nodded eagerly, and her high, blonde hairdo bobbed. "Remember, carnivorous flowers and a demonic sun."

"I don't think so." Looking down, Erin noticed a spot of yellow paint on her olive drab Army-style t-shirt. At least she had a dozen more of them at home. If any paint had gotten on her Army camouflage pants, she couldn't see it among the gray and brown splotches of fabric.

"This is only your second try," said the teacher. "And hey, it's better than your first draft, right? The one with the fluffy bunnies and kittens?"

"I don't want to work on it anymore," said Erin. "I'm done with this one."

"Then how about starting over? Third time's the charm, right?" Mrs. Mulligan grabbed a big brush from a tray on a nearby ladder. "Paint over what you've got there and show us something better suited to the holiday."

Erin's short brown pigtails flicked back and forth on her shoulders as she shook her head slowly. "Maybe I should just quit."

"Not yet." Mrs. Mulligan leaned close and locked her gaze with Erin's. "Just give it one more try, honey, okay?"

Erin recognized the tone of deep concern and encouragement. She'd heard it many times in the past year, ever since the Bad Thing had happened.

She knew it was well-intentioned. Other people were just trying to help by showing sympathy for her loss and giving her a little special treatment.

So why did it still make her want to kick over a couple of paint cans and run away?

"Come on, Erin." The teacher pressed the big brush toward her. "Show us what you can do. Bring home that first prize and make us all proud."

"Okay." Erin took the brush. She would give it another try, though she knew in her heart it would just be another waste of time.

"Great." Mrs. Mulligan grinned. "I can't wait to see what you come up with."

With that, the teacher marched off, pulling a pack of cigarettes out of a pocket in her dress as she headed across the street to Central Park.

Leaving Erin to sigh, then dunk the brush in a can of white paint and slap the start of a fresh coat over the flowers and butterflies on the window.

"WHAT'LL IT BE, SWEETIE?" The little brown-haired woman in the red smock smiled behind the soda fountain counter in the Glosser Bros. Department Store Cafeteria. "The usual?"

Erin nodded. "Yes, please, Ruby. One chocolate milkshake."

"And what else?" Ruby's kind smile widened, and her eyebrows lifted. "Should I make it a double?"

"No thanks." Erin didn't smile back. It just showed how bad her mood was, that one of her favorite people couldn't cheer her up.

Ruby and her sister Ruth had been there for Erin since she was a little girl, the first time she'd lived in Johnstown. She'd moved to Ohio with her mom and brother six years ago, then had come back to Johnstown one year ago after the Bad Thing happened. She'd needed friends more than ever at that point, and had picked up right where she'd left off with Ruby and Ruth. It was good having some supportive adult friends, since Mom was still a mess from the Bad Thing, and Erin's father had never been in the picture from the beginning.

"Here you go." Ruby lowered her voice to a whisper as she handed over the chocolate shake. "And I gave you something extra, after all."

Looking down at the shake, Erin saw it had three maraschino cherries on top instead of just one. It was enough to get a small smile out of her at last. "Thanks, Ruby." She reached over with two dollar bills to pay for the shake.

"On the house." Ruby wouldn't take the cash. "So what's got you down, anyway?"

Erin sighed. "I'm disqualified from the window-painting contest. My paintings weren't scary enough."

Ruby shook her head. "They just threw you out?"

"They gave me three chances." Erin thought of her third painting, which had turned out to be the stylized face of the lady from the ads for the Gee Bee stores (also owned by Glosser Bros.), smiling at a basket of puppies. "Three strikes, and I'm out."

Ruby picked up a parfait glass and polished it with a white rag. "I'll bet they were all wonderful." She leaned forward across the counter. "It's their loss, disqualifying you like that."

"Thanks." Erin sipped the shake through her straw. It was delicious as always.

"You can come and paint *my* windows," said Ruby. "I'd love anything you paint."

"Thanks, Ruby." Erin sipped some more shake.

"I'll bet there are lots of people who appreciate you," said Ruby. "People who make you feel better instead of worse."

Erin smiled. One other person did come to mind, one person beside Ruby and Ruth who might help her feel better.

Maybe now was a good time to go see her.

"MORE SLIME OVER HERE! And somebody get me another bucket of blood!"

When Erin walked her ten-speed bicycle into the big garage where the Halloween float was taking shape, her best friend Donna's voice was the first thing she heard. It was a big voice, impossible to ignore, much like the girl it belonged to.

As soon as Erin walked into view, that voice was aimed point-blank at her. "Hey, wait a second! Did somebody order a creature from the black lagoon?"

Erin's mood still sucked, but she smiled anyway. "Hi, Donna."

"Get outta here!" Donna hurried over and shooed her toward the door. "Tell them to send us the Bride of Frankenstein we ordered!"

"They're fresh out." Erin shrugged as she leaned her bike against the wall. "I guess you'll have to settle for me."

Donna, who was six feet tall and played on Johnstown's varsity girls' basketball team, glared down at her in mock disgust. "We'll just have to make do, then. Come on and I'll drape some fake intestines over you."

"I'll bet you say that to all your friends," said Erin.

Donna smirked. "You know I do." She brushed her dirty hands on her mismatched sweats—red top, black pants—which were covered in paint smears, sawdust, and glitter. Her long, black hair, which was tied in a ponytail, was full of the same stuff. "So what brings you to this *neck* of the woods, as Dracula might say? I thought you were painting windows."

"Not anymore," said Erin. "I got disqualified."

"Good!" Donna spun and headed for the float-in-progress, where two younger girls were hard at work with paint brushes. "I could use another pair of hands around here!"

As Erin followed, she took a closer look at the float, which consisted of a red base on a four-wheeled flatbed surrounded by cut-out waist-high flames of red, orange, and yellow. The girls' basketball teams were putting it together, using a spare bay at Donna's father's auto repair center.

"So what's this going to be, then?" asked Erin.

"It's Hell, baby!" Donna threw her arms in the air dramatically. "A *special* Hell for the people of Johnstown! We're gonna have Morley's Devil-Dog poking people with a pitchfork, and Mr. Flood dumping buckets of water on the crowd, wearing a powder-blue leisure suit!"

"Buckets of water?" Erin fiddled with the dog tags. "Won't that make people mad?"

"Okay, okay," said Donna. "Buckets of confetti, then."

"I like it," said Erin. "Maybe you could have a steel mill demon pouring make-believe hot metal on the damned. Or an Inclined Plane torture rack that keeps going up and down, like it's crushing them to a pulp."

"Yes!" Donna jabbed a finger in Erin's direction. "Perfect! And *that's* why I need your help! You've got that sick creativity, Eerie!"

Erin waved at one of the girls who was painting the base of the float—a redhead and cousin of Donna's from the JV girls' basketball squad. The girl smiled and waved back. "Well, I don't know what good it'll do your float. You might be better off without me."

"Why would you think that?" asked Donna. "Sick creativity is *always* a good thing."

"Not lately, it isn't." Erin watched as the other girl, a blonde who was also a JV basketball player, mixed a big bucket of some kind of slimy green goo. "My window painting sure didn't come out very sick."

"Why?" Donna went to work shaping a wire frame that looked like it might be the skeleton of a papier-mâché boulder. "What did you paint?"

"Bunnies and kittens," said Erin. "Flowers and puppies. And the Gee Bee lady."

Donna laughed. "I love it! You were totally rebelling against the system! Breaking the rules to stick it to the man!"

"Not really."

"Then you were making a statement!" said Donna. "An artistic or political statement!"

Erin shook her head. "That's not it, either."

Donna stopped working on the wire frame and looked up at her. "Then what gives, Eerie?"

"I just..." Erin frowned. "I just couldn't do it."

"Okay." A look of sympathy flashed across Donna's paint-speckled face, quickly replaced by a sarcastic smile. She, more than just about anyone, understood where Erin was coming from and what the Bad Thing meant to her. They'd been friends since the first time Erin had lived in town, six years ago, and they both knew everything about each other. "Then I say, get back on the horse." She gestured at a pile of Styrofoam heads, the kind department stores used to display wigs for sale. "Start painting those disembodied heads, wouldja? Make 'em nice and gruesome, and stick 'em on those pikes for the gates of Hell."

"Okay." Erin still didn't feel like she could do the job right, but she thought she'd give it a try.

"Now get cracking!" Donna clapped her hands loudly. "Hell wasn't built in a day, y'know!"

IT WAS WELL after dark by the time Erin walked through the door of the Hornerstown apartment she shared with her mother...late enough to earn her a scolding for missing dinner.

In the old days, that is. The days before the Bad Thing happened.

Now, Mom wasn't even home. The lights were off, and

the place was quiet as a tomb. Which, considering the way things were going, was very appropriate.

Erin slammed the door behind her and flicked the switch for the living room light...but nothing happened. "Great." She tried again with the same result.

The same thing happened when she tried turning on the TV. Sadly, it wasn't a surprise. It wasn't the first time Mom had forgotten (or been unable) to pay the electric bill. There were lots of things she didn't take care of anymore.

Not that Erin really blamed her. The Bad Thing had hit Mom worse than anyone, and it hadn't happened that long ago. A single mother, she'd moved back to Johnstown, where she and the kids had lived until six years ago—anything to make a change. But it hadn't helped much. She was still a wreck, and Erin was enough of a mess herself that she hadn't been able to help her heal. It was totally understandable that she was still struggling, trying to deal with it by drinking a little too much and staying out a little too late.

Totally understandable.

With a sigh, Erin kicked off her combat boots and padded out to the kitchen. She ate a few Ritz crackers dipped in peanut butter—just enough to stop her stomach from growling—and washed them down with grape Kool Aid.

Then, she ducked through a doorway around the corner into her bedroom. Getting down on her knees, she slid a beat-up black backpack out from under the bed and took a moment to go through the contents by the glow of the streetlight outside her window.

At a glance, it looked like everything was there...everything she needed for her mission that night. Four candles, matches, a flashlight...

...incense, an incense burner, a little brass bowl...

...a Ouija board and planchette pointer...

...three baseball cards...

...a lock of hair from her dead brother, Bobby...

...and a letter he'd written long ago.

All set.

Erin zipped up the backpack and pulled it over her shoulders, then paused before getting to her feet. Without warning, a tear formed in the corner of her left eye, then rolled down her cheek.

And she stopped it, swiping it away with the back of her hand.

"Come on." She took a deep breath and released it slowly, fighting to keep more tears from falling. It shouldn't be a problem, she knew.

Tonight wasn't an occasion for sadness, was it? It was a night for joy.

After all, she was about to see someone she hadn't seen in quite some time. She was about to see her big brother, Bobby, who'd died in Vietnam a year ago.

That was what the Bad Thing had been—Bobby's death in the war at the age of 19. And getting to see him again was the only thing that had kept her going since it happened. Knowing it was coming soon had been the only thing keeping her sane.

Though three years apart in age, the two of them had always been close. They'd done everything together, at least until he'd been drafted and gone off to boot camp. Even then, all the way to Vietnam, he'd stayed in touch faithfully, sending her lots of letters. Then, the letters had stopped, and the news of his death had come soon after.

In the year since then, she'd been heartsick, counting down the days until she could see him again...until the agreement they'd made as kids could be fulfilled.

Now, finally, tonight was the night. Was it any wonder she'd been distracted at Glosser's window painting contest and not much better at the garage decorating the float with Donna?

Jumping to her feet, she hurried out of the room. She pulled on her combat boots and rushed out the front door, slamming it shut on her way to what she was sure would be the first happy night she'd known in months.

ERIN WAS BREATHING hard as she rode her ten-speed into the alley between the main building of the Glosser Bros. Department Store and the annex that housed the cafeteria. She was pretty sure no one had seen her; it was after 11 o'clock, so town was pretty quiet, and there hadn't been any traffic on Franklin Street when she'd turned down the alley.

The store and cafeteria had been closed for hours, and the windows were all dark. When she got to the end of the alley, she saw that the loading dock area located there was dark, too.

Stopping the bike to listen, she didn't hear any telltale sounds of anyone lurking nearby. Reaching into the backpack, she pulled out the flashlight and shone its beam into the shadowy corners of the dock area, but saw no one.

Perfect. It was just the way she'd hoped it would be.

Dismounting the bike, Erin parked it against a wall. Then, she proceeded to walk the last few steps to the middle of the open space around the loading dock, framed by the back of the Glosser Building and the buildings behind it along Washington Street.

Looking down, she saw a red X spray-painted on the pavement. "Right here." It marked the exact spot where the ritual would take place. She and Bobby had put it there six years ago, when this had been their favorite hiding place during their explorations around town.

Sitting cross-legged beside the X, facing Glosser's loading dock, she unloaded her backpack and set up her tools. The Ouija board went over the X. She lit a votive candle at each of the board's four corners, then set up the incense burner at the top edge. She loaded the burner with a stick of Nag Champa incense and lit that, too.

Finally, she was ready. Taking a deep, shaky breath, she held up one of the baseball cards. One of *Bobby's* baseball cards—Willie Mays of the San Francisco Giants.

"Bobby, I'm here." She lit the card with a match and watched as it burned. When it was almost down to her fingertips, she dropped it in the little brass bowl and let it burn the rest of the way to ash.

Then, she set fire to another card—Roberto Clemente of the Pittsburgh Pirates, Bobby's all-time favorite player. "I'm here, just like we said." Again, she let it burn to ash in the brass bowl.

She burned one more card after that—Catfish Hunter of the Oakland A's. Then she lit the lock of Bobby's hair and dropped that in the bowl, too.

Next, she reached for the letter and read it for what must have been the ten thousandth time. And then she pressed it to her chest and closed her eyes.

"Bobby." Her voice, when she spoke, was a whisper. "We always said, whichever one of us died first would come back on the night of that person's birthday...right here, at our favorite place, behind Glosser's." Her heart was beating so fast, she had to pause and take a breath to keep going. "Well, I know it's a long way from Vietnam, but here I am. It's your birthday, the night before Halloween, and I'm right here, Bobby. And I need to talk to you." Her whisper grew fainter. "I need to *see* you."

Just then, a car whooshed by on the street, breaking her mood...but only for a moment. She closed her eyes again and continued whispering. "So here goes, Bobby. Just the way we talked about it...before you went to Vietnam. Just the way we agreed it would be."

Erin folded the letter once and put it on her lap. Leaning forward, she took the glass planchette from her backpack and placed it on the Ouija board. Then, she rested her fingertips lightly on the planchette, careful not to apply too much pressure.

"Okay, Bobby," she said. "Let's start with a question. Are you here?"

She waited, her senses keenly focused on the planchette, but it didn't budge.

Heart pounding in her chest, she tried again. "Bobby, just answer yes or no. Are you here with me?"

Still, there wasn't the slightest movement from the planchette, or anything else for that matter. Even the flames of the candles seemed perfectly frozen, pointing straight up at attention.

Erin waited a little longer, but it was hard. She'd already waited so long, and now she was *right here,* at the appointed time and place, and she needed to see her brother so badly. She needed to tell him how much she missed him, and how sorry she was that she'd never said goodbye, and how Mom was falling apart without him. Most of all, she needed him to make her *feel better* somehow, like she wasn't always about to shatter into a million pieces even as she walked around pretending she was fine.

But none of that was happening yet. The planchette remained steady, as if glued to the board.

"Bobby, please," said Erin. "Why won't you talk to me?"

Still nothing. How many times had she and Bobby played with the Ouija board, and they'd always gotten some kind of response, no matter how slight? But now, when she needed it the most, there was nothing.

"Talk to me, Bobby!" Tears ran down her face, but she didn't dare take her hands off the planchette to wipe them away. "Just say *something* so I know you're all right!"

Just then, a man's voice rose up suddenly out of the night. "Excuse me."

Adrenaline shot through Erin as her head swung up in the direction of the voice.

"Are you all right?" The man, who'd come down the alley, stepped into the moonlight so she could see him.

Instantly, a tidal wave of disappointment rushed through her. The guy wasn't Bobby. He was a hippie, and he didn't look or sound anything like him.

Instead of short, brown hair, he had long, blond hair. Instead of a broad-shouldered, muscular frame in Army fatigues, he had a scrawny, knobby body in a suede fringe jacket, white V-neck t-shirt, and torn jeans. Instead of a strong, deep voice, he had a raspy, gravelly one.

And he wore glasses, wire frames. Bobby had had perfect vision until the day he'd died. Not to mention, the hippie was carrying a bottle in a bag...and Bobby never drank.

"Yes, I'm fine." Erin scrambled to her feet and dusted herself off. "Thanks for asking."

"So what'cha doin'?" The hippie frowned a little as he stared at the Ouija board, candles, and incense. "Trying to channel the ghosts of the original Glosser Brothers?"

Erin shook her head, feeling suddenly self-conscious, embarrassed...and also a little worried about being alone with a strange guy at a deserted loading dock around 12 o'clock midnight.

"Hey, it's cool if you are." The hippie put his hands up in front of him, one still holding the bottle in the bag. "It's groovy. Whatever floats your boat, I always say."

"I'm trying to contact my brother." The words rushed out of her by surprise, before she could call them back. "He died in Vietnam a year ago."

Slowly, the hippie lowered his hands. "So how's it going? Any luck?" He gestured at the Ouija board setup.

"No," said Erin. "Nothing."

"Damn." The hippie wagged his shaggy head. "Maybe he just can't cross over, y'know? Maybe he really wants to, but he can't."

Erin shrugged. "I guess."

The hippie swigged whatever was in the bottle in the bag, then wiped his mouth on the sleeve of his jacket. "Or maybe he's already come to see you, and you just didn't know it. Maybe you just didn't recognize him."

Erin frowned, considering what he'd said. "I hadn't thought of that."

"So what do you want from him anyway?" asked the hippie. "What do you expect? Some kinda message, maybe?"

"I guess so," said Erin.

The hippie smiled and sipped from the bottle again. "Well, what if it was you, talkin' from the other side? What kind of message would you send if you could?"

Erin thought for a moment. "I don't know. 'Don't worry,' maybe? 'Everything will be okay?'"

"Okay, good," said the hippie. "You know what mine would be? 'Peace.' That's all. Just 'peace,' man."

"'Peace.'" Erin narrowed her eyes. "What kind of peace?"

"Every kind." The hippie spread his arms wide. "*All*

kinds. Peace for everyone, everywhere, in every way." Lowering his arms, he started to back away down the alley. "What better message could there be, huh?"

With that, he gave her a two-fingered peace symbol salute. As he turned and shuffled off into the shadows, Erin saw the cartoon face of the lady from the Gee Bee ads on the back of his suede jacket. She couldn't help smiling; the whole time she'd been talking to him, she hadn't even known it was there.

Then, he was gone, leaving her alone in the moonlight again.

Erin stood there for a while, thinking about what he'd said. What if he was right, and Bobby had already come back? After all, he would've done everything in his power to keep his solemn promise to her. What if she just hadn't recognized him?

Lost in thought, Erin slowly sat down at the Ouija board...then suddenly sprang to her feet. "Oh my God." Heart hammering, she ran down the alley and out onto Franklin Street, looking for the hippie.

But he was gone.

Erin ran up the block and turned the corner of Washington Street, but saw no sign of him there. Then, she ran back down the block and around the corner of Locust Street, again to no avail.

She ran through Central Park, too, looking behind every tree and monument. She bolted onto Main Street and peered in both directions, looking for that suede fringe jacket with the Gee Bee lady's face on the back.

And finding nothing. The hippie was gone.

Or was he ever a hippie in the first place? What if he'd been someone else in disguise all along?

"Oh, Bobby." She couldn't prove it. He'd said nothing, in fact, to lead her to think it was true. She might live her whole life forever wondering, never knowing for certain if that had been him.

But for now, for tonight, when she needed it most, she chose to believe.

And that meant taking his message to heart, didn't it?

"Peace." Fingering the dog tags at her throat—*his* dog tags, Bobby's dog tags—she considered the word. Wondered what it might mean to her.

Peace of mind, maybe...finally accepting that Bobby was gone and learning to move on. But there was more to it, wasn't there? *Peace for everyone, everywhere, in every way.* That's what the hippie had said.

So what exactly could she do with that?

By the time she'd walked back to the loading dock behind Glosser's, she knew. She knew exactly what she wanted to do with that message.

"Thank you, Bobby." She blew out one candle, then another. "Thank you for keeping your promise. And thank you for sending me a message."

Then, she blew out the third candle. "Now wait till you see what I do about it." And then she blew out the fourth candle, too.

Early the next morning—Halloween morning—Erin skidded her bike into the parking lot in front of Donna's father's garage. She hopped off and let it fall to the pavement without a second thought, in too much of a hurry to worry about leaning it against a wall.

The garage door was up, but she didn't see anyone inside. It was just after eight, so it was possible the float-making team hadn't arrived yet.

"Donna?" As Erin walked into the garage, her eyes went straight to the big, red float. It looked closer to being finished than it had the day before, with lots of papier-mâché boulders scattered around and a hellish altar draped in a red tablecloth in the middle. The "gates of Hell" were done, too—poles at the front corners of the float, spiked with the Styrofoam heads she'd decorated. Each head was painted with gruesome features and had patches of hair and rubber insects stapled in place. They looked pretty good, she thought, though she hadn't been at her best when she'd worked on them.

"Hey there, Eerie." Donna strolled out from behind the float with a steaming Styrofoam cup in her hand. "Welcome back to Hell."

Erin smiled. "I feel like I never left."

"Coffee?" Donna raised her cup.

"Yes, please," said Erin. "I didn't get much sleep last night."

Donna narrowed her eyes suspiciously. "And why is that, young lady?"

"There was something I had to take care of," said Erin.

Donna cocked her head to one side. "What was his name, pray tell?"

"Nothing like that." Erin brushed a hand through the air. "More like...trying to find someone I hadn't heard from in a long time."

"And did you?" asked Donna.

"I don't know. Maybe." Erin shrugged. "It's complicated."

"If you say so." Donna turned and walked around the back of the float, leading Erin to a coffeemaker set up on a dirty, cluttered workbench. She filled a Styrofoam cup with the steaming black brew from the pot and handed it to Erin, then topped off her own cup. "I'm just glad you're here. The girls who were helping me called in late, so I could use the help."

Erin sipped the bitter black coffee and bobbed her head toward the float. "Looks like you're almost done."

"I wish." Donna rolled her eyes. "I've still got a *ton* to do."

"Oh yeah?" Erin had another sip. "So, uh...I guess you wouldn't mind a little *redesign* then?"

Donna's expression instantly turned into a scowl. "What *kind* of redesign?"

Cup in hand, Erin walked over to the float. "Oh, you know. A little tweak here, a little tweak there."

"How *many* tweaks?"

Erin cleared her throat. "All of them."

"*All* of them?"

"Yeah, you know." Erin spread her arms wide. "Everything."

"Everything?"

"Pretty much."

"Are you *crazy*? We have to be in line by 6:00 for the parade tonight!"

"I know," said Erin. "But it'll be great. It's the best idea ever."

Donna stormed over, spilling coffee from the rim of her cup, and landed in front of Erin. "We don't have *time,* Erin!"

"But it's my sick creativity, remember?" Erin grinned. "You said you love it."

"I do, but we can't do this! It's just too late!"

"No it's not," said Erin. "I know exactly how we can make it work. Trust me."

"But I...but we..."

"Trust me." Erin reached over and laid her hand on Donna's shoulder. "This will be the best float in the parade by far. The best float *ever*."

"But Johnstown Hell was gonna be great! What about Morley's Demon Dog? What about Mr. Flood throwing buckets of water at the crowd?"

"That would've been great, too," said Erin. "But people will *never* forget this float. Trust me."

At that, Donna scrunched her eyes shut and let loose a cry of frustration. "This is nuts!"

"Donna, please." Erin gave her friend's shoulder a squeeze. "I need to do this. It's important."

"Gah!" Donna shook her head hard. "I can't believe I'm doing this!" She opened her eyes. "All right, Eerie! You win! But this better be as great as you say, or I swear to God I'll *murderize* you!"

"It will be," said Erin. "Now here's what we need to do..."

THAT NIGHT, not long after dark, the Fifth Annual Glosser Bros. Halloween Parade made its way up Main Street in downtown Johnstown. The sidewalks and curbs were packed with hundreds of spectators, crowding in for a look at the marching bands and Halloween-themed floats...crowding in also to catch some of the treats that were being thrown from the goodie bags of passing masqueraders.

Little did they know it, but they were in for something very different in the middle of the parade. That was where the float that Erin had redesigned was located, smack between the Windber High School marching band and a troop of boy scouts dressed up like Indians.

The float didn't look like much at first, though. Set up on the flatbed towed by Donna's dad's pickup, it was nowhere near as lively as the other floats that came before it. No one was waving at the crowd or throwing candy or acting out a skit. It was almost like no one was aboard the float at all, like the crew hadn't bothered to show up.

But they were there, all right. Erin, Donna, and half the varsity and JV girls' basketball squads were up there, hunkered down amid the abundant greenery that covered the flatbed.

Just as Erin had envisioned, the float was completely different from its original concept. Instead of a barren, red-slathered Hell surrounded by flames, it had become a jungle, piled with simulated (and not-so-simulated) vegetation.

The fiery cutouts around the edges had been wrapped in a tangle of leafy vines and limbs. Two palm trees stood at the rear, brown papier-mâché trunks topped with green-painted cardboard fronds. Down the middle, there were heaps of freshly-cut brush, piled together like little hills.

The only things remaining from the original design were the poles spiked with gruesome Styrofoam heads, one at each corner of the front of the flatbed.

The float rolled up Main Street for a few blocks, getting plenty of puzzled stares and comments from the crowd. What was it supposed to be? Why wasn't there anyone aboard? Why wasn't there a sign at least, so people would know who'd sponsored it?

But for a while, no explanations were forthcoming. The float just glided along, still and silent, as spectators complained and made fun of it.

Then, when it got to Central Park, the float stopped in the street. The parade behind it had no choice but to stop there, too.

That's when Donna's dad pushed the 8-track tape into the player in the cab of his truck and hit the play button.

Suddenly, "War, What Is It Good For?" by Edwin Starr came blasting out of the pickup's windows.

That was the cue Erin had been waiting for. As the music played, she popped up from under one of the piles of brush on the flatbed, dressed in a combat uniform straight out of Vietnam, complete with helmet and toy rifle from Glosser's Halloween costume department.

Turning slowly, she surveyed her surroundings as if she were in the jungle. She looked left, then right, keeping her rifle raised at all times.

Then, when her back was turned, Donna popped up from under the brush behind her. She was dressed the same way (courtesy of the clearance racks at the Army Navy Store up the street) except her helmet had "VC" painted on it in white letters...and she also had a toy rifle, which she swung up and pretended to fire.

Erin lunged forward as if she'd been shot, then dropped to the flatbed. Meanwhile, another girl in combat gear from the Army Navy Store, this one with a "US" helmet, popped up and pretended to fire at Donna, who also went down.

One after another, the varsity and JV girls—half with "US" helmets, half with "VC"—popped up and fell down before make-believe gunshots, until no one was left. For a moment, they all stayed down, concealed in the foliage, as the music continued to blare.

Then, one by one, they rose up—only now they had no guns and were wearing ghoulish, glow-in-the-dark green masks. Groaning loudly, they shambled around the float like zombies with their arms extended.

The music reached a crescendo and stopped, and so did the zombies. They stayed like that, frozen, as the next song started playing in the truck. It was "Imagine" by John Lennon.

Rain started to fall as the zombie soldiers all joined hands and sang along. It was just as Erin had imagined it, a perfect ending to get across the message that the hippie in the alley had given her.

"How'd I let you talk me into this?" whispered Donna. "It's about the corniest thing ever."

Erin didn't care. All that mattered was that she felt like she'd done something good for Bobby, something he would've loved if he'd seen it.

Not that everyone in the crowd appreciated it, though. Lots of people glared and booed and waved dismissively at the float. Some even stomped off angrily into the night. They didn't seem to understand what Erin was trying to say—that in death, everyone's the same, no matter which side they're on. Imagine if enemies could realize that before killing each other; maybe good men like Bobby wouldn't have to die. That's what Erin was saying.

She wasn't really taking a stand against the war or the people who were in favor of it. She was against what it had done to her brother and so many other people's loved ones. She was against letting it happen again.

She thought it was a good message, even if so many people in the crowd were against it. But the good news was, they weren't all like that. Some people—younger ones, mostly, but some older ones, too—were even singing along.

That included Erin's friends, Ruby and Ruth Shaffer. They were right there in the front of the crowd in their coats and babushkas, smiling and waving excitedly at Erin.

And all of them were there together in that moment in the rain, listening to John Lennon singing about a different world while the lights of the Glosser Bros. Department Store glowed softly through the red-and-gold-leafed trees of Central Park.

Glosser bros inc.

THANKSGIVING AT GLOSSER'S

Jessie Preston jumped when the big box on the floor of the elevator at Glosser Bros. Department Store talked to her...though of course she shouldn't have been surprised.

The box was a friend of hers.

"Lady?" A young man's voice spoke from inside the box, muffled by the cardboard. "Yeah, you. Could you help me out, ma'am? I'm feelin' kind'a *boxed in* here."

Grinning, Jessie fell back against the wall of the elevator, combing her fingers through her short, black hair. "Oh my God, you scared me!"

The elevator dinged as it passed the second floor on the way up. The box shifted as the person inside bumped around against the sides.

"Well, you've been a good sport," he said. "Now smile! You're on *Candid Camera*!"

Jessie laughed as the lid of the box flew open and Dick Boyle popped out, grinning, his brown hair mussed. Just then, the bell dinged again, and the car stopped on the third floor. The doors slid open just in time for a heavyset woman with dark-framed horn-rimmed glasses to see the man duck back into the box. Frowning, she let the doors slide closed without stepping inside.

As the elevator started climbing again, Dick stayed in the box. "I really blew my cover, didn't I?"

"I don't know about that." Giggling, Jessie looked down into the box. "She might be too afraid to tell anyone in case they think she's crazy."

"I hope you're right." Dick held up a hand, pinching the thumb and forefinger close together. "I am *this close* to catching the *wrapping paper* bandit."

Dick, who worked in security at Glosser's, used props like the big cardboard box to disguise himself while watching for shoplifters. Most people wouldn't look twice at a box like that—but Dick could see their illegal acts quite well thanks to the eyeholes cut in the sides of the box. All it took was for a shoplifter to check out his or her loot on the elevator with Dick watching from inside his box, and the jig was up.

The bell dinged again, and the doors opened on Jessie's destination, the fourth floor. Stepping forward, she stood on the threshold, keeping the doors from sliding shut again.

"Well, I have faith in you," she said. "Like they always say, no one foils Doyle."

Dick looked over the top of the box, eyes shifting from side to side. "Nothing can stop the master of disguise," he said. "Except maybe rain or a boxcutter knife."

Jessie's dark eyes twinkled as she laughed. She loved his sense of humor, and she loved the art of disguise. He'd been teaching her about it, in fact, and all the ins and outs of department store security at Glosser Bros.

She had a flair for it, though she was only 17 years old. As for Dick, he was 25.

"See you later, box boy." She waved and stepped back out of the elevator.

"Meet me in the bargain basement at one," said Dick as he sank out of sight in the box. "*If* you can figure out where I'm hiding *this* time. Hint: it won't be inside a *box.*"

With that, the doors bumped shut, and the car started back down the shaft toward the lower floors.

JESSIE HEADED STRAIGHT for the personnel department, which was located among the other offices on the fourth floor. Co-workers smiled as they whisked past her on the way to errands elsewhere in the store. It was Saturday, the busiest day of the week, and the place was jumping.

Before she could reach the personnel office, however, a familiar voice called out from another office—the big one on the corner.

"Jessie Preston! Hello!"

Turning, she saw the president of Glosser Bros., Alvin Glosser, grinning in the doorway of his office. As always, he looked friendly and unassuming, a middle-aged man who could just as easily have been a salesman in one of the departments as president of the entire company.

Upbeat as ever, he waved her over and headed for his desk. "So this is the big day, isn't it?" Alvin dropped into his leather swivel chair behind the desk. "I'm going to miss seeing you around!"

Jessie frowned. "What do you mean, Mr. Glosser? I'm not going anywhere."

He frowned back, scrunching up his eyes behind his dark-framed glasses. "But I thought you were leaving us! Isn't today your last day?"

Jessie shook her head. "No, sir."

"Well, good!" Alvin reached up and scratched his head, which was mostly bald with a fringe of brown hair from ear to ear. "I'm glad to hear it! Did your dad dodge the layoff after all, then?"

Again, Jessie shook her head.

"Sorry to hear that," said Alvin. "So many people are in the same boat these days."

It was true. Thousands of workers had been cut from the steel mills in Johnstown, and the layoffs kept coming. Jessie's dad had been one of the fortunate ones, making it all the way to November 1983...but his luck had finally run out.

"I'm so sorry." Alvin leaned forward, folding his hands on the desk.

"It's all right," said Jessie. "He found a job in Buffalo."

"So your family *is* moving out of town," said Alvin.

"*They* are," said Jessie. "But *I'm* not."

Alvin looked puzzled. "You're not?"

Jessie shook her head. "I'm staying here to finish out the school year."

"Staying here?" asked Alvin. "With whom?"

"Friends." Jessie smiled. "And I'd like to keep working here, if that's okay."

Alvin grinned. "Jessie Preston, you are *always* welcome at Glosser's."

When Jessie found Dick, he was in his priest outfit, rifling through dress socks on a rummage table in the bargain basement.

She couldn't help smiling when she spotted him, though she was careful not to blow his cover. For all she knew, one of the old ladies at the nearby tables might be in his crosshairs, about to be snared for shoplifting.

That was the whole reason for the disguises—to enable Dick to get close enough to shoplifters to catch them in the act. There was another reason, too, though, as Dick would be the first to admit.

It was *fun*.

Jessie appreciated *that* reason more than ever, as Dick trained her to follow in his footsteps. Sneaking around in disguise was a blast, and she loved it.

She was *good* at it, too, and that was a good thing. Her sneaking-around-the-store days were about to become a much bigger part of her life.

Though even Dick didn't know just *how* big.

"Bless you, my child." Dick saw her coming and made the sign of the cross in midair with two fingers. "Come closer, and we will pray our thanks to the Lord for these bargains."

Jessie stifled her giggles and joined him at the table. "Thank you, Father. These savings are indeed miraculous, are they not?"

"Verily," he said, and then he dropped his voice to a low whisper. "See that old lady in the black overcoat at the table by the steps?"

Without making too big a show of it, Jessie took a look. "I see her."

"She's got at least a dozen wristwatches stuffed up her sleeves," said Dick. "She just keeps pushing them up her arms when she thinks no one's watching."

"No kidding. She just looks like a law-abiding little old lady."

"Think you can take her, my child?"

Jessie shrugged. "Sure. Why do you ask?"

"How would you like to help with the bust?" asked Dick. "Your very first bust."

"Yes!" said Jessie. "As long as I don't have to get in the *cardboard box*."

"Forget the box." Dick brushed a sock through the air dismissively. "The box is in the back room. No disguises necessary for this bust, Jess."

"I like it so far!"

"It's time." Dick nodded. "Time for the little bird to leave the nest."

"Okay." He was right. He'd been training her for weeks, and it was time.

She waited another moment, until she saw the lady shove another watch up her arm under her sleeve. Then, clearing her throat, she approached her.

"Ma'am?" she said. "Please come with me."

The woman looked up from behind a pair of round spectacles. "Why is that, sweetheart? What do you need?"

"We need to talk to you about something." Jessie waved toward the door that led to the back rooms of the basement. "If you'll just come this way, please."

"If you'd just tell me, we could work it out right here." The woman spread her arms.

"It's regarding some merchandise." Again, Jessie gestured toward the back room. "Please, ma'am."

Without another word, the old lady bolted up the steps. Stunned that she could move so fast, Jessie hesitated, then charged after her.

The woman stumbled halfway up the stairs, and Jessie caught her, knocking her down. When they hit, the woman's hair flew off—it was a wig—and Jessie saw what she really looked like underneath.

She looked like a *he*.

For a second, the two of them froze, and she got a good look at him. He had blond hair and blue eyes and looked like he was in his 20s or early 30s. He actually grinned at her under the old lady makeup he had caked on his face...and then he winked.

Right before he pushed her off, scrambled back to his

feet, and raced up the rest of the steps without looking back.

Jessie tumbled down the steps and hit bottom, where Dick was waiting to catch her. Both of them watched as the old lady made it up the last few steps and barreled out of the store through the doors that led to Locust Street.

"Well how do you like that?" asked Dick. "Another master of disguise!"

Jessie frowned as she dusted herself off. "That jerk!"

"Maybe so, but he was *convincing* as hell!" Dick shook his head in admiration. "I really thought he was an old lady! And it isn't *easy* to fool *me*."

"I just wish I could've caught him."

"I don't think you've seen the last of him." Dick clapped her on the shoulder. "He'll be back."

"What makes you think so?" asked Jessie.

"He's your *archenemy* now," said Dick. "*Every* hero has one!"

LATER, long after her shift had ended and the sun had gone down, Jessie sat behind the wheel of her beat-up olive-green Dodge Dart and ate dinner—a cheeseburger and fries from a McDonald's paper sack.

It was times like these when she really missed her family—when she was completely alone, eating dinner out of a bag by the glow of a battery-powered camping lantern in her car.

Which was parked under the carport of the house where she used to live.

Sometimes, it was so sad, she almost couldn't stand it. Just days ago, she'd been living *inside* that very house with her family, doing the things that normal 17-year-olds did.

But that was all over now. Her family was gone, starting new lives in Buffalo, New York—and she'd been left behind.

By choice.

As she nibbled the last cold fries from the bottom of the bag, she thought back to the morning when they'd left town. The rented moving truck was full and idling in the driveway, the family car hitched up behind it. Dad had stood in the dim morning light, chugging coffee, and looked at her with fatherly concern.

"Are you sure you don't want to come with us?" he'd asked.

Jessie had nodded. "I'm sure. I want to finish the school year here, with my friends."

Dad had slugged back more coffee and stared grimly up the street. "I still don't like it."

"Come on, Dad," she'd said. "You know Judy Lynne and I get along like sisters. And her mom told you herself how she doesn't mind putting me up till the end of the school year."

"I know, but..." Dad had scowled and shaken his head. "A family shouldn't split up like this."

"It's okay, Dad. We'll see each other at Christmas time."

"And I don't like not being able to pay for your room

and board," Dad had told her. "We shouldn't expect the Lynnes to cover your expenses."

"Just till you get back on your feet, Dad. Isn't that what Mrs. Lynne told you?"

Dad's face had been flushed as he looked down and nodded.

"Meanwhile, I'll give them what I can from my Glosser's pay," Jessie had said. "It's all good. Don't worry about it."

Grudgingly, Dad had nodded. It had made Jessie feel good, knowing she'd taken a burden off his shoulders...given him one less thing to worry about in this difficult time.

Even if she'd had to lie to do it.

The truth was, Judy and her family were about to leave town, too, heading south. Judy's dad had just lost his own job at the Freight Car Division of Bethlehem Steel, and their family was leaving to stay with relatives in North Carolina.

Luckily, Judy's mom had trusted Jessie to tell Dad that she couldn't stay with the Lynnes after all, and Dad had been too distracted getting ready for the move and new job to check personally and make sure the arrangements were still in place. And Jessie, who wanted to stay in town no matter what and had a plan up her sleeve for doing so, kept Dad in the dark with a few white lies. It was all working out just fine.

Thinking about it had made her feel better, as sad as she'd been that day. Taking some of the burden off her father's shoulders had been a big part of the reason she'd decided to stay behind. He'd had it tough since her mom had died a year ago; the last thing Jessie wanted to do was make it tougher for him.

"Just remember," he'd told her. "If you need anything, call me. In fact, I want you to call me every day or two to catch up, all right? Just so I know you're okay."

"All right." A cool breeze had blown through the driveway, making her shiver. Fall was coming fast, and the cold weather was fast behind it.

But the thought of her father, little brother, and little sister warm and toasty in their new apartment made her feel warmer.

"Okay then, honey." Dad had held out his arms for a hug, smiling. "Wish us luck."

"Good luck." A tear had crawled down her cheek as she'd hugged him back.

"Take care of yourself," he'd said, and then he'd broken away and headed for the truck.

Leaving her to wave and watch as it pulled away, exhaust smoke puffing into the chilly air from the tailpipe.

Thinking about that moment again made her feel sick to the stomach. So did thinking about the way things used to be in the house beside the carport.

She remembered eating dinner with her dad, her sister, Eve, and her brother, Jack. She remembered watching T.V. in the living room, brushing her teeth in the bathroom, and sleeping in her bedroom on a mattress under clean sheets and blankets.

Now, she was going to sleep in her car, wrapped up in

a sleeping bag...no more than a few yards from the very house that had once been hers.

If only the realtor hadn't changed the locks and sealed the place tight. If only she could have gotten inside, returning to the little world she knew so well.

Though as empty as it was inside, it probably would have just made her feel sicker at heart.

At least she had a better life to look forward to. She had a way to get by, if she played her cards right.

Making sure the doors were locked, she crawled into the back seat of the Dart and stretched out, pulling the sleeping bag over her. She yawned and pressed her head down into the pillow, already feeling drowsy.

As she started to drift off, she hoped she'd be okay for the night. It was warm for November, in the 50s, so at least she wouldn't freeze. As long as no one bothered her, she thought she'd be fine.

After that, if her plan worked out, she wouldn't have to spend another night in her car.

The thought of it made her smile as she slept, covered by the sleeping bag under the carport of the home she'd once lived in and loved.

Where was Jessie's archenemy, the criminal master of disguise? She spent most of the next day watching for him during her afternoon shift at Glosser's, to no avail.

Sometimes, she searched the store in disguise, hiding

as Dick had taught her to. Other times, she hunted in plain sight, not even trying to conceal herself or what she was doing.

No matter what she tried, her archenemy wouldn't show himself. Was he lying low because he'd almost gotten caught? Or was he right in front of her, so cleverly concealed that she didn't sense his presence on any level?

Whatever he was up to, Jessie was determined to bring him in. One way or another, she would stop his shoplifting campaign and prove who the better disguise artist was.

Though it was also possible that Dick might take him down first. Sunday was supposedly Dick's day off, but Jessie kept seeing him around the store, lurking in various disguises. Coming in on his free time to hunt the bad guy was just the kind of thing Dick would do, she thought, even knowing she was on duty in his place.

She meant to ask him about it when she spotted him in the menswear department on the third floor, but she didn't get the chance. Before she could approach him, she saw a middle-aged guy stealing some neckties, and she had to cover that situation instead. She grabbed a salesman and confronted the guy, then called security on the store phone and had them send someone up to take custody of the tie-stealer...who, unfortunately, was *not* the archenemy master of disguise.

By the time the action was all over, Dick was gone.

She saw him again, later, in hardware on the fourth floor, but couldn't talk then, either. A sales associate summoned her for what turned out to be a false alarm, and Dick vanished by the time she looked for him again.

She finally gave up around 5:00—closing time—as other concerns weighed on her mind. It was the big night, after all, the test run she'd been getting ready for for weeks.

Stepping outside, she hurried down Locust Street to check on her car, which was parked in front of the offices of the *Tribune-Democrat* newspaper. She made sure the Dart was locked and safe for the night, then rushed back into the store.

After punching out at Personnel on the fourth floor, as other employees headed down in the elevators, Jessie headed up the stairs to the fifth floor.

Dick had shown her around every corner of Glosser Bros., so she knew the fifth, top floor like the back of her hand. Leaving the stairwell, she darted into the receiving department, where new stock arrived after it was shipped to the store. The place was deserted now, and she hid between boxes of merchandise in the far corner.

An hour later, when she thought the coast was clear, she emerged from her hiding place. Even then, she stayed a little longer in Receiving for good measure.

Not that she liked it much in there. The big room, with its creaky wood floors and piles of boxes, was creepy when no one else was around. To make matters worse, she bumped into something when she was backing through a dark corner and nearly screamed when she saw a human face peering back at her. Fortunately, it was only a mannequin perched on a stool, staring blankly into space.

Blonde hair gleaming in the last of the day's sunlight from the windows across the room, the mannequin nearly fell until Jessie caught and restored it to its original position.

Heart pounding, she hurried out of Receiving, then, and paused outside the door, listening. From what she could hear, the top floor was entirely silent and empty.

The entire store should be just as deserted. There wouldn't even be a guard in the house; the night watchman, Steve, was in the hospital, according to Dick. The Glossers hadn't found the right person to fill in for him, so the store was temporarily unguarded at night.

Still, Jessie was nervous as she pulled the silver flashlight from her pocket and switched it on. If a watchman was on duty after all, and she got caught, she'd be in a world of trouble. In her experience, the Glosser family had only been kind and understanding, but what she was doing now might push the bounds of even their generosity.

Swallowing hard, she eased open the door to Receiving and started down the hall. As she passed the Shipping department and headed for the dim red glow of the Exit sign over the stairwell door, she heard nothing but her own footsteps. Other than the Exit sign, she didn't see a single light anywhere on the fifth floor.

Easing open the metal door, Jessie followed the beam of her flashlight into the stairwell. She closed the door carefully, then worked her way down the steps to the fourth floor.

As on the top floor, she found the fourth floor was deserted, silent, and dark. No lights were visible among the home furnishings, housewares, or paint, or under any of the office doors.

She found the same conditions on the third and second floors, though the glow of streetlights leaking through the windows brightened both levels. The ground floor was even better lit from outside, though shadows moved in the flow of headlights from passing cars on Locust and Franklin streets.

As for the Bargain Basement, it was pitch black as she gazed down into it from the top of the stairs. Chills ran up her spine as she thought of going down there, so she decided to give it a pass for now.

Turning, she threw up her arms and let out a little whoop. Finally, she was alone in Glosser's after hours. She had the entire store to herself.

Feeling a little giddy, she twirled around and danced across the floor. Though she was locked in, she felt completely free. The place was all hers, and she could do anything she wanted.

Though, of course, that wasn't *entirely* true. Whatever she did, she couldn't leave traces for anyone to find later.

And she had to be gone before anyone came to work the next day.

Humming a tune, Jessie headed for the candy and nuts counter. It was closed but not locked, and she was able to open the access doors behind the glass display case. She helped herself to a handful of cashews, just enough to quell the hunger pangs she felt. They were usually served warm, and she loved them like that...but the sweet nuts were almost as good without being heated at all.

After the cashews, she had a piece of chocolate from the back of the case, one she didn't think anyone would miss. The milk chocolate and buttercream filling were delicious.

Staying clear of the windows as much as she could, Jessie roamed the big ground floor, playing among the merchandise. In the ladies' shoe department, she tried on high heels and boots, admiring herself in the mirror. She draped herself in accessories, wrapped herself in hose, even tried on men's ties and hats and gloves. With no one around to watch—and no security cameras installed in the place—she could goof around as much as she wanted, acting like a kid playing dress-up.

Jessie ran up the stairs, then, to the second floor. (She didn't want to take the chance of using the elevators in case she got stuck.) On Two, she ran between the racks with flashlight in hand, putting on lingerie over her clothes, then throwing men's suit coats over that.

But she had the most fun on Three, where the teen girls' department was located. She tried on one outfit after another—dresses, jumpers, blouses, slacks, jackets. It was her own private fashion show, performed by the glow of her flashlight.

Eventually, though, she grew tired and took the stairs to the fourth floor. She cleaned up in the ladies' bathroom, taking a sink bath with a washrag and towel from Domestics and brushing her teeth with a toothbrush and toothpaste she'd taken from the Toiletries Department. She'd have to bundle them up and hide them in the morning, leaving no trace of her overnight stay to be found—but she knew of the perfect spot in a far corner of the drop ceiling where she thought it unlikely that the things would be found.

Next, Jessie grabbed a pillow in Domestics and an alarm clock in Housewares and made her way to the bed that was furthest back in the furniture showroom, closest to the wall. She stretched out on it, yawning with exhaustion.

Jessie wound the clock and set it for six in the morning. According to Dick, that was a half-hour before anyone showed up for work at the store. It was early enough for her to sneak out in time to get to school by seven, as well.

With the clock ticking away at her side, she drifted off to sleep, smiling. It was good to be sleeping somewhere other than the back seat of her car.

It was *great* to be sleeping somewhere that felt like home.

"SWEETIE? HONEY?"

At the sound of a woman's voice, Jessie stirred from a deep, deep sleep. She fought to open her eyes but couldn't; she was just too totally exhausted to manage it.

"Come on, honey. Wake up now."

She felt herself being gently shaken, and that finally did it. Jessie's eyes fluttered open, and she looked up to see a familiar face.

"There you go." The round, friendly face, surrounded by a nimbus of white hair, smiled down at her. "Wakey wakey, eggs and bakey."

"Mary?" Jessie rubbed her eyes and yawned.

"The one and only!" She was known around the store as Hunt Room Mary because she'd worked in the Hunt Room restaurant at Glosser's for decades, though she also helped in the cafeteria as well.

Shaking off the sleepiness, Jessie sat up and looked for the alarm clock. It was next to her on the bed, where she'd left it—and the time was just before six o'clock.

Clearly, she'd been misinformed about the earliest arrival of employees at Glosser Bros. Mary was there a half-hour before the first workers should have shown up, according to Dick.

"Oh no." Jessie swung her legs over the edge of the bed. "I'm so sorry."

Mary, who wore a white uniform blouse and skirt and name tag, sat down beside her. "Honey, what are you doing here at this hour? If you're the acting night watchman, you're not doing a very good job of watching the store."

"I didn't know you came in this early," said Jessie.

"Someone has to have the kitchen ready for breakfast." Mary shrugged. "I don't always come over to *this* building so early, but I had to drop off some paperwork for Accounting first thing. I'm just glad I did, because I happened to see you over here."

"Thank you, Mary. I guess I lost track of time." Jessie started to get up from the bed.

But Mary held on to her arm. "Honey, you still haven't told me why you're here right now."

Dozens of lies flickered through Jessie's mind as she wondered what to say. She didn't know Mary that well, didn't know if she could trust her—but maybe truth was her best option in the end.

"Mary, I..." What she most wanted to do was run away, but she knew she had no choice but to face up to the situation. "I needed somewhere to sleep."

"But your family..."

"Left town," said Jessie. "My dad got a job in Buffalo."

Mary frowned. "And they *left* you here?"

"I insisted. I wanted to finish the school year here, with my friends and teachers."

"And you don't have *anywhere* to stay?" Mary's frown deepened.

"No." Tears trickled down Jessie's face as she shook her head. "I thought I did, but it fell through. My friend Judy and her family had to move after her dad got laid off. Now I'm...I'm just so alone."

At the sight of Jessie's tears, Mary's expression softened. She put her arm around Jessie's shoulders and pulled her close. "Shh, it's okay. It'll be all right, honey."

"I just didn't want to sleep in my car again." Jessie let the tears and sobs come; it felt good to let it out against a sympathetic shoulder. "I thought maybe...just for a little while...I could stay *here*."

"It's against the rules, dear," said Mary.

"I know, I'm sorry."

"But...sometimes rules are made to be broken." Mary

rocked a little, squeezing Jessie's arm. "As long as you're not damaging anything, and you're up and gone before the bosses get here..."

"I will be, I promise," said Jessie.

"Or maybe we could talk to the Glossers," said Mary. "They're good people, you know. They've always helped out others in need."

"No, please." Jessie pulled away. "I don't want them to know. Can't we just keep it between *us*?"

"All right." Mary reached over and dabbed tears off Jessie's face with her fingertips. "For now, we won't tell the Glossers—but it won't be just between *us.*"

"What do you mean?" asked Jessie.

Mary smiled. "I'm not the *only* one who comes in this early, and I'm not the only one who can help."

THE LIGHTS in the cafeteria were already shining bright when Mary led Jessie inside. The air was filled with cooking smells and the sound of pots and pans banging in the kitchen.

"Welcome to the Early Risers gang!" said Mary. "We gotta be ready for the breakfast crowd when they come through the door at eight."

Just then, the kitchen door behind the snack bar swung open, and a brown-haired woman in a white uniform emerged. She stood there, staring at Jessie—and then an identical woman in an identical uniform walked out to stand beside her.

Jessie recognized them instantly. *Everyone* who worked or shopped at Glosser's knew Ruth and Ruby, the Shaffer twins. Like Mary, they'd been working there for decades, running the snack bar, and were practically an institution.

"On your best behavior, girls! We've got company!" said Mary. "You both know Jessie, right?"

Ruth and Ruby both nodded, small smiles on their faces...though Jessie wasn't sure how well they *did* know her. She'd eaten at the snack bar many times but had never been overly friendly with either of them.

"Jessie needs a place to stay, just for a little bit," said Mary. "She'll be spending the night in the store for a while, and I told her we'd watch out for her. What do you say, girls?"

Ruth and Ruby looked at each other and seemed to come to a decision without saying a word.

"Okay," said Ruth. "As long as she doesn't cause any trouble."

"I would never do that." Jessie shook her head hard. "I promise."

"Then that's okay," said Ruby. "We believe in watching out for each other around here, don't we?"

"Glosser's is a family." Mary patted Jessie on the back. "A *crazy* one, maybe...but still *a family*. And family don't let each other down, especially at this time of the year."

"Thank you." Jessie was moved by her words. "Thank you all so much."

"Now then." Mary clapped her hands. "How about we get some food in your tummy, you poor thing? We can't have you getting so skinny, you make the rest of us *look* bad, can we?"

Jessie shook her head. "I don't want to put you out..."

"Nonsense! What say we get Dorothy to whip up some eggs and toast for Jessie here?"

Ruth and Ruby both nodded, waved, and headed into the kitchen, leaving the door swinging behind them.

"As for you..." Mary peered at Jessie from the corner of her eye. "What time do you have to be at school, young lady?"

"Seven," said Jessie.

"And how long does it take to get there?"

"Hardly any time at all. I go to Johnstown High."

Mary nodded thoughtfully. "Then that gives you plenty of time to eat...*and* pay for your breakfast."

"Pay for it?" asked Jessie.

"No freeloaders in *this* joint, honey." Mary chuckled as she led Jessie across the cafeteria by the elbow. "I have *plenty* of potatoes for you to peel."

Peeling potatoes at six in the morning was *not* Jessie's idea of fun, even using a potato-peeling machine...but she thought it was more than fair. Hunt Room Mary and the Shaffer twins could have given her the boot or turned her in; repaying their kindness with some manual labor was the least she could do.

The extra work also helped smooth the way for her to

stay at Glosser's in days to come. With the restaurant ladies looking out for her, she'd be less likely to get caught...and more likely to have a full stomach.

She also wouldn't have to sneak out a window to get out of the store before business hours the way she'd planned. The snack bar, cafeteria, and Hunt Room were in a separate building called the Annex, connected to the main store building by a second-floor walkway, and Mary had a key, at least until Steve the watchman returned to duty. She could simply let Jessie out the front door of the Annex (after Jessie took a quick trip to the fourth floor of the main building to clean up in the bathroom and cover her tracks), and she'd be on her way without crawling out of a ground-level window on her hands and knees.

All in all, it seemed like the perfect arrangement. Getting caught by Hunt Room Mary had been the best thing that could have happened to Jessie.

"Breakfast's ready," said Dorothy Bello, one of the cooks, from across the kitchen. "Do you want to eat at a table or booth, dear?"

"I'll just eat back here, thanks." Jessie smiled and patted the stainless-steel table beside her.

"Okay then." Dorothy brought over the plate of eggs and toast and put it on the table. "You want anything else? A cup of coffee or tea?"

"Coffee, please, with double cream and sugar." Jessie dropped her latest peeled potato in a black plastic bin and reached for the plate of food.

"Here you go. Fay will bring you your coffee." Dorothy gave her a fork and knife and smiled warmly. "And welcome to Glosser's morning family. We're glad to have you."

"Yeah, welcome!" shouted Loretta Nana, the head cook, who stomped over and grabbed the bin of peeled potatoes from her. Loretta was on the rough-and-tumble side, and Mary called her by the nickname "Gorilla." "We can always use another pair of hands around here."

"Thank you." Jessie picked up a piece of buttered toast and nibbled the corner. "It's good to be here."

"When you're done with the potatoes, how about giving me a hand with chopping the onions?" asked Loretta.

"I could use her help wiping down tables, too," said Mary as she hurried past. "Don't you be hogging her, Gorilla!"

"Will do!" Jessie smiled as she wolfed down her breakfast. Feeling wanted was a good thing. So was having food in her stomach and a place to sleep other than her car.

Her plan to stay at Glosser's was working out just fine, though she knew it couldn't last forever. Steve the night watchman would be back on the job at some point, or the Glossers would get someone to fill in for him. What Jessie would do after that, she didn't know.

But until then, at least, her new family at Glosser's was taking her mind off her old one in Buffalo.

"Save room for dessert, please." Ruth Shaffer approached with a glass parfait dish of vanilla ice cream in her hands, drizzled with fudge topping.

"Oh, thank you!" Jessie felt tears burning her eyes as she accepted the ice cream. "You really shouldn't have."

"Well, it's too late to put it back now, so enjoy." Ruth shrugged and headed back through the door to the snack bar.

Leaving Jessie to wish she could live at Glosser Bros. forever.

"ARE you sure you want to work *every* day, Jess?" Bill Glosser, the director of personnel (and Alvin's cousin), looked up at Jessie through a cloud of pipe smoke.

Jessie nodded from the other side of his desk. She'd gone straight to his office after school to get her schedule worked out...and, therefore, make sure she'd be in the store every evening so she could sleep on the premises. "I just wish I could work Thanksgiving Day, too."

"Well, if you're serious, maybe I could arrange to keep the store open that day." Bill smirked. "But you'd be the *only* employee on the job. Would that be okay with you?"

It *would*, but Jessie knew he was kidding. Bill was that kind of guy, always teasing—but he had a heart of pure gold.

"I guess six days out of seven will be all right," she told him.

"If that's what you want." A trim man in his mid-50s with gray-brown hair and dark-rimmed eyeglasses, Bill stared at the schedule chart on the desk in front of him. "Well, you picked a good week for it—one of the busiest of the year. Have you ever worked Black Friday before?"

"No, sir."

"It gets pretty wild. Are you sure you want to give it a try?"

"Yes, sir."

"Okey-doke then." Bill wrote her name in several boxes on the schedule, along with the shift hours she'd be assigned. Then he handed the schedule across the desk, looking up at her with eyes narrowed. "So why do you want all the work, sweetheart?"

"My dad got laid off from the mill," said Jessie. "I want to save up as much as possible so I can still pay for college."

Bill nodded as she took the schedule. "Well, that's very admirable of you. Be sure to let me know if there's anything I can do."

You just did it, she thought. "Thank you, Mr. Glosser. I will."

"Good, good," said Bill. "Have Arlene make you a copy of that and send the original back in here."

"I will." Jessie started through the door, then stopped and turned. "By the way, how's Steve the night watchman doing?"

"Better," said Bill. "Thanks for asking. You security people really stick together, don't you?"

"We really do," said Jessie, and then she left him there and headed off to start her shift in the store. She was all set now, scheduled to work almost every day of the week. That left her with just one unanswered question:

Where was she going to sleep on Thanksgiving night?

"HEY, YOU," said the male mannequin on the display pedestal in Menswear. "Yeah, you."

Looking up, Jessie couldn't help giggling. The supposed mannequin, dressed in a white driver's cap, button-down purple silk shirt, and tight white trousers, was Dick Doyle in disguise.

Dick stood perfectly still, with one arm at his side and the other raised as if in a wave to someone he knew. His smile was frozen in place, and even his skin had a tan, plastic cast to it. Honestly, if he hadn't gotten her attention, Jessie might have walked right by, never realizing it was him.

"Dick!" she said. "What a great disguise!"

"Shhh! Don't blow my cover!" He said it in a loud whisper without visibly moving his lips. "I'm waiting to ambush your archenemy...if he ever shows his *face* in here again, that is."

"I've been looking." Jessie whispered, too. "But I haven't seen him, either."

"He has to come back," said Dick. "He can't resist the *challenge*."

"I hope you're right." Jessie looked around but didn't see anyone who looked remotely like the other master of disguise. "I owe him some serious payback."

"I'm *ready* for him this time," said Dick. "He *won't* get away."

"I wonder if he's making the rounds at the Gee Bee

stores and the Richland Mall," said Jessie. "That would explain why we haven't seen him since that first time."

"It wouldn't surprise me," said Dick.

"Should we alert security at the mall? Tell them he's working in disguise?"

"I already have. They're on the lookout."

Jessie was impressed he was a step ahead of her. "I hope they let us know if they catch him first."

"They will. One of their guards is a protégé of mine."

"Good," said Jessie. "That's good to know."

"Don't worry, we'll get him, and we'll bring him to justice. Crime doesn't pay, Jessie. *No one* is above the law."

Jessie wondered what he'd say if he knew she was living on the sly at Glosser's, eating and sleeping free of charge.

THAT NIGHT, after Jessie's shift, things weren't quite as free and easy as they'd been the night before. She did no dancing among the racks, didn't try on any clothes or check herself out in the mirrors. She simply waited through closing time in the Receiving department on five, picked out a magazine from the racks across from the tobacco counter on the ground floor, then got herself cleaned up for the night in the ladies' room and returned to her comfy bed in the back of the furniture showroom on Four.

Flipping through the magazine by the light of a lamp

she'd set up on the bedside table, Jessie yawned, feeling exhausted. Between working in the cafeteria that morning, going to school, and working in the store that night, she'd worn herself out.

But she still felt happy. She loved the store, and she liked being among friends in her own little world. Except for the mystery of her archenemy, things were simple and relaxed there.

Her family's problems were far from her mind. So were her own thoughts of what the future might hold.

Putting aside the magazine, she wound and set the alarm clock, switched off the light, and rolled over on her side. Safe within the walls of the Glosser Bros. Department Store, she fell fast asleep, dreaming of her adventures with Dick, Hunt Room Mary, Gorilla, Dorothy, and Ruth and Ruby Shaffer—the surrogate family who were taking care of her while her real family struggled to survive in a faraway town.

THE NEXT MORNING, after finishing her duties—and breakfast—in Glosser's cafeteria, Jessie cleaned up, hid her things, hopped into her car on Locust Street, and drove to Johnstown High School. She only got midway through first period, though, before she was summoned to the office over the P.A. system.

"Hello?" She stepped up to the counter and spoke to

the closest secretary, who was typing something. "I'm Jessie Preston. I was just called in a minute ago?"

"Good morning, Jessie." The secretary, a middle-aged woman with short brown hair, was very businesslike. According to the nameplate on her desk, her name was *Mrs. Rager*. "We called you here because there's a problem."

Suddenly, Jessie felt nervous. "What's that?"

Mrs. Rager held up a sealed white envelope. "This letter was sent to your house, but it came back undelivered."

Jessie's insides clenched as she stared at the envelope. It was a problem, all right. Her father must not have ordered mail forwarding to the new address in Buffalo.

Swallowing hard, she tried to act like nothing was wrong. "Oh, that happens sometimes. Our mailman gets confused and delivers our mail to the wrong house or returns it to the sender for no good reason."

"Really?" Mrs. Rager flapped the letter, looking suspicious.

Jessie fought to stay on an even keel. If the school found out her family had moved out of town and she was living in a department store, she was sure her happy little world would come to an end.

"Yes, it's true," she said, sounding as convincing as she could. "It drives us all crazy. Dad's registered complaints at the Post Office, but it hasn't done any good."

Mrs. Rager stared at her for another moment, giving the envelope one more flick. Then, she got up from her chair. "Well, here." She handed the letter over the counter. "I'll ask you to deliver it to your father, then."

"I'll take care of it." Jessie nodded earnestly. "Thank you."

"No problem." Mrs. Rager nodded once and returned to her desk. "Now hold on till I write you a hall pass."

"Sure." Waves of relief washed over Jessie as she waited for the pass. She'd come oh so close to being found out, but she'd dodged the danger in the end. As far as Mrs. Rager was concerned, her family just had a bad mailman.

The coast was clear...but how long would it stay that way?

IT MUST HAVE BEEN Jessie's day for getting called to offices.

Two hours into her shift at Glosser's that evening, she was called over the in-store P.A. to Personnel. Frowning, she broke character (as a mother-to-be, complete with baby belly, shopping in the infants' department on the third floor) and headed for Personnel on Four.

"Hi, Jessie." Bill Glosser's secretary, Arlene Goss, pointed at the phone on her desk. "There's a call for you."

"Who is it?" asked Jessie.

"Your dad." Arlene gestured at a nearby desk that was empty except for a phone. "You can take it over there."

When Jessie got to the other desk, the phone there rang. She hesitated, sitting down behind the desk, and then she picked up the receiver. "Hello?"

"Hi, Jess." It was Dad, all right. "I finally tracked you down."

"Hi, Dad." Jessie lowered her voice. "How's everything?"

"How's everything with *you,* Jess?" asked Dad. "I haven't heard a peep out of you since we left!"

"I'm good," said Jessie. "Everything's great. Just busy with school and work. You know how it is."

"Jess, are you sure everything's okay? Because I tried calling your friend, Judy Lynne, and the line was disconnected. Didn't you say you were staying with her?"

"That was just a mix-up," lied Jessie. "The bill was a little late, and the phone company cut off service."

Dad was quiet on the other end of the line. When he finally spoke, he sounded deeply concerned. "Is there anything you want to tell me, Jess? Anything you think I should know?"

"No, no," she told him. "It's all good. Nothing to worry about."

Again, he was quiet for a moment. "Do you want me to come get you, honey? I mean, it's almost the holiday anyway. You should be with your family on Thanksgiving, right?"

"Thanks, but I'm fine," said Jessie. "And I don't want to miss work. Black Friday is the biggest day of the year at Glosser's."

"Okay, then." Dad didn't sound convinced...but at least he was backing down. "But if you change your mind, let me know. Call any time, Jess."

"Thanks, Dad," said Jessie. "Now I'd better get back to work. I'm in the middle of my shift."

"All right, honey." Dad cleared his throat. "Talk to you soon. Love you."

"Bye, Dad." Jessie hung up the phone, then lingered for a moment at the call desk. She suddenly felt her old life pressing in on her, the life of layoffs and sadness and worries. It was a life she *never* wanted to go back to.

Even so, Dad's voice echoed in the back of her mind.

THE NEXT MORNING, Jessie woke and crawled out of bed when the alarm went off. As always, she cleaned up in the ladies' room, then gathered up and hid her things. Yawning, she made her way to the cafeteria.

"Jess honey!" Hunt Room Mary said when she walked through the door. "Am I glad to see you! Come on and help me get these tables prepped!"

"Why?" asked Jessie. "What's going on?"

"We're closed Thursday for Thanksgiving, and Thursday is always the day we serve turkey for lunch," explained Fay Frick, the gray-haired head waitress, as she pushed up a cart full of things for the tables. "Since our turkey lunches are so popular with customers, the bosses decided to serve turkey on *Wednesday* for a change. They'd rather bump our Wednesday special instead...so *everyone* will be here today. This place will be *jumping* all day!"

Jessie followed Fay and Mary's lead, arranging placemats, water glasses, and bundles of napkin-wrapped silverware on tables in the cafeteria area. "I've always loved Turkey Thursdays," she said. "My parents brought me here a lot when I was a little girl."

"I'll bet we waited on you many times," said Fay. "Ain't that something?"

"We got an employee discount." Jessie reached for more placemats from the cart. "Mom used to work at Glosser's, actually."

"She did? What's her name, dear?" asked Fay.

"Linda Preston," said Jessie. "Though you might have known her by her maiden name, Hall."

"You're Linda Hall's little girl?" Mary grinned. "Oh, hon, she was such a sweetie! She worked the perfume counter for years!"

"Thanks." Jessie placed a water glass upside-down on the top right corner of each placemat, then put the rolled-up silverware on the left side. "I just...I really miss her."

Mary's expression turned sad. "I saw the obituary, hon. I'm so sorry."

"Me, too," said Jessie.

"But you know how proud she'd be right now, don't you? If she could see you working at Glosser's like she did?"

Jessie didn't answer. Breast cancer had taken Linda too soon, but Jessie felt like a part of her was still alive within the walls of the store.

"It's not easy, I know." Mary walked over and gave her shoulder a squeeze. "This time of year, especially. But you just have to get through it."

Tears burned Jessie's eyes, and she dabbed them away.

"You just have to be grateful for the time you shared

with her," said Mary. "And the family you have now. Count your blessings, hon. Try to focus on that."

"I will." Jessie sniffed, fighting off the tears.

"Keeping busy helps, too," said Mary. "In fact, I've got just the thing. Are you free at all tomorrow? On Thanksgiving Day?"

Jessie shrugged. "I guess so."

"Well, I could sure use your help." Mary winked. "It's a big project, and we need all the volunteers we can get."

"What exactly is it?" asked Jessie. "What would I be doing?"

"It's very worthwhile, hon...and it's about the same kind of work you've been doing in the kitchen already." Mary squeezed Jessie's shoulder again. "So what do you say?"

Jessie thought it over for a moment, but the decision wasn't hard. She'd already been wondering what she'd do for Thanksgiving, after all. "Okay, sure. Count me in."

"Don't be so stingy with that paint," said Dick. "Go ahead and get more on your brush."

Jessie couldn't help giggling, because the can of paint he was telling her to dip into was nothing but water.

Of course, she played along, because it was all part of their undercover act. She and Dick sat atop a scaffolding on the ground floor of the store, overlooking the jewelry department. They pretended to paint a wall, when in reality, they were just brushing water around while keeping an eye on potential shoplifters in Jewelry.

"That's better," said Dick, swiping his brush up and down as he observed Jessie's technique. "Nice, even strokes. Now you're getting it."

As Jessie dipped her brush into the can for more "paint," she stole a look at a young blonde woman who was milling around the earring racks below. The woman's purse was on the counter, wide open, near the racks—the perfect spot for earrings to "accidentally" drop inside.

"So what are you doing for Thanksgiving?" Dick asked her, keeping his voice on the low side. "Any plans?"

"Helping Mary with some secret project in the cafeteria," said Jessie.

"Good for you," said Dick. "You'll have a blast."

"So what is it, exactly? Mary wouldn't tell me much."

Dick smiled as he dipped more "paint" from the can. "You'll be helping people in need. That's especially important *this* year, with all the layoffs. At the rate they're going, there won't even *be* a Bethlehem Steel in town before long."

"So you'll be volunteering, too?" asked Jessie.

Dick shook his head. "Not this year. I'll be traveling out of town. In fact, this is my last shift for a week. I'm leaving *you* in charge." Smiling, he dabbed her arm with the wet tip of his paintbrush. "But I was *really* hoping to catch your archenemy before I left." He looked down, scanning the sales floor from side to side. "I guess it'll be up to you, though. I don't see a trace of him."

"I'll do my best," said Jessie.

"You might want to focus in on the furniture showroom on Four," said Dick. "I've noticed some things missing and moved around up there."

Jessie's blood suddenly ran cold. "You have?"

"Yep." Dick nodded. "Makes me wonder if this guy is somehow hiding out in the building."

"Wow." Jessie dipped her brush in the can again, trying not to make it too obvious that her hand was trembling. "That's hard to believe, right?"

"Maybe not," said Dick. "There are plenty of places to hide in this old store."

"Huh." Jessie's heart was hammering in her chest. Did Dick already know she was the one hiding out in the building?

"Well, do your best to find him while I'm away," he said. "Keep your eyes open for anything out of the ordinary. Not just shoplifters in disguise. *Anything.*"

"I will."

"And don't worry," said Dick. "If you don't catch him, we'll do it when I get back. Steve ought to be back on night watch duty by then, so we won't be so understaffed."

"Okay, great." Jessie held her breath as she swabbed more water on the wall. Maybe Dick wasn't onto her after all...or if he was, maybe he was giving her a veiled warning that the jig was up. Either way, one thing was clear.

Her safe haven at Glosser's would soon come to an end.

THAT EVENING, Jessie was extra-careful and quiet when sneaking out of her hiding place on the fifth floor and making her way downstairs. She was also more cautious than usual in retrieving the things she needed for the night and resolved not to leave the slightest trace when she put them away the next day.

She set up on a different bed, too, in the hope of throwing off anyone who might be following her trail. As careful as she thought she'd been from the start, it was time to be even more methodical in covering her tracks.

The whole thing left her troubled and uncertain of the future, unable to fall asleep. Tossing and turning on the bed, she thought about her meeting at the school office that morning, her phone call from Dad, her conversation with Mary about Mom, and Dick's warning that time was running out for whoever was hiding in the store. The alarm clock ticked loudly on the bedside table, and it seemed to her like an ominous countdown.

Maybe she'd known in her heart that her special refuge couldn't last, that she couldn't live in the Glosser Bros. Department Store forever. Maybe she'd known that at some point in the future, she would have to find another way of life somewhere else. But now, on just her fourth night sleeping at Glosser's, she realized how little time she seemed to have left in her happy little haven away from the sadness of the world.

Maybe her father had felt the same way, she thought, when he'd gotten his layoff notice from Bethlehem.

Mind racing, she continued to toss and turn, wide awake. Finally, she sat up in bed, utterly frustrated, and wondered if she could find something that would help her sleep—some warm milk, maybe, in the cafeteria.

It was then that she heard the loud bang from one of the lower floors.

Heart pounding, Jessie sat and listened, waiting for whatever came next. With any luck, if something had just fallen, there would be nothing, and she could relax.

BAM!

But she was out of luck.

For a long moment, Jessie shivered and wondered what she should do next. Maybe it was Dick down there, or Steve the night watchman had come back earlier than expected from sick leave. If someone had come to catch whoever was hiding in the store at night, she'd be in huge trouble.

But what if it wasn't security at all? What if Jessie was actually in physical danger?

CRASH!

As worried as she was, Jessie forced herself to move. She crawled off the bed, slipped on her sneakers, grabbed the flashlight, and started toward the stairs.

Maybe she could see what was going on without being noticed. Maybe she could even make it outside and run away if she had to.

Or she could always hide on the fifth floor until whoever was downstairs finally left. She thought about it as she opened the door to the stairs, thought about going up instead of down. It was probably the smart thing to do; at least it gave her a better chance of remaining undiscovered.

She almost did it, too, when she heard another bang from below—but then she decided to go down after all. As scared as she was, her curiosity compelled her to find out what was happening. Her sense of duty pushed her along, too; after all, she was still part of the Security team at Glosser's, even if she wasn't officially on the clock. If someone was breaking in, she couldn't just turn her back and run away without at least investigating and reporting the incident.

She took the stairs slowly, her sneakers softly scuffing the linoleum tile treads. When she'd descended two flights, she stopped at the door to the third floor and slowly pushed it open.

Except for the exit sign over the door and some streetlight glow from the windows, the third level was dark. Jessie ventured out a little way, watching and listening—and stopped dead when she heard another loud bang.

One thing was clear: the noise had *not* come from the third floor.

Returning to the stairwell, Jessie eased the door open and followed the beam of her flashlight down two more flights. When she peered into the shadows on the second floor, she found the same conditions as on the third. The entire level was silent and still.

BAM!

And, again, she heard noise from below.

By the time she slipped out of the stairwell on the ground floor, she was having a hard time staying calm. She was shivering, her gut twisting in knots, her breath coming in short, shallow bursts. She was terrified of going forward—but she had to.

Gently closing the stairwell door, she crouched and crept across the ground floor. Flashlight switched off so as not to draw unwanted attention, she looked in every direction, probing the shadows for a clue to what was happening.

CRASH!

The latest noise came from nearby, and she froze. If she stood up straight, she was sure she would have a good look at whoever was causing it.

SKRISSH!

Jessie winced as the sound of shattering glass filled the air. Then, it happened again.

SKRISSH!

Gathering her courage, she got ready to leap up from behind the clothing racks for a look—but before she could, the flashlight slipped from her hand and clattered to the floor.

A second later, she heard a male voice cry out in pain, and something heavy and metallic hit the floor. Then, the ground level of the Glosser Bros. Department Store fell deathly silent.

Paralyzed with fear, she stayed where she was, hunkered down behind a rack of men's coats. She heard nothing, sensed no movement at all in the big room. The intruder, whoever he was, must have been as frozen as Jessie; either that, or he was incredibly stealthy, able to move without making the slightest sound.

Finally, Jessie couldn't stand the suspense anymore.

Retrieving the flashlight, she prepared to rise, determined to see what she could.

Tensing, she counted down in her head: *three, two, one.* Then, she hesitated and counted down again.

Three, two, one...

This time, she sprang up, flashlight blazing in the direction of the jewelry cases.

Her heart was in her throat as she swung the beam back and forth. If someone was over there, however, she saw no trace of him, just the glare of the flashlight on the glass cases and glittering jewelry.

Slowly, Jessie emerged from behind the rack and crossed the floor to the jewelry department. Part of her wanted to turn around and run out of there, getting as far from the intruder as she could...but the rest of her needed to see, and know, and try—at least *try* to stop the damage to her safe haven, her happy place, her Glosser Bros.

When she reached the first of the glass cases, she looked around either side and into the middle—the square well with cases all around. Some of the cases were smashed, with shards of glass scattered around empty display stands. Other cases were undamaged and filled with jewelry, twinkling in the beam of the flashlight.

But the intruder was nowhere to be found...just shadows and racks and cases and tables, all the usual items in the middle of Glosser's ground floor.

Swinging the beam wider, she found a bare evergreen standing in the aisle—an undecorated Christmas tree. Someone had hauled it out of storage, along with cartons of ornaments and other decorations, in preparation for

Black Friday. Employees would come in early that day to decorate for the Christmas shopping season, decking the halls in every conceivable way to get customers in the mood to shop.

Jessie took a deep breath and let it out slowly, guiding the flashlight's beam over the cardboard boxes stacked in the middle of the floor. The boxes overflowed with wreaths, holly, and glittering garlands; festive signs and cardboard cutout standees leaned among them.

She came to a face, then, and sucked in a startled breath—but it was only the jolly face of a full-size Santa Claus figure. Jessie recognized it from window displays of years past, suited up in the usual red cap and jacket with furry white trim.

She relaxed, scolding herself for being easily spooked.

Then, Santa suddenly lurched forward. She let out a shout of surprise as the figure crashed into her, not so harmless after all, knocking her back into one of the unbroken jewelry cases.

The flashlight dropped to the floor, and Santa's bulk pinned her against the glass. As she fought to break free, she quickly realized the figure wasn't flesh and bone, though; it was the same molded plastic Santa Claus she remembered from the window display, propelled from behind by human hands.

Slumping against the jewelry case, Jessie marshaled her strength. She shifted left, as if she were going to make a push in that direction—then lunged right with everything she had.

Her attacker was fooled, and Jessie burst free. Before

he could make another move, she plowed into him, blasting him back into the cartons of decorations.

She tackled him right off his feet, knocking him into a huge carton filled with tinsel. Then, she quickly leaped away, leaving him sprawled there with his sneakered feet dangling over the edge.

"Who *are* you?" she shouted, backing away out of reach.

The man, who was masked and dressed in black, braced himself on the sides of the box and thrashed around, but he couldn't easily get out. Looking around, Jessie saw a crowbar on the floor, lit by the beam of the flashlight that had fallen nearby, and grabbed it—then swung it menacingly toward him.

With a heavy sigh, he settled back into the carton.

"I said, who *are* you?" she snapped.

Reaching up, the man pulled off the mask. "You already know."

Jessie snatched up the flashlight from the floor and aimed the beam at her captive.

Blinking at the sudden burst of light, he threw an arm up to shield his eyes. Even with his arm in the way, Jessie could see that he was older than she was, somewhere in his 20s or 30s, with a thin face and dark beard stubble. Now that she could put a face to him, he didn't seem so threatening—though she knew better than to let her guard down.

"Seriously? Don't you recognize me?" he asked.

"Should I?" asked Jessie.

The man cleared his throat, then did a bad impression

of an old lady's voice. "You chased me once already, dearie. I guess you finally caught me."

Realization flashed through Jessie's brain. "You're *him*? The disguise guy?"

Her archenemy chuckled from the box, returning his voice to normal. "Yeah, that's me. Mr. Disguise."

"What's your *real* name?"

"Joe," said the man in the box. "And you're Jessie, right?"

She frowned. "How'd you know?"

Again, he chuckled. "Now what kind of master of disguise would I be if you recognized me every time I came in the store?"

Jessie's frown became a scowl. "You're telling me you were here without us knowing it?"

"Precisely."

Jessie was annoyed. "You jerk." She wanted to give him a whack with the crowbar just for tricking her like he had. "You sure went to a lot of trouble just to rob a department store."

"I had to do *something*," said Joe. "I got laid off from the mill and can't feed my *family*."

Jessie lost the edge of her anger when she heard that. His story hit close to home for her.

"*Lots* of people are laid off these days," she said. "They don't *all* rob Glosser Bros."

Joe shrugged. "What can I say? I worked here years ago and know the place inside out. I knew what to do and figured I could get away with it."

"Well, you figured *wrong*, didn't you?"

"I guess I did." Joe chuckled. "And my sources on the inside were wrong about there not being a night watchman. Though I wonder why they didn't mention you specifically?"

Jessie ignored the question. "You have sources on the inside?"

"How do you think I managed to stroll in during business hours with a crowbar up my pants leg and hide out till the middle of the night?"

"Who's your inside source?"

"An old buddy of mine, all right? Part of the cleaning crew. He's a good guy, leave him out of it." He blew out his breath. "So what do we do now, Jessie? You going to cuff me and take me in or something?"

She thought for a moment. Trying to manage him physically was a chance she wasn't willing to take, and she couldn't leave him there while she found the nearest phone and called for help. He was stuck in the box, but she figured he could smash his way free if he wanted to, in a few unguarded moments. "I guess we'll just have to wait around till someone shows up."

"Sounds boring, don't you think?" said Joe.

"I guess that depends," said Jessie, "on how boring *you* are."

No, Jessie wasn't going to let him go free. It was an answer she had to give repeatedly, as Joe kept bringing it up...but eventually, he stopped asking.

The conversation was much less annoying that way. Joe told her about his family—a wife, three kids, and two dogs—and where they lived and what their lives were like. He told her about his 15-year career at Bethlehem Steel and how it had ended, leaving them all dependent on unemployment compensation and food stamps. He told her how, one day, when things had started getting bad, he'd decided on a life of crime—and he hadn't looked back ever since.

It almost made her feel sorry for having caught him. Her own path wasn't so different, really; she'd been living at Glosser's without permission, stealing (or at least borrowing) here and there to get by. She'd concealed the truth to keep from getting caught, and she'd turned to store insiders to help her with her plan.

The two of them weren't so different after all...but she still couldn't just cut him loose, even if it meant the end of her happy little world at Glosser's.

That was exactly what it meant, and she knew it. When she turned him in and reported what he'd done, she'd have to explain why she was there in the store late at night, and the full truth of her life at Glosser's would emerge. Not only would her overnight stays at the store come to an end, but she would probably lose her job. As good as the Glossers had been to her, she knew there were limits to what they'd turn a blind eye to.

To make matters worse, it didn't take long for Joe to

pick up on the situation. "You weren't supposed to be here, were you?" he asked. "That's why my sources didn't give me a heads-up about you."

"You don't know as much as you think you do," she told him.

"Sure I do," said Joe. "It's *also* why we're sitting here waiting around instead of you handling this like a *real* night watchman."

Jessie yawned. "I'm getting bored talking to you after all. Maybe we should give it a rest."

"Maybe we should come to an *arrangement* instead," said Joe. "Like we *both* get out of here, and *neither* of us gets in trouble."

"No deal." She smacked the crowbar again a metal pillar. "Now shut up."

It was true, though, that she considered his offer. He didn't seem like such a bad guy, after all, and they were both in similar situations. Wouldn't she want someone to help *her* if their positions were reversed?

She was still thinking about it two hours later, at four in the morning...and then it was too late. That was when the lights came on, earlier than she'd ever known them to come on.

At which point, Hunt Room Mary walked in, stunned at the scene before her, and rushed over to help.

"Jessie!" she said. "You caught a *burglar?*"

"Why don't you ask her what she's *doing* here at four in the morning?" said Joe.

"Shut up, you," hissed Mary. "You're just mad you got caught."

"That's not it!" said Joe. "She isn't supposed to—"

Mary cut him off. "Jessie, are you okay?"

Jessie nodded. "I'm just not sure what to do with him without anyone here but us."

"Oh, don't worry, hon." Mary put an arm around her shoulders and gave her a reassuring squeeze. "Alvin and Mr. Bill will take care of this tout sweet, baby!"

MARY PLACED a call on a phone at one of the checkouts, keeping an eye on Joe from across the store as she spoke.

Moments later, the elevator dinged, and Alvin and Bill Glosser hurried out. It was the first time Jessie had ever seen them in the store so early—and wearing white aprons over t-shirts and blue jeans, to boot.

"Happy Thanksgiving!" Alvin said it to Mary and Jessie...but then his smile became a scowl when he saw Joe. "Though not such a happy day for *you*, my friend."

"I was just trying to make ends meet after the layoff," said Joe. "Desperate times, y'know?"

It was then that Bill leaned in for a closer look at him. "You used to work here," he said, nodding. "Years ago. You were a decent employee at the time, too, as I recall."

"Good to be remembered," said Joe.

"Sure, I remember you." Bill turned to Alvin. "His name's Joe Snyder. He was an okay guy back in the day."

"And now here you are, robbing our store." Alvin

folded his arms over his chest and shook his head. "Right before Thanksgiving and Black Friday, yet."

"Bad timing," said Bill, staring Joe in the eye. "We're struggling too, you know. Folks get laid off, they don't spend as much in our store. This holiday season, we're just hoping to get back on our feet."

"Well, I'm sorry about that." Joe actually seemed contrite for the first time since Jessie had met him. "I guess I thought the insurance would cover your losses."

"Insurance doesn't cover everything, pal," said Bill. "And theft drives up our premiums. It takes money out of our pockets, and then we have less to pay our employees."

"I guess I didn't look at it like that." Joe frowned and rubbed his head. "I'm sorry. I really am."

"That doesn't solve our problem, though, does it?" asked Alvin. "Now that we've caught you, what do we do with you?"

"We have to involve the police." Bill shrugged. "We need a record of our losses and his role in the criminal activity."

"*Do* you?" Jessie was as surprised as anyone when she spoke up. "Could there be another way?"

Joe looked up at her but didn't say a word.

"What do you have in mind, young lady?" asked Alvin.

"I don't know, exactly," said Jessie. "But I don't think he's a *terrible* person."

"Careful, Jess," Joe said sarcastically. "You don't want to go way out on a limb there."

"He's in a bad situation," continued Jessie. "Just like so many people these days."

"True," said Alvin. "But *they* didn't break into our store and smash things up, did they?"

"He made a mistake, but he did it for the right reasons," said Jessie. "I think a lot of us can identify with that."

"You're right about that, certainly." Alvin nodded thoughtfully. "And it *is* Thanksgiving."

Just then, Mary cleared her throat. "Speaking of Thanksgiving, we need to get to work in the kitchen ASAP. We're falling behind schedule on our special project, fellas."

"We are, aren't we?" Alvin smiled. "Would it help if we had an extra set of hands?" He looked at Joe.

"Yes, it would," said Mary. "Assuming those hands don't get up to no good, and the feet that go with them don't skedaddle out the door when my back is turned."

"All right then." Alvin planted his hands on his hips as he looked down at Joe. "I'm going to make you an offer, Mr. Snyder. If you don't like it, your only alternative is being turned over to the Johnstown Police."

"Shoot," said Joe. "I mean, let me rephrase that..."

"The offer is this," said Alvin. "If you join our team for the Thanksgiving special project today, we'll cut you some slack."

"Great, fine, perfect," said Joe. "That's not asking for much."

Alvin held up an index finger. "Oh, but there's more. We need your help today, and then you'll need to work off the damages to the store after that."

Joe frowned. "You mean you're giving me a job?"

"Correct," said Alvin. "Starting Black Friday."

Bill grinned wickedly. "Working on Black Friday is a punishment in itself."

"Your pay will mostly go toward the damage you did, at least until it's repaired and paid off. Then it all goes in your pocket." Alvin reached down for a handshake. "Fair enough?"

Joe thought for a moment, then returned the handshake. "Fair enough."

Alvin looked at Jessie next. "Happy now? We did find another way."

Jessie smiled. "Happy, Mr. Glosser."

He stepped over and shook her hand, too. "And you'll notice," he said softly, "I'm not asking why certain people were here after closing time in the middle of the night when they shouldn't have been."

"Yes, Mr. Glosser," said Jessie.

"Please, call me Alvin," he said, and then he released her hand. "Now let's go, everyone. We'd better get back to the kitchen before Hunt Room Mary comes after us with a *skillet*."

As soon as everyone got to the kitchen, Mary put them to work...and kept them that way.

The objective was to prepare multiple Thanksgiving dinners for early afternoon service. Other volunteers were already hard at work—including Loretta, Dorothy, Fay, the Shaffer twins, and Alvin's wife, Joan—but there was still more than enough to keep Jessie, Joe, Alvin, and Bill busy.

Basting the turkeys was one of Jessie's jobs. There were four of them in the two big ovens; they'd already been cooking for hours thanks to Loretta, who'd dropped by and gotten them started in the middle of the night. They smelled so delicious, Jessie's stomach growled as she squirted water onto their golden skins with the baster.

When she wasn't basting turkeys, Jessie helped Mary, Dorothy, and the others with peeling, boiling, chopping, and mashing sacks of potatoes. Alvin, Bill, and Joe worked harder at that than anyone, turning it into a competition to see who could mash the most in the shortest time.

Jessie worked with Loretta on the candied yams, too, laying them into trays, covering them with sauce and marshmallows, and sliding the trays into the ovens with the turkeys.

They all made vats of corn and peas, too, and mixed up huge pans of cranberry-walnut Jell-O salad and put them in the refrigerator to set.

They only stopped for a quick breakfast of scrambled eggs, toast, and coffee served in the cafeteria. They all sat around a row of pushed-together tables, chatting and laughing regardless of their station in life. Even Joe, who'd tried to rob Glosser's just hours before, was talking and eating as if he and the others were the best of friends.

Then *bam*, they were back to work in the kitchen. More potatoes were boiled and mashed, more yams were candied and baked, and more veggies were cooked. Mary and Mr. Bill made rolls from scratch and lined them up on trays, ready to bake. Joe and Dorothy made fresh green salads in big bowls and stretched plastic wrap tight as a drum over top of them.

In between basting the turkeys, Jessie helped Ruth and Ruby Shaffer fix pumpkin pies, one after another. The filling was made from fresh pumpkins delivered from Dorothy's farm in Tire Hill, spiced with nutmeg.

Everything was ready to go on schedule at noon as planned. That was when Jessie finally got to see what the rest of the Thanksgiving project entailed.

"Load 'em up, gang!" said Mary. "Let's get these goodies to the folks who need them!"

With that, the cooking team pulled everything out of the ovens and refrigerators, covered it with plastic wrap and foil, and marched outside with it. Four Glosser Bros. delivery trucks were waiting there for them, parked on Locust Street with their engines running.

The trucks were painted with brown and white stripes like Glosser Bros. shopping bags and bore the company logo on their sides. They delivered shoppers' purchases far and wide without a shipping charge of any kind, with no size limitations or restrictions.

And now they were going to deliver Thanksgiving dinner.

Bowls and trays and pans were arranged on the shelves inside each truck, held in place by cords and rails. When the loading was done, each truck carried everything needed for meals for at least one large family or several small groups.

"Move 'em out!" said Loretta. "Go feed those hungry folks!"

"You tell 'em, Gorilla!" said Mary. "Get this show on the road!"

Jessie ended up in the front seat of a truck with Alvin, who was doing the driving. He handled the truck like a pro, weaving through the streets of Johnstown as if he drove the same vehicle on the same route every day.

"This was Joan's idea, you know," said Alvin. "She's always thinking of ways to help people in need."

"Well, I think it's pretty great," said Jessie.

"Taking Thanksgiving dinner to folks affected by the layoffs." Alvin nodded. "It's the least we can do."

"I'm glad to be part of it," said Jessie. "It feels good."

"Even though your own family's been through hard times lately," said Alvin. "Good for you. That's what we call true *tzedakah*."

Jessie frowned. "What's that?"

"Acts of charity. A Jewish tradition. Our family has done good works for as long as we've lived in this town. We know how important it is to give to others."

"Cool tradition," said Jessie.

He pulled up at a stoplight then and turned to her. "But I'm sorry, that doesn't mean you can keep living at the store."

Someone must have told him the full truth, and Jessie didn't bother denying it. "I understand."

"Maybe we can figure something else out, though." The light changed, and Alvin pulled forward. "But first, let's get this food delivered and served."

JESSIE AND ALVIN served Thanksgiving dinner to a group of families at a church hall in Moxham Borough. They set up a buffet line for most of the food, with Alvin carving and dishing out the turkey at a special station.

It turned out there was more than enough to go around, so the families called in some needy friends and relations to polish it off. Soon enough, every tray, pan, bowl, and plate was empty and ready to be carted away.

Alvin and Jessie loaded the truck and returned to Glosser's Cafeteria, where Mary, Loretta, Dolores, Fay, the Shaffer Twins, and the other restaurant staff were waiting with more food (including a turkey that Mary had cooked and brought in from home). Joe Snyder was still there, too, helping with cleanup.

"C'mon, Joe." Alvin took him by the arm. "Give us a hand loading this stuff on the truck, will you?"

When they'd gotten the last of the food aboard, Alvin told him to sit up front. "You can come, too, Jessie, if you don't mind squeezing into the cab."

"I don't mind," she told him.

When the three of them had packed into the front compartment, Alvin started the truck and pulled away from the curb. "Two more stops," he said. "Then you're both home free."

The first stop turned out to be Joe's house in the West End, which surprised Jessie. Even after everything Joe had done, the president of Glosser Bros. was personally delivering Thanksgiving dinner to his family?

If also surprised Joe, who teared up when he saw where they were going. He even gave Alvin a big hug after they'd unloaded dinner and set it up in the dining room.

"Thank you," he told Alvin. "You've really given me something to be thankful for."

"That's good to know," said Alvin. "You and your family enjoy the holiday, and I'll see you Friday at the store."

The second stop was also familiar—to Jessie, this time. But Alvin didn't get out of the truck at first.

"Home sweet home," he said, smiling.

Jessie almost didn't get out of the truck, either. "My old house? But nobody's here."

Alvin gestured at the house. "Look again."

It was then that Jessie saw the rear-end of a familiar car in the carport.

"Oh my God." She saw a door open on the driver's side of that car, and a figure got out. Turning, she looked at Alvin with tears in her eyes. "How did you...? When did you...?"

"Trade secret." Alvin grinned. "Now get out there and be thankful!" He shooshed her out with a wave of his hand.

As Jessie got out of the truck, the figure emerged from the shadows of the carport. Grinning, he opened his arms wide for her.

She ran to him and let his arms wrap around her. She'd missed him more than she'd thought since he'd gone away.

Living at Glosser's and being with friends like Hunt Room Mary, Gorilla, Dolores, Mr. Bill, Dick Boyle, and the Shaffer Twins had been wonderful, just what she'd needed...

But seeing her flesh-and-blood father on Thanksgiving Day was like coming home.

"I missed you, honey," said Dad. "We all did."

He turned and gestured, and the rear doors of the car swung open. Her little sister and brother, Eve and Jack, darted out and excitedly joined the hug.

Jessie laughed. "I missed you all, too. But you shouldn't have driven all the way from Buffalo like this."

"Sure we did!" said Jack. "It's not right for a family to be apart on Thanksgiving Day!"

"That's what we're most thankful for, isn't it?" chimed in Eve. "Each other!"

"We still have that," said Dad. "No matter how tough life gets."

Jessie let her head fall against his shoulder. "But I didn't want to be a burden. I wanted to take care of myself."

"You goof." Dad patted her back. "You were more of a burden by *not* being with us. The longer we were apart, the more we worried about you."

"But I did all right, Dad," said Jessie. "With a little help from some friends."

"Good for you, honey," said Dad. "But I hope you'll consider coming home with us anyway. We *need* you, Jessie."

"No one makes us laugh like you do!" said Jack.

"And no one's as good at playing games," said Eve.

"But I'd have to change schools in the middle of the year," said Jessie. "And I'd have to find a new job and friends."

"We'll work it out," said Dad. "After what we've been through, there's nothing we can't handle together."

Jessie leaned back, wiping tears from her eyes. "Can I think about it? Today, at least?"

"Sure," said Dad. "We'll hold off going back to Buffalo until Friday. There's just one problem. We can't exactly stay *here* tonight." He gestured at the house that had once been theirs.

Jessie turned to Alvin, who by now had gotten out of the truck and was standing nearby, listening. She couldn't exactly ask if her whole family could stay at Glosser Bros., could she? But money was tight, so a motel was out of the question, and she didn't know where else they could stay.

Alvin, fortunately, had it figured out. "If you're looking for somewhere to stay the night, you should talk to Mary," said Alvin. "When I told her your family was coming to town, she offered to put you all up."

"She did?"

"Joan and I wanted to, but Mary wouldn't take no for an answer," said Alvin. "And she already has more than enough Thanksgiving dinner cooking for *all* of you."

Fresh tears ran down Jessie's cheeks, and she dabbed them away. "Oh, thank you! I can't thank you enough!"

"Thank Mary," said Alvin. "She might not be Jewish, but she's all about the *tzedakah*."

Jessie ran over then and gave him a hug, too. As she

did, she thought about her days living at Glosser's, dancing and trying on clothes and eating and sleeping in that magical place. She thought about the friends who'd helped her, and the archenemy master of disguise who'd given her a run for her money. She thought about pitching in in the kitchen and cafeteria and Hunt Room, seeing a different side of the store and the people who worked there.

And she thought about how it had helped her get back on her feet, feel better about life, and feel hopeful again about facing its challenges. She didn't feel so scared or boxed-in anymore.

Thanks to Glosser's, she felt ready to face whatever came next in her world, side-by-side with the people who loved her most.

"Happy Thanksgiving," she told Alvin. "Thank you for everything."

"Happy Thanksgiving, Jessie," he said. "*Mazel tov* to you and your family, for such a reunion is truly something to be grateful for on *any* day of the year."

GLOSSER BROS
GLOSSER BROS

CHRISTMAS AT GLOSSER'S

WHAT HAPPENED in the secret sub-basement of Glosser's department store in Johnstown, Pennsylvania every Christmas Eve? Jack Perkins found out in 1975, when he was eleven years old.

And then, he found out what it felt like to die.

"WHERE DID you say you were going?" Mom stared at Jack through slitted eyes, holding one hand over the phone receiver in her grip.

"The library." Jack scrubbed his fingers through his short sandy hair in frustration. Mom had been talking on the phone and hadn't heard him the first two times he'd said it. "There's a book I need to get."

Mom waved him off. "Go on, then." She didn't ask if he

was sure the library was open on Christmas Eve, didn't tell him to be careful or hurry home. She wasn't always big on that sort of thing, since her latest boyfriend had moved out.

Jack pulled on his navy blue jacket over his red sweatshirt and blue jeans. "See ya."

Mom didn't answer. Her hand was already off the receiver.

As Jack zipped up the jacket and marched toward the front door, he heard her talking excitedly into the phone again. "He'll definitely be at church tonight, Deb? You really think he'll like me?"

Scowling, Jack threw the door open and slammed it shut behind him. As he ran off down the street, all thoughts of Mom's dating life shot right out of him. He had bigger things on his mind, a mystery he needed to solve.

One involving the only man he truly cared about in the whole world.

THE DOOR on the yellow-sided house two blocks from where Jack lived opened slowly, and a heavy tread came down on the front porch. As Jack watched from behind a tree on the other side of the street, a tall man with wavy silver hair stomped down the four steps from the porch to the sidewalk.

The man wore a dark gray jacket, zipped halfway up

over a big pot belly. Under the jacket, he wore the same thing he wore every day—a crisp white button-down shirt and black tie. His trousers were black, too, and so were his immaculately shined Oxford shoes.

If Jack had called out to him at that moment—*Hey, Bub!*—the man would have grinned and waved him right over. Not only was he Jack's grandfather, Mom's dad, but he was Jack's biggest supporter, always there when he needed him.

Except for one night out of the year, that is. One night when he was nowhere to be found.

Christmas Eve.

Jack waited for Bub to get half a block down the street, then followed, taking care to stay far enough back that he wouldn't likely draw Bub's attention. Whenever he could, he lingered behind trees or lamp posts or parked cars, ever ready to duck down if needed...but Bub never looked back.

He just kept rambling down the street, eyes dead ahead, steering toward his mysterious errand.

Suddenly, a neighbor lady, Mrs. Williams, pushed open her car door in front of Jack. "Well, hello there, Jackie." She was in her eighties and stooped with arthritis but got around fine, even drove herself on errands. "Do you think you might help me with my groceries?"

Jack shook his head. "I'm sorry, Mrs. Williams, but I can't. I'm in a hurry."

"But it will just take a minute, Jackie."

"Next time, sorry." Jack's guts jittered when he looked up ahead where Bub should be. He was nowhere in sight.

Mrs. Williams was saying something, but Jack ran off without another word. No way was he going to wait another year to find out Bub's secret.

There was an intersection up ahead, and Jack charged toward it. Stopping on the corner, he looked right, then left, then stomped his foot angrily. He saw no sign of Bub in either direction.

Thinking fast, Jack sprinted forward, hoping for a glimpse of Bub down one of the cross-streets or alleys. He didn't spot him at the first street or even the second, but he caught a glimpse at the third—a flash of Bub's silver hair and gray jacket sliding past.

Jack gasped in relief and veered right down the side street. Reaching the end, he leaned out in time to see Bub disappear around a corner.

"Geez!" Jack panted as he darted after him. The old man was giving him a run for his money as he navigated the maze of the neighborhood in Dale Borough, not far from downtown Johnstown.

Peeking around the corner, Jack saw Bub continue straight ahead. He fell in behind him, keeping his distance as before.

And wondering what exactly Bub intended to do downtown, since that was where he was headed.

SNOW FLURRIES FLICKERED down around Jack as he followed Bub out of Dale. The closer he got to downtown, the more flurries fell, and the colder the wind got.

The skies darkened, too, as afternoon spun toward evening. Plenty of the cars whisking past on Bedford Street had their headlights on, though the streetlights above remained dark.

The snow picked up, and so did Jack's curiosity. Where could Bub be heading on Christmas Eve, alone? Why was he going there?

Every year, he did the same thing, without explanation. Jack always ended up going to midnight mass at St. John's with his grandmother, Gram. As for Mom, she never came along, either, but her travels weren't so mysterious; there was always a new boyfriend in the picture, complete with drama or celebration or both.

Bub left the bigger gap, as far as Jack was concerned. He'd been Jack's father figure and best friend for the past seven years, for most of Jack's life. Not having Bub around cast a shadow on Christmas Eve; he was always back for Christmas Day, but it was never enough.

And every year, the mystery of his whereabouts haunted Jack a little more. It had become one of the overriding mysteries of his life, right up there with *Why did my Dad leave when I was four years old and is he ever coming back?*

Now, as Jack got closer to an answer, his heart beat faster. He was on the verge of discovery, he could feel it; nothing would be the same after that.

Bub ambled across Haynes Street and kept going,

making a beeline into town. He glanced in the front window of the Bedford Street Newsstand, waved at someone inside, but didn't slow down.

When Jack reached the newsstand, he looked in and saw an old-timer looking back at him, scrawny and shriveled in a pale blue polyester leisure suit. The old man eyed him as he passed, giving a little half-nod before returning his attention to the magazine rack.

By the time Jack looked forward again, Bub was two blocks ahead, rounding the corner of Main Street. No question, he was making good time; for a man with a big pot belly, he could really move when he wanted to.

Imagining he was Colonel Steve Austin, the bionic hero from his favorite TV show, *The Six Million Dollar Man,* Jack broke into a full-tilt run. Arms and legs pumping, he blasted across Vine Street—getting honked at by a car about to make a left turn—and covered the remaining distance to Main in nothing flat.

Worried that he might have lost Bub, he eased around the corner for a look down Main...and felt a wave of relief. Bub had stopped a block away, across from the McDonald's restaurant, and was talking to an old woman dressed in red. Her hat, coat, dress, and shoes were all red; maybe she was going to a holiday function...but if so, where was the green to go with the red?

As Jack watched, Bub reached out and put a hand on her shoulder. Had this been his goal from the start? Meeting up with a secret girlfriend?

But then, with a few more words, he let go of her and

continued on his way down Main Street. Meeting the woman wasn't his last stop after all.

Jack still thought there was something funny about her, though. As he walked past her on his way to follow Bub, he took a good look...and felt a shiver up his spine. Her eyes, when he gazed into them, were misaligned, each looking off to either side instead of straight ahead. Jack couldn't tell if she was looking right at him or not.

He was all too happy to get past her, especially as Bub was already turning another corner. He was a block ahead on the other side of Main, zipping right on Franklin Street.

Channeling the Six Million Dollar Man, Jack bolted after him. As he ran, he heard the sound effect from the TV show in his head, the sound like high-tech motors and parts cranking and straining in artificial legs: *ch-ch-ch-ch-cha, ch-ch-ch-ch-cha.*

The latest course change brought him to the heart of the action, the middle of town. Central Park, on the left, was filled with little cottages, each decorated with Christmas paraphernalia. The trees in the park were all decorated, too; just as Jack rounded the corner, every one of them lit up at once, hundreds of bulbs glowing blue, red, yellow, and green amid the falling flurries.

The park and the sidewalks around it were busy with people, most of them hurrying with arms full of shopping bags. The bags were all stamped with a familiar logo, a name printed with a flourish on the brown-and-white-striped paper. It showed where they'd been...and where Bub was now headed. Whether it would be his last destination remained to be seen, but Jack knew it was where he was going right now.

Glosser Bros. The big department store facing the park, on the corner of Franklin and Locust.

Bub was crossing Locust, marching toward Glosser Bros. department store...for what reason, Jack still didn't know.

AS JACK HUNG BACK, staying on the park side of Locust, Bub ambled up to the door on the corner. Another old-timer was standing there, spindly as a scarecrow in a black-and-white houndstooth sport coat, bright green Alpine hat with a big white feather in it, and brown-and-red plaid pants.

Grinning, the old-timer shook Bub's hand with gusto. Jack couldn't hear a word they said, but they rattled on like old buddies for a while.

Then, the old-timer hugged Bub and shuffled into the store with a jaunty wave. Bub didn't follow him in, to Jack's surprise; instead, he walked down Locust Street along the side of the dark brick building, weaving between the knots of last-minute shoppers and people gazing at the window displays.

That was Jack's cue. Darting across Locust, he threaded through the crowd in Bub's wake.

But he didn't make it past the windows as fast as Bub did. They were one of his favorite Christmas traditions;

every year, Glosser's employees decorated them to the hilt, filling them with holiday scenes centered around mechanical figures.

Jack had already seen this year's editions, but he couldn't help stealing glances again. There was one with Santa checking names off a giant list with an orange quill pen while elves built toys around him. In another, a drummer in a tall black hat and red uniform beat a drum in front of a Christmas tree dripping with white lights and tinsel. Another window was done up like an undersea kingdom with a blue backdrop; Santa, wearing scuba gear, rode a sleigh pulled by dolphins, surrounded by branches of coral draped with glittering lights.

Jack didn't consider himself a little kid anymore, but he still loved those windows. They brought back memories of years gone by, gazing through that same glass with Bub and Gram...or, further back, with Dad. Sometimes, he felt like he could just reach right through and touch them, if the moment was right and no one was looking. Or maybe he could just ask Dad a question, get him to lip-read if he couldn't hear the sound...then Jack could lip-read his answer in return. He'd looked for that moment, looked for Dad's reflection more than a few times.

Just as he now looked away from the windows for the answer to the Christmas Eve mystery. Up ahead, he saw Bub hang a sharp right, entering the store through the last door on Locust Street.

Pacing himself, Jack took his time getting to that door. He didn't know exactly where Bub was going and didn't want to get caught following too closely.

When he got to the door, he cupped his hands around his eyes and peered through the glass. Bub was nowhere to be seen.

As soon as Jack opened the door, his nose filled with the smell of tobacco and roasting nuts. It was the smell that always came to mind when he thought of Glosser Bros., the rich aroma that permeated his favorite part of the store, the last lobby on Locust Street.

The tobacco counter was on his left, a nook where pipe tobacco, cigars, and cigarettes were sold. Magazine racks lined the wall on his right; two white wire spinner racks stood in front of them, stuffed with bags of comic books. Jack had gotten comics there for as long as he could remember, three to a bag; sometimes, he picked them out himself, and other times, Bub brought them home as a treat. None of the comics had covers, which was why they were sold so cheap, but Jack loved them just the same.

It looked like the racks were freshly stocked, and Jack had to force himself to look away. Moving on, he paused at the candy and nut counter, the source of the aroma of roasting peanuts and cashews wafting through the lobby. His mouth watered at the sight of the trays of candy and piles of nuts behind the glass case.

Tearing himself away, Jack ran up the few short steps leading out of the lobby. A bustling trio of women loaded with packages nearly knocked him over as he stepped out into the spacious ground floor of the store.

There it was, in all its glory: the heart of the Glosser Bros. department store. To the left of where Jack was standing, shoppers jostled among displays of shoes and boots, shouting and waving for the attention of overwhelmed salespeople. Straight ahead, in the big middle section, people crowded around tables overflowing with merchandise—everything from hats and gloves to shirts and socks. On the far side of the store, shoppers swarmed racks of menswear and coats, inspecting items from top to bottom and trying them on, then slinging them over forearms or tossing them aside.

The place was a madhouse, packed with people grabbing last-minute gifts...but Bub was nowhere among them. Jack saw plenty of familiar faces in the crowd under the glittering decorations, heard the chorus of voices mingling with the Christmas music piped in over the intercom system...but neither saw nor heard a trace of his grandfather.

Bub was in there somewhere, though. He had to be, unless he'd ducked out another door. If he wasn't on the ground floor, he must be on another level of the store.

Jack darted left, weaving through the mob like a football player navigating downfield. Cutting off a fat lady with a baby in each arm and a shopping bag hanging from each hand, he hopped on the escalator heading up.

When the moving stairs reached the second floor, Jack jumped off. Women's clothing and lingerie occupied most of level two; maybe Bub was looking for a last minute present for Gram.

Giving up on caution, Jack sprinted all around the second floor. He snaked between the clothing racks and tables, craning his neck for a glimpse of Bub's telltale silver hair. Every step of the way, he ducked shoppers casting glares in his direction, especially when he cut them off or bumped into them.

By the time he'd finished his circuit of the women's department, he was out of breath...but maybe not out of luck. Grimly determined, he bolted down the short hallway into the Annex, an adjacent building connected to the main body of the store.

The second floor of the Annex seemed like a better choice than the women's department...not because it was home to the notions department with all its sewing supplies, but because it was also home to Glosser's Cafeteria.

As Jack passed through Notions, a sales clerk frowned at him—an old woman he'd seen there often, who'd worked there for ages. As always, her lipstick extended beyond the middle section of her upper lip, forming a double arch of deep red that reached up under her nose.

Jack ignored the dirty look she gave him and continued on to the cafeteria. He knew the place well; he'd been there many times with Bub over the years. It was one of their favorite places to eat, right up there with Stuver's Crispy Chicken and the Bradford Room in Grant's Department Store in Richland, a Johnstown suburb.

Bub wasn't anywhere in sight today, though. The airy,

brightly lit dining area was full, but Bub wasn't sitting there. He wasn't in the cafeteria line, either, or standing at the ice cream counter.

Jack hurried over there anyway. As he approached the counter, the twins who worked there—who'd worked there as long as he could remember—both gave him a bright smile.

"What would you like?" The two women said it at the same time, with identical high-pitched voices.

"Uh, hi." Jack had never been able to tell them apart; they were both short, with deep brown eyes and black hair pulled back in a bun. They wore matching uniforms, too—pink and white striped aprons over white dresses with short, puffy sleeves. "Have you seen my grandfather here today? He's tall, with white hair, and..."

"Of *course* we know your grandfather," said one of the twins.

"Rocky Road in a waffle cone is his favorite," said the other twin. "He's always in here."

"But not today," said the first twin. "Sorry."

Jack slumped. "Thanks anyway."

"So sorry." The second twin patted the side of the freezer beside her. "Would you like a sample on the house?"

Jack glanced over his shoulder, feeling jumpy. His only goal was finding Bub and solving the mystery.

But when one of the twins handed him a flat wooden spoon topped with a clump of chocolate hard-packed ice cream, he didn't turn it away.

He licked the spoon clean in a heartbeat, then dropped it in the little trash can beside the counter. "Thanks!"

"And what else?" Both twins asked the question at the same time.

Jack couldn't help grinning. "Nothing, thanks." Turning, he hurried back toward the elevators. "Merry Christmas!" He shouted it to them as an afterthought.

In reply, the twins started singing Christmas songs—one, "White Christmas," the other, "Santa Claus Is Coming to Town." Their high, piping voices sounded strange singing different things at the same time instead of speaking in unison.

Jack sprinted back down the hallway into the main building, running a serpentine course through overloaded shoppers. Charging straight for the elevators, he punched the button with the arrow pointing up. Since the escalator only reached the second floor, this was the quickest way to the upper levels.

The bell dinged, and the door closest to Jack slid open on a full car. Jack squeezed in anyway, hearing shopping bags crumple as people shifted to make room. At least he didn't have to reach across for the buttons; the one labeled with the number 3 was already lit.

When the door opened again, Jack popped out of the crowded car onto the third floor. Just as he started searching the housewares department, a woman's voice spoke over the storewide intercom system, interrupting the holiday music.

"Glosser's will close in fifteen minutes," she said. "Thank you for shopping at Glosser's, and have a very Merry Christmas."

So now the clock was ticking. If Jack didn't find Bub soon, he would have to end the search and get out of the building.

Adrenaline sizzling in his bloodstream, Jack hurtled among the blankets and pillows, the curtains and cookware and blenders and sweepers. Moving on, he barreled through the furniture department, hoping for a glimpse of Bub on a sofa or rocker/recliner.

But he came up short again. That left the fourth floor, Jack's next favorite place after the candy and comics lobby.

When an elevator didn't come right away, he went for the stairs. He took them two at a time, climbing fast to the store's top floor, where they kept the good stuff.

The toys. Bursting through the door, Jack found himself facing a mother lode of them...a Fort Knox of playthings, a Scrooge McDuck vault overflowing with every cool toy his heart desired. Right there on an endcap display—*right there*—was the fabled Colonel Steve Austin, the Six Million Dollar Man doll, 12 inches tall, complete with a plastic silver engine block for Steve to toss around like a feather and a rocket capsule to reenact the accident that led to him becoming bionic. Jack wanted that doll so bad he could taste it, wanted it more than anything for Christmas '75.

Except for the answer to the mystery of where Bub went on Christmas Eve, that is.

Snapping back to the mission at hand, Jack dashed through the toy department, looking right and left...seeing nothing but toys and late shoppers.

Skidding to a halt by the elevators, Jack punched the only button there, a down button. There was only one more place where he might find Bub, assuming Bub hadn't left the store or backtracked to one of the floors Jack had already searched.

This time, when the elevator door opened, the car was empty. Jack leaped inside and hammered the bottom button on the control panel, the one with a big letter "B" printed on it.

He was going all the way down now, all the way to the bargain basement.

As soon as the elevator door opened at the last stop, the woman's voice came over the intercom again.

"Glosser's will close in five minutes," she said. "Thank you for shopping at Glosser's, and have a very Merry Christmas."

Jack's heart pounded faster than ever now, as time kept running out. Frantically, he scanned the basement...though he wasn't feeling hopeful. It was starting to look like Bub would get to keep his secret another year after all.

Though, truthfully, Jack couldn't say that for sure at first. The basement was a madhouse as always; the crowd down there was thicker than anywhere else in the store.

Men, women, and children—mostly women—swarmed the rows of tables lining the space under bright fluorescent lights. The mob of shoppers tussled over heaps of merchandise, everything from purses to underwear to razors, all of it deeply discounted.

The bargain hunters didn't seem to be slowing down, either. If anything, the five-minute warning seemed to have ratcheted up their frenzy. People bumped and elbowed each other to grab the best junk from the piles. The hubbub they made was loud enough to drown out the piped-in Christmas music.

Careful not to get hit by a deal-crazed grandma, Jack worked his way across the room, checking one face after another. Some were familiar, but none belonged to Bub.

By the time Jack crossed back to where he'd started, he felt the crush of impending defeat. He started thinking of other places he could look, places other than Glosser's; Bub must have given him the slip and gone elsewhere.

Maybe he was at a bar with his old buddies from Bethlehem Steel, where he'd worked for 40 years. He'd retired from Bethlehem five years ago, but he still liked drinking with the guys whenever he got the chance.

Or maybe he was playing cards at the retired men's club, where he also liked to hang out. Or maybe he'd gone to a movie at the Embassy or State theaters on Main Street. Anything was possible.

Then, suddenly, it wasn't.

Jack made one last trip across the basement and turned to work his way to the exit. At that instant, his eyes grazed past the crowd to the far wall...just in time to catch sight of an open elevator there.

Jack's eyes widened. He couldn't believe what he was seeing. Bub was right there in the elevator, calmly staring into space.

Heart racing, Jack started forward. He'd only taken three steps when the elevator door slid shut, and Bub disappeared from view.

But at least he wasn't far. At least Jack finally knew where he was and had a chance to catch up.

Breathless, he ran the rest of the way across the basement to the elevator. He glanced up at the arrow light beside the closed door. The arrow pointed upward, as always; it should have been lit to indicate the car was heading to an upper floor.

Except it wasn't.

Jack frowned. There was only one direction to go from the basement, and that was up. Bub had to be heading for an upper level. Therefore, the light must be broken.

Jack flicked his eyes to the indicator bar above the elevator door, the one that showed what floor the car was on according to what number was illuminated. He expected to see the number 1, 2, 3, or 4 lit up, indicating that Bub had stopped on one of those upper floors. Instead, he saw something he'd never seen before, something he couldn't explain.

For a split-second, Jack saw the letter "X" appear and

light up to the left of the numbers. He blinked hard, then looked again, and it was still there.

X.

Then it was gone, and all the numbers on the indicator bar were dark.

"GLOSSER'S IS NOW CLOSING," said the woman's voice over the intercom. "Thank you for shopping at Glosser's, and have a very Merry Christmas."

As shoppers hurried out of the bargain basement with their merchandise, Jack slumped in the corner, moping. His secret mission was over; the store was closing, and he had to leave.

The chase across town had been for nothing. Jack would have to go another Christmas without solving the mystery.

He hated the thought of giving up and going home. He knew his failure would hang over him all through Christmas Eve and Christmas Day. Even a 12-inch Colonel Steve Austin the Six Million Dollar Man doll under the tree wouldn't make him feel better...not all the way better.

Because Jack would still have to wonder, as he did every year, if Bub was sneaking off to see someone important. Someone who might want to keep tabs on the family once a year at least...especially on Jack.

After all, Bub and Jack's dad had always gotten along

really well, hadn't they? Even though Mom was Bub's own daughter, and Dad had skipped out on her, Bub had never seemed to hate him, had he?

Jack knew it was probably a childish pipe dream—he'd always known it in his heart—but still, he'd held on to his hope. He'd imagined, if he followed Bub on Christmas Eve, that Bub might lead him to Dad in the flesh. And maybe, in the spirit of the season, they might settle some things between them.

But now, that childish dream was melting away like ice between his fingers. He had to let go of it, at least for another year.

Pushing away from the corner, Jack stuffed his hands in the pockets of his jacket and started for the steps leading out of the basement. The rest of the crowd and employees had already climbed up out of there, leaving Jack as the last straggler.

Or was he?

Just as he was about to put his foot on the bottom step, he heard two familiar, high-pitched voices chirping in unison behind him. "We can send you to him, if you like."

Whirling, Jack saw the twins from the ice cream counter standing five feet away, smiling at him. Each of them held a waffle cone of double-scooped Rocky Road hard-packed ice cream.

Jack looked around and frowned. "Where did you come from? I didn't see..."

"The Annex, silly." The twin on the right laughed. "Here." She pushed her cone of Rocky Road in his direction.

Jack took it, feeling creeped out. He hadn't seen or heard a trace of the twins until they got his attention. "No, I meant..."

"Right this way, please." Both twins said it at once as they turned and started walking. "We will send you to him."

Jack followed...though deep inside, a warning bell was going off like crazy. He'd known the twins forever—known them to buy ice cream from them, anyway—but something didn't seem right about what was happening. "What do you mean, 'send?'"

The twins led him across the room to a silver aluminum Christmas tree in the far corner. A device on the floor cast light on the tree from a bulb behind a slowly turning color wheel. The tree turned red, then yellow, then blue, then green...then red again.

"The ice cream will help you pass the time," said one of the twins.

Jack's frown deepened. "What do you mean, 'pass the time?' How much time am I going to have to pass?"

Without answering, the twin who'd given Jack ice cream bent down and picked up the color wheel device. Walking away from the tree, she aimed the device under one of the bargain tables, casting colored light into the shadows.

As the wheel kept turning, the cement floor under the table changed from yellow to blue to green. When it turned red, a rectangular outline appeared, five feet long by three feet wide...only to disappear when the color returned to yellow.

"What the heck?" Jack bent down for a closer look, but the rectangle was gone. He couldn't see the faintest trace of it, at least when the light was yellow, blue, or green.

But when the red beam shone again, it came back. And this time, Jack saw more detail than before. In the middle of the edge closest to him, there was an indentation—four inches long, cut into the substance of the rectangle.

Jack's ice cream was dripping, but he didn't notice. "What *is* this?"

"Something you must swear never to breathe a word of to anyone," said the twin with the color wheel.

"If you make it back," said the other twin.

"*If*? What do you *mean, if*?" asked Jack.

"Do you swear it?" asked both twins at once.

Jack knew he was in over his head. This craziness was like something out of a movie or TV show...like something Colonel Steve Austin might face. It was exciting, but a whole lot scarier than he'd ever imagined an adventure could be.

"Do you swear it?" repeated the twins.

"Will I find my grandfather if I don't?" asked Jack.

The twins smiled and shook their heads.

"Then fine," said Jack. "I swear it."

"Hold this, please." The twin who still had an ice cream cone handed it over.

Jack took it, leaving him holding two cones...one of which was dripping. Raising the dripping cone, he took a half-hearted lick around the rim, stopping the worst of the leak...then suddenly couldn't care less if every bit of both cones melted at once.

Because one twin was opening a door that shouldn't have existed. Crouching alongside the table, she reached down, touching her fingertips to the floor. When the color wheel turned red again, the indentation reappeared, less than an inch from her hand. She pushed her fingers into it and pulled up with a loud grunt.

And the rectangle of floor lifted up, revealing a hole. A doorway.

"There you go." The twin stopped pulling when the slab of floor was canted at a 45-degree angle. It couldn't go any higher unless someone moved the table out of the way.

"Now hurry," said the other twin, taking one of the ice cream cones back from Jack. "Move it or lose it." She looked over her shoulder as if expecting trouble.

"I don't know." Jack swallowed hard. "You're sure he's down there?"

Both twins raised their eyebrows. "Have we ever served you bad ice cream?" they asked.

"Well, no." Jack shook his head.

"And we're not serving it to you now," said the twins. "Everything you want to know is through there." They pointed at the doorway in the floor.

Suddenly, the woman's voice spoke over the intercom again. "Glosser's is now closed. All associates, please escort any remaining guests out of the store."

"Time's up," said the twin with the ice cream. "Close it."

As the other twin took hold of the door, Jack's heart pounded. What if this was his last chance to find out where Bub had gone? "Wait!"

"No time," said the twin at the door.

Footsteps clacked in the distance; someone was coming down the stairs...an associate, maybe, looking for stray shoppers.

"Here!" Jack gave his cone to the twin who didn't have one. Dropping to his knees, he scooted under the table to the edge of the hole. Looking down, he saw dimly lit spiral stairs winding around a shaft walled with gray stone blocks. "Where do I go?"

"All the way down," said the twins. "To the bottom."

Jack had a split second of indecision...then slid his feet over the edge. He dangled them into the shaft, stretching to reach the first step with his toes, and lowered himself down.

Ducking, he eased down a second step, then a third and a fourth. By the time he got to the sixth, the top of his head was just above floor level in the bargain basement.

"Don't forget your ice cream." The twin Jack had given his cone to handed it down to him. "Use it to pass the time."

Jack didn't really want it, but he took it anyway. "Thanks. Thanks for everything."

"Good luck!" said the twins.

Then, as Jack continued downward, they shut the door after him. When he looked up, he couldn't see a trace of it.

JACK SHIVERED as he descended the spiral stairs...as much because of the cold as because he was scared of what he might find at the bottom. A chilly draft swirled up from below, moaning in the passageway and cutting right through his clothes. He wished he'd put on a heavier coat when he'd left the house on Bub's trail.

Needless to say, he wasn't really in the mood for ice cream anymore. He still held on to the cone, though, because there wasn't a good place to leave it. He thought better of putting it down behind him, just in case he had to get back up those narrow stairs in a hurry.

Not that he was in a hurry going down. The stone steps were worn smooth, as if lots of people had walked them in the past. It wouldn't take much to slip and fall, especially in the dim, flickering light.

Jack thought it looked like torchlight on TV or in the movies, dancing up through the stairwell from below. It didn't amount to much near the top but got a little brighter as he descended. Even so, it left deep shadows along the inner wall and played tricks with his eyes. Several times, he thought he saw something moving in the gloom, slithering beyond the next bend...only to realize it was just the flickering glow.

Or was it?

The whole time Jack walked deeper underground, every hair on the back of his neck stayed standing at attention. Ever since the twins had revealed the door in the basement floor, he'd had the feeling he was moving into uncharted territory, a twilight zone in which anything might be possible. He half-expected to see Rod Serling himself appear around the next turn.

Jack had always loved shows like *The Twilight Zone,* had watched them religiously. It had been so much better to dive into fantasy and science fiction than deal with the problems of his own broken family and crappy life. But being in the middle of a creepy scenario himself didn't seem like quite as much fun as watching one on TV. In spite of the twins' assurances about what awaited him downstairs, he couldn't help dreading the outcome.

But he had to keep moving anyway. He couldn't turn back, the door was gone...and he needed to see for himself if Bub was at the bottom.

The question was, how far down did Jack have to go to get there? The stairs just kept leading him deeper and deeper; he wasn't counting, but he knew he'd already gone down lots more than it should have taken to get from one basement to another. There were so many, he needed a break after a while and stopped to sit down for a moment. He even had a lick of the ice cream, which wasn't melting as fast in the cold.

Continuing onward, Jack wondered when it would end. Had the twins led him into some kind of bizarre supernatural trap? What if he spent all eternity just walking down those steps, trying to get somewhere that didn't exist?

When he took a second break, though, he heard something...some kind of sounds in the distance. Was it just his imagination, or was he hearing faint voices wafting up from down below?

As Jack resumed his descent, he moved slower than before, listening intently. Just as the flickering light kept brightening the further down he went, so did the sounds get louder.

A few more steps, and he could tell for sure: they were voices, all right. He didn't know what they were saying, but he could tell they were human voices.

Heart pounding, Jack continued to creep toward them. He realized his long trip down was almost over, though he still had no idea if that would be a good thing. Whatever Bub was mixed up in, it was unusual, to say the least. If Jack's ominous descent down that dim, dank stairway was any indication, it might be dangerous, as well.

As Jack got closer, the voices got louder, until he could finally distinguish between them. There were three: an old man's voice, high and gravelly; a woman's, deeper and throatier; and a younger man's, deeper and louder than the rest.

"What do you want us to say?" asked the woman. "Times are changing."

"New times, new terms," said the old man. "You understand."

"It's nothing personal," said the younger man. "Just business."

Suddenly, a fourth voice spoke. "It's *personal,* all right." This voice, Jack knew by heart. "It's nothing *but* personal."

Bub. It was *Bub.* The twins had not steered Jack wrong, after all.

But what were Bub and the others talking about? Jack had to get closer to find out.

"It's a *negotiation,* Ben," said a fifth voice, that of another old man. "Same as it is *every* year."

"You're not negotiating," said Bub. "You're doing the *opposite*. You're not giving me a leg to stand on."

"Did you think you could keep doing this *forever*?" asked the woman. "Postponing the inevitable one year at a time?"

"Yes," said Bub. "Now tell me what I need to do to make this deal. Tell me what you want from me to make it worth your while."

"Honestly?" The first old man, the one with the high-pitched voice, cackled. "You're wasting your *breath.* We want *nothing* from you anymore."

"This town is doomed to *die,* and there's nothing you can do to save it."

FINALLY, Jack reached the end of the shaft. As he walked off the bottom step onto a floor of dusty cobblestones, the old man's last words echoed in his mind.

This town is doomed to die, and there's nothing you can do to save it.

Jack wondered what it meant. What had he stumbled into here?

And how exactly was Bub involved? What had the woman meant when she'd said he'd been "postponing the inevitable, one year at a time?"

No doubt about it, Jack needed to get closer. He needed to hear more, to understand what was happening.

Taking care not to make a sound, Jack tiptoed toward the voices. He saw an entryway in the gray stone wall ahead, a gap through which the flickering light was flowing, and he headed straight for it.

There was a curved rim along the base of the gap, a crescent-shaped lip with a large stone in the middle. Breathing fast, Jack stepped over it, watching carefully to make sure he didn't trip and fall.

But when he got both feet on the other side and looked up, he almost fell over anyway. He felt instantly dizzy and light-headed when he took in the scene around him; it was a miracle he managed to stay upright.

Because somehow, everything and everyone but him was upside-down.

Jack stood at the edge of a large chamber hewn of the same gray block as the stairway. The voices that had drawn him there were coming from the middle of that chamber, and the people they belonged to were upside-down, seated or standing on the ceiling. The circular table and chairs they occupied were upside-down, too.

So were the blazing torches and the framed paintings and photos on the walls. So was the statue of the big red dog across the room—Morley's dog, a legendary canine from the 1889 flood.

Everything had been flipped...or, maybe, it was all perfectly *normal.* Looking back at the entrance he'd come through, Jack suddenly thought of an explanation for the curved lip along the bottom. What if that was the *top* of an *archway* instead of some kind of inexplicable low ledge?

But what Jack was thinking couldn't be true, could it? Wasn't it impossible to defy the law of gravity like that?

Apparently not. As Jack stood there, trying to adjust to the off-kilter scene, a stream of ice cream melted from his cone...and ran straight *up*. It dribbled past his head and kept on going, running toward what seemed to be the ceiling from his point of view.

Except it was the floor. And Jack was the only occupant of the room who was truly upside-down.

JACK HASTILY LICKED at the ice cream cone to keep any more from falling. Somehow, doing that made him feel less dizzy and light-headed, as if something in the ice cream was a cure for vertigo.

Meanwhile, the group at the table up above (down below?) kept talking. Luckily, the room was an echo chamber; the people were in the middle of the room, at least thirty feet away, but their voices carried so well that they sounded like they were right next to him.

"There must be *something* you want," said Bub. "There always is." He was standing in the open well in the middle of the circular table. His jacket was gone; his bright white button-down shirt took on a reddish glow in the torchlight.

"Not this time," said the old man with the high-pitched,

gravelly voice. Now that Jack had a clear view of him, he could see he was the old-timer Bub had waved at in the Bedford Street Newsstand, the one in the pale blue polyester leisure suit.

Jack recognized two others at the table, also: the old lady in red whom Bub had spoken to on Main Street and the old man in the houndstooth sport coat and brown-and-red plaid pants whom Bub had hugged in front of Glosser's.

"Events have been set in motion," said the lady in red. "Events that have been too long delayed already."

"The death of Johnstown, Rachel?" Bub shook his head angrily. "That can *never* be delayed too long."

"Now, now." The old man in houndstooth fiddled nervously with his green Alpine hat on the table in front of him. "It will only be temporary, Ben."

Suddenly, the younger man spoke, the one with the deepest, loudest voice. "Damn right!" When he jumped to his feet, Jack could see he was tall and broad-shouldered, rippling with muscles like a bodybuilder. "You can't keep Johnstown down! It'll be *back*, baby, bigger and better than ever!"

"You tell 'im, Steel Toe!" The man in the powder blue leisure suit clapped his hands.

"Which is, of course, the whole point, isn't it?" said the man in houndstooth.

"The cycle of death and rebirth," said Rachel. "There can be no true progress without it."

"At a cost of how many lives?" asked Bub.

"A drop in the bucket, Benny." Powder blue leisure suit

leaned back in his chair and hoisted his feet on the table. "*Less* than a drop. A *drip*."

"Those people out there are your *charges*." Bub gestured up at the ceiling, which was also Jack's floor. "Isn't that what you've *told* me?"

"I'm Mr. Flood!" Powder blue leisure suit pumped his gnarled fists in the air. "*My* only charges are the storm clouds and lightning bolts!"

"No, it's true," said houndstooth. "We're like parents to them...and as such, we know what is *best* for them."

"Which is *death*?" Bub threw his arms open wide. "For how many, Joe? Hundreds? Thousands?"

Houndstooth—Joe—shrugged and looked away. "I can't say."

"Whatever it *takes*," snapped the muscle man.

"Whatever the flood waters can carry." Mr. Flood's feet jiggled around in their white buck shoes as if the idea tickled him.

For a long moment, no one spoke. Above them, Jack watched in amazement, trying to sort out what he'd heard.

Who *were* these people? Were they actually talking about flooding Johnstown? Could they *do* it?

And how had Bub come to try to talk them out of it? Was this really what he did every Christmas Eve?

Jack shivered. There he was, in a scenario worthy of the Six Million Dollar Man, and he just wanted to get out of it. He just wanted to get back to his boring, crappy life again and forget about life-or-death deals in sinister hidden lairs.

He was starting to think he would've been better off not knowing Bub's secret after all.

RACHEL WAS the one who finally broke the silence. "You need to accept reality, Ben. The covenants are yesterday's news."

"I wouldn't say that." Bub turned in her direction. "We've negotiated them every year since I was, what...25? And my father did the same before me."

"You *had* to bring *him* up, didn't you?" Mr. Flood swung his legs off the table and lunged halfway out of his chair. "That sweet-talking son of a gun!" He stood all the way up and wriggled his hands in front of his chest effeminately. "'Ohh, that terrible flood in 1889!'" he said in a falsetto, mocking voice. "'Johnstown can't stand another disaster like that! Please, can't we make a bargain to keep this town safe?'"

"It was a *hard* bargain," said Bub. "You've only ever agreed to it a year at a time."

"Poor baby!" shouted Mr. Flood. "Do you have any *clue* how *lucky* you were to get even *that*?"

"What about '36?" said Bub.

"Ah, '36." A broad grin stretched across Mr. Flood's cadaverous face. "A good year. A *very* good year."

"So that's what *this* is?" said Bub. "1936 all over again? Tear up the covenant, flood the city, get your jollies?"

"Why the hell not?" Mr. Flood slammed his palms

down on the table. "You've been holding this town back for too long, Benny! How do you expect this place to *grow up* if we keep *babying* it?"

Bub leaned in and locked eyes with him. "You don't need to kill thousands of people for this town to grow up."

"You're spoiled!" Mr. Flood sneered. "You've been getting what you want for too long. Well, the gravy train stops *here,* my old not-friend."

Bub leaned closer. He had an expression of fury on his face that Jack had seen only a handful of times in his life. "You twisted, miserable..."

"Hey!" Steel Toe jumped up and threw down a fist between Bub and Mr. Flood. "Back off, Ben! I don't *care* if you're a *union man,* I'll smack you *down* if you lay a hand on him!"

For a moment, Bub stayed right where he was, glaring at Mr. Flood. "*You* don't want progress. *You* don't want this town to grow up." He leaned a little closer then, making Steel Toe tense up. "You might have fooled the others, but you haven't fooled *me.*"

"Says the biggest fool in the room." Mr. Flood howled at his joke and threw himself down in his chair.

"That's enough!" shouted Joe. "There will be no further conflict here." He picked up his green Alpine hat and plunked it on his head. "This matter is settled."

"You must accept what has been ordained." Rachel looked around the table grimly with her misaligned eyes. "The next great flood will strike Johnstown next year, in July of 1976."

"Just in time for America's Bicentennial." Mr. Flood let out a little whoop. "Talk about fireworks!"

"Consider yourself fortunate, Ben," said Joe. "You've been given enough warning to move your loved ones elsewhere."

Bub backed away from Mr. Flood and slumped. "Please." He held out his hands to Joe and Rachel. "Please, no. All those people..."

"Will be a tragic loss," said Rachel. "And none of us takes joy in that."

Mr. Flood cleared his throat loudly.

Rachel ignored him. "But it doesn't change the fact of what is coming. We all must accept and look beyond it to the new and stronger Johnstown that will rise up in the wake of this disaster."

"Till the next one." Mr. Flood snickered.

"No, wait," said Bub. "There must be something we can do. There must be something I can give you."

Just then, at that exact instant, a blob of Rocky Road ice cream hit the floor at the edge of the room with an echoing splat.

JACK HAD FORGOTTEN about the ice cream. He'd been too caught up in the conversation to remember to keep licking it.

The melting had slowed in the cold underground chamber but never stopped completely. Eventually, the

Rocky Road had turned to mush and dropped right out of the cone.

So now, his secret surveillance was at an end. All eyes in the room were locked on him.

"Jack, no!" shouted Bub.

"Again with the drama?" Mr. Flood scowled like a rotting peach. "Would someone please get that brat out of here?"

"Jack, run!" Bub waved frantically, trying to shoo him from the room. "As fast as you can!"

"No need to be inhospitable," said Joe. "This is your grandson?"

"Aren't you going to introduce us?" asked Rachel.

Bub wouldn't take his eyes off Jack. He jerked his head, signaling him once more to leave.

But Jack was frozen where he stood. He knew he should do what Bub told him and run—he *wanted* to get away—but he felt pinned down by the pressure of all those eyes upon him.

"Well?" said Rachel.

"This is Jack," said Bub. "Let him go. He isn't a part of this."

"That remains to be seen," said Rachel. "How long have you been standing there, Jack?"

Still gaping at Jack, Bub drew his thumb and index finger across his lips as if he were pulling a zipper across them. The message was clear.

Jack kept his mouth shut.

"How much have you heard?" asked Joe.

Bub shook his head. Jack got the clear impression it wouldn't be good for him to say anything.

So why did he feel such a powerful compulsion to speak? Why did he have to fight so hard to keep himself from answering the question?

"Shy child." Rachel smiled. "Perhaps we should finish the introductions first. Ben, will you do the honors?"

Bub flicked his eyes hard to the side, another signal. But when Jack didn't run, he sighed and spoke. "Jack, this is Rachel Adams."

"I'm kind of a local legend," said Rachel. "You've heard of Rachel Hill?"

Jack nodded. Of course he knew about Rachel Adams, everyone did. She was a settler...in the 1700s.

Killed by Indians.

"This is Joseph Johns," said Bub, gesturing at the man they'd been calling Joe.

"Yes, *the* Joseph Johns." Joe laughed. "Founder of Johnstown. *Late* founder, as far as most people know."

Jack swallowed hard. He'd guessed there was magic at work here, some kind of supernatural forces...but *dead people?*

"This is Steel Toe." Bub gestured at the man with the superhero build.

"Spirit of the steel mills," said Steel Toe, grinning and waving. "Any grandson of a steelworker is okay in my book."

"And this..." Bub gestured at Mr. Flood.

"Is your worst nightmare!" Mr. Flood lunged up and hissed loudly, baring his teeth.

"We're all local legends, Jack," said Rachel. "We have an *influence* around here, and we use it for the greater good of Johnstown."

"Your grandfather here has been a...consultant of ours for some time now," said Joe.

"More of an advocate," said Rachel, "for certain local interests."

"Until he done got *fired*," said Mr. Flood.

"There are men like him all over the world," said Rachel. "Pleading their case with people like us. Keeping it all from falling apart for one more year."

"So, Jack," said Joe. "Is there anything you'd like to ask us?"

Bub's eyes widened, and he shook his head once.

Jack remained silent at first. He knew he shouldn't say anything that might get him in any deeper than he already was.

But then, suddenly, he wanted to talk. As scared as he was, a mob of questions pressed to be let out. This might be his only chance to get answers.

Shaking and sweating and breathing fast, Jack opened his mouth and spoke. "Can you really do it? Flood Johnstown, I mean?"

"Can we *do* it?" Mr. Flood smacked the table with both hands. "How'd you like a lungful of *water*, you disrespectful *guttersnipe?*"

"Hey!" Bub whirled around to glare at Flood.

"Enough!" snapped Joe. "Both of you!"

"The answer to your question is yes, Jack," said Rachel. "We can indeed make such a thing happen."

Jack thought it over for a moment...and another question came to mind. This time, he directed it at Bub. "What did you give them?"

Bub frowned, looking puzzled. "What do you mean?"

"Every year, when you made the deal," said Jack. "The one to hold off the flood. You said they wanted something to make it worth their while."

Bub started to say something, but the others cut him off.

"He gave us his youth," said Joe. "And his energy."

"He gave us his *dreams*," said Rachel. "His dreams to be anything other than a shop steward in a steel mill in the town where he was born."

"He stayed *here*." Joe tapped the table with a bony finger. "He put Johnstown first."

"It's called *sacrifice*, boy." Mr. Flood sneered. "Giving up something *important*, something you want more than *anything*. It's what you're *supposed* to do, to keep people like us happy."

"But you're not happy now?" Jack pointed at Bub. "You don't want what he has anymore?"

"*Now* you're catching on," said Mr. Flood. "Grampa's all used up. He's circling the drain."

Jack fell silent. As crazy as the situation was, he thought he understood it.

A great flood would strike Johnstown in 1976, killing hundreds or thousands of people. Bub, who'd always managed to put it off before, couldn't stop it this time. It looked as if no one else could...but maybe it was just that no one else had tried.

An idea was forming in Jack's mind. He knew Bub wouldn't like it; Jack didn't like it much himself. But Jack and Bub weren't the ones who mattered, were they?

The thousands of people in the path of the flood were the ones who mattered.

"Well, Jack?" asked Joe. "Have we answered your questions?"

"Why don't you come down from there and have a proper visit then?" said Rachel.

"I've got some crazy *mill stories* you're gonna love," said Steel Toe.

The longer Jack considered his idea, the more frightening it became...and the more *real*. He trembled at the thought of it, shivered fiercely from the inside out.

"Come on down, Jack," said Joe. "Just walk down the wall."

"But don't knock off any of the pictures, of course," said Rachel.

Mr. Flood chortled. "Unless you'd rather *we* come up *after* you?"

Jack opened his mouth to speak, then closed it. He knew he was about to make a huge mistake.

But he also knew one other thing. When he asked himself what Colonel Steve Austin, the Six Million Dollar Man, would do in this situation, he only came up with one answer.

Anything he could.

"Wait." The word sprang out of Jack before he could call it back in. "What about me?"

"What *about* you, you ugly little urchin?" asked Mr. Flood.

Jack's voice shook. The enormity of what he was doing left him quaking in his sneakers. "What if *I* sacrificed something?"

For a moment, the room was dead silent. All eyes were glued to Jack again...though only Bub's were wide with horror.

Finally, Joe spoke up. "What do you have in mind?"

JACK SWALLOWED HARD. "What if I stay here like Bub did? What if I put Johnstown first like you said?"

"That's a nice thought, dear," said Rachel. "But didn't you hear what we said about events being set in motion?"

"This has already been decided," said Joe. "We've made up our minds."

"No, wait." Jack's mind raced. "What about my youth and energy? I've got plenty of both."

"Jack, stop," blurted Bub. "You don't know what you're saying!"

"Doesn't matter." Joe adjusted his Alpine hat. "The cycle of death and rebirth must continue."

"We've put it off long enough," agreed Rachel.

"You heard the lady." Mr. Flood hiked a thumb in her direction. "Take your youth and energy and stick 'em where the sun don't shine."

Jack felt like he was losing ground fast...but like

Colonel Steve Austin, he had to do everything in his power to save innocent lives. "*Dreams*." The word shot out of him like a cannonball.

"Jack, no!" shouted Bub.

"I'll give you my *dreams*, too," said Jack.

"They're *using* you," said Bub. "They'll take *everything*, if you let them!"

"Why don't you put a sock in it?" snapped Mr. Flood. "You're dead wrong, anyway. There's nothing he or *anyone* could offer to delay this glorious flood!"

"Actually..." said Joe. "Let's not be hasty."

"*What?*" Mr. Flood's eyes bugged out of his knobby skull.

"I'm just saying." Joe shrugged. "Now that I think about it, an infusion of new dreams and vitality might not be such a *bad* thing, would it?"

"Yes!" said Mr. Flood. "If it means putting off the flood of the century *again*, then yes it *would* be."

"You might be onto something, Joe," said Rachel.

Mr. Flood leaped out of his chair. "You're not actually *considering* this, are you?"

"What else could you give us, Jack?" asked Rachel. "*If* our minds weren't already made up, that is."

"Nothing!" said Bub. "Don't listen to him! He's just a child!"

"I can't believe I actually agree with *Benny* about something," said Mr. Flood. "Don't listen to that kid!"

Joe ignored him. "What else could you offer us, Jack? What else could you offer for a new covenant?"

Jack thought hard, trying to block out Bub and Mr.

Flood, who were both yelling. What could he, an 11-year-old kid, possibly have to offer to save hundreds or thousands of lives?

He could think of nothing on the same scale, nothing that might be worth trading for all those lives. But then he remembered what Mr. Flood had said about sacrifice...how it had to be something important, something you wanted more than anything.

"The 12-inch Six Million Dollar Man doll," said Jack. "With rocket capsule and engine block." Even as he said it, he hated the thought of doing without it. "I asked for it for Christmas this year."

"And you want it that badly, Jack?" asked Joe. "It means that much to you?"

Jack nodded emphatically. "Oh, yeah." He didn't have to exaggerate his sincerity at all. "It means everything." That toy was at the top of his Christmas list; it had dominated his dreams and daydreams for months, ever since he'd first seen it in the Sears Christmas catalogue.

"Hmm." Joe looked at Rachel. "What do you think?"

Rachel shrugged. "We already agreed not to postpone the flood any longer."

"Damn skippy!" hollered Mr. Flood. "'76 is set in stone!"

"On the other hand," said Rachel, "I suppose I'm not averse to spicing things up." She turned her misaligned eyes on Joe. "What about that wild card we talked about?"

"Hollywood." Joe nodded. "The hockey movie."

"I loved that idea!" Steel Toe pounded the table and grinned. "Lots of opportunities for union work!"

"A new local legend," said Rachel. "One that ripples around the world and far into the future. Some will call it one of the greatest sports movies of all time."

"Yes!" Steel Toe slammed the table again.

"No!" wailed Mr. Flood.

"But the patterns are clear," said Rachel. "It can only happen in 1976. If there's a flood, there will be no *Slapshot,* or any of the movies that come after."

Joe stared into space with eyes narrowed. "It's a different approach, that's for sure."

"A *stupid* approach!" said Mr. Flood.

"But surprises can jump-start evolution," said Rachel. "And this movie will certainly be a great surprise."

"You want a surprise?" snapped Mr. Flood. "How 'bout a couple million gallons of water roaring through town at once?"

Joe ran a finger back and forth along the brim of his Alpine hat. "I don't like changing course once a decision has been made..."

"You tell 'em!" said Mr. Flood.

"But in this case, it might be worth exploring the permutations." Joe smiled up at Jack. "The deal you've proposed has merit."

"No, please," said Bub. "He's a child, he doesn't know..."

Joe looked around at the other occupants of the table. "All in favor of making this deal?"

Everyone but Mr. Flood and Bub raised their right hands.

"Wait!" shouted Bub. "*Stop!*"

All eyes turned to him.

Bub's shoulders heaved, and his face was flushed with stress. For a moment, he said nothing, just stared up at Jack.

"If you insist on doing this, I suppose I can't stop you," said Bub. "But you need to know something." He looked down at the people around the table. "He needs to know something."

Joe made a sweeping gesture with one arm, giving him permission to continue.

Bub looked back up at Jack. "Before you sign anything, you can ask for something else. Something for *yourself,* Jack, to sweeten the deal."

"I can?" said Jack.

"But you don't *have* to," said Joe. "Isn't another year's reprieve from a devastating flood enough for you?"

"*No,*" snapped Bub. "Jack, no. Listen to me. Ask for something else. You won't get another chance."

Jack thought about it. "Anything? I can ask for anything?"

"What do you have in mind, child?" asked Rachel.

"Put off the flood longer," said Jack. "How about that? Make it *ten* or *five* years instead of *one*."

"Never!" howled Mr. Flood. "If it were up to *me*, you wouldn't even get *five minutes*!"

"Sorry, but no," said Joe. "The contract is for one year. That's non-negotiable."

Jack looked at Bub, who shrugged and nodded. "Can I *warn* people, at least? Tell them to move away before it hits?"

"Warn whomever you like," said Rachel. "They won't believe you without some kind of proof."

"Jack," said Bub. "You're a good boy, wanting to buy more time and save people's lives...but you need to ask for something for *yourself*."

Jack frowned.

"You're paying a steep price for this deal," said Bub. "Much steeper than you know." He nodded gravely. "Isn't there something you've always wished for? Something that could make up for all the things you're giving away?"

"I don't know." Jack shook his head. "I don't know what to say."

"There must be *something*," said Bub. "Something that could make your life better in spite of the burden you're taking on."

Jack wracked his brain...and then he found it. "Wait...yes." He came up with the one thing he wanted more than the Colonel Steve Austin doll. "I know what I want."

When he said it out loud, he knew it was right. It was perfect. It was what he'd *always* wanted most in his deepest heart of hearts.

And everyone at the table, except Mr. Flood, agreed to it.

"It's a deal." Smiling, Joe plucked the white feather from his Alpine hat. "Now just hold still a moment, young man."

"Why?" Jack asked with a frown.

"Our covenant can only be sealed one way." Joe held up the feather, quill first, and pitched it at Jack like a paper airplane. The feather spiraled its way up to him in lazy loops, white tufts fluttering along its length. "In *blood*."

Jack's eyes widened. Before he could back away or defend himself, the feather suddenly shot toward him. The tip of its quill punctured his left thumb, shocking him with a pinprick of pain...then popped free and zipped back down to Joe.

"Very good." Joe reached up and snagged the feather from the air, then turned to Rachel. "Contract, please?"

Rachel snapped her fingers, and a parchment scroll appeared on the table between them. "Sign here." She unrolled the scroll and pointed to a line on the bottom with a big black "X" beside it.

Joe positioned the bloody feather above the line, then let go of it. The feather stayed hovering in place, its bloody tip just above the start of the line. "Jack? Pretend you're signing your name, won't you? The feather will do the rest."

Hesitantly, Jack raised his right hand, pinching his thumb and forefinger together as if he were holding a pen. Then, he scribbled an imaginary signature in thin air.

Glancing down below, he saw the feather scratch across the scroll in exactly the same way, leaving a bright red scrawl on the line beside the "X."

"Done." Joe grabbed the feather, pricked his own left thumb, and signed on the line below Jack's name. "And done."

Rachel waved her right hand in a circle, leaving a trail of glittering sparks that hung in midair. "Now this next part might feel a little uncomfortable."

"What next part?" asked Jack.

"Tough it out, li'l guy!" said Steel Toe. "It'll be over before you know it!"

"But what part are you talking about?" asked Jack.

"When you make a deal with us, you're reborn," said Rachel. "But you can't be reborn if you don't die first." With that, she leaned forward and blew out a big gust of breath.

It sent the sparks flashing toward Jack, expanding as they went. By the time they reached him, they'd become a cloud big enough to engulf him...which they did.

Instantly, Jack's feet left the floor. As he floated upward in the grip of the glittering cloud—or downward, from the point of view of those around the table—he became paralyzed. No matter how hard he tried, he couldn't move a muscle.

Drifting further, Jack felt his body stiffen and go cold. His breathing stopped, and so did his heart.

Am I dying? As the thought came to him, Jack saw a fresh burst of sparks which might have been in his head. Then, a curtain of blackness fell over his vision, and he couldn't see outside himself anymore.

A rush of memories rushed up to take the place of Jack's darkened sight. He remembered the first time he'd gone to a Pirates baseball game at Forbes Field in Pittsburgh. He remembered the first time he'd gone camping in a tent at Prince Gallitzin State Park. He remembered getting his tonsils out and eating Rocky Road ice cream in his hospital bed while watching cartoons.

With his father. In every one of the memories that came to him, his father was there.

He was part of lots more, too...so many moments that Jack hadn't thought about in ages. Going grocery shopping at the supermarket; skinning a knee on a gravel driveway; sitting in church on a Sunday morning; crying on a shoulder over something unimportant. Dad was there every time, his face and voice and presence woven through the fabric of Jack's life in ways Jack had forgotten.

Then Dad was gone, too, and so were those moments. And so was Jack.

He had a distant awareness of touching down, settling onto the floor that had been his ceiling. Then that, too, faded, as did his awareness of himself.

All was dark and silent and still, a vacuum. Nothing remained of Jack or anything he knew or thought or wanted, not even the faintest impression of an absence in the void, like a wisp of perfume left behind in a room.

THE FIRST THING Jack saw when he opened his eyes was the giant Christmas tree decoration on the corner of the Glosser Bros. building. It was made up of V-shaped rows of white lights, broad at the bottom and narrower further up. An eight-pointed star perched atop the peak, glowing softly in the falling snow.

Watching that tree, which had towered over Christmas for as long as Jack could remember, he felt completely at peace. He didn't have a single worry, didn't have a single need.

He smelled the icy air of a winter's night, felt snowflakes gently falling on his face. His body bobbed up and down, carried away from Glosser's glowing tree in someone's strong and steady arms.

The only thing he heard was the soft buzz of Glosser's lights and the labored breathing of whoever was carrying him. Turning his head, he looked up and saw a familiar face staring straight ahead—eyes squinting against the snow, cheeks and forehead flushed and glistening with sweat, silver hair fluttering in the wind.

"Bub?" Jack's voice was a squeak.

Bub looked down at him, his smile as warm as the air was cold. "Welcome back, Jack." A familiar parchment scroll brushed his cheek; the scroll was sticking up from his shirt pocket under his jacket, rolled up and tied with a shiny red ribbon.

Seeing that scroll started bringing back Jack's memories of what had happened in the secret chamber under Glosser's. "I'm...alive?"

Bub nodded. "Alive and kicking, Fauntleroy." It was a nickname he sometimes used for Jack. "On your way home in time for Santy Claus to come."

Jack heard church bells in the distance and frowned. He felt exhausted, as if he might drift off at any moment. "Bub?"

"Yes, Jack?"

"Did it really happen?"

Bub's expression turned grim. "You shouldn't have followed me, Jack. You shouldn't have been there."

Jack yawned loudly. "But did it really happen?"

Bub didn't say anything for a long moment. He kept his eyes focused ahead, blinking away snowflakes.

"Yes, Jack." Bub nodded toward the rolled-up scroll in his pocket. "The contract with your signature on it is right there."

"Huh." Jack's eyes fluttered shut. He wanted to stay awake but couldn't seem to make it happen. "I could've sworn it was all a crazy dream."

"No, Jack." Bub's voice sounded sad as well as strained from carrying his grandson. "I'm sorry to say it wasn't a dream at all."

JACK WOKE the next morning to the sound of "Step Into Christmas" by Elton John playing on his clock radio. Though he'd slept like a rock through the night, he was still so exhausted that he let the song play through to the end.

When he finally managed to reach over and switch it off, he dropped right back into a deep sleep. His experiences of the night before had left him so drained, he couldn't even drag himself out of bed on Christmas morning.

A knock on the door nearly woke him up again, but Jack ignored it. He was lost in a dream about Penn Traffic, the other department store in downtown Johnstown; Colonel Steve Austin was there playing Santa, fighting reindeer terrorists with laser-emitting noses.

But then the knock at the door repeated, followed by a voice. "Jack?" It was Bub. "Jack, can I come in?"

Jack groaned and rolled over on his side, wishing Bub would leave him alone. He wasn't ready to deal with human contact yet, not until he'd slept a while longer and sorted out his bizarre memories from last night.

But Bub wasn't ready to give up. "Jack?" He knocked louder. "Are you okay in there?"

Jack flopped on his back and scowled at the ceiling. The room was awash in bright white light, the kind that flares around the edges of the curtains on a snowy morning. He guessed it was after ten even before he looked over at the numbers displayed on the face of his clock radio: *10:15.*

There was a long pause until the next knock. "I'm coming in, Jack."

The doorknob turned slowly, and the bolt clicked free of the jamb. Jack wished he'd locked it the night before...but the truth was, he didn't even remember getting home. He had a vague recollection of gazing up at Glosser's Christmas lights and being carried in Bub's arms; then nothing.

Had Bub carried him all the way home and put him in bed? It would explain why Jack was still fully dressed under the blankets, wearing the same red sweatshirt and blue jeans he'd worn to Glosser's. Only his navy blue jacket had been removed.

"Are you all right?" Bub opened the door halfway and peered in with a look of concern.

Jack nodded. "Just tired."

"Good, good." Bub eased in the rest of the way and shut the door behind him. As always, he was wearing a white button-down shirt, black tie, black trousers, and black Oxfords. "What you went through last night..." He lowered his voice. "It can be pretty rough on you."

"Tell me about it," said Jack.

Just then, the radio popped back on, blasting "Santa Claus Is Comin' To Town" by Bruce Springsteen. With a loud grunt, Jack smacked the off switch on top of the device, silencing the music.

"You look okay otherwise, though," said Bub. "That's a good sign."

"I guess so," said Jack.

Bub looked uncomfortable. "If you ever want to talk, let me know." He paced to the window at the foot of Jack's bed and tugged back the edge of the curtain, peeking outside. "I've been through it all at this point. I can answer your questions."

Jack sat up and swung his legs off the edge of the bed. Now that he was awake, certain questions did come to mind. "How will they take them?" he asked. "The things I said I'd sacrifice?"

"A little at a time." Bub sighed. "You won't even notice they're gone...for a while, at least."

"But I promised to give them my youth, my energy, and my dreams. How can I *not* notice they're gone?"

"I misspoke." Bub turned from the window and

narrowed his eyes. "What you'll notice...the way you'll give those things up...is by never leaving this town. Then your youth and your energy will fade over time as they always do."

"I'll never leave town?" said Jack.

"You'll never *want* to leave," said Bub. "One day you'll wake up, and you'll be 65 years old...and you'll realize you're still here. You'll just end up stuck here."

"Stuck here?" Jack had never thought much about the future, had never thought about leaving or where he might want to live someday. But thinking about it now gave him a funny feeling in the pit of his stomach.

"It won't be so bad, Jack," said Bub. "Johnstown's a good place. A *decent* place. It's worth saving. It's worth *staying*."

Jack frowned. "But the deal's only for one year. I can leave after that, can't I?"

Bub shrugged. "Why would you, if there's still a chance you can save everyone? A chance you can buy another year?"

"I could do that?"

"Why not?" Bub's eyes twinkled. "My first contract was only for a year, too."

Seeing the look on his grandfather's face made Jack smile. Maybe things would work out okay after all. Maybe it wouldn't be so bad following in the footsteps of Bub, and Bub's father before him. There were huge responsibilities and a price to be paid, but it might all be worth it in the end. After all, saving lives was its own reward, wasn't it? Wouldn't Colonel Steve Austin be proud?

And there was another reward, too, that Jack had

forgotten until now. "What about that thing I asked for? The one to sweeten the deal?"

Bub peeked outside again. "What about it?"

"You don't think they'll go back on their word, do you?"

Bub snorted and let the curtain fall back into place. "Not a chance." He headed for the door. "Steel Toe won't let them take away a good union man's fringe benefits."

Just as he said it, the doorbell rang.

Bub opened the bedroom door. "C'mere a minute, Fauntleroy. There's something you should see." He nodded for Jack to follow and stepped out into the hallway.

As the two of them walked downstairs, the doorbell rang again. No one else was running to get it; Jack guessed Mom was at her boyfriend's place.

Turning a corner at the bottom of the stairs, Jack stole a glance at the Christmas tree in the living room. Even from a distance, he could see that the telltale red-and-white box of the Six Million Dollar Man 12-inch doll wasn't among the few gifts scattered under the tree. Jack spotted books and clothes and a basketball, but no Six Million Dollar Man. So the local legends had held him to the terms he'd agreed to; Jack had said he'd sacrifice that toy—which had been at the top of his list, so he'd been sure he was going to get it—and they'd taken him up on the offer.

But that was okay. Jack was willing to give it up, if it meant saving Johnstown.

And anyway, he wasn't even thinking about it thirty seconds later. It was the furthest thing from his mind when Bub opened the door, and Jack saw who was standing there.

"Hi, Jack." The man at the door was a little older than Jack remembered. His dark brown hair was frosted with gray, and his eyes crinkled when he smiled. "Merry Christmas."

Jack was dumbstruck. He stood there staring at the man on the front stoop, not knowing what to say or do next.

His heart was racing like Colonel Steve Austin chasing down a speeding motorcycle. His eyes were locked on the man's face, zooming in and scanning every detail as if they were bionic.

"So how are you?" asked Bub as he shook the man's hand. "What brings you back to these parts?"

"Actually..." The man shrugged and shuffled his feet, uncertain. Then, he straightened and smiled. "I'm moving back to town."

"Is that so?" Bub looked at Jack. "How do you like that?"

Jack was still tongue-tied. He'd gotten what he'd asked for in the chamber under Glosser's, and he'd gotten it right away...like magic. This was exactly what he'd asked for to sweeten the deal, the one thing he'd wanted more than anything in the depths of his beating heart.

"I've been thinking," said the man, nodding as snowflakes fell gently around him. "Maybe I could see you once in a while, Jack. If you'll let me."

Jack just kept staring.

"Maybe we could talk a little first," said the man. "I could explain a few things. Clear the decks, so to speak."

"What do you say, Jack?" asked Bub.

Jack had been brave enough to face down Joseph Johns, Rachel Adams, Steel Toe, and Mr. Flood in the mystery basement under Glosser's, but he still held back from talking to this one ordinary man. There was so much history between them, so much hurt, so much loss. And now, there was a chance to start over, and Jack wanted it more than he'd ever wanted anything in his life.

But seeing the man in front of him was so much different than daydreaming about it. The pressure of reality made it all so much sharper and more dangerous.

"Well, Jack?" said the man. "Do you have time to talk?"

It was Christmas Morning, and a potentially wonderful gift had landed on Jack's doorstep. The question now was, what should he do about it?

Exactly what Colonel Steve Austin would do.

"Sure, Dad." Jack stuck out his hand. When Dad shook it, he felt an electrical tingle run up his arm, like the power surge in a bionic limb performing a superhuman feat. "I'm not going anywhere, am I?"

WELCOME
BACK !

NEW YEAR'S EVE AT GLOSSER'S

Nurse Lizzie's Christmas tree sweater blinks in colors when she comes to the door of my father's house, which is also the house where I grew up. Though Christmas Day was a week ago, she's still in a festive mode…though I wonder how much my dad appreciates it, given how out-of-it he is these days.

"Hello, Jason." With her rosy cheeks and curly silver hair, Lizzie has the look of a sweet old lady—a Mrs. Claus type—but I know she's more than tough enough to handle my dad on even his worst days. "Happy New Year's Eve, hon."

"To you as well, Lizzie." I nod, brushing the fresh snow off my navy pea coat.

"Looks like we're getting the white stuff we missed out on for Christmas." She backs in, pulling the door wide for me to enter. "At least the roads weren't bad for your drive from Pittsburgh to Johnstown."

"Not yet, anyway." I brush off more snow as I step into the foyer of the house where I grew up. It feels weird being here, like stepping back in time in a dream…though it's not the same as the old days, of course. For one thing, there isn't a holiday decoration in sight. Lizzie likes to keep things simple that way to avoid adding to Dad's confusion.

"No Desiree?" She looks over my shoulder.

I shake my head. I could've sworn Lizzie knew about the breakup, which happened back in September. "We're not together anymore. We couldn't work things out."

"Sorry to hear that, hon." She closes the door. "I know your dad enjoyed her visits."

She's right, but I don't want to dwell on the subject of my ex-fiancée. The wound feels too fresh, and I still haven't pulled myself together in the aftermath. I recently lost my job as a software developer, and depression over my run of bad luck is dragging me down a dark, dark hole.

Dad's worsening condition certainly isn't helping matters.

"So how is he today?"

"It's a good day for Raymond." Lizzie nods. "Relatively speaking, of course."

I smile as I shrug off my pea coat and straighten the plain gray crewneck sweater and black denim jeans underneath. The news hasn't often been good since the diagnosis came down three months ago. I've learned to be grateful for the small blessings when they happen.

Though there are parts of my life where the blessings never come.

"He hasn't been talking about your *mother,* either." Lizzie leans closer and lowers her voice. "Or talking *to* her, for that matter."

"Good. That's great." The fact is, talking to Mom is impossible these days. No one's seen hide nor hair of her for the past five years, four months, two weeks, and three days…unless you count Dad, though he only *thinks* he sees her.

Lizzie leads me left, through the dining room. Cleaning isn't part of her job, but the place looks immaculate from what I can see.

"I'll fix you a cup of tea," she says, heading for the kitchen doorway. "You go ahead back."

"Thanks, Lizzie." I veer off, aiming for the entrance to the short hallway running along the rear of the first floor. Dad's bedroom is back there; it has been since his knees got bad and he moved downstairs two years ago.

Suddenly, it looms before me…the doorway to what has become his last little corner of the world. The sound of the TV wafts from inside, the comforting theme song of *The Andy Griffith Show* whistling unmistakably over the airwaves.

"Hello?" His voice sounds shockingly the same as it ever did, just as strong and vital—not at all gritty and hoarse as it often seems when we talk over the phone. "Is that you, Arlene?"

He calls me by Mom's name, which makes me feel

weirdly awkward. He's having a *good* day, I remind myself…and take a step inside.

"Hi, Dad." I swallow hard, fighting back a wave of strong emotion. Talking on the phone is one thing; seeing him in the flesh, in his current condition, is quite another.

"You made it!" Crumpled into his motorized recliner, swaddled in an overabundant red flannel shirt and blue jeans, he looks small. His eyes look huge, on the other hand, hypermagnified by his Coke bottle spectacles. "Happy New Year's Eve, Miss Tourmaline!"

"Not sure who that is, Dad." This is what's it's like to be happy just to see someone alive, yet annoyed and even angry at what they've become…remembering how they used to be and wishing, impossibly, that you could revisit that robust past self. "I'm Jason, your son."

His look of surprise holds for a moment, then settles into a smile. "Jason! Welcome home, son!" He extends his arms for contact.

I lean in for a hug, completing the circuit. "Good to see you, Dad." His body's as bony as a bundle of dry sticks. "Sorry I couldn't make it in for Christmas."

"You didn't miss much." He smells of Binaca, Old Spice, and Ben Gay. "Though Lizzie brought over some cookies and eggnog…without the hootch."

He clings to me as I pull away. "Glad to hear it, Dad. She sure is good to you."

Dad frowns. "Who's that?"

I skip over his mental hiccup, as I often do. His particular dementia makes linear conversations nearly impossible, but jumping down every rabbit hole would leave me almost as dazed and confused as he is.

"Watching *Andy Griffith,* huh?" I sling my pea coat on the foot of his bed and gaze at the flat-screen TV on the wall. Good ol' Andy's strumming a guitar while little Opie sings along adorably—the picture of nostalgic perfection. At a time like this, especially, the past beckons with enticing appeal.

"I want to go shopping at Glosser's." Dad pulls out the chair's remote control and hits what I jokingly refer to as the "ejection seat" button—the one that starts the recliner pushing forward, angling to deposit him on his feet on the floor. He can still walk, thankfully, but getting up out of a chair unassisted is more of a challenge. "Your mother's meeting us there."

"Glosser's Department Store is closed, Dad." It's been closed for thirty-odd years, though I won't belabor the point. As for Mom…

I make it a practice these days to avoid mentioning her whenever possible. It hurts too much, reminding myself that she's gone.

And knowing I've lost Dad, too—*most* of him, at least—and he might have good days now and then, but he isn't really coming back.

"Glosser's is open if you know how to get there." Dad nods emphatically as the chair keeps moving him forward. "That's what Miss Tourmaline says."

As often happens these days, I wonder what the heck he's talking about, but I refuse to get dragged into the maze. "We'll spend the day together tomorrow, Dad, for the New Year." I swoop over, slip the remote from his grasp, and punch the button to reverse the motion of the chair. "I'll make us some pork and sauerkraut for luck."

Just then, the doorbell rings. I ignore it, assuming Lizzie will answer. My face-to-face time with Dad is short, as always, and I don't like it being interrupted.

Suddenly, his eyes dart to the doorway, and a look of fear swims onto his face. One withered hand lashes out and snaps onto my left forearm with unexpected strength.

"Will you go with me to Glosser's?" His voice is meek as a frightened child's. "Will you help me go through with it, no matter what?"

"Sure, Dad." Is this the same man who built a business, raised a family, and survived the loss of a wife under unexplained circumstances? Usually, my memories of who he used to be balance the awareness of his current fallen state—but right now, all I see is someone to be pitied. "Whatever you want."

He looks relieved, but only for a second. At the sound of a knock on the door jamb, the look of terror leaps back on his face, and his grip tightens so painfully on my arm that I nearly cry out.

"Raymond?" Lizzie leans into view. "Someone's here to see you." She sounds puzzled.

"It's you!" Dad's voice is an urgent whisper. "I mean him! I mean it's the man I thought you were when you first got here!"

But the next voice doesn't sound at all like the voice of a man. "Hello, Ray." The face that peeks in through the doorway is that of a young woman, perhaps in her twenties, with copious freckles and curly red hair swinging over her left shoulder. "Aren't you going to introduce me?" Her bright green eyes dart over to light upon me.

"I, uh..." Dad's flustered, to say the least. "This is, uh..." He gestures at her, but he can't seem to make the connection.

"Hope." The young woman, who is tall and slim and dressed in layers of exotically printed veils, strides in and reaches for my hand. "Hope Tourmaline. Pleased to meet you."

I feel dazed as we shake. "Jason Mahoney. Ray's son."

"You said you were coming to take me shopping at Glosser's, didn't you?" Dad flounders, gaping up at her. "But Jason says the store is *closed*."

Hope giggles and winks at him. "Have no fear, my friend. I know *exactly* how to get to Glosser's...though we might have to do a *little* improv en route."

"Improv?" asks Dad. "What are you talking about?"

"I'm talking about the *when*." Hope shoots me a look. "The *where* is not a problem, but the *when* is another story."

"LET'S GET GOING." Dad takes the remote control back and starts the chair moving forward again. The fear that dominated him just moments ago seems to have fled; it's true, his moods can be pretty fluid these days in the grip of dementia. "I just need to make a quick pit stop at the john first."

"Good idea." Hope giggles. "We've got a busy night ahead."

"I can't wait." He sounds excited as the chair pushes him to his feet, and he shuffles toward the door. "And I can't believe we're really *doing* this."

"What exactly *are* you doing?" As Lizzie takes Dad's arm, she casts a suspicious look at Hope. "Some kind of fantasy role-play involving Glosser Bros. Department Store?"

"Heavens, no." Hope grins as she whips her head from side to side. "I wouldn't *dream* of wasting precious time on silly *games*."

"Then what *is* this about?" Lizzie asks darkly. "You *do* know this man requires vital medications administered on a precise schedule, don't you?"

"Yes, *Mom.*" Hope blows out her breath, puffing up a lock of curly red hair on her forehead. "You're not the *only* one who knows things around here."

"Come along, Elizabeth." Dad tugs Lizzie out the bedroom door. "There's no need to make our guest feel unappreciated." He winks at Hope just before he rounds the corner, heading toward the bathroom with Lizzie in tow. Though Dad's usually okay on his own in there, he sometimes needs assistance if the dementia flares up at an awkward moment.

Hope giggles and waggles her fingers in a two-handed wave, though Dad isn't in the room to see it. "What a sweetie!"

"Okay, Ms. Tourmaline." Now that we're alone, I'm done holding back for Dad's benefit. "What's going on here, exactly?"

Suddenly, she's all business. "Two things you need to know." Leaning forward on the balls of her feet, she holds up two fingers, a little too close to my face. "One, whatever happens today is *real* and *true*, and you need to accept it."

"Accept what?" I'm getting annoyed.

Hope flicks down her middle finger, leaving her index finger upright. "Two, if you or your father disobey my instructions *in the slightest*, a *terminal situation* could ensue." She proceeds to push that index finger into my face with great urgency. "Per the terms of my agreement with your father, I will *not* be held responsible for such situations or their ultimate ramifications, which can be *exceedingly* unpredictable." She pokes me between the eyes with her fingertip. *"Are we clear?"*

For once, I feel more confused than Dad is. "What the *blazes* are you *talking* about?"

"You heard your old man." Suddenly relaxed and glib, she bounces back on her heels, folding her hands behind her back. "Just a li'l ol' shopping trip, as advertised."

"At Glosser's. A department store that's been closed for decades."

Hope scrunches up her nose. "Has it, though? Has it really?"

A spark of anger surges to life within me. "I'm shutting this down. I refuse to let you take advantage of my father in his current condition."

"Just stop." Calmly, she raises an eyebrow. "Don't ruin this for him."

Whatever "this" is, it won't matter. He won't remember it anyway. The thought comes to me quickly, but I don't say it aloud.

"How did you even *meet* my father?" I ask. "And why haven't I heard about you before?"

"Not sure why he never mentioned me." Hope shrugs. "But I do tarot readings at the senior center sometimes. He was there one morning—maybe his nurse dropped him off—and I did a reading for him. We got to talking, and he told me about your mom."

"You must've thought he was an easy mark." I know I'm scowling, and I don't care. "A sad old man whose wife went missing, and now he's losing his mind, too."

"That's not how it was."

"Then, what? You told him a fairy tale about how you'll take him to a department store he's fixated on, even though it's been closed for decades?"

Hope smiles knowingly, as if *I'm* the crazy one. "It's not a fairy tale. I have...certain abilities. I can *find* people. Those who are *lost*."

"Oh, really?"

"It's run in my family for generations," insists Hope. "Helping those who are lost is our *legacy*."

"Lost?" My scowl deepens. "You must be talking about my mother."

Hope nods. "I can find her."

"Now I *know* you're full of crap."

"Not at all." She jabs a finger at her chest. "I *will* find her."

"With your 'abilities.'"

"Don't you *want* to see her again?" asks Hope. "Don't you want to bring her *home*? Well, I can do it."

"For a price, I'm guessing. How much?"

Hope sighs. "No price, Jason. We don't monetize our mission."

"Then what *is* the catch?"

"None. Zero."

"You get nothing out of it?"

"Just the satisfaction of helping someone," says Hope.

I stare at her for a long moment, peering into her glittering green eyes. "How dare you?" I'm so angry, I shiver a little as I speak. "Taking advantage of an old man? Getting his hopes up to feed your own need for some kind of sick thrill?"

"That's not it at all."

"Well, it's a good thing I got here when I did, before you took this any further."

"Before we find your mother, you mean?"

"Enough already! Just because Dad thinks it's possible doesn't mean *I* do."

"But what if it *is* possible?" She narrows her eyes and tips her head to one side. "What if there's a *chance* I can make it happen? Should you be so quick to throw it all away?"

As her words sink in, I stiffen. Does her argument outweigh all my concerns?

I would be a complete idiot to let this play out longer,

wouldn't I? Without somehow vetting this woman and her story, I could *never* justify putting my father in what might turn out to be harm's way just to see if her impossible story holds water.

Except I *can* justify it, after all. I *have* to. If Mom *is* still out there somewhere, and Hope indeed has the key to retrieving her, I *can't* say no to her proposal. Endangering Dad is a risk I'm willing to take, at least while I'm along for the ride.

I know it's nuts, but I can't pull the rip cord just yet. Not until we go a little further down this road.

"I'm driving!" Just then, Dad returns on Lizzie's arm, wearing blue jeans instead of sweatpants and sounding crazy coherent. "Who wants to ride shotgun?"

All I can think is, *why doesn't he act this alert when it's just the two of us in the picture?* All I say, though, is, "Shotgun."

Lizzie shoots me a scowl that could fry an egg, and I brush it off with a smirk that says, *Never in a million years will that man be driving a car.*

I don't think I convince her, though.

"It's almost dinner time." Smiling at Hope, Lizzie gestures at the doorway. "Perhaps you could visit again tomorrow or some other day." She nods encouragingly, stopping short of sweeping Hope out the door with a broom.

"That depends," says Hope. "Will it be New Year's Eve then?"

"Well, no..."

Hope shrugs. "Then the answer is..."

"It *has* to be New Year's Eve!" Dad's sudden, angry shout comes as a surprise. "It *has* to be tonight! There's no other way!"

For a moment, we all stand silent, each of us weighing our own private concerns. Was the outburst a flash of dementia? Is Hope manipulating Dad for some evil end she has yet to reveal? Or is there indeed more happening here than meets the eye, and not necessarily in a bad way?

I feel us teetering as on the tip of a fulcrum, tipping this way and that. Which way should we lean? Which future should we choose?

For me, though, there is only way to go. I know I couldn't live with myself otherwise, not after what Hope said moments ago.

What she said about Mom.

"All right then." I walk over and pat Dad's shoulder, smiling reassuringly. I'll humor him, at least for now, until I know more…or realize there's nothing to know after all. "I'll go on one condition."

His eyes narrow. "What's that?"

"You buy me a bag of those roasted nuts." I grin, and he smiles back at me. "The ones you can smell every time you walk in Glosser Bros."

Dad's head bobs on his spindly neck as he chuckles. Whatever else might happen, it's worth the possible inconvenience to see him so coherent and reinvigorated for once. "It's a deal."

As I drive my blue Subaru SUV from our suburban home in Westmont, an upscale borough in the hills around Johnstown, Dad is as jazzed as a kid on Christmas Eve. Riding shotgun beside me, he keeps humming and snapping his fingers, leaning forward against the seat belt as if he imagines he can speed our progress through sheer force of will.

At the same time, he and Hope talk about Glosser Bros. Department Store and what made it such a wonderful place—the selection, the prices, the friendly staff, the personal touch…the roasted nuts. This puts me off because she's much too young to ever have been there when it was open; it's impossible for her to know what the place was like in any but the most abstract sense.

I, on the other hand, remember it well. The place closed when I was a teenager, and I loved it, for the most part—but I don't add my own recollections to the mix. I'm too busy thinking ahead, wondering what comes next in Hope's plan and how to make the most of it without Dad getting hurt in any way.

"Remember the grilled cheese at the snack bar?" asks Dad. "It was the *best*, wasn't it?"

"Always perfectly done, yes." Hope reaches forward and touches his shoulder. "And the tomato soup was to *die* for."

"So delicious." Dad lets out a sigh of contentment. "I used to dip my sandwich in it."

"What a great idea," says Hope. "The perfect combination."

"What was *your* favorite, Lizzie?" asks Dad, though Lizzie isn't in the car.

"She didn't come with us, remember?" says Hope. "She went home early to spend the holiday with family."

"Oh, right." Dad nods. "I guess I forgot."

"No worries. It's all good, Raymond." Hope touches his shoulder again, and he beams.

Glancing at her smiling face in the rear-view mirror, I'm annoyed all over again at the response she's getting. I can't remember the last time I saw Dad this alert, happy, and composed...but it sure wasn't because of anything *I* said or did.

"There it is!" Dad jabs a finger at the windshield. "Let me out right here!" We're over a block away, but he starts tugging on the door handle.

"Hold on." I tap the control that locks all four doors at once, ensuring he can't jump out. "Just let me get a space, and we can go in together."

He jimmies the handle some more with increasing frustration. "Door's broken," he snaps.

As we roll up Franklin Street along Central Park, the five-story building looks much the same as it ever has—a big brick shoebox, each level defined by rows of windows. It mostly consists of offices now, and a few retail businesses, but if you came back to town after years away and didn't know any better, you might just as easily believe the old department store still sprawled throughout its interior.

As we draw closer, the differences between the modern building and its past incarnation become more evident. There's no Glosser Bros. signage running above the big picture windows on either side of the corner. Instead of providing unobstructed views of festive displays designed by Glosser's window dressers, those windows are covered with Christmas-themed paintings executed by local schoolchildren. Also different from the store's heyday, no streams of customers flow into and out of the ground-level doors, carrying Glosser Bros. shopping bags with the familiar brown-and-white-striped motif and the name of the store in cursive script lettering.

How Hope intends to take Dad on a shopping trip in there is beyond me.

Turning left off Franklin Street, I pull into a space on Locust, right in front of that side of the store. In the old days, it would have been a prime spot, nearly impossible to get because of its proximity to the main entryways of the place.

"This is it." I flick the switch on the control panel on the driver's side door, popping all the locks, fully expecting Dad to leap right out.

But he doesn't. Instead, he just sits there, staring straight ahead, lost in thought.

"Raymond?" Hope leans forward between the seats. "Is something wrong?"

Dad takes a deep breath and lets it out slowly. "I'm scared. That's all."

"Don't worry, Raymond." She gives his shoulder a squeeze. "Jason and I will be with you every step of the way."

"But what if…what if it doesn't work? What if I can't *make* it?"

"Trust me, you'll be fine," she tells him. "This isn't my first rodeo, remember?"

"But what if something goes wrong?"

"Then we throw *him* under the bus." She giggles and hikes a thumb at me. "Don't you know *cannon fodder* when you see it?"

I shoot her a glare, but she doesn't seem to notice.

Dad chuckles, then clears his throat and sits up straighter. "Thank you." Already, his voice is stronger. "I think I'm ready now."

"That's the spirit." Hope pops forward, presses a quick kiss on his cheek, then surprisingly brushes one on mine as well—the first a woman's lips have made contact with me since Desiree flew the coop.

"RIGHT THIS WAY, FELLOW GLOSSERITES. GLOSSERTONIANS?" Hope holds the door to the ground floor open as I help Dad over the threshold. "The shopping experience of a lifetime awaits!"

As we pass, I notice she's carrying a big hardcover book with the title *Long Live Glosser's* on the spine. I wonder why she brought it, but I don't ask about it yet.

"This is where the magic happens, guys." She zips past as we slowly make our way up the entry ramp. "Gives me a chill just thinking about it."

I'm not sure if it's the power of suggestion, but I get a chill myself as I look around. We're entering a big, open lobby that I instantly recognize as part of what used to be the first floor of Glosser Bros.

With memories, and a little imagination, it isn't hard to see the outlines of the original ground level of the store. Some parts have changed little from the old days, like the bank of elevators along one wall or the big central well leading into the basement. Other things have been greatly redone, like the offices on one side of the space or the restaurant (now closed) on the other. Walk straight back and hang a left, and you'll run into an appliance rental place occupying the back half of the ground level.

It isn't the same as the old Glosser Bros. store, and yet, it fills the same space. It echoes with the vibrations of a million million bargains, a billion billion shoppers, an infinite number of brown-and-white-striped bags.

On this December afternoon, however, so many years after the store's final closing, the foot traffic is much more limited, and no one carries Glosser Bros. bags. Other than the three of us, only a handful of people drift through the lobby area—a woman in business attire and winter coat leaving and locking up one of the offices; a young man walking out of the rental place with a microwave oven in hand; a female security guard rounding a corner and stepping into a public bathroom, pulling the door shut. Things are winding down before the holiday; the old excitement of the former retailer's annual New Year's Eve sales no longer permeates these walls.

How in the world does Hope thing she can bring it back...and why?

"Do you remember that old song from the commercials?" Hope walks to the middle of the room, opens the book, and flips through the pages. "'*We're all going to Glosser's.*' Remember that?"

Dad starts singing it as I lead him over to her. I'm not sure why, but he seems more energized all of a sudden. *"We're all going to Glosser's. We're all going to Glosser's."*

"That's the one." Hope gets to almost the end of the book and stops, holding it wide open for us to see. "Now here's what I want you to do. Focus your eyes on this photo and sing that song, again and again."

The photo is a full-page image of the Glosser Bros. Department Store on a winter night, a big arrangement of lights in the shape of a Christmas tree draped over the corner of the building. The streets around it are covered in newfallen snow, a car driving past like something out of the 1970s. A man and woman stand in the foreground, backs to the camera, getting ready to cross Franklin Street.

"Is this some kind of hypnosis technique or something?" I frown, wondering if it's time to pull the plug on this little adventure.

"Does this *look* like a Vegas stage show?" Hope giggles and wags her head. "You *really* need to expand your ideas of what's *possible*, Jason."

My frown deepens. "Then what exactly are we doing here? What is this all about?"

"Finding your mother," says Hope.

"But the last place she was seen was the Galleria Mall in Richland," I tell her. "Nowhere *near* here."

"Which means *nothing* according to your father," she insists. "He's been having *visions* of her, and the visions are *memories* of his *younger* self meeting her *older* self in the *past.* Within these recovered memories, she looks the *same* as she did just before she *disappeared*...only the flashbacks are from *decades* ago."

I shake my head in disbelief as her impossible story sinks in. "You're trying to tell me she's somewhere *back in time*? That's where she disappeared to?"

Hope nods. "However, we don't know the exact *year*... just that Ray remembers meeting with her on New Year's Eve at Glosser's, and she was the same age in that memory as when she was last seen five years ago. *Now* is our chance to go back and find that particular New Year's Eve from Ray's memory before she slips even farther away."

"Well, that sounds easy enough." I snort sarcastically. "You're *nuts,* you know that?"

"Am I?" She grins at Dad. "What do *you* think, Ray?"

"We're all going to Glosser's." Dad's singing again and staring at the Christmas photo in the book as instructed. *"We're all going to Glosser's..."*

"At least *he* has the right idea," whispers Hope...and then she sings, too. *"We're all going to Glosser's. We're all going to Glosser's."*

I'm losing my patience. Not sure what I expected when I agreed to come here with Dad, but my tolerance for this silliness is wearing thin.

"Look deep into the picture, guys," says Hope. "Gaze

into the doors and windows on the corner of the store. Imagine walking inside, entering that magical place… leaving today's world and all its troubles behind."

"Okay, enough." I back away. "It's 4:30 in the afternoon. They'll be locking up the building soon for the holiday."

"Give it a *chance,* Jason." She grabs my wrist and reels me back in. *"Look.* Just *look* in those *doors.* You can practically reach out and *touch* them, can't you?"

I do look deeper then, almost against my will. The image is so clear, I can see inside the store—can make out two shoppers in the doorway, each carrying a Glosser's striped shopping bag. Behind them, I glimpse displays and decorations leading toward the very spot where we now stand.

Hope is right about the reaching out part. This photo is a window on a lost and distant past, nearly as clear and solid as the world entrenched around us.

"Sing it just once, Jason." Hope jabs me in the side with her elbow. "Just one time, please. We all need to sing it."

I can't help rolling my eyes…but then I do as she's asked, resolving it will be my final act of cooperation before whisking my father away from this con artist or nut. *"We're all going to Glosser's."*

Just then, I swear, the photo *moves.* Snowflakes swirl in the wind. The people in the doorway step outside. The people in the foreground step onto the street.

This, of course, is my imagination in action. I *knew* she was working some kind of hypnosis on us.

But then how do you explain the sudden *rush* of cold

air, the feeling of my feet *leaping* free of the floor, and the overwhelming sensation of *spinning* taking hold of me? What about the blurs of rapid motion in all directions, punctuated by the flashing of bright lights?

And what about the *sudden* impact of my feet landing hard on a solid surface, knocking the breath out of my lungs?

"Jason?" Hope's voice seems to come from miles away as it seeps through the haze in my head. "Jason, take some deep breaths."

I shake my head hard but can't clear it. I try to look around, but there seem to be curtains of gauze blocking my vision.

"Jason." Her voice is closer and stronger now. "Listen to me. You're going to be fine, but you need to focus. You need to complete the transition."

I clamp my eyes shut and take a deep breath as instructed, then let it out. After that, I draw and release another breath, then another.

Focus. I reach deep, fighting to wrap my head around whatever has happened, straining to grasp *just one thing* I might use as a guidepost. A sound, a touch, a taste, that's all I need...just one single ray of light to pull me through the fog.

Then, suddenly, I have it. *A smell.*

As it wafts into my nose, I recognize it instantly. Though it's been a while since last I smelled this scent, I know it intimately. It awakens intense feelings within me, stirs something deep that I'd somehow forgotten...something I can *focus* on with every fiber of my being.

The smell is that of *roasting nuts*—and not just *any* roasting nuts. This particular mix, prepared a particular way with particular seasonings and roasting conditions, exists in only one place, to my knowledge, in all the world.

It only exists *here*.

"What the—?" My eyes spring open, and my vision clears. Gazing around, I see the only place I've been expecting since the smell of roasting nuts hit my nose, the only place this could possibly be, as impossible as it seems.

I'm on the ground floor of the Glosser Building, and the department store is open for business.

LOOKING AROUND, I see Glosser Bros. as I remember it—the racks of clothes, tables of accessories, shelves of shoes. Price signs are everywhere, proclaiming New Year's holiday deals—and the prices themselves are remarkably low, straight out of a long-gone decade.

Amid Christmas and New Year's decorations—Santa Claus coexisting with Father Time, Baby New Year, and bottles of champagne—shoppers make the rounds, perusing the merchandise. Their outfits and hairstyles look like something from the early-to-mid 1970s, all floral prints, leisure suits, primary colors, sideburns, and feathered shags.

I swallow hard as I take it all in. If this is a hypnotically-induced hallucination, it's a startlingly real one, almost enough to make me believe I've traveled back in time to…

"Jason?" Suddenly, Hope blocks my view, pushing something into my hands—the hardcover *Long Live Glosser's* book. "Hold this for me and keep it safe. No matter what you do, don't let *anyone* read it."

"What? Why?"

She leans in close and lowers her voice. "Because it could change the past, which we want to avoid if possible."

Then, she darts off between the racks, calling Dad's name. Only then does it sink in that he isn't in sight.

Heart pounding, I look around frantically for some sign of him—and instead come face to face with a middle-aged Black woman in a green coat with a dark fur collar. "Where can I find one of *those*?" She points at the book in my hands.

Looking down, I see I've been holding it with the front cover out, the title in plain sight. The artwork on the cover is framed along the spine with brown vertical stripes like those on the store's trademark shopping bags.

"Oh, uh, you can't. Not yet." Flustered, I turn the book, see the title's on the back cover, too, then lower it in front of me, futilely hiding as much of the typography as I can with my outspread hands.

"Is it some kind of history of the store?" The woman reaches for the book. "Can I just have a quick look, at least?"

"Nope, sorry." I manage a nervous smile as I back away —then run into a rack of men's shirts. "It's a galley, you know. Just a draft, really. A very *rough* one."

"I don't mind." She steps forward and reaches again. "It looks so interesting."

"Bye!" I twist out of the way, stuff the book under my peacoat, and head off through the racks after Hope. "Have a happy New Year's!"

I have a moment of pure panic, then, as I wind my way across the ground floor of Glosser's. Not only is Dad nowhere to be seen, but Hope has disappeared, too.

A wave of sheer terror washes over me, driving my heartbeat to fresh hammer-blow heights. Until now, I've never imagined this fate was possible—but here I am, apparently in the middle of it.

I'm stuck in the Glosser Bros. Department Store in the 1970s, and those who traveled back here with me are gone.

WHAT IF I can't get home to the time where I belong? What if Dad is lost in this bygone era? What will become of the two of us?

These are the questions racing through my brain when I hear someone whistle up ahead, from above. Eyes lurching in that direction, I see the whistling's coming from the old-fashioned wooden escalator. Hope's halfway up, trying to get my attention.

Relief replaces the terror washing over me. Hope waves urgently for me to join her, and I quicken my pace, eager to catch up before she loses me again.

Along the way, I have to dodge several customers, each dressed in classic 70s garb, and a male employee toting two stacks of shoeboxes. He nearly drops them when I pass but somehow manages not to, tossing curses in my wake as I keep going.

"Sorry!" I tell him over my shoulder, but I don't dare slow down with so much at stake. Hope is my lifeline; I can't afford to let her slip away.

And Dad, who's on the way to having the mind of a child, is lost in a department store in the 1970s, though honestly, I have to wonder if he might feel right at home here…more at home than I do.

WHEN I STEP off the escalator, Hope has eluded me again…but not for long. I spy the back of her head across the second floor, her curly red hair catching the light from the overhead fluorescents.

As I get closer, I feel a fresh surge of relief, for I can see she's talking to Dad. His head's down, and he looks confused, but at least he's present and safe.

They keep talking as I jog up to them. He has something in his hand—an avocado green knit shirt, sized for a child.

"She's not here." He sounds halfway like he's sobbing. "We missed Arlene! She's gone, gone forever."

"We did miss her, you're right," says Hope. "But she's not gone forever. She's just somewhen else, that's all."

"I thought this was it," says Dad. "I thought I remembered standing here with her today...talking." He lifts the shirt on its hanger, then lowers it, looking lost. "But I guess I was wrong, wasn't I?"

"We'll give it a few more minutes to be sure." Hope takes the shirt from him and hangs it on the nearest rack. "Just relax, Ray. We're not nearly done searching, I promise you."

Dad leans heavily on a table covered with boys' socks and underwear. "But what if I'm wrong about all of it? How will we know?"

"I'll know." She reaches for him. "You'll just have to trust me on this."

As they hug, I step away and bob my head, summoning her to follow. She joins me across the aisle, leaving him looking around forlornly amid the children's clothes.

"None of this makes sense." I gesture at the very-much-open store around us. "None of this is possible."

"How can you say that?" asks Hope. "The evidence of your own eyes tells a different story, doesn't it?"

I frown, watching a young woman in a peasant blouse, bell-bottom jeans, and Earth shoes stroll past, looking at clothes on the racks. "But it *can't* be real. Time travel is a *fantasy.*"

"Only to the closed-minded." Hope smiles. "It's a good thing none of us fits that description."

I blow out my breath, unable to deny what I'm experiencing though I badly want to reject it out of hand. "You really think Mom is lost in time somehow?"

"It happens more often than you realize," says Hope.

"There are holes, you know...holes in the time-space continuum. People fall through them, usually without realizing it. They blink, and they're suddenly decades in the past, with no way home."

I frown. "And you think Dad's recovered memory proves that's what happened to Mom?"

"We can't ignore the possibility, can we?"

"But his memory is awful these days, you know."

"Not in this case," says Hope. "His recollection of their meeting is *extremely* vivid."

"Really? He has *dementia*."

"Doesn't matter," says Hope. "Dementia patients and the elderly with memory loss can still remember certain things with amazing accuracy. In fact, it's common for old folks who can't remember what they did five minutes ago to *clearly* remember something that happened decades ago in childhood."

"And you say this particular memory just *came back* to him?" I still don't trust her. "There were no drugs or hypnotic regression involved?"

"Correct."

I watch as Dad steps out from the racks of children's clothes and wanders down the aisle, looking this way and that. "If his memory's so clear, then where *is* she? How'd he get it wrong?"

Hope blows out her breath and folds her arms over her chest. "Just because a memory's *clear* doesn't mean it's *perfect*."

"Sounds like you're talking in circles," I tell her.

"Ray remembers certain details like they happened

yesterday, but *other* details are *fuzzy*. He recalls meeting her at Glosser's around closing time on New Year's Eve, but he doesn't recall *which* New Year's Eve."

"How is that even possible?"

"Nothing in his memory is identifiable as belonging to a specific year," she explains. "As far as he remembers, your mother's clothes and hairstyle during their encounter were nondescript. The decorations and layout of the store could have belonged to any of a number of eras. What he remembers of the products on the shelves and racks is also non-specific."

"What about what she said to him? There weren't any hints in that?"

"Apparently not," says Hope. "She didn't seem to recognize his younger self. She did know him when he was younger—they married in their twenties—but maybe she was disoriented or just didn't make the connection because he was out of context to her older self."

"Huh." I watch as Dad continues his circuit of the second floor, pausing near the lingerie department to stare at a middle-aged woman shopping for bras. "So this is a real crapshoot, is what you're trying to tell me?"

Hope shakes her head. "I have a system. We'll narrow it down."

"What system?" I know I sound skeptical, and I don't care. "What *system?*"

Hope walks off without answering, scooting Dad away from the bra-buying woman. Judging from the bra buyer's annoyed body language, I'd say Hope's rescue was timely.

As the two of them work their way back to me, I

grapple with my sense of disbelief. Nothing she's said about our situation has any basis in what I know as reality. Her explanations get more far-fetched every time she opens her mouth.

But *none* of this seems based in reality, does it? And if any of it is fake in any way, I have yet to determine what that might be.

As far as I can tell, we have indeed traveled back in time to the Glosser Bros. Department Store in the 1970s, and Hope and her "system" are our only chance of finding Mom and getting home. Those are the facts as I know them.

"Hello, shoppers." Just then, a woman's voice speaks over the store's public address system. *"Glosser Bros. will close for the holiday in five minutes. Please complete your purchases and enjoy a wonderful New Year's Eve with your family and friends."*

"That's our cue, fellas," says Hope as she and Dad return to the boys' clothing department. "Time to move on down the line."

"Are you sure?" Dad looks around again, eyes darting from one department to the next. "She definitely isn't here?"

"You're the Geiger counter," says Hope. "You tell me."

He looks around some more, then closes his eyes. When he opens them again and speaks, he looks and sounds disappointed. "She's gone."

"Must have fallen through another portal," says Hope, "and entered another time."

"That can happen?" I ask.

Hope nods. "Sometimes, there are whole chains of interlinked portals, leading from era to era, for reasons I don't pretend to understand. I've known people who've spent their entire *lives* hopelessly lost in those chains, unable to get home."

A chill races up my back at the thought of poor Mom wandering lost through time, desperate but unable to return to us. "We have to save her. We have to try."

"Then let's find our next destination." Hope reaches for the Glosser Bros. book, which I'd nearly forgotten I was carrying under my peacoat. "Time to consult this mystic tome once more."

She flips the book open and points at one of the pages. It's a newspaper story about the store's 50th anniversary, though I can't quite make out the year in the header of the reprinted clipping.

"Just like before, guys." Hope raises the book and pokes her finger at the artwork that accompanies the story—an illustration of the Glosser Building with *GLOSSER BROS. 50TH* in bold text superimposed over it. "Focus on the doors leading into the store. Imagine walking through them and going inside. Sing it with me: *We're all going to Glosser's."*

"We're all going to Glosser's." Dad's singing sounds a little less spirited this time. *"We're all going to Glosser's."*

I still don't fully buy into whatever magical process we're supposedly triggering—but I also don't like the idea of possibly being left behind in the 1970s. Cooperation seems like the lesser of evils, so I focus on the image in the book and repeat the words softly...speaking, not singing them.

"We're all going to Glosser's."

And it works.

Just like before, I experience a sudden rush of cold air, and my body leaves the floor. I spin like a top, dazzled by a blur of bright lights streaking past.

This time, though, when my feet slam back to the floor, and the impact kicks the breath out of my lungs, the jarring arrival doesn't rattle me as much as it did when we arrived in the 70s. Maybe I'm getting used to time travel, or whatever this is.

But what I see when I finish my landing on Glosser's ground floor and look around is quite different from what I saw in the 70s. Men in business suits and women in fancy dresses and hats linger around racks and tables, looking at merchandise. The lettering on the sale signs is old-fashioned, using basic fonts that were out of fashion by the 70s. In general, everything looks newer, less worn and weathered. The song playing over the P.A. is light popular music from a simpler time, performed by a male crooner and a big band orchestra.

The only thing that hasn't changed, the thing I latch onto and use as an anchor, is the smell of roasted nuts wafting through the store.

Just as I wonder *when* we've landed, I spot a decoration on the wall—a Baby New Year being carried in a white cloth bundle from the beak of a stork, a year stamped on his diaper. This, then, must be the year to which we've come on this stage of our journey—a year that was long gone before I was ever born.

1956.

"I DON'T SEE HER." Dad looks around frantically. "She isn't here!"

"Don't give up yet, we just got here." Hope gives his shoulder a squeeze. "Let's look around a little, first."

"Is it definitely the right time and place?" I ask her. "The one we were aiming for?"

"Absolutely." Even as she says it, a male customer in a gray flannel suit marches by and wishes us all a Happy New Year's Eve with a tip of his snappy hat.

"But why 1956?" I gesture at the Baby New Year decoration with the datelined diaper. "What's the significance?"

"It's because Ray sensed this would be Arlene's next stop," explains Hope. "He's *connected* to her, even across the time-space continuum."

"The store's 50th anniversary is on New Year's Eve, then?"

"No," says Hope. "The book pulls us into the correct general vicinity—in this case, the year 1956. Then, Ray's link to Arlene helps us zero in on the exact date we want, which is New Year's Eve."

At that moment, Dad moves past us with eyes narrowed.

After his disappointment in the 70s, he looks alert and engaged again, not at all weakened by age or dementia. "There are still traces of her." He tips his head to one side as if listening for a distant signal. "But they feel...*different*."

Following Dad's intuition, the three of us cross the ground floor and board the escalator to the next level. The wooden handrails and treads aren't brand-new, but they're in better shape than I've ever seen, less nicked and worn. How strange it is, seeing the process of aging in reverse, restoring the long-lost luster to objects that are destined for decay and disrepair. I wonder if Dad's newfound vitality is in some way the result of that reverse aging process.

We disembark on the second floor and resume our search, weaving through the racks of clothes that reflect the era's styles. I see more women in outfits that look like what I'd expect to be their Sunday finest, complete with understated, finely-tailored dresses, color-coordinated hose, and sensible yet classy pumps. Men match the mannequins in the suit department, framed in double-breasted jackets, monochromatic neckties, and trousers with creases so sharp, they could slice a stick of butter. The children wear their own conformist uniforms—button-down plaid shirts and blue jeans with rolled cuffs for the boys, and sweaters, skirts, dresses, caps, and buckled patent leather flats for the girls.

Overall, it's a very different look than the 70s, much more of a culture shock situation for me. I feel much less at ease here, more out of my element...though Dad seems right at home. He plows through the second floor as if he belongs there, as if he never left in the first place.

I'm guessing Mom felt the same way when she was here, though that doesn't seem to have kept her anchored in this era. We cover the entirety of the second floor in a matter of minutes, yet still she is nowhere to be found.

"Nothing." Dad wags his head in frustration...then gestures at the elevator bank behind the piece goods and notions department. "Maybe we should try upstairs."

He hits the button, and a car arrives a moment later.

"What floor, please?" asks the black-haired, middle-aged female attendant seated inside, wearing a dark brown Glosser Bros. smock.

"Three, please," says Dad...but then he surprises me.

Something catches his eye just as the door starts sliding closed. Moving with amazing quickness for someone of his age and poor health, he slips out just before the door shuts and the car rises.

I shoot a look at Hope, whose eyes are wide as saucers.

When the car reaches the third floor, we stay aboard and ride it back to two. The attendant smiles knowingly just before the door slides open again.

"Good luck with your dad," she says. "Old-timers can give us a run for our money, can't they?"

"You don't know the half of it," says Hope as the two of us bolt out of that car as fast as we can, looking every which way for the man who isn't there.

"WHAT ARE the chances he fell through a hole in the time-space continuum like Mom did?" That's what I ask after Hope and I have combed the entire second floor with no luck.

"Anything's possible," says Hope. "Maybe the hole that pulled her out of here sucked him in, too."

"If that's what happened, how would we find them?"

"We wouldn't," she tells me. "Game over."

"Game over?"

"But the good news is, there's one place left to look on this floor." She leads me past the boys' department and into a short passageway leading out of the main Glosser Building.

We emerge from the end of the passage into an adjacent structure known as the Annex. I recognize the place from childhood, though the décor is very different; the space is occupied by Glosser's Cafeteria, the Hunt Room Restaurant, and my personal favorite, the soda fountain.

That's where we find Dad, leaning against the wall, eyes glued to a young mother and a little girl of about six or seven with gleaming blonde hair streaming over the hood of her quilted red-and-black winter coat.

"Dad?" He doesn't look up as I approach, just keeps watching the mother and child. "Are you okay?"

"Found her," he says softly. "Right there. There she is."

I've known the day will come when he'll lose it completely, and I'm thinking this might be it. "Dad, no. That woman isn't her. That's not Mom."

"Not the woman." Dad chokes out a sob and brushes a tear from his cheek.

"The little girl?" says Hope. "You really think that's her?"

"I *know* it is," says Dad. "I've seen plenty of old photos...and I *feel* her presence. That is *her.*"

"This is what you meant when you said she felt *different,*" explains Hope. "That is her *younger* self, as she originally existed in 1956."

We all watch as the child gets a dish of ice cream from the dark-haired waitress at the counter. "And what else?" asks the waitress, whose name tag reads *Ruby*.

"That's all, thanks," says the child's mother, popping open her purse.

As she pays, Dad starts forward...and I grab him by the arm, holding him back.

"Dad, no," I tell him. "Don't do it."

"But it's *her*."

"Maybe it is," says Hope. "But if so, what can you accomplish by approaching her? She's not the Arlene you're looking for, is she? She's not your *wife*...not the woman from the future who fell through a hole in the time-space continuum and got lost in the past."

Dad frowns, watching as the little girl dips a white plastic spoon in the vanilla ice cream, then lights up as she tastes it. I can tell he wants to run to her.

And I can empathize. Though I don't recognize her at all in that form, the thought of meeting her as a child is tempting. After all, it's been years since I last saw her as an adult; seeing her in *any* form is enough to tug at my heart-strings.

But both of us manage to hold back, with a little help

from Hope. "We can't risk changing history any more than we have to," she says, keeping her voice low. "Who *knows* what damage we might do with a single slip of the tongue? We might trigger a time paradox and inadvertently erase *both* of you from *existence*."

"You're right." I sigh as Arlene and her mother—my grandmother—head for a table in the dining room. "We can't take the chance."

"Let's go." Dad lurches out the door with tears staining his cheeks.

Leaving the cafeteria behind, the three of us emerge from the passageway to the second floor of the main building.

Before we can figure out what our next move should be, a woman's voice booms over the P.A. system, announcing the store is about to close for the holiday. *"Happy New Year's Eve to one and all from your Glosser Bros. family,"* she says.

We all know that's the *time's-up* signal. Reflexively, I raise the book that will lead us to our next destination.

This time, Hope opens *Long Live Glosser's* to an early page and brings down her fingertip on a black-and-white photo of what to me are prehistoric times. It's a shot of the grocery store that once occupied Glosser's basement, complete with shelves stocked with various foods in truly vintage packaging. The lights and furnishings have a streamlined, art deco style, a look evoking old late-late-show movies I've seen.

"*That's* where she is?" I ask. "The Roaring Twenties?"

"More like the early 30s," says Hope, lifting the book higher for our benefit. "Now *focus*. Imagine yourself in that grocery department, walking among those counters and shelves. You can practically pick up a ripe peach and bite into it, letting the juice run down your chin."

"Is there any way we could skip this one?" I'm having trouble focusing. The Great Depression isn't an era I particularly want to visit…or risk getting trapped in.

"It's where the trail leads." Hope looks at Dad, who nods. "Ray confirms it. The latest hole in the time-space continuum deposited the future version of Arlene in the era pictured in that photo. Our paths might finally intersect with hers there."

I sigh and stare at the photo, fighting to concentrate. Dad does the same, though the words of the song come more easily to his lips. He doesn't even wait for Hope's prompting to start singing.

"We're all going to Glosser's. We're all going to Glosser's."

The familiar changes happen around us as our trip through time initiates…but then things take an unexpected turn.

Just as the cold wind gusts and I start to feel lightheaded, Hope drops the book. It lands on the floor at our feet, and I scoop it up—but the world is already spinning. By the flickering lights whirling around us, I see the book is open to a different page, a much earlier one.

The photo there, at the bottom of page 26, holds my

attention, drawing me in. I'm aware of Hope and Dad fading from view, leaving me alone in the heart of the storm…and then the whirling takes my breath away, and everything goes black.

I WAKE ON A HARDWOOD FLOOR, my neck and back killing me. Instead of hot roasted nuts, I smell sawdust and tobacco smoke.

Blinking my eyes open, I see a single, glowing light bulb hanging from a stamped tin ceiling above me. Looking left, I see a glass display case filled with men's dress shirts; a display case on my right is occupied by old-fashioned dresses, the kind with long sleeves and hems that reach the top of women's shoes.

Only when I sit up do I realize I'm in a one-room store in the *very* old days—and I'm not alone. A dark-haired, dark-eyed young man in a black suit and bow tie leans against a table stacked with folded sheets and towels. He doesn't look at me right away because his attention is elsewhere…focused on the pages of a book.

An all-too-familiar hardcover book.

A wave of dread washes over me as I take in the scene —and realize he's the only other person in the room. Dad and Hope aren't there; they must not have made it back this far, perhaps because they were more focused on the grocery department photo from the 1930s.

I, on the other hand, must have gotten a big enough

dose of the *other* image, the one that came up when I retrieved the dropped book, that I ended up somewhen very *else.* Based on what little I saw of the text on the page, I'd say I've traveled back to the *original* Glosser Bros. store, and I'm nowhere *near* the early 30s.

The calendar on the wall behind the dark-haired man confirms it. The big, bold number at the top of the panel is shockingly ancient, so long ago it might as well be biblical to me.

According to the calendar, the year is *1906.* Not only have I been separated from my traveling companions—one of whom was doing the driving on this trip through time—but I've ended up near the turn of the 20th Century, a decidedly low-tech time that would *not* have been my first choice when it comes to eras in which to be marooned.

"You all right?" asks the guy without looking up from the book.

"Sure." As I get to my feet and get a better look at the copy of *Long Live Glosser's* spread on the counter, I get a sick feeling. From what I can see, the book is open to almost the very end.

Hope's words come back to me. *No matter what you do, don't let anyone read it,* she said. *It could change the past, which we want to avoid if possible.*

Houston, we have a problem.

"You whacked your head pretty good," says the guy. "When you popped up outta nowhere, that is."

I brush the sawdust from my peacoat, choosing not to

respond to his comment. "Have you seen a redheaded woman and an old man, by any chance?"

"No sir." The guy can't tear his eyes away from the book, and I can't blame him. He's getting a good, long look at the future...and the future of this store. I just have to hope he's not in a position to put that foreknowledge to use.

"I'm Jason, by the way," I tell him, walking over to the book on the counter.

"Pleased to make your acquaintance." The guy shakes his head slowly as he turns another page. "You can call me Nate...short for Nathan. Nathan Glosser, actually."

"Ah, okay," I say. "And that's 'Glosser' as in..."

"The sign outside, yep." He points toward the front of the place, still without looking up from the book. "I'm the 'N' in the 'N. Glosser Store.'"

So much for him not being someone in a position to change history. I'm not a Glosser Bros. expert, but I know enough to recognize the name of the very first Glosser store in Johnstown...meaning the guy in front of me is the actual founder of the Glosser retail empire.

"So, uh...how long was I out?"

"Not long." He turns another page, frowning at something he sees there. "An hour or so."

"You let me lie there *on the floor* in the middle of your *store* for an *hour?"*

"I checked, and you were breathing." He flips back to the previous page to check something. "Besides, I was busy."

"I can see that. You're quite a reader, aren't you?"

"Depends on the book." He flips forward again. "And I really like this one, for some reason."

"Uh-huh." Approaching the counter, I clear my throat. "Nice tie, by the way. Got a date?"

"New Year's Eve party," says Nate. "I'm going straight there after work."

"Good for you. Sounds like fun."

"I hope so." He flashes a smile. "What about you? Got any plans?"

"I'm not big on New Year's, actually." That's true but ironic, considering the number of New Year's Eves I've been to recently. "We'll see how things shake out, I guess."

"'Shake out.'" Nate chuckles. "That's a new one."

Leaning over the counter, I point at *Long Live Glosser's*. "You do know that's mine, right?"

"I don't think so." He closes the book and holds it up, gesturing at the title. "My name's on the cover."

I smile. If I were in his shoes, I'd want to claim that book for my own, as well. "That may be true, but it's still my property. You don't get to keep it just because you were conscious when I got here and I wasn't."

"It's quite a story, isn't it?" He drums his fingers on the cover.

I wrack my brain for some kind of excuse to explain away the book's vision of future events. "Actually, it's a work of fantasy…a marketing tool. An example of the kind of 'future history' we've produced to promote other retail establishments such as your own."

"Seems pretty realistic to me," says Nate. "More like prophecy than fantasy."

"Thank you." I take a slight bow. "Then I've done my job well and created a believable, enjoyable fiction."

"I didn't say I *enjoyed* it." Nate leans back casually and deposits the book on a high shelf on the wall, then slips a cigarette case from the vest pocket of his black jacket.

"You didn't? And why is that?"

Nate opens the case, slips out a hand-rolled cigarette, and lights it with a match. "Lousy ending, of course. Not a happy one at all."

Clearly, Nate has absorbed a lot of the book's content. I'm not thrilled, to say the least. "What didn't you like about it?"

"The end of the company, of course. The closing of the store." He puffs on the cigarette, then blows out a cloud of smoke. "So much success, and it was all for nothing in the end."

"What about all the people whose lives were better because of the store?"

Nate puffs thoughtfully on the cigarette. For the first time, his dark-eyed gaze meets mine. "How would you like to work for me?" The question seems to come out of the blue.

I'm dumbstruck, but I can't let on. "That's a generous offer," I tell him. "But I'm just passing through Johnstown."

"You've given me a remarkable gift." He reaches up and pats the book. "Please allow me to repay you in this small way."

Smart guy that he is, I'm sure he'd love to have me stick around and reveal more secrets of the future. I figure

I've already changed history enough for one lifetime... though I doubt he'll appreciate the sentiment.

Then there's the matter of Mom, Dad, and Hope, whenever *they* are. Pretty sure I won't have much chance of finding them if I hang around here too long.

My best strategy is clear. I need to get the heck outta Dodge.

And to do that, I need a certain book—assuming I can even get it to work without help from Hope.

"No need to repay me, Nate," I tell him. "But there *is* a bit more to the story...an interesting piece we left out of the book."

He frowns. "What kind of piece?"

"Let's call it an epilogue." I gesture at the book. "In fact, why don't I just add it in for you?" I give him a wink. "Then you'll have the *complete* story."

He hesitates, and rightly so. Would *you* take a chance with something so precious that just magically fell in your lap?

But then, temptation gets the better of him. He stubs out his cigarette in a tin ashtray on the counter, then turns and slides the book off the shelf.

"Great, thanks," I say as he places the book on the counter. "Now I just need a pencil."

Without taking his eyes off me and the book, he reaches back and pulls a red-painted pencil out of a cigar box on a shelf behind him. He hands it over without comment...but I get a strong feeling that his muscles are tightly coiled and ready to burst into action if I make a wrong move.

"Okay, great." I open to the blank end papers at the back of the book, then start sketching with the pencil. I'm not much of an artist, but I manage a drawing that vaguely resembles the corner of the future Glosser Building, the main entrance of the department store of tomorrow. "So the ending of the story turned out *not* to be the end, after all. A few years after the store closed, it was reborn."

"How?"

"A group of investors." I sketch a few stick figures near the storefront and add dollar signs floating over their heads. "They loved Glosser's Department Store so much, they banded together to bring it back."

"Just like *that*?" He snaps his fingers. "They threw good money after bad just because they loved the store?"

"Hey, I'm just telling you how it happened."

"In your *fictional* story," says Nate. "You did say this is just a marketing tool, right?"

"Isn't everything?" I shrug, adding details to the sketch of the building—shading in bricks in the walls, dropping stick-figure shoppers in the doorway, writing GLOSSER BROS. above the windows on either side of the corner. It's not exactly a high-resolution photo, not even a quality piece of artwork, but I'm hoping it might serve the purpose.

"So did the store live happily ever after?" asks Nate. "Or did it end up going under all over again?"

"It became *spectacularly* successful." I scribble *Glosser's International* atop the page and sketch little block buildings in a ring around the central drawing, each labeled with the letters *G.I.* "The company opened *thousands* of stores everywhere, becoming the number one retailer in the world."

"And it all started here." Nate looks around the one-room store and grins. "Isn't that something?"

"There's a theme song, you know. Everyone on Earth learns it when Glosser's International takes off. Would you like to hear a little?"

"Sure, why not?"

I add a few more details to the sketch, including the year *2023* scrawled in one of the display windows. Dad and Hope could be anywhere in the timestream; in lieu of knowing their exact location, I think it's best to return home (if possible) as my next step. Either the two of them are already waiting for me there, on the date when we started our travels, or I can take a break in that familiar comfort zone to devise and launch the rest of my search.

"It goes like this." I gaze at my sketch, trying to convince myself it's a time travel guidepost like certain photos in the book. *"We're all going to Glosser's. We're all going to Glosser's."*

Though I feel no mystic energies coursing through me, and Hope isn't around to facilitate the spell, I keep hoping there might be enough lingering magic in the book to send me diving back into the ages. If not, and I'm trapped in 1906, I might take up Nathan Glosser on his job offer, after all.

"We're all going to Glosser's." Nothing happens, and I sing it again. *"We're all going to Glosser's."*

"That's pretty catchy." Nate grins and bobs his head. "Can I use it? For the store?"

"Sure, why not?" I lean closer to the book and try harder to focus on the sketch. I really double down, fighting to imagine that the sketch is a doorway to the future and I'm about to step through it.

Still, there's no icy, cyclonic wind, no change in the air, no chill up my spine. Has the magic run out? Will I indeed be stuck here, decades from anyone I know, forced to survive in a simpler time? And would that be a *bad* thing, necessarily? With my knowledge of future history and technological advancements, couldn't I live like a *king* in this backward era?

What if this is the life I was meant to live all along? Starting over here, far from the pain of losing Desiree and my job, might be the perfect fresh start for me.

I'm just about to give up trying to conjure a portal and embrace my new 1906 lifestyle when something finally changes.

It all starts with the song. For some reason, nothing happens when I sing it.

But when Nate chimes in, it's a different story. *"We're all going to Glosser's. We're all going to Glosser's."*

As soon as he starts singing, the cold wind rises and swirls around us. The air itself seems charged, and a chill shoots up my back.

"We're all going to Glosser's." We both sing it in unison. *"We're all going to Glosser's."*

Bright lights flash around us, flickering amid blurs of motion. I feel light-headed and cold enough to see my own breath emerge as puffs of mist.

It's then that Nate gets a panicked look on his face and stops singing. "What is this? What's happening?"

I clamp my hands on the book, afraid he might grab it away, and keep singing. *"We're all going to Glosser's."* The frigid wind whirls faster, and I feel my feet leave the floor.

"Stop this!" He makes a grab for the book then, landing both hands on it. "Let go!"

I wrench the book away hard, sending him stumbling backward. He falls against shelves of merchandise, bringing them down on top of him.

"Give it back!" shouts Nate. "That's *my* book!"

But the *Long Live Glosser's* is coming with me, though it probably doesn't matter much. Depending on how much Nate retained from his rapid trip through its pages, he may already know more than enough to shape the future of his company.

"Good luck!" I shout as he scrambles out from under the pile of women's blouses and hats. "Have a great life!"

The last thing I see in 1906 are his outstretched hands reaching for the book. Then, I'm whisked away from the N. Glosser Store in a rush of wind, spinning off into the greatest unknown I've yet faced.

Though I've ridden the time stream before, my heart is gripped with a tidal wave of fear bordering on pure terror. Without Hope to guide me and with no real time travel knowledge of my own, who knows when I'll end up?

This time, I land on my feet, and awake...but my senses are overwhelmed.

At first, I'm shellshocked by the tumult of light and color and noise raging around me. I just stand in one place, awash in the chaos, struggling to sort it all out.

Then, after a moment, it comes into focus. I realize I'm in the middle of a crowd, and everyone's laughing and shouting. Colored lights swoop this way and that, illuminating the people and the vast space around them. Rhythmic dance music blares at levels so loud they are almost deafening. Clearly, I'm in the middle of a party.

And the party is in a very familiar place. The smell confirms it—the aroma of roasting nuts in the air, overriding the swirl of perfume and cologne.

The giant, holographic sign hovering overhead leaves no room for doubt. *Glosser Bros. New Year 2023,* it says in glowing red letters and numbers.

As my dazed condition settles, I realize I'm back where I started, location-wise. The portal deposited me on the ground floor of Glosser's Department Store. The outline of the room is correct, though the décor is very different from what I remember—all glittering, hyper-modern furnishings and fixtures, a mix of gleaming silver, gold, and crystal.

The mere fact of the store's existence, though, is most surprising of all. It shouldn't *be* here, in 2023. It closed *decades* ago in the history I remember.

Which tells me one thing: Nathan Glosser retained *a lot* of what he read in *Long Live Glosser's,* and he wasn't afraid to put it to use.

I shake my head and mutter a curse. I guess I changed history after all, creating a future in which the Glosser Bros. Department Store is still open in the 21st century. Thanks to me, the store never closed…and based on what I see around me, it's in better shape than ever.

For the life of me, I can't think how that could possibly be a bad thing.

"Ladies and gentlemen!" says a man's voice over the P.A. system. "We are nearly at the top of the hour! Get ready to welcome in the new year of 2024!"

The crowd roars its approval, hoisting champagne glasses high.

"Everybody outside!" says the P.A. announcer. "Let's do this up in style!"

Everyone heads for the corner door, and I'm caught up in the rush. I can't help being swept outside into the surprisingly warm night air, carried by the crowd's momentum into the middle of Franklin Street.

"Get ready!" shouts the announcer. "It's almost time to watch 'the ball' drop!"

The outside of the building takes my breath away. The old brick walls have been covered with what looks like gleaming, silvery mercury. With each passing second, the liquid surface flows and ripples, reshaping itself into huge patterns and decorations—everything from a giant clock face to Baby New Year to champagne flutes tapping together. The images and patterns are complemented by elaborate showers of light and holographic projections, merging to create a symphony of shifting visual artistry.

Above all of it, a darkened sphere hovers motionless

over the roof, shrouded in shadows. Is that "the ball" referred to a moment ago by the announcer?

My heart pounds as I tug up the collar of my peacoat against the cold and take in the scene unfolding around me, marveling at what this place has become. Even in its heyday in the original timeline, Glosser Bros. was never like *this*.

"Jason?"

At the sound of that voice, I lose all interest in the spectacle before me. I whirl with a name on my lips, even before I see the face I know so well.

"Mom?"

IT'S *HER!* The woman standing before me, gray-haired and bespectacled, is the same one who disappeared more than five years ago, the original, elderly Mom we've been searching the time-space continuum for since we left our chronological home base of 2023 (the original 2023, in which Glosser's Department Store was long closed). After all the travels through time, I've finally found her.

I've found her!

Tears stream down my cheeks as we embrace. Everything else seems to fade away as this impossible moment unfolds.

"Oh my God!" I know I'm sobbing, and I couldn't care less. "It's you! It's really *you!*"

"You took the words right out of my mouth, Jason." Mom is crying, too.

"Where have you *been*?"

Leaning back, she cradles my face in her hands. "That's what I was going to ask *you*, honey. I've been here all along!"

My eyes burn as I parse what she's told me. "You have?"

"Where else would I be?" Mom's smiling face looks exactly the same as it did the last time I saw her, over five years ago. "But where have *you* been all this time?"

"You wouldn't believe me if I told you."

"So Hope was right?" asks Mom. "You fell through some kind of time portal?"

I frown. "Hope said that? Hope Tourmaline?"

Mom nods. "And thank God she did." Hopping forward, she pecks me on the cheek. "So where are they?"

"They?" Confusion is setting in, I can't deny. "Hope, you mean?"

"Well, yes." Mom looks around expectantly. "Hope and your father, of course. They brought you back, didn't they?"

"Well, actually…" I get a sinking feeling in my belly as the implications of what she's said settle in. Apparently, the changes to the destiny of Glosser's had a ripple effect that changed other parts of history, as well. "It's kind of a long story, Mom."

She pulls out her phone and flips through the contacts. "I need to text Lizzie and let her know!" She starts thumb-typing a text message on the onscreen keypad. "She's been worried sick about your father since he left to look for you, given all his health problems. She wanted to go along, being his nurse and all, but Hope wouldn't hear of it. She said time travel's too dangerous and unpredictable to put anyone else's life in danger if she didn't have to."

I reach over and rest my hand atop Mom's, stopping her from finishing the message in progress. "You might want to hold off on that text a little longer, Mom."

"Why?" Suddenly, she looks suspicious. "Has something bad happened to Raymond?"

"They're fine, they're fine..." The truth is, they could be just about anywhen, going through any number of difficult or dangerous scenarios...and it's all because of me.

In the timeline that now exists, Hope and Dad set out to search for *me,* not Mom. *I* was the missing one this time.

But thanks to a loophole, the *me* from the original timeline—*my* timeline, the one where Mom went missing—has crossed over into this one and returned to 2023...*alone. I* returned alone. Meanwhile, those who set out in search of me are still out there somewhere. For all I know, they could be stuck in one era in the past, unable to travel on without a copy of *Long Live Glosser's*...and they need help.

Can I give it to them? I, at least, still have the *Long Live Glosser's* book in hand—the guidepost that got me this far. And I have *some* knowledge of how to travel through time without Hope to run the show. I wouldn't have made it here otherwise.

Will any of it do me any good, though? Will I be able to find Dad and Hope and bring them home? What if I end up changing history again, but *not* for the better?

I don't have the answers...not yet, anyway. All I know for sure is I'm not going to worry about them for the next thirty seconds or so.

"It's almost time!" shouts the announcer. "Let's all count down together!"

The crowd counts down from thirty, thousands of voices booming over Central Park and the buildings around it (which are all part of Glosser Bros. Department Store now). When they hit the last ten seconds, the darkened sphere above the Glosser Building starts to drop, drifting lower with each shouted number.

Five...four...three...two...

When the count hits zero, the ball flares with golden light. Only then do I see it has the heart-shaped face of Miss Gee Bee on it, complete with floral derby hat—the logo of the Gee Bee Discount Department Store division.

"Happy New Year!" shouts the announcer, as everyone goes wild.

"Happy New Year, Mom." I hug her and kiss her on the forehead, so glad to have her back that I think I might burst.

"Happy New Year, Jason," she says, smiling...though her joy can't conceal a current of deep concern for her husband, who hasn't returned to her yet. Though I haven't told her the full story of his plight, she senses that all is not entirely copacetic. "You'll never know how happy I am to have you here with me tonight."

"I think I know. Now come here." I have no intention of leaving Dad and Hope out there in the time-space continuum for long, lost in the past…no matter how nostalgic and special that past may be. "There's something I need you to do."

Mom frowns. "What are you talking about?"

People shout and kiss and blow noisemakers around us as I open my copy of *Long Live Glosser's*. "You and I are going on a little trip. We're mounting a search party for Dad and Hope." I flip through the pages of the book, watching the succession of images pass before my eyes.

Reaching out with my mind, I focus on Mom's link to Dad and using it to home in on his location in the timestream. Then, when I feel a flash of intense heat from one of the photos, I stop flipping and touch the image on page 328 with my fingertip—a black-and-white shot of the store's exterior from the 1980s. "Take a look at this picture here. Imagine walking inside the store as you see it in that picture.

"Now sing along with me. *We're all going to Glosser's. We're all going to Glosser's...*"

THE LAST DAY OF THE GLOSSER BROS. STORE

MAY 26, 1989

WHAT WAS the last item sold at the Glosser Bros. Department Store? Who was the customer who bought it? Who was the cashier who rang it up?

No one seems to know anymore. All that matters now is that there *was* a last item sold, and a final customer.

And then Glosser's was gone.

It had had a good run, all the way from 1906. It had fallen and risen again and again, like Johnstown itself. It had been a gathering place, a shelter, an institution, and the greatest show in town. In so very many ways, it had been a *home*...and now, that home was finished.

Friday, May 26th, 1989 was the end of its era.

ONE LAST CUP OF COFFEE

The closing actually happened a day earlier than Glosser Bros., Inc. had originally announced.

Maybe it didn't matter. Maybe it didn't make that much difference in the grand scheme of things that The Store closed on May 26th instead of May 27th.

Or maybe it just made it that much tougher to take. Maybe it made it that much harder for the employees and patrons who already had precious little time to say goodbye.

Still, they did the only thing they could, going through the last scenes of the tragedy together. They smiled sadly, they shook hands, they hugged, they laughed, they cried. They reminisced about days gone by and wondered how the good times had gotten away from them so fast.

Some customers had said their goodbyes earlier, avoiding the sadness of the last day. Those who'd wanted one last visit to the cafeteria, for example, had had to come Thursday, the last day the cafeteria was open to customers. One of those final cafeteria visitors, Albert Zawallah of Upper Yoder Township, had come for one last cup of coffee after having one in the cafeteria every day for the past 50 years.

Chances are, he might have nursed that last cup of coffee and had a refill or two.

ONE MORE TIME TOGETHER

Glosser Bros. employees gathered in the cafeteria on Friday for a free lunch, courtesy of the company. It was a somber occasion, as men and women who'd spent so much time together through the years came together once more to share a meal.

When would they all be together in the same place like that again? Maybe never, though people talked about staying in touch and keeping up friendships.

Soon enough, the last of the lunch guests trickled back to their work stations in The Store, leaving the cafeteria employees to clean the place up...one last time.

Leaving them to share their own memories and hopes and regrets as the little world in the Annex they'd known so well for so long continued to darken around them.

HUNT ROOM MARY LOCKS UP

After the last meal had been served, one of the managers handed a set of keys to Mary Schuster—aka Hunt Room Mary. "He gave me the keys to the Hunt Room, the freezers, everything," remembers Mary. "He said, 'Give the girls anything they want, get rid of everything, then lock up.'

"So that was what I did. The employees in the Hunt Room and cafeteria took all the food that was left, so it wouldn't go to waste.

"I gave the window curtains to the girls, too," says Mary. "The manager had given me the clock off the wall and a special plaque, so I took those myself."

When the place was empty, Mary did as she'd been told and locked it up. Then, trying not to think about how much her life was about to change and how hard it would be for her, she handed the keys to the doorman and walked off down the street.

THE LAST SHOPPER

Who was the last shopper to walk out of The Store? Did he or she stop on the way out and turn for one last look around? Did he or she brush away a tear at the thought that it was all coming to an end forever?

Who closed and locked the front door the last time? Who turned out the lights and walked off into the shadows, footsteps echoing across the deserted ground floor?

Maybe, when that last person was gone, the lights flickered up once more, and the past came to life again. Who's to say it didn't?

Maybe the big room filled with bustling shoppers again, shoppers from all the years, all the ages of The Store, mingling in a giddy, ghostly swirl.

Maybe holiday music filtered from the P.A. system, and the sound of laughter rippled through the shimmering air. Maybe the display windows flowed like kaleidoscopes with Halloween paintings and Christmas decorations—maybe even a monkey or two.

Maybe it all danced and swirled for a while, a gossamer calliope of price tags and cellophane and starlight. Maybe the elevators rose and fell of their own accord, doors opening and closing to admit spectral passengers. Maybe the escalator returned, built of silvery moonbeams and mist, carrying customers up and down, up and down.

Maybe, in the heart of it all, four men stood and smiled, surveying the scene...four familiar faces, four brothers from Antopol. Maybe they smiled wistfully, or proudly, or sadly, arms around each other's shoulders, eyes glistening more brightly than any of the flickering, otherworldly lights that spun and twinkled like pinwheels through the room.

And then, maybe a car's headlights blazed through the windows, dispelling that glorious whirl of times gone by like dust in a Johnstown wind.

Leaving only the sweet smell of roasting cashews to linger in the air within those silent walls.

GLOSSER BROS
GLOSSER BRO

ABOUT THE AUTHOR

Author and editor Robert Jeschonek grew up in Johnstown, Pennsylvania and spent many happy hours as a kid at Gee Bee and the Glosser Bros. Department Store. Since then, he has gone on to write lots of books and stories, including *Long Live Glosser's, Penn Traffic Forever, Christmas at Glosser's, Easter at Glosser's, Fourth of July at Glosser's, Halloween at Glosser's, A Glosser's Christmas Love Story, Thanksgiving at Glosser's, Valentine's Day at Glosser's, Richland Mall Rules,* and *Death By Polka*. He has written lots of other cool stuff, too, including *Star Trek* and *Doctor Who* fiction and Batman comics. His young adult fantasy novel, *My Favorite Band Does Not Exist,* won a Forward National Literature Award and was named a top ten first novel for youth by *Booklist* magazine. His work has been published around the world in over a hundred paper books, e-books, and audio books. You can find out more about them at his website, www.bobscribe.com, or by looking up his name on Facebook, Twitter, or Google. As you'll see, he's kind of crazy...in a *good* way.

facebook.com/usa.today.bestseller
twitter.com/TheFictioneer
instagram.com/robertjeschonek
bookbub.com/profile/robert-t-jeschonek

SPECIAL PREVIEW: LONG LIVE GLOSSER'S

THE FULL, TRUE STORY OF A CLASSIC DEPARTMENT STORE

Can you smell the roasting peanuts?

The Glosser Bros. Department Store has reopened, just for you, just in the pages of this one-of-a-kind book. For the first time, the whole true story of Glosser's has been told, on the 25th anniversary of the fabled department store's closing. Step through the famous doors on the corner of Franklin and Locust Streets and grab a brown-and-white-striped shopping bag. You're about to embark on a journey from the humble beginnings of Glosser Bros. to its glory days as a local institution and multi-million dollar company...and the thrilling battle to save it on the eve of its grand finale. Read the stories of the executives, the employees, and the loyal shoppers who made

Glosser Bros. a legend and kept it alive in the hearts and minds of Glosser Nation. Hundreds of photos, never before gathered together in one place, will take you back in time to the places and people that made Glosser's great. Experience the things you loved best about the classic department store, from the roasted nuts to the Shaffer twins to the Halloween windows and the amazing sales. Discover secrets and surprises that have never been revealed to the general public until now. Relive the story of a lifetime in a magical tour straight out of your memories and dreams, a grand reopening of a store that never really closed in your heart and will open its doors every time we shout...*Long Live Glosser's!*

SPECIAL PREVIEW: PENN TRAFFIC FOREVER

THE FULL, TRUE STORY OF ANOTHER CLASSIC DEPARTMENT STORE

Meet you on the mezzanine...

The Penn Traffic Department Store is back in business in the pages of this one-of-a-kind book. Now's your chance to revisit this Johnstown, Pennsylvania landmark or experience its magic for the very first time. The whole true story of the legendary store, its employees, and the shoppers who loved it is right here, complete with all your favorite treats and traditions. Help yourself to Penn Way candies...have a burger and fries in the Penn Traffic restaurant...relax on the mezzanine...and wait on the sidewalk on a cold winter's night for the grand unveiling of the most spectacular Christmas window in town. You'll never forget this trip through history, from the store's pre-Civil War beginnings to its dramatic finale 123 years later, with three devastating floods, an epic fire, and a high-stakes robbery in between. Hundreds of photos, never before gathered in one place, will whisk you back in time to the people and events that made Penn Traffic great...and carry you forward for a special tour of the Penn Traffic building as it stands today, complete with traces and treasures from the store's glory days. You'll feel like you've returned to the store of your dreams, especially when you cook up the authentic goodies in the Penn Traffic recipe section, handed down from the store's own bakery and candy kitchen all-stars. If you've ever longed to go back to the magical department store where you always felt at home, or you just long for a simpler, sweeter place where the air smells like baking bread and the customer is always right, step inside. Welcome to the grand reopening of the store that comes to life every time we shout the magic words...*Penn Traffic Forever!*

Penn Traffic Forever

Order now from your favorite online or in-person bookstore!

Also available from Pie Press Publishing at

www.piepresspublishing.com

SPECIAL PREVIEW: RICHLAND MALL RULES

THE FULL, TRUE STORY OF A BELOVED SHOPPING MALL

You can smell the caramel popcorn and taste the clown sundaes...

Once upon a shopping center, the Richland Mall was the place to shop, eat, meet, play, and be seen in suburban Johnstown, Pennsylvania. Decades after its closing, this classic mall returns to life in the pages of this one-of-a-kind book. For the first time, the true story of the Richland Mall, its creators, its employees, and the shoppers who loved it has been told, complete with surprising secrets and inside stories from those who knew it best. You'll never forget this trip through an unforgettable period of retail history, from the Mall's miraculous beginnings to its glory days in the 70s and 80s to the struggle to save it from going out of business. Hundreds of rare photos and images, never before gathered in one place, will whisk you back to the people and moments that made the Richland Mall great, then carry you forward to modern-day reunions of Mall employees where the disco music and nostalgia never stop. Relive the story of a lifetime on a magical journey straight out of your favorite memories and dreams. If you've ever longed to return to the Mall where you always felt at home, or you just crave a simpler, sweeter place where the Super Chick sandwiches, Capri pizza, and Sweet William clown sundaes are always delicious, and the customer is always right, step inside. Richie the Pook invites you to the grand reopening of the Mall that comes to life every time we shout...*Richland Mall Rules!*

www.ingramcontent.com/pod-product-compliance
Lightning Source LLC
Chambersburg PA
CBHW070645310726
48982CB00001B/426
9798985776935